A REIGN OF TERROR . . .

"Sweet Sixteen" by Robert Bloch—They appeared out of nowhere, invading the quiet country town, destroying its peace with their noise and fury. But the time to truly fear them was when they left the town behind . . .

"The Compleat Werewolf" by Anthony Boucher—A professor's discovery that he is a werewolf sends him on a rendezvous with the secret underworld of terror.

"Such Nice Neighbors" by Chelsa Quinn Yarbro—The children had come to a new life in a new home, and Halloween was about to take on a whole new meaning for them this year . . .

These are just a few of the chillingly devilish encounters to be found in—

DEVIL WORSHIPERS

DEVIL WORSHIPERS

EDITED BY
MARTIN H. GREENBERG AND
CHARLES G. WAUGH

DAW BOOKS, INC.
DONALD A. WOLLHEIM, PUBLISHER

375 Hudson Street, New York, NY 10014

DAW Book Collectors No. 817.

First Printing, May 1990

2 3 4 5 6 7 8 9

Printed in Canada

ACKNOWLEDGMENTS

CONTENTS

WARNING—

by Frank D. McSherry Jr.

Flame.

Whipped by the night winds, the torches flare over the black-robed congregation, bowing on a wooded hilltop before an altar bearing the nude body of a beautiful woman. Above her a priest, his face masked by a horned animal's skull, leads the witches' worship, the Black Mass, reciting the Lord's Prayer backward, lifting a small baby up in the air—

His knife flashes in the torchlight.

Blood spurts crimson—

and the gathered witches shriek in terror and adoration as a monstrous shadow with burning red eyes rises against the stars—here is the Prince of Evil, the Father of Lies, the Lord of the Sorcerors—

The Devil!

Or so the Inquisition claimed.

Devil worship appears again and again in the thousands of confessions of witches during the fifteenth century, when the Inquisition, the arm of the Church designed to extirpate heresy, harried the witches with fire and sword and torture in a giant witch persecution that swept over Europe like a forest fire. A hundred thousand died in Germany; Llorente, the historian of the Inquisition, claims it executed more than 340,000 witches in Spain alone—

Yet many historians of the twentieth century have wondered if actual Devil worship reached anything remotely like that number; if Devil worship really began in the sick minds of its persecutors. The confessions, they point out, were obtained under a torture so insane

9

that even the Gestapo and the Russian secret police could only imitate, and never exceed it. Did Satanism, as an organized religion, appear first in the sick minds of Christian witch hunters (Christian, for Protestants had their torture chambers and witch hunts, too): Satanic and Christian ritual are strikingly alike—

Christianity in a black mirror?

Religious fanaticism fueled the fury. In the Dark Ages a man's religion *was* his politics. The 1500s saw the last Mohammedans driven out of Europe by the sea battle of Lepanto, the destruction of the giant Spanish Armada by Protestant guns and Atlantic storms, the Thirty Years War between Lutherans and the Church of Rome. Witchcraft and heresy also meant treason.

Thus the numbers and powers of the Devil Worshipers grew. When the poor and powerless were persecuted and tortured, driven from home to starve, when God Himself seemed to have turned his face from them, there was yet one Being they could turn to. . . .

Others genuinely worshiped the Fallen Angel, sought from Him the supernatural power to kill silently, swiftly, from a distance. The mentally unbalanced were attracted to such cults, in order to do their own persecuting; willing to sacrifice children for supernatural power.

Thus neither the practice nor the persecution of Devil worship ever quite died out. In 1680, at the court of Louis XIV, his lovely mistress, Mme. de Montespan, performed Black Masses in the hope that the Devil would keep her eternally young and thus forever in the Sun King's favor; 1692 saw the notorious witchcraft trials in Salem.

The dark diamond of Satanism has countless facets, and the stories included here show many of them. There's the kids that live in a town where children disappear every Halloween, who find they have ''Such Nice Neighbors;'' there's Seabury Quinn's bittersweet love story of a modern man whose mind makes contact with a beautiful girl in witch-haunted Italy of centuries past, not realizing until too late that her frightened townspeople will believe this to be witchcraft. There's the boys' school where more is being taught than the administration ever dreamed, where a dark worship of Satan had begun, in a shivery story by Manly Wade Wellman. A good Christian attends a Black Mass held in the nighted hills above Salem and is surprised to see who's among the worshipers, in "Young Goodman Brown," by Nathaniel Hawthorne, who as a child heard tales of the witchcraft days in Salem from actual witnesses.

In a novelette of Hollywood and academia, a Devil worshiping cult is used as a front for a Nazi spy ring; the Black Widower's Club of Isaac Asimov's story faces a puzzling problem indeed when it tries to convince a woman member of a Satan cult that its leader, Lucifer, Son of the Morning, is a con artist who lies when he says he saw Earthrise while on the planet Mars. Robert Bloch, author of "Psycho," gives us a scary portrait of a teenage witch who is "Sweet Sixteen"—and more . . . His Imperial Majesty Himself appears in many of these stories.

These tales were chosen, of course, for their entertainment value, for the artistic skill with which they produce a good icy scare. But recent events provide another rationale for this anthology.

In April 1989, a twenty-five-year-old American tourist, Mark Kilroy, a pre-medical student at the University of Texas, was kidnapped in Matamoros, Mexico, during the university spring break. His mutilated body was found about a month later, along with twelve others, including two Mexican policemen and a sixteen-year-old boy. All had been murdered as part of the ritual of a devil-worshiping cult led by a Cuban-born American citizen, Adolfo de Jesus Constanzo, police said, adding that Constanzo had had his cult followers cross the border into Texas to kidnap one of their victims. Until the Kilroy killing, the cult's very existence had been unknown. . . .

"They believed," Texas Attorney General Jim Mattox said, "the human sacrifices . . . put a magical shield around them."[1]

Remember how long the cult of Thuggee, who strangled innocent travelers in India, preferably entire families at a time, as part of their religious ritual, thrived before being stamped out?

Don't think of this as just a group of horror stories, especially if you travel—

Think of it, say, as a kind of Distant Early Warning Line. . . .

[1]Wire Reports, in *Tulsa World*, 13 April 1989, v 84, n 209, pg. A–11.

SWEET SIXTEEN
by Robert Bloch

Everything was peaceful the night before the trouble came.

Ben Kerry perched on the porch rail outside his cottage, blinking like an owl in the twilight. He peered across the wide rolling expanse of the Kettle Moraine country and flapped his arms as if he were about to take off.

"There's gold in them thar hills," he muttered. "I never knew it, but I could have gotten in on the ground floor, too."

Ted Hibbard grinned at him. "You mean, when the glaciers swept down and made them? You're not *that* old."

Kerry chuckled and lit his pipe. "That's right, son. And I wasn't here when the glacier rolled back and the Indians came, either. They used the hills for signalling posts or for their ceremonial rituals. No money in that, I grant you."

"I know," Hibbard said. "I read your book about it."

Kerry chuckled again. "No money in *that,* either. If it wasn't for the university presses, we anthropologists would starve to death waiting for a publisher. Because we never see what's right under our noses." He stared out at the hills again, far into deepening dusk.

"Of course the farmers didn't see, either, when they arrived here. They preferred to settle on level land. And their sons and grandsons sought still better soil, down around the waterways. So all these rockstrewn hills with their boulder outcroppings, stood deserted until maybe thirty years ago. Then the automobile brought the first hunters and fishermen from the cities. They put up cheap cabins on cheap land. And they didn't see the gold any more than I did, when I came here just before the War. All I wanted was a summer place where I could get away from people.''

Ted Hibbard chuckled, now. "Strikes me as funny," he said. "An anthropologist who hates people."

"Don't hate 'em," Kerry insisted. "At least, not most of 'em. Even today, we know, the majority of the inhabitants of the earth are still savages. I've always gotten along with *them* very well. It's the civilized who frighten me."

"Such as your students and former students?" Hibbard smiled up at him. "I thought I was welcome here."

"You are, believe me. But you're an exception. You aren't like the others. You didn't move out here for a fast buck."

"Oh," Hibbard said. "So that's what you mean by the gold, is it?"

"Of course. What you see out there isn't hill country any more. It's real-estate. Development property. Right after the War the city people came. Not the hunters and the fishermen now, but the exurbanites. The super deluxe exurbanites, who could afford to move forty miles out of town instead of just fifteen. They've been pouring in ever since, putting up their ranch-houses and their double garages for the station wagons."

"Still looks like a pretty lonely region to me," Hibbard mused. "Too damned lonely, after dark."

"The Indians were afraid of the hills at night," Kerry told him. "They used to huddle inside their te-pees around the fire. Just like today's citizens huddle inside their ranch-houses around the TV set."

"I suppose you have a right to be resentful," Hibbard said. "All these property-values going up. If you'd anticipated the boom you might have picked up choice locations and made a fortune.''

Kerry shrugged. ''Wouldn't need a fortune. Just enough to move on. By now I could have a little *cabana* down along the barren stretches of the Florida Keys. I'd call it the *Key Pout*.''

A white face popped around the corner of the porch. ''Hey, Dad! Mom says it's almost time for supper.''

''Okay,'' Hibbard answered. ''Tell her I'll be along soon.''

The face disappeared.

''Nice boy you have there,'' Kerry said.

''Hank? We think so. Crazy about math, all that sort of thing. Can't wait to start school in the fall. I guess he's a lot more serious about things than I was at his age. A lot more than most kids are, nowadays.''

''That's why I like him,'' Kerry tapped his pipe against the porchrail. ''You know, I'm not really such a misanthrope. This hermit pose of mine is mostly pretense. But some of it is defense, too. Defense against the mobs taking over our cities, our culture. I saw it coming, fifteen years ago. That's why I got out. It's bad enough having to stay in town during the school year, to teach. Once that's over, I come back to the cottage here. Now even this little bit of privacy is being invaded. The hot dog stands are taking over Walden Pond, I guess.''

Hibbard stood up. ''I hope you don't resent my hanging around this way,'' he said.

''Good heavens, no! When you bought your place last month I was mighty pleased to see you. I'm still a member of the human race, remember, even though I find the average rural resident as much of an alien as I do the city troglodyte or his suburbanite cousin. You're more than welcome here, at any time. I like your wife, and I like that boy of yours. They're real people.''

''Meaning that the rest are not?''

''Don't bait me,'' Kerry said. ''You understand very

well what I'm talking about. That's why you moved
out here yourself, isn't it?''

Hibbard moved to the edge of the porch. ''Well, I
guess so. Actually, we came out here because of Hank,
mostly. Didn't like the city schools. Didn't like the
kind of kids he ran around with back in town.
They're—I don't know—different. All these juvenile
delinquents. You know.''

Kerry nodded. ''Indeed I do. As a matter of fact,
I've been spending most of the summer taking notes
for a little monograph. Nothing pretentious, understand—sociology's out of my line—but it's an interesting study. And this happens to be an ideal spot for
anthropological field-trips.''

''You mean there's a lot of rural delinquence around
here?'' Hibbard looked distressed. ''We were hoping
to get away from that.''

''Don't worry,'' Kerry reassured him. ''From what
I've seen, the farm areas are still pretty well untouched. Of course, we have the usual percentage of
barnyard sadist truants, maladjusted types. But Hank
won't run into too many; at his age most of them have
either gone off to the armed services or the Industrial
Home for Boys. It's the city youngsters I've been investigating.''

''You're talking about exurbanite kids like mine? Or
is there some kind of boy's camp around here?''

''Neither. I'm speaking about our weekend visitors.
Don't tell me you haven't seen them in town during
the summer.''

''No, I haven't. Actually, I've been so busy getting
our place straightened out that I don't get into town
very often. About once a week I stock up on supplies,
usually on a Wednesday. I heard it's pretty crowded,
weekends.''

''You heard correctly,'' Kerry told him. ''But perhaps you might be interested in seeing just what I'm
talking about. I plan to take a run in tomorrow morning, about nine or so. And you're welcome to ride
along.''

"Will do." Hibbard waved his hand in salute.

Kerry stood on the porch and watched his guest walk down the hillside path, his shoulders silhouetted against the sunset.

From the far horizon came a low, rumbling sound. It might have been the mutter of distant thunder—at least, that is what both men mistook it for at the time.

Neither of them knew that it heralded the arrival of the trouble.

They must have been coming in all through the night, and they were still gathering around ten in the morning when Ben Kerry drove Hibbard into town in his old Ford.

Their first encounter occurred on the highway just outside the town limits, between the *Welcome to Hilltop* sign and the notice which read *Speed Limit 25 m.p.h.*

It came in the form of a rumbling again, but this time there was no mistaking it for thunder. The motorcycle roared along the road behind them, then swerved past without slackening speed. As it zoomed by, Hibbard caught a glimpse of a squat figure in a black leather jacket, with a monkey on his back. At least, it looked like a monkey in the dusty passing blur; not until a moment later did he realize that what he had seen was a girl with cropped hair who was clinging with arms entwined about the cyclist.

As they speeded ahead, Hibbard saw the girl raise her right hand as though in a gesture of greeting. Automatically he started to return her wave, then froze as Kerry gripped his shoulder.

"Look out!" he shouted, and ducked his head.

At that instant something struck the windshield of the car and bounced off with a clatter. It fell in a silvery arc to the side of the road, and Hibbard understood. The girl had not been waving. She had hurled an empty beer can at them.

"Why, she could have broken the windshield!" he exclaimed.

Kerry nodded. "Happens all the time. By tonight you'll find the roadside paved with empties."

"But they aren't even supposed to *buy* beer, are they? Isn't there a state law?"

Kerry jerked his finger over his shoulder. "Sign says you cut down to twenty-five miles an hour when you enter town, too," he muttered. "But they're doing close to fifty."

"You talk as if you expected such things."

"I do. It's like this every weekend, all summer long. Everyone knows what to expect around here."

"And nobody tries to do anything about it?"

"Wait and see," Kerry told him.

They were entering town now, passing a row of motels. Although it was still mid-morning, a surprising number of cars were parked before the various units. Hibbard gazed at them curiously, noting a strange incongruity. Virtually none of the vehicles were cognizable as standard units. Painted junkers, restyled hot rods, ancient sports cars predominated. And there were dozens of motorcycles.

"I see you notice our weekend visitors' choice of transportation," Kerry said. "I'm afraid it's apt to strike you as a bit unconventional. As a group they seem to dislike what I believe is called 'Detroit iron'— you might gather from that that they utilize the motor car as a symbol of protest. As I remark in my notes, there seems to be an automotive in their madness."

He slowed to a snail's pace as they proceeded up the short thoroughfare known, inevitably, as Main Street. The sidewalks were jammed with the usual Saturday throng of farm-folk, but intermingling with them was the unusual throng of teen-age visitants.

There was no difficulty in separating them from the local youngsters; not these swaggering, guffawing figures in their metal-studded jackets and skintight jeans. Their booted feet thudded along the pavement, their visored caps bobbed. Some of them were bareheaded, choosing to display shaven skulls, crewcuts, and the more outlandish coiffures known as "Mohawks" or—

for polite abbreviation—the "d.a." An occasional older lad in the crowd was more apt to affect the other extreme; long, greasy locks and exaggerated sideburns. Several of the latter youths wore spade beards, which gave them an oddly goatish appearance. The resemblance to satyrs was perhaps increased by the presence, and the attitudes, of their female companions. Virtually all of them were indistinguishable from the girl on the motorcycle; the cropped hair, overpainted face, and tight sweater and jodhpurs seemed to be standard equipment.

Their boisterous babble rose and echoed from the artificial amphitheatre created by the store-fronts lining either side of the narrow street; from the end of the block came the sound of a juke box blaring away at full volume inside the root beer stand and drive-in.

A large crowd of juveniles congregated before it, and several couples were dancing on the sidewalk, oblivious of those who had to step out into the street in order to pass by. The sun's rays reflected from a score of beer cans held in a score of hands.

Hibbard turned to his companion. "I think I get it now," he said. "I remember reading something about this a couple of years back. Wasn't there a motorcycle convention in some small town in California? A gang took over, almost started a riot?"

"There was," the older man confirmed. "And it happened again, last year, in another state. Then I read of another instance, this summer. If you wanted to check on such things, I imagine you'd find the phenomenon has become commonplace all over."

"Is this what you wanted to show me?" Hibbard asked. "That cyclist gangs are coming in here and terrorizing the citizens?"

Kerry shook his head.

"Don't be melodramatic," he murmured. "In the first place, this isn't a 'cyclist gang.' Any more than it's a 'hot rod crowd' or a 'sports car mob' or a congregation of Elvis Presley fans. These youngsters come from all over; the big city, the outlying suburbs, the

smaller industrial communities nearby. There's no outward indication that they belong to any formal group,
club, or organization. They just congregate, apparently. And if you look closely, you'll see they're not
terrorizing the citizens, as you put it. In fact most of
the local merchants are delighted to have them here."
He waved his arm in the direction of the beer-drinkers.
"They're good customers. They leave a lot of money
in town over a weekend."

"But you said yourself that they break the laws. They
must stir up trouble, get into fights, do damage."

"They pay for it, I guess."

"What about the local authorities? What do they
think?"

Kerry smiled. "You mean the mayor? He's a
plumber here in town, gets a hundred dollars a year to
hold the title as a part-time job. He doesn't worry
much."

"But the police—"

"We have a local sheriff, that's all. The place isn't
even big enough to have its own jail. That's over at the
county seat."

"Don't the citizens who aren't merchants do any
complaining? Are they willing to sit back and just let
a bunch of strange young hoodlums run wild?"

"I guess they complain. But so far there hasn't been
any action taken. For my selfish purposes, it's just as
well. You'd be surprised what I've managed to observe
during this summer alone. What I want to do now is
get over and see one of their race meetings."

"Race meetings?"

"That's right. You didn't think they come here just
to walk up and down Main Street, did you? Saturday
or Sunday afternoons you'll generally find them off in
the hills, on one of those little side roads back behind
the county trunk highways. They rent a spot from a
local farmer and hold drag races, hill-climbing con-
tests, that sort of thing. This week they'll be gathering
in our neighborhood, I think. They were always west
of town before this, but I guess something happened

and they got run off from their usual spot. Now old Lautenshlager is going to let them use the big hill behind his property. We ought to be able to see the bonfire tonight.''

"Bonfire?"

Kerry nodded. ''They usually have them.''

"What do they think they are, Indians?" Hibbard stared at a trio on the nearby corner; a skinny boy epileptically contorted over a guitar and a writhing couple who seemed to be executing an impromptu wardance. He had to grin at the sight. ''Maybe they are, at that,'' he admitted. ''They sure sound like savages.''

"Rock-and-roll," Kerry shrugged.

Suddenly Hibbard's grin faded. ''Look at that,'' he snapped pointing up the street ahead.

A beat-up convertible was screeching down the avenue towards them, loaded with youngsters whose voices competed more than successfully with the mechanical din. As the car moved forward, a cat moved quickly out of its path. But not quickly enough, for the car swerved purposefully to the side. There was a jarring thump and a louder screech, followed by howls of laughter.

"Did you see what they did?" Hibbard demanded. ''They deliberately went out of their way to run it down! Let me out of here! I'm going to—''

"Oh no you're not." Kerry put his foot down on the accelerator and the Ford moved on. ''The poor thing's dead. You can't help it now. No sense starting trouble.''

"What's the matter with you?" Hibbard's voice was shrill. ''You aren't going to let them get away with this, are you?'' He stared as the convertible skidded to a halt and its inmates poured out across the sidewalk. ''It's bad enough when small boys torture an animal out of childish curiosity, but these aren't children. They're old enough to know what they're doing.''

"That's right," Kerry agreed. ''Like you say,

they're savages. Remember the riots. You can't win."
Kerry drove in silence, turning off at the end of the
street and cutting back along a side-road which circled
the edge of town and joined the highway once again.
Even at a distance it was possible to hear the blare of
music, the cough of exhaust pipes, the yammer of
horns and the snarl of the cycles.

"They must have noise wherever they go," Kerry
said, at last. "I suppose it's what the psychiatrists call
oral aggression."

Hibbard didn't reply.

"Rock-and-roll is another manifestation. But then
again, there was swing in your salad days and jazz in
mine. In fact you see a lot of parallels if you look for
them. Eccentric dress and hair styles, the drinking—
the whole pattern of rebellion against authority."

Hibbard stirred restlessly. "But not the senseless
cruelty," he said. "Sure, I remember frat initiations
and how wild we got after football games. But there
was nothing like this. There were a few bullies or maladjusted kids with mean streaks—now they all behave
like a pack of psychos."

"Your boy isn't like that," Kerry answered. "Lots
of them are normal."

"Yes. But there seem to be so many of the other
sort. More and more each year. Don't tell me you
haven't noticed. You told me you've been studying
these kids. And just now, back in town, you were
afraid."

Kerry sighed. "Yes, I've studied them. And I am
afraid." He paused. "How about coming home for
lunch with me? I think I ought to show you a few
things."

Hibbard nodded. The noonday countryside was silent, or almost silent. It was only by listening very
closely that they could hear the faint rumbling, moving along the roads in the direction of the distant hills.

Kerry spread the scrapbooks on the table after lunch.
"Started these myself some time ago," he said. "But
recently I've signed up with a clipping service."

He riffled the pages of the topmost book. "Here's your motorcycle riots, and a section on gang fights. Rumbles, they call them. A report from the Police Commissioner of New York on the rise of delinquency. A list of weapons taken from a group of high-school freshmen in Detroit—switch-blade knives, straight razors, brass knuckles, two pistols, a hatchet. All of them used in a street battle. A section on narcotics, one on armed robbery, quite a few stories of arson. I've tried to eliminate what seem to be run-of-the-mill occurrences, so the clippings involving sex-crimes mostly concern forcible rape, gang assaults, and sadistic perversion. Even so, you can see there's a frightening assortment. This second book is devoted exclusively to news stories of torture and murder. I warn you, it's not pleasant reading."

It wasn't. Hibbard found his gorge rising. He'd noticed such items, of course, while skimming through his daily paper, but had never paid too much attention to their frequency. Here, for the first time, he encountered a mass accumulation, and it was an anthology of horror.

He read about the teen-age kidnappers in Chicago who mutilated and then killed an infant; the youngster down South who butchered his sister; the boy who blew off the head of his mother with a shotgun. Case after case of parricide, fratricide, infanticide; instance after instance of apparently senseless slaughter.

Kerry glanced over his shoulder and sighed.

"Truth is stranger than fiction, isn't it?" he muttered. "You'll look a long time before discovering any Penrods or Willie Baxters in those news clippings. This isn't a Booth Tarkington world any more. For that matter, you'll search in vain for an Andy Hardy."

"I believe it," said Hibbard. "But I can't understand it. Of course, there were always juvenile delinquents. Dead End Kids, that sort of thing. Only they seemed to be the exceptions, the victims of the Depression. And the zoot-suiters during the War were supposed to be the result of lack of parental supervision. The youngsters in these cases seem to be the products of normal upbringing; I notice the stories make quite a point out of the fact that most of them come from nice homes, prosperous backgrounds. What's happened to our kids?''

"You'll still find nice children around. Hank isn't that way, remember?''

"But what's influencing the majority? Why has there been such a terrible change in the last few years?''

Kerry puffed on his pipe. "Lots of explanations, if you want them. Dr. Wertham, for example, blames a lot of it on the comic books. Some psychotherapists say television is the villain. Others think the War left its mark; kids live in the shadow of military service, so they rebel. They've taken new heroes in their own image—James Dean, Marlon Brando, the torn-shirt totem rules their clan. Oh, there's already a most impressive literature on the subject.''

"Well, it doesn't impress me," Hibbard declared. "Maybe it sounds good, but how does one of those fancy theories explain a thing like this? Listen." He jabbed his finger at one of the clippings pasted on the page opened before them. "Here's a case from just last month. A fourteen-year-old boy, down South. He got up out of bed in the middle of the night and killed his parents in cold blood, while they slept. No rhyme or reason for it, he admits he had no reason to hate them, and the analysts' reports seem to show he's perfectly normal, had an ordinary home-life. His story is that he just woke up out of a sound sleep and felt a sudden 'urge to kill somebody.' So he did." Hibbard thumbed through the book. "Come to think of it, that's what a lot of them say. They just get an 'impulse,' or 'something comes over them,' or they 'want to see what it's like.' And the next day the cops are beating the bushes for the bodies of missing babies, or digging up fragments of dismembered corpses in gravel-pits. I tell you, it doesn't make sense!''

He closed the scrap book and stared at Kerry. "You've gone to a lot of trouble to collect these clippings,'' he said. ''And you say you've been studying this juvenile delinquent problem all summer. You must have come to some conclusions.''

Kerry shrugged. ''Perhaps. But I'm not quite ready to commit myself. I need further data before presenting a hypothesis.'' He gave Hibbard a long look. ''You were a pretty fair student, as I recall. Let's see what you make of it all.''

''Well, there's a couple of things that occur to me. First, this insistence, in case after case, over and over again, that a youngster suddenly experiences an irrestible impulse to commit murder. Generally, in such examples, the child is alone and not part of any gang. Come to think of it, he's often an only child, isn't he, or lives an isolated life?''

Kerry's eyes narrowed. ''Go on.''

''That seems to take care of one group. But there's another—the gangs. The ones that go in for the uniforms, and the regalia. I notice there's quite a bit of reference to initiations and secret society mumbo-jumbo. They've got a jive-talk language of their own, and fancy names, that sort of thing. And they seem to be premeditated in their crimes.'' He hesitated. ''On the face of it, we're dealing with two totally different types. ''No, wait a minute—there's one thing all these kids seem to have in common.''

Kerry leaned forward. ''What's that?''

''They don't *feel* anything—no shame, no guilt, no remorse. There's no empathy towards their victims, none at all. Time after time the stories bring that point out. They kill for kicks, but it doesn't really touch them at all. In other words, they're psychopaths.''

''Now we're getting somewhere,'' Kerry said. ''You call them psychopaths. And just what *is* a psychopath?''

''Why, like I said—somebody who doesn't have normal feeling, who lacks responsibility. You've studied up on psychology, you ought to know.''

Kerry gestured towards the row of bookshelves lining the sides of his fireplace. ''That's right. I've got quite a collection of psychotherapy tests up there. But you can search through them in vain for a satisfactory definition of the so-called psychopathic personality. He isn't considered a psychotic. He doesn't respond to any form of treatment. No psychiatric theory presently offers a demonstrable explanation of how a psychopath evolves, and for lack of contrary evidence it's often assumed that he's born that way.''

''Do you believe that?''

''Yes. But unlike orthodox therapists, I have a reason. I think I know what a psychopath is. And—''

''Dad!''

Both of them turned at the cry.

Hibbard's son stood in the doorway, the rays of the late afternoon sun reflecting redly from the bright blood streaming down the side of his face.

''Hank! What happened? Did you have an accident?'' He moved towards the boy.

''No, I'm all right. Honest I am. I just didn't want to go home and scare Mom.''

''Sit down.'' Kerry led him to a chair. ''Let me get some hot water, clean you off.'' He went over to the sink and returned with a cloth and a basin. Skillfully he sponged the blood away, revealing the lacerations on the scalp.

''Not too deep,'' he told Hibbard. ''A little peroxide and a bandage, now.''

The boy winced, then subsided as Kerry finished his ministrations.

''Better?''

''I'm all right,'' Hank insisted. ''It's just that they hit me with the tire-chain—''

''Who hit you?''

''I don't know. Some guys. I went for a walk this afternoon, and I heard all this racket up on the hill behind old Lautenshlager's place, you know. And I saw all these guys, and some dames, too. They were riding motorcycles up and down, making a lot of noise. I wanted to see what was going on, that's all, I just wanted to see what was going on—''

His lower lip trembled and Hibbard patted his shoulder. "Sure, I understand. So you went up there, eh? And then what happened?"

"Well, I started to go up. But before I could get very close, these big guys jumped me. There must have been five or six of them; they just come out from around some bushes and grabbed me. And one of them had a stick and another one had this tire-chain, and he swung it at me and hit me alongside of the head, here. The others let go of me to get out of the way, and that's how I got loose. I started to run, and they were chasing me, only I got across the fence and then I ducked down behind Lautenshlager's barn so they couldn't see me."

"Did you get a good look at the fellows?"

"Well, one of them had a beard. And they were all wearing these black leather jackets and some kind of boots."

"It's the gang, all right. Our friends, the psychopaths." Hibbard stood up. "You can walk, can't you? Then come on."

"Where are we going?"

"Home, of course. I'm going to see to it that you get to bed. You got quite a knock there. And then I think I'll hop in the car and take a little run over to the county seat. Seems to me this is a matter for the State Police."

Kerry put down his pipe. "Are you sure it's wise to stir up trouble?" he asked quietly. "No telling what might happen."

"Something has happened already," Hibbard answered. "When a bunch of hoodlums knock my son over the head with a tire-chain, that's trouble enough for me. Come on, Hank."

He led the boy out of the front door and down the path, without a backward look.

Kerry grimaced, then shook his head. For a moment he opened his mouth to call after them, then closed it. After that he just stood there, his eyes intent on the far hills. No smoke rose from them in the waning horizon-light, but the sound of racing exhausts was plainly audible. Kerry stood there listening for a long time. Then, slowly, wearily, he walked into the front room. He kindled a fire in the fireplace and sat down before it, balancing a notebook on his lap. From time to time he scribbled a few words, sitting stiffly, head poised as though listening for an unexpected sound. His face bore the tight, strained look of a man who had been waiting for trouble—and found it.

It must have been almost an hour before the sound came. Even though he'd been tensed and alert, Kerry jumped when he heard the footsteps. He rushed to the door, reaching it just as Hibbard burst in.

"Oh, it's you!" His voice rose in relief. "So dark I didn't recognize who it was at first."

Hibbard didn't respond for a moment. He stood there, panting, waiting to regain his breath.

"Ran all the way," he wheezed.

"What's the matter? Is it Hank?"

"No. The kid's all right, I guess. We put him to bed when I got him home, and my wife doesn't think there's any concussion. She used to be a nurse, you know. So I decided to grab a sandwich before I drove in for the police. We had the door shut, so I guess that's why I didn't hear anything. They must have sneaked in and out of the yard again very quietly."

"Who?"

"Our young friends. Guess they figured out where Hank lived and decided I might be going after them. Anyway, they weren't taking any chances. They slashed all my tires."

Hibbard's voice rose. "They could see there are no telephone wires around our place, and I suppose they thought if they fixed the car I couldn't do anything. But I'll show them!"

"Take it easy, now."

"I am taking it easy. I'm just here to borrow your car, that's all."

"You still intend to get the police?"

"What do you mean, *still?* After what happened, nothing could stop me. I made sure everything was locked good and tight when I left, but even that's no guarantee. For all I know, they'll be around to burn the house down before the night is over."

Kerry shook his head. "I don't think so. I think if you just go back home and stay there quietly there won't be any more trouble. All they want now is to be left alone."

"Well, what they want and what they're going to get is two different things. I'm going to round up every police officer in this part of the state. We're going to put an end to this sort of thing—"

"No. You won't end it. Not that way."

"Look, I'm not here to argue with you. Give me your car keys.

"Not until you listen to me, first."

"I listened to you long enough. I should have got tough the minute I saw those kids run over the cat." Hibbard wiped his forehead. "All right, what is it you wanted to say?"

Kerry walked over and stood next to the bookshelves.

"We were talking about psychopaths this afternoon. I told you that psychiatrists didn't understand them, but that I did. Sometimes it takes an anthropologist to know these things. In my time I've studied a great deal concerning the so-called 'gang-spirit' and the secret societies of many cultures. You find them in all regions, and there are certain similarities. For example, did you know that in some places, even the young women have their own groups? Lips says—"

"I'm not interested in a lecture."

"You will be. Lips says there are hundreds of such societies in Africa alone. The Bundu group, in Nigeria, wears special masks and costumes for their secret rituals. The male adventurer who dares to spy on them is disciplined, or even killed."

"Listen, a gang of crazy kids around a bonfire isn't any secret lodge!"

"You noted the similarity yourself, this afternoon."

"I said some kids ran in gangs, yes. But others don't. What about the 'loners,' the ones who just get the urge to kill?"

"They don't know what they are, that's all. They haven't recognized themselves. For that matter, I don't think the gangs do, not consciously. They think they're just out for thrills. And I only pray that they go on that way, that they don't realize what brings them together."

"We know what brings them together. They're psycho."

"And what *is* a psychopath?" Kerry's voice was soft. "A psychotherapist couldn't tell you, but an anthropologist can. A psychopath is a fiend."

"What?"

"A fiend. A devil. A creature known in all religions, at all times, to all men. The spawn of a union between a demon and a mortal woman." Kerry forced a smile. "Yes, I know how it sounds. But think a moment. Think of when all this started—this wave of sudden, unnatural juvenile crime, of psychopathic cruelty. Only a few years ago, wasn't it? Just about the time when the babies born in the early years of the War started to enter their teens. Because that's when it happened, during the War, when the men were away. And the women had nightmares—the kind of nightmares some women have throughout the ages. The nightmare of the incubus, the carnal demon who visits them in sleep. It happened before in the history of our culture, during the Crusades. And then followed the rise of the witch cults all over Europe—the witch-cults presided over and attended by the spawn of the night-fiends, the half-human offspring of a blasphemous union. Don't you see how it all fits into the pattern? The unholy love of cruelty for its own sake, the strange, sudden maniacal urge to torture and destroy which comes in sleep, the hideous inability to respond to normal sentiment and normal feelings, the seemingly irrational way in which certain youngsters are irresistibly drawn

together into groups who thrive on violence? As I said
I don't think that even the gangs realize the truth about
themselves yet—but if they ever do, you'll see a wave
of Satanism and Black Magic which will put the Middle Ages to shame. Even now, they gather about fires
in the summer night, seeking the hilltop haunts—''

"You're batty!" Hibbard grabbed Kerry by the
shoulder and shook him roughly. "They're just kids,
that's all. What they need is a damned good beating,
the whole lot of them, and maybe a couple of years in
reform school.''

Kerry shook him off. "Now you're talking like the
authorities—the truant officers and the police and the
get-tough school of welfare workers. Don't you see,
that's just the way they've tried to handle the problem,
and it never works? Any more than psychotherapy can
work? Because you're dealing with something you're
no longer conditioned to believe in. You're dealing
with fiends. What we need is exorcism. I can't let you
go up there, tonight. The police will just start a riot,
it will be murder—''

Hibbard hit him, then, and he went down. His head
struck the edge of the fireplace and he lay silent, an
ugly bruise rising along the side of his right temple.
Hibbard stooped, felt his pulse, then gasped in relief.
Quickly he explored the contents of Kerry's jacket-
pockets. His hands closed over the car-keys.

Then he rose, turned, and ran from the cottage.

Kerry woke to the pain of a terrible throbbing in his
head. He grasped the mantel, pulled himself erect.
The throbbing intensified. But it wasn't all in his head;
part of it pounded in rhythm from a distance. He recognized the sound, the roaring that came from the
hills.

He rubbed his forehead, then walked slowly in the
direction of the porch. The distant darkness was dissolved in a reddish glow, and he could see the flames
rising now from the far hilltop.

Kerry felt in his pocket, then swore and started for

the door. He hesitated in the doorway, then returned
to the living room and stooped over his desk. His hand
scrabbled in the right top drawer; closed over a small
revolver. He slipped it into his jacket-pocket and
headed for the door once again.

It was dark on the path, but the faint flicker of flames
guided his descent. When he reached the bottom of
the hill and made sure that his car was gone, he swore
again, then squatted until he discerned the fresh tire-
tracks and the direction in which they led. Hibbard
had chosen to take the back road, the nearest approach
to the highway which led to the county seat. The road
was rough and it skirted directly behind the big hill
on the Lautenshlager property, but it would be the
fastest route. Kerry wondered if he'd reach the highway in time to head off the police. He hadn't been able
to convince Hibbard, but he was willing to try again.
The police weren't going to solve the situation. There'd
just be more violence. If he only had time to work on
the problem *his* way, to talk to those who still retained
faith in the age-old remedy of exorcism, the casting-
out of demons—

Kerry lengthened his stride, smiling wryly to himself. He couldn't blame Hibbard for his reaction. Most
men were of the same mind today. Most *civilized*
men—that is to say, the small minority of our western
culture who go their way blindly, ignoring the other
billion and a half who still know, as they have always
known, that the forces of darkness exist and are potent. Potent, and able to spawn.

Perhaps it was just as well they didn't believe. He'd
told Hibbard the truth—the only immediate hope lay
in the fact that the changelings themselves weren't fully
aware of their nature. The fiends didn't know they were
fiends. Once they came to learn, and united—

He put the thought away as he worked around behind the hill where the fire flared. Kerry sought the
shadows at the side of the road for concealment; the
noise of racing motors and the sound of shouts muffled
his passing.

Then he rounded a sharp turn and saw the car looming drunkenly in the ditch. Through narrowing eyes he recognized the vehicle as his own. Had there been an accident? He started forward, calling softly. "Hibbard—where are you?"

The figure emerged from the edge of darkness. "Kind of thought you'd be along."

Kerry had just time enough to wonder about the oddly altered voice; time enough for that and no more. Because then they were all around him, some of them holding and some of them striking, and he went down.

When he came to he was already on top of the hill; yes, he must be, because the big brush-fire was leaping and roaring around it.

Why it was like the old woodcuts, the ones showing the Sabbat and the Adoration of the Master. Only there was no Master in the center of the fire—just this burned and blackening figure, a charred dummy of some sort, thrust upright against a post. And the youngsters were dancing and capering, somebody was plucking the guts of a guitar, it was rock-and-roll, just a gang of kids having a good time. Some of them were drinking beer and a few had even started up their motorcycles to race in a circle about the flames.

Sure, they'd panicked and hit him, but they were only teenagers, he told himself, it had to be that way. And he'd explain, he'd tell them. He had to thrust the other thought from his mind, had to. Now they were pulling him into the circle and the big kid, the one with the beaver-tails dangling from his cap, was grinning at him.

"We found the other one," he called. "Clobbered him before he got away."

"Man, he's all shook up."

"Must be hip. He was on his way to town."

"If he got there, we'd really have a gasser."

"Ungood."

"What'll it be?"

Kerry whirled, seeking the source of the voices. He stared at the circle of goatish, grinning faces in the firelight. A girl danced past, bop-fashion, her eyes wild.

"How about the sacrifice bit?"

And then they were all shouting. "The sacrifice bit, that's it! Yeah, Man!"

Sacrifice. Man. The *Black Man* of the Sabbat.

Kerry fought the association, he had to fight it, he couldn't believe that. And then they were pushing him closer to the fire, and he could see the blackened dummy, see that it wore glasses.

When he recognized what was burning there he couldn't fight the knowledge any more, and it was too late to fight the hands which gripped him, held him, then thrust him forward into the flames.

It was the Sabbat, he knew it now; the olden ways with new celebrants and a new tongue for the rituals. Kerry winced in pain, the smoke was suffocating him, in a moment he'd fall.

A mighty shout went up and he made one last effort to retain his faculties. If only he could hear what they were screaming—at least then he'd learn the final truth. *Did they or did they not know what they really were?*

But he fell forward, fainting, as the motorcycles began to race around and around the fire.

Their roaring drowned out every other sound, so even at the end Kerry never heard the chanting.

THE MISSING ITEM
by Isaac Asimov

Emmanuel Rubin, resident polymath of the Black Widowers Society, was visibly chafed. His eyebrows hunched down into the upper portion of his thick-lensed spectacles and his sparse gray beard bristled.

"Not true to life," he said. "Imagine! Not true to life!"

Mario Gonzalo, who had just reached the head of the stairs and had accepted his dry martini from Henry, the unsurpassable waiter, said, "What's not true to life?"

Geoffrey Avalon looked down from his seventy-four inches and said solemnly, "It appears that Manny has suffered a rejection."

"Well, why not?" said Gonzalo, peeling off his gloves. "Editors don't have to be stupid all the time."

"It isn't the rejection," said Rubin. "I've been rejected before by better editors and in connection with better stories. It's the reason he advanced! How the hell would he know if a story were true to life or not? What's he ever done but warm an office chair? Would he . . ."

Roger Halsted, whose career as a math teacher in a junior high school had taught him how to interrupt shrill voices, managed to interpose. "Just what did he find not true to life, Manny?"

Rubin waved a hand passionately outward. "I don't want to talk about it."

"Good," said Thomas Trumbull, scowling from under his neatly waved thatch of white hair. "Then the rest of us can hear each other for a while. Roger, why don't you introduce your guest to the late Mr. Gonzalo?''

Halsted said, ''I've just been waiting for the decibel level to decrease. Mario, my friend Jonathan Thatcher. This is Mario Gonzalo, who is an artist by profession. Jonathan is an oboist, Mario.''

Gonzalo grinned and said, ''Sounds like fun.''

''Sometimes it almost is,'' said Thatcher, ''on days when the reed behaves itself.''

Thatcher's round face and plump cheeks would have made him a natural to play Santa Claus at any Christmas benefit, but he would have needed padding just the same, for his body had that peculiar ersatz slimness that seemed to indicate forty pounds recently lost. His eyebrows were dark and thick, and one took it for granted that they were never drawn together in anger.

Henry said, ''Gentlemen, dinner is ready.''

James Drake stubbed out his cigarette and said, ''Thanks, Henry. It's a cold day and I would welcome hot food.''

''Yes, sir,'' said Henry with a gentle smile. ''Lobster thermidor today, baked potatoes, stuffed eggplant . . .''

''But what's this, Henry?'' demanded Rubin, scowling.

''Hot borscht, Mr. Rubin.''

Rubin looked as though he were searching his soul and then he said grudgingly, ''All right.''

Drake, unfolding his napkin, said, ''Point of order, Roger.''

''What is it?''

''I'm sitting next to Manny, and if he continues to look like that he'll curdle my soup and give me indigestion. You're host and absolute monarch; I move you direct him to tell us what he wrote that isn't true to life and get it out of his system.''

''Why?'' said Trumbull. ''Why not let him sulk and be silent for the novelty of it?''

''I'm curious, too,'' said Gonzalo, ''since nothing he's ever written has been true to life. . . .''

"How would you know, since you can't read?" said Rubin suddenly.

"It's generally known," said Gonzalo. "You hear it everywhere."

"Oh God, I'd better tell you and end this miasma of pseudowit. Look, I've written a novelette, about fifteen thousand words long, about a world-wide organization of locksmiths. . . ."

"Locksmiths?" said Avalon, frowning as though he suspected he had not heard correctly.

"Locksmiths," said Rubin. "These guys are experts, they can open anything—safes, vaults, prison doors. There are no secrets from them, and nothing can be hidden from them. My global organization is of the cream of the profession and no man can join the organization without some document or object of importance stolen from an industrial, political, or governmental unit.

"Naturally, they have the throat of the world in their grip. They can control the stock market, guide diplomacy, make and unmake governments and, at the time my story opens, they are headed by a dangerous megalomaniac. . . ."

Drake interrupted even as he winced in his effort to crack the claw of the lobster. "Who is out to rule the world, of course."

"Of course," said Rubin, "and our hero must stop him. He is himself a skilled locksmith. . . ."

Trumbull interrupted. "In the first place, Manny, what the hell do you know about locksmithery or locksmithmanship or whatever you call it?"

"More than you think," retorted Rubin.

"I doubt that very much," said Trumbull, "and the editor is right. This is utter and complete implausibility. I know a few locksmiths, and they're gentle and inoffensive mechanics with IQ's . . ."

Rubin said, "And I suppose when you were in the army you knew a few corporals and, on the basis of your knowledge, you'll tell me that Napoleon and Hitler were implausible."

The guest for that evening, who had listened to the exchange with a darkening expression, spoke up. "Pardon me, gentlemen, I know I'm to be grilled at the conclusion of dinner. Does that mean I cannot join the dinner conversation beforehand?"

"Heavens, no," said Halsted. "Talk all you want— if you can get a word in now and then."

"In that case, let me put myself forcefully on the side of Mr. Rubin. A conspiracy of locksmiths may sound implausible to us who sit here, but what counts is not what a few rational people think but what the great outside world does. How can your editor turn down anything at all as implausible when everything . . ." He caught himself, took a deep breath, and said, in an altered tone, "Well, I don't mean to tell you your business. I'm not a writer. After all, I don't expect you to tell me how to play the oboe," but his smile as he said it was a weak one.

"Manny will tell you how to play the oboe," said Gonzalo, "if you give him a chance."

"Still," Thatcher said, as though he had not heard Gonzalo's comment, "I live in the world and observe it. *Anything* these days is believed. There is no such thing as 'not true to life.' Just spout any nonsense solemnly and swear it's true and there will be millions rallying round you."

Avalon nodded magisterially and said, "Quite right, Mr. Thatcher. I don't know that this is simply characteristic of our times, but the fact that we have better communications now makes it easier to reach many people quickly so that a phenomenon such as Herr Hitler of unmourned memory is possible. And to those who can believe in Mr. von Däniken's ancient astronauts and in Mr. Berlitz's Bermuda Triangle, a little thing like a conspiracy of locksmiths could be swallowed with the morning porridge."

Thatcher waved his hand. "Ancient astronauts and Bermuda Triangles are nothing. Suppose you were to say that you frequently visited Mars in astral projection and that Mars was, in fact, a haven for the worthy souls of this world. There would be those who would believe you.''

''I imagine so,'' began Avalon.

''You don't have to imagine,'' said Thatcher. ''It *is* so. I take it you haven't heard of Tri-Lucifer. That's t-r-i.''

''Tri-Lucifer?'' said Halsted, looking a little dumbfounded. ''You mean three Lucifers. What's that?''

Thatcher looked from one face to another and the Black Widowers all remained silent.

And then Henry, who was clearing away some of the lobster shells, said, ''If I may be permitted, gentlemen, I have heard of it. There were a group of them soliciting contributions at this restaurant last week.''

''Like the Moonies?'' said Drake, pushing his dish in Henry's direction and preparing to light up.

''There is a resemblance,'' said Henry, his face a bit thoughtful, ''but the Tri-Luciferians, if that is the term to use, give a more other-worldly appearance.''

''That's right,'' said Thatcher, ''they have to divorce themselves from this world so as to achieve astral projection to Mars and facilitate the transfer of their souls there after death.''

''But why—'' began Gonzalo.

And Trumbull suddenly roared out with a blast of anger, ''Come on, Roger, make them wait for the grilling to start. Change the subject.''

Gonzalo said, ''I just want to know why they call them . . .''

Halsted sighed and said, ''Let's wait a while, Mario.''

Henry was making his way about the table with the brandy when Halsted tapped his water glass and said, ''I think we can begin the grilling now, and Manny, since it was your remark about true-to-lifeness that roused Jonathan's interest over the main course, why don't you begin.''

''Sure.'' Rubin looked solemnly across the table at Thatcher and said, ''Mr. Thatcher, at this point it would be traditional to ask you how you justify your existence, and we would then go into a discussion of the oboe as an instrument of torture for oboists. *But* let me guess and say that at this moment you would consider your life justified if you could wipe out a few Tri-Luciferians. Am I right?''

"You are, you are," said Thatcher, energetically. "The whole thing has filled my life and my thoughts for over a month now. It is ruining . . .''

Gonzalo interrupted. "What I want to know is why they call themselves Tri-Luciferians. Are they devil worshipers or what?''

Rubin began, "You're interrupting the man. . . .''

"It's all right," said Thatcher. "I'll tell him. I'm just sorry that I know enough about that organization to be able to tell him. Apparently, Lucifer means the morning star, though I'm not sure why. . . .''

"Lucifer," said Avalon, running his finger about the lip of his water glass, "is from Latin words meaning 'light bringer.' The rising of the morning star in the dawn heralds the soon-following rising of the Sun. In an era in which there were no clocks that was an important piece of information to anyone awake at the time.''

"Then why is Lucifer the name of the devil?'' asked Gonzalo.

Avalon said, "Because the Babylonian King was apparently referred to as the Morning Star by his flattering courtiers, and the Prophet Isaiah predicted his destruction. Can you quote the passage, Manny?''

Rubin said, "We can read it out of the Bible, if we want to. It's the Fourteenth Chapter of Isaiah. The key sentence goes, 'How art thou fallen from heaven, O Lucifer, son of the morning!' It was just a bit of poetic hyperbole, and very effective too, but it was interpreted literally later, and that one sentence gave rise to the whole myth of a rebellion against God by hordes of angels under the leadership of Lucifer, which came to be considered Satan's name while still in heaven. Of course, the rebels were defeated and expelled from heaven by loyalist angels under the leadership of the Archangel Michael."

"As in *Paradise Lost?*" said Gonzalo.

"Exactly as in *Paradise Lost.*"

Thatcher said, "The devil isn't part of it, though. To the Tri-Luciferians, Lucifer just means the morning star. There are two of them on Earth, Venus and Mercury."

Drake squinted through the curling tobacco smoke and said, "They're also evening stars, depending on which side of the Sun they happen to be. They're either east of the Sun and set shortly after sunset, or west of the Sun and rise shortly before sunrise."

Thatcher said, with clear evidence of hope, "Do they have to be both together, both one or both the other?"

"No," said Drake, "they move independently. They can be both evening stars, or both morning stars, or one can be an evening star and one a morning star. Or one or the other or both can be nearly in a line with the Sun and be invisible altogether, morning or evening."

"Too bad," said Thatcher, shaking his head, "that's what *they* say. Anyway, the point is that from Mars you see *three* morning stars in the sky, or you can see them if they're in the right position; not only Mercury and Venus, but Earth as well."

"That's right," said Rubin.

"And," said Thatcher, "I suppose then it's true that they can be in any position. They can all be evening stars or all morning stars, or two can be one and one can be the other?"

"Yes," said Drake, "or one or more can be too close to the Sun to be visible."

Thatcher sighed. "So they call Mars by their mystic name of Tri-Lucifer—the world with the three morning stars."

"I suppose," said Gonzalo, "that Jupiter would have four morning stars, Mercury, Venus, Earth, and

Mars, and so on out to Pluto, which would have eight morning stars."

"The trouble is," said Halsted, "that the farther out you go, the dimmer the inner planets are. Viewed from one of the satellites of Jupiter, for instance, I doubt that Mercury would appear more than a medium-bright star, and it might be too close to the Sun for anyone ever to get a good look at it."

"What about the view from Mars? Could you see Mercury?" asked Thatcher.

"Oh yes, I'm sure of that," said Halsted. "I could work out what the brightness would be in a matter of minutes."

"Would you?" said Thatcher.

"Sure," said Halsted, "if I've remembered to bring my pocket calculator. Yes, I have it. Henry, bring me the Columbia Encyclopedia, would you?"

Rubin said, "While Roger is bending his limited mathematical mind to the problem, Mr. Thatcher, tell us what your interest is in all this. You seem to be interested in exposing them as fakers. Why? Have you been a member? Are you now disillusioned?"

"No, I've never been a member. I . . . ." He rubbed his temple hesitantly. "It's my wife. I don't like talking about it, you understand."

Avalon said solemnly, "Please be assured, Mr. Thatcher, that whatever is said here never passes beyond the bounds of this room. That includes our valued waiter, Henry. You may speak freely."

"Well, there's nothing criminal or disgraceful in it. I just don't like to seem to be so helpless in such a silly . . . It's breaking up my marriage, gentlemen."

There was a discreet silence around the table, broken only by the mild sound of Halsted turning the pages of the encyclopedia.

Thatcher went on. "Roger knows my wife. He'll tell you she's a sensible woman. . . ."

Halsted looked up briefly and nodded. "I'll vouch for that, but I didn't know you were having this . . ."

"Lately, Carol has not been social, you understand,

and I certainly haven't talked about it. It was with great difficulty, you know, that I managed to agree to come out tonight. I dread leaving her to herself. You see, even sensible people have their weaknesses. Carol worries about death.''

"So do we all," said Drake.

"So do I," said Thatcher, "but in a normal way, I hope. We all know we'll die someday and we don't particularly look forward to it, and we may worry about hell or nothingness or hope for heaven, but we don't think about it much. Carol has been fascinated, however, by the possibility of demonstrating the actual existence of life after death. It may have all started with the Bridey Murphy case when she was a teenager—I don't know if any of you remember that . . .''

"I do," said Rubin. "A woman under hypnosis seemed to be possessed by an Irishwoman who had died a long time before.''

"Yes," said Thatcher. "She saw through that, eventually. Then she grew interested in spiritualism and gave that up. I always relied on her to understand folly when she finally stopped to think about it—and then she came up against the Tri-Luciferians. I never saw her like this. She wants to join them. She has money of her own and she wants to give it to them. I don't care about the money—well, I do, but that's not the main thing—I care about *her*. You know, she's going to join them in their retreat somewhere, become a daughter of Tri-Lucifer, or whatever they call it, and wait for translation to the Abode of the Blessed. One of these days, she'll be gone. I just won't see her anymore. She promised me it wouldn't be tonight, but I wonder.''

Rubin said, "I take it you suppose that the organization is just interested in her money.''

"At least the leader of it is," said Thatcher grimly. "I'm sure of it. What else can he be after?''

"Do you know him? Have you met him?" said Rubin.

"No. He keeps himself isolated," said Thatcher,

"but I hear he has recently bought a fancy mansion in Florida, and I doubt that it's for the use of the membership."

"Funny thing about that," said Drake. "It doesn't matter how lavishly a cult leader lives; how extravagantly he throws money around. The followers who support him and see their money clearly used for that purpose never seem to mind."

"They identify," said Rubin. "The more he spends, the more successful they consider the cause. It's the basis of ostentatious waste in governmental display, too."

"Just the same," said Thatcher, "I don't think Carol will ever commit herself entirely. She might not be bothered by the leader's actions, but if I can prove him *wrong*, she'll drop it."

"Wrong about what?" asked Rubin.

"Wrong about Mars. This head of the group claims he has been on Mars often—in astral projection, of course. He describes Mars in detail, but can he be describing it accurately?"

"Why not?" asked Rubin. "If he reads up on what is known about Mars, he can describe it as astronomers would. The Viking photographs even show a part of the surface in detail. It's not difficult to be accurate."

"Yes, but it may be that somewhere he has made a mistake, something I can show Carol."

Halsted looked up and said, "Here, I've worked out the dozen brightest objects in the Martian sky, together with their magnitudes. I may be off a little here and there, but not by much." He passed a slip of paper around.

Mario held up the paper when it reached him. "Would you like to see it, Henry?"

"Thank you, sir," murmured Henry, and as he glanced at it briefly, one eyebrow raised itself just slightly, just briefly.

The paper came to rest before Thatcher eventually and he gazed at it earnestly. What he saw was this:

Sun	—26
Phobos	—9.6
Deimos	—5.1
Earth	—4.5
Jupiter	—3.1
Venus	—2.6
Sirius	—1.4
Saturn	—0.8
Canopus	—0.7
Alpha Centauri	—0.3
Arcturus	—0.1
Mercury	0.0

Thatcher said, "Phobos and Deimos are the two satellites of Mars. Do these numbers mean they're very bright?"

"The greater the negative number," said Halsted, "the brighter the object. A –2 object is 2½ times brighter than a –1 object, and a –3 object is 2½ times brighter still, and so on. Next to the Sun, Phobos is the brightest object in the Martian sky, and Deimos is next."

"And next to the Sun and the two satellites, Earth is the brightest object in the sky, then."

"Yes, but only at or near its maximum brightness," said Halsted. "It can be much dimmer depending on where Mars and Earth are in their respective orbits. Most of the time it's probably less bright than Jupiter, which doesn't change much in brightness as it moves in its orbit."

Thatcher shook his head and looked disappointed. "But it *can* be that bright. Too bad. There's a special prayer or psalm or something that the Tri-Luciferians have that appears in almost all their literature. I've seen it so often in the stuff Carol brings home, I can quote it so exactly. It goes, 'When Earth shines high in the sky, like a glorious jewel, and when the other Lucifers have fled beyond the horizon, so that Earth shines alone in splendor, single in beauty, unmatched in brightness, it is then the souls of those ready to receive the call must prepare to rise from Earth and cross the gulf.' And what you're saying, Roger, is that Earth *can* be the brightest object in the Martian sky.''

Halsted nodded. ''At night, if Phobos and Deimos are below the horizon, and Earth is near maximum brightness, it is certainly the brightest object in the sky. It would be 3½ times as bright as Jupiter, if that were in the sky, and 6 times as bright as Venus at its brightest.''

''And it could be the only morning star in the sky.''

''Or the only evening star. Sure. The other two, Venus and Mercury, could be on the other side of the Sun from Earth.''

Thatcher kept staring at the list. ''But would Mercury be visible? It's at the bottom of the list.''

Halsted said, ''The bottom just means that it's twelfth brightest, but there are thousands of stars that are dimmer and still visible. There would be only four stars brighter than Mercury as seen from Mars: Sirius, Canopus, Alpha Centauri, and Arcturus.''

Thatcher said, ''If they'd only make a mistake.''

Avalon said in a grave and somewhat hesitant baritone, ''Mr. Thatcher, I think perhaps you had better face the facts. It is my experience that even if you *do* find a flaw in the thesis of the Tri-Luciferians it won't help you. Those who follow cults for emotional reasons are not deterred by demonstrations of the illogic of what they are doing.''

Thatcher said, ''I agree with you, and I wouldn't dream of arguing with the ordinary cultist. But I know Carol. I have seen her turn away from a system of beliefs she would very much like to have followed, simply because she saw the illogic of it. If I could find something of the sort here, I'm sure she'd come back.''

Gonzalo said, ''Some of us here ought to think of something. After all, he's never *really* been on Mars. He's got to have made a mistake.''

''Not at all,'' said Avalon. ''He probably knows as much about Mars as we do. Therefore, even if he's made a mistake it may be because he fails to understand something we also fail to understand and we won't catch him.''

Thatcher nodded his head. "I suppose you're right."

"I don't know," said Gonzalo. "How about the canals? The Tri-Luciferians are bound to talk about the canals. Everyone believed in them and then just lately we found out they weren't there; isn't that right? So if he talks about them, he's caught."

Drake said, "Not everybody believed in them, Mario. Hardly any astronomers did."

"The general public did," said Gonzalo.

Rubin said, "Not lately. It was in 1964 that Mariner 4 took the first pictures of Mars and that pretty much gave away the fact the canals didn't exist. Once Mariner 9 mapped the whole planet in 1969 there was no further argument. When did the Tri-Luciferians come into existence, Mr. Thatcher?"

"As I recall," said Thatcher, "about 1970. Maybe 1971."

"There you are," said Rubin. "Once we had Mars down cold, this guy, whoever he is who runs it, decided to start a new religion based on it. Listen, if you want to get rich quick, no questions asked, start a new religion. Between the First Amendment and the tax breaks you get, it amounts to a license to help yourself to everything in sight. I'll bet he talks about volcanoes."

Thatcher nodded. "The Martian headquarters of the astral projections are in Olympus Mons. That means Mount Olympus, and that's where the souls of the righteous gather. That's the big volcano, isn't it?"

"The biggest in the solar system," said Rubin. "At least, that we know of. It's been known since 1969."

Thatcher said, "The Tri-Luciferians say that G. V. Schiaparelli—he's the one who named the different places on Mars—was astrally inspired to name that spot Olympus to signify it was the home of the godly. In ancient Greece, you see, Mount Olympus was . . ."

"Yes," said Avalon, nodding gravely, "we know."

"Isn't Schiaparelli the fellow who first reported the canals?" said Gonzalo.

"Yes," said Halsted, "although actually when he said *canali* he meant natural waterways."

"Even so, why didn't the same astral inspiration tell him the canals weren't there?" asked Gonzalo.

Drake nodded and said, "That's something you can point out to your wife."

"No," said Thatcher, "I guess they thought of that. They say the canals were part of the inspiration because that increased interest in Mars and that that was needed to make the astral projection process more effective."

Trumbull, who had maintained a sullen silence through the discussion, as though he were waiting his chance to shift the discussion to oboes, said suddenly, "That makes a diseased kind of sense."

Thatcher said, "Too much makes sense. That's the trouble. There are times when I want to find a mistake not so much to save Carol as to save myself. I tell you that when I listen to Carol talking there's sometimes more danger she'll argue me into being crazy than that I'll persuade her to be rational."

Trumbull waved a hand at him soothingly. "Just take it easy and let's think it out. Do they say anything about the satellites?"

"They talk about them, yes. Phobos and Deimos. Sure."

"Do they say anything about how they cross the sky?" Trumbull's smile was nearly a smirk.

"Yes," said Thatcher, "and I looked it up because I didn't believe them and I thought I had something. In their description of the Martian scene, they talk about Phobos rising in the west and setting in the east. And it turns out that's true. And they say that whenever either Phobos or Deimos cross the sky at night, they are eclipsed by Mars's shadow for part of the time. And that's true, too."

Halsted shrugged. "The satellites were discovered a century ago, in 1877, by Asaph Hall. As soon as their distance from Mars and their period of revolution were determined, which were almost at once, their behavior in Mars's sky was known.''

"*I* didn't know it," said Thatcher.

"No," said Halsted, "but this fellow who started the religion apparently did his homework. It wasn't really hard.''

"Hold on," said Trumbull truculently, "some things aren't as obvious and don't get put into the average elementary-astronomy textbook. For instance, I read somewhere that Phobos can't be seen from the Martian polar regions. It's so close to Mars that the bulge of Mars's spherical surface hides the satellite, if you go far enough north or south. Do the Tri-Luciferians say anything about Phobos being invisible from certain places on Mars, Thatcher?''

"Not that I recall," said Thatcher, "but they don't say it's always visible. If they just don't mention the matter, what does that prove?''

"Besides," said Halsted, "Olympus Mons is less than twenty degrees north of the Martian equator, and Phobos is certainly visible from there any time it is above the horizon and not in eclipse. And if that's the headquarters for the souls from Earth, Mars would certainly be described as viewed from that place.''

"Whose side are you on?" growled Trumbull.

"The truth's," said Halsted. "Still, it's true that astronomy books rarely describe any sky but Earth's. That's why I had to figure out the brightness of objects in the Martian sky instead of just looking it up. The only trouble is that this cult leader seems to be just as good at figuring.''

"I've got an idea," said Avalon. "I'm not much of an astronomer, but I've seen the photographs taken by the Viking landers and I've read the newspaper reports about them. For one thing, the Martian sky in the daytime is pink, because of the fine particles of the reddish dust in the air. In that case, isn't it possible that the dust obscures the night sky so that you don't see anything? Good Lord, it happens often enough in New York City.''

Halsted said, "As a matter of fact, the problem in New York isn't so much the dust as the scattered light from the buildings and highways, and even in New York you can see the bright stars, if the sky isn't cloudy.

"On Mars, it would have to work both ways. If there is enough dust to make the sky invisible from the ground, then the ground would be invisible from the sky. For instance, when Mariner 9 reached Mars in 1969, Mars was having a globewide duststorm and none of its surface could be seen by Mariner. At that time, from the Martian surface, the sky would have had to be blanked out. Most of the time, though, we see the surface clearly from our probes, so from the Martian surface, the sky would be clearly visible.

"In fact, considering that Mars's atmosphere is much thinner than Earth's, less than a hundredth as thick, it would scatter and absorb far less light than Earth's does, and the various stars and planets would all look a little brighter than they would with Earth's atmosphere in the way. I didn't allow for that in my table.''

Trumbull said, "Geoff mentioned the Viking photographs. They show rocks all over the place. Do the Tri-Luciferians mention rocks?''

"No," said Thatcher, "not that I ever noticed. But again, they don't say there aren't any. They talk about huge canyons and dry riverbeds and terraced ice-fields.''

Rubin snorted. "All that's been known since 1969. More homework.''

Avalon said, "What about life? We still don't know if there's any life on Mars. The Viking results are ambiguous. Have the Tri-Luciferians committed themselves on that?''

Thatcher thought, then said, "I wish I could say I had read all their literature thoroughly, but I haven't. Still Carol has forced me to read quite a bit since she said I ought not defame anything without learning about it first.''

''That's true enough,'' said Avalon, ''though life is short and there are some things that are so unlikely on the surface that one hesitates to devote much of one's time to a study of it. However, can you say anything as to their attitude toward Martian life from what you've read of their literature?''

Thatcher said, ''They speak about Mars's barren surface, its desert aridity and emptiness. They contrast that with the excitement and fullness of the astral sphere.''

''Yes,'' said Avalon, ''and of course, the surface *is* dry and empty and barren. We know that much. What about microscopic life? That's what we're looking for.''

Thatcher shook his head. ''No mention of it, as far as I know.''

Avalon said, ''Well, then, I can't think of anything else. I'm quite certain this whole thing is nonsense. Everyone here is, and none of us need proof of it. If your wife needs proof, we may not be able to supply it.''

''I understand,'' said Thatcher. ''I thank you all, of course, and I suppose she may come to her senses after a while, but I must admit I have never seen her quite like this. I would join the cult with her just to keep her in sight but, frankly, I'm afraid I'll end up believing it, too.''

And in the silence that followed, Henry said softly, ''Perhaps, Mr. Thatcher, you need not go to that extreme.''

Thatcher turned suddenly. ''Pardon me. Did you say something, waiter?''

Halsted said, ''Henry is a member of the club, Jonathan. I don't know that he's an astronomer exactly, but he's the brightest person here. Is there something we've missed, Henry?''

Henry said, ''I think so, sir. You said, Mr. Halsted, that astronomy books don't generally describe any sky but Earth's, and I guess that must be why the cult leader seems to have a missing item in his description of Mars. Without it, the whole thing is no more true to life than Mr. Rubin's conspiracy of locksmiths—if I may be forgiven, Mr. Rubin.''

''Not if you don't supply a missing object, Henry.''

Henry said, ''On Earth, Mercury and Venus are the morning and evening stars, and we always think of such objects as planets, therefore. Consequently, from Mars, there must be three morning and evening stars, Mercury, Venus, plus Earth in addition. That is memorialized in the very name of the cult and from that alone I could see the whole thing fails.''

Halsted said, ''I'm not sure I see your point, Henry.''

''But, Mr. Halsted,'' said Henry, ''where is the Moon in all this? It is a large object, our Moon, almost the size of Mercury and closer to Mars than Mercury is. If Mercury can be seen from Mars, surely the Moon can be, too. Yet I noticed it was not on your list of bright objects in the Martian sky.''

Halsted turned red. ''Yes, of course. The list of planets fooled me, too. You just list them without mentioning the Moon.'' He reached for the paper. ''The Moon is smaller than Earth and less reflective, so that it is only one seventieth as bright as the Earth, at equal distance and phase, which means—a magnitude of 0.0. It would be just as bright as Mercury and in fact it could be seen more easily than Mercury could be because it would be higher in the sky. At sunset, Mercury as evening star would never be higher than 16 degrees above the horizon, while Earth could be as much as 44 degrees above—pretty high in the sky.''

Henry said, ''Mars, therefore, would have four morning stars, and the very name Tri-Lucifer is nonsense.''

Avalon said, ''But the Moon would always be close to Earth, so wouldn't Earth's light drown it out?''

''No,'' said Halsted. ''Let's see now—never get a pocket calculator that doesn't have keys for the trigonometric functions—the Moon would be, at times, as much as 23 minutes of arc away from Earth, when viewed from Mars. That's three quarters the width of the Moon as seen from Earth.''

Henry said, ''One more thing. Would you repeat that verse once again, Mr. Thatcher, the one about the Earth being high in the sky?''

Thatcher said, ''Certainly. 'When Earth shines high in the sky, like a glorious jewel, and when the other Lucifers have fled beyond the horizon, so that Earth shines alone in splendor, single in beauty, unmatched in brightness, it is then that the souls of those ready to receive the call must prepare to rise from Earth and cross the gulf.' ''

Henry said, ''Earth may be quite high in the sky at times, and Mercury and Venus may be on the other side of the Sun and therefore beyond the horizon—but Earth cannot be 'alone in splendor.' The Moon has to be with it. Of course, there would be times when the Moon is very nearly in front of Earth or behind it, as seen from Mars, so that the two dots of light merge into one that seems to make Earth brighter than ever, but the Moon is not then beyond the horizon. It seems to me, Mr. Thatcher, that the cult leader was never on Mars, because if he had been he would not have missed a pretty big item, a world 2,160 miles across. Surely you can explain this to your wife.''

''Yes,'' said Thatcher, his face brightening into a smile, ''she would have to see the whole thing as a fake.''

''If it is true, as you say,'' said Henry quietly, ''that she is a rational person.''

THE COMPLEAT WEREWOLF

by Anthony Boucher

Author's Note: In my criminological researches, I have occasionally come across references to an agent of the Federal Bureau of Investigation who bids fair to become as a great a figure of American legend as Paul Bunyan or John Henry. This man is invulnerable to bullets. He strikes such terror into criminals as to drive them to suicide or madness. He sometimes vanishes from human ken entirely, and at other times he is reported to have appeared with equal suddenness stark naked. And perhaps the most curious touch of all, he engages in a never ceasing quest, of Arthurian intensity, for someone who can perform the Indian rope trick.

Only recently, after intensive probings in Berkeley, where I have certain fortunate connections particularly with the department of German, and a few grudging confidences from my old friend Fergus O'Breen, have I been able to piece together the facts behind this legend.

Here, then, is the story, with only one important detail suppressed, and that, I assure you, strictly for your own good.

The Professor glanced at the note:

Don't be silly—Gloria.

Wolfe Wolf crumpled the sheet of paper into a yellow ball and hurled it out the window into the sunshine of the bright campus spring. He made several choice and profane remarks in fluent Middle High German.

Emily looked up from typing the proposed budget for the departmental library. "I'm afraid I didn't understand that, Professor Wolf. I'm weak on Middle High."

"Just improvising," said Wolf, and sent a copy of the *Journal of English and Germanic Philology* to follow the telegram.

Emily rose from the typewriter. "There's something the matter. Did the committee reject your monograph on Hager?"

"That monumental contribution to human knowledge? Oh, no. Nothing so important as that."

"But you're so upset . . ."

"The office wife!" Wolf snorted. "And pretty polyandrous at that, with the whole department on your hands. Go 'way."

Emily's dark little face lit up with a flame of righteous anger that removed any trace of plainness. "Don't talk to me like that, Mr. Wolf. I'm simply trying to help you. And it isn't the whole department. It's . . ."

Professor Wolf picked up an inkwell, looked after the telegram and the *Journal,* then set the glass pot down again. "No. There are better ways of going to pieces. Sorrows drown easier than they smash . . . Get Herbrecht to take my two o'clock, will you?"

"Where are you going?"

"To hell in sectors. So long."

"Wait. Maybe I can help you. Remember when the dean jumped you for serving drinks to students? Maybe I can . . ."

Wolf stood in the doorway and extended one arm impressively, pointing with that curious index which was as long as the middle finger. "Madam, academically you are indispensable. You are the prop and stay of the existence of this department. But at the moment this department can go to hell, where it will doubtless continue to need your invaluable services."

"But don't you see . . ." Emily's voice shook. "No. Of course not. You wouldn't see. You're just a man—

no, not even a man. You're just Professor Wolf. You're Woof-woof.''

Wolf staggered. "I'm what?"

"Woof-woof. That's what everybody calls you because your name's Wolfe Wolf. All your students, everybody. But you wouldn't notice a thing like that. Oh, no. Woof-woof, that's what you are.''

"This," said Wolfe Wolf, "is the crowning blow. My heart is breaking, my world is shattered, I've got to walk a mile from the campus to find a bar; but all this isn't enough. I've got to be called Woof-woof. Good-bye!"

He turned, and in the doorway caromed into a vast and yielding bulk, which gave out with a noise that might have been either a greeting of "Wolf!" or probably an inevitable grunt of "Oof!"

Wolf backed into the room and admitted Professor Fearing, paunch, pince-nez, cane and all. The older man waddled over to his desk, plumped himself down, and exhaled a long breath. "My dear boy," he gasped. "Such impetuosity."

"Sorry, Oscar."

"Ah, youth . . ." Professor Fearing fumbled about for a handkerchief, found none, and proceeded to polish his pince-nez on his somewhat stringy necktie. "But why such haste to depart? And why is Emily crying?"

"Is she?"

"You see?" said Emily hopelessly, and muttered "Woof-woof" into her damp handkerchief.

"And why do copies of the *JEGP* fly about my head as I harmlessly cross the campus? Do we have teleportation on our hands?"

"Sorry," Wolf repeated curtly. "Temper. Couldn't stand that ridiculous argument of Glocke's. Goodbye."

"One moment." Professor Fearing fished into one of his unnumbered handkerchiefless pockets and produced a sheet of yellow paper. "I believe this is yours?"

Wolf snatched at it and quickly converted it into confetti.

Fearing chuckled. "How well I remember when Gloria was a student here! I was thinking of it only last night when I saw her in *Moonbeams and Melody*. How she did upset this whole department! Heavens, my boy, if I'd been a younger man myself . . ."

"I'm going. You'll see about Herbrecht, Emily?"

Emily sniffled and nodded.

"Come, Wolfe." Fearing's voice had grown more serious. "I didn't mean to plague you. But you mustn't take these things too hard. There are better ways of finding consolation than in losing your temper or getting drunk."

"Who said anything about . . ."

"Did you need to say it? No, my boy, if you were to . . . You're not a religious man, are you?"

"Good God, no," said Wolf contradictorily.

"If only you were . . . If I might make a suggestion, Wolf, why don't you come over to the Temple tonight? We're having very special services. They might take your mind off Glo—off your troubles."

"Thanks, no I've always meant to visit your Temple—I've heard rumors about it—but not tonight. Some other time."

"Tonight would be especially interesting."

"Why? What's so special about April 30th?"

Fearing shook his gray head. "It is shocking how ignorant a scholar can be outside of his chosen field . . . But you know the place, Wolfe; I'll hope to see you there tonight."

"Thanks. But my troubles don't need any supernatural solutions. A couple of zombies will do nicely, and I do *not* mean serviceable stiffs. Good-bye, Oscar." He was halfway through the door before he added as an afterthought, " 'Bye, Emily."

"Such rashness," Fearing murmured. "Such impetuosity. Youth is a wonderful thing to enjoy, is it not, Emily?"

Emily said nothing, but plunged into typing the proposed budget as though all the fiends of hell were after her, as indeed many of them were.

The sun was setting, and Wolfe's tragic account of his troubles had laid an egg, too. The bartender had polished every glass in the joint and still the repetitive tale kept pouring forth. He was torn between a boredom new even in his experience and a professional admiration for a customer who could consume zombies indefinitely.

"Did I tell you about the time she flunked the midterm?" Wolf demanded truculently.

"Only three times," said the bartender.

"All right, then; I'll tell you. Yunnerstand, I don't do things like this. Profeshical ethons, that's what's I've got. But this was different. This wasn't like somebody that doesn't know just because she doesn't know; this was a girl that didn't know because she wasn't the kind of girl that has to know the kind of things a girl has to know if she's the kind of girl that ought to know that kind of things. Yunnerstand?"

The bartender cast a calculating glance at the plump little man who sat alone at the end of the deserted bar, carefully nursing his gin and tonic.

"She made me see that. She made me see lossa things and I can still see the things she made me see the things. It wasn't just like a professor falls for a coed, yunnerstand? This was different. This was wunnaful. This was like a whole new life like."

The bartender sidled down to the end of the bar. "Brother," he whispered softly.

The little man with the odd beard looked up from his gin and tonic. "Yes, colleague?"

"If I listen to that potted professor another five minutes, I'm going to start smashing up the joint. How's about slipping down there and standing in for me, huh?"

The little man looked Wolf over and fixed his gaze especially on the hand that clenched the tall zombie glass. "Gladly, colleague," he nodded.

The bartender sighed a gust of relief.

"She was Youth," Wolf was saying intently to where the bartender had stood. "But it wasn't just that. This was different. She was Life and Excitement and Joy and Ecstasy and Stuff. Yunner . . ." He broke off and stared at the empty space. *"Uh-mazing!"* he observed. "Right before my very eyes. *Uh-mazing!"*

"You were saying, colleague?" the plump little man prompted from the adjacent stool.

Wolf turned. "So there you are. Did I tell you about the time I went to her house to check her term paper?"

"No. But I have a feeling you will."

"Howja know? Well, this night . . ."

The little man drank slowly; but his glass was empty by the time Wolf had finished the account of an evening of pointlessly tentative flirtation. Other customers were drifting in, and the bar was now about a third full.

"—and ever since then—" Wolf broke off sharply. "That isn't you," he objected.

"I think it is, colleague."

"But you're a bartender and *you* aren't a bartender."

"No. I'm a magician."

"Oh. That explains it. Now like I was telling you . . . Hey! Your bald is beard."

"I beg your pardon?"

"Your bald is beard. Just like your head. It's all jussa fringe running around."

"I like it that way."

"And your glass is empty."

"That's all right, too."

"Oh, no, it isn't. It isn't every night you get to drink with a man that proposed to Gloria Garton and got turned down. This is an occasion for celebration." Wolf thumped loudly on the bar and held up his first two fingers.

The little man regarded their equal length. "No," he said softly. "I think I'd better not. I know my capacity. If I have another—well, things might start happening.''

"Lettemappen!"

"No. Please, colleague. I'd rather . . ."

The bartender brought the drinks. "Go on, brother," he whispered. "Keep him quiet. I'll do you a favor sometime."

Reluctantly the little man sipped at his fresh gin and tonic.

The professor took a gulp of his *n*th zombie. "My name's Woof-woof," he proclaimed "Lots of people call me Wolfe Wolf. They think that's funny. But it's really Woof-woof. Wazoors?"

The other paused a moment to decipher that Arabic-sounding word, then said, Mine's Ozymandias the Great." "That's a funny name."

"I told you I'm a magician. Only I haven't worked for a long time. Theatrical managers are peculiar, colleague. They don't want a real magician. They won't even let me show 'em my best stuff. Why, I remember one night in Darjeeling . . ."

"Glad to meet you, Mr. . . . Mr. . . ."

"You can call me Ozzy. Most people do."

"Glad to meet you, Ozzy. Now about this girl. This Gloria. Yunnerstand, donya?"

"Sure, colleague."

"She thinks being a professor of German is nothing. She wants something glamorous. She says if I was an actor now or a G-man . . . Yunnerstand?"

Ozymandias the Great nodded.

"Awright then! So yunnerstand. Fine. But whatddayou want to keep talking about it for? Yunnerstand. That's that. To hell with it."

Ozymandias' round and fringed face brightened. "Sure," he said, and added recklessly, "let's drink to that."

They clinked glasses and drank. Wolf carelessly tossed off a toast in Old Low Frankish, with an unpardonable error in the use of the genitive.

The two men next to them began singing "My Wild

Irish Rose," but trailed off disconsolately. "What we need," said the one with the derby, "is a tenor."

"What I need," Wolf muttered, "is a cigarette."

"Sure," said Ozymandias the Great. The bartender was drawing beer directly in front of them. Ozymandias reached across the bar, removed a lighted cigarette from the barkeep's ear, and handed it to his companion.

"Where'd that come from?"

"I don't quite know. All I know is how to get them. I told you I was a magician."

"Oh. I see. Pressajijijation."

"No. Not a prestidigitator; I said a magician. Oh, blast it! I've done it again. More than one gin and tonic and I start showing off."

"I don't believe you," said Wolf flatly. "No such thing as magicians. That's just as silly as Oscar Fearing and his Temple and what's so special about April 30th, anyway?"

The bearded man frowned. "Please, colleague. Let's forget it."

"No. I don't believe you. You pressajijijated that cigarette. You didn't magic it." His voice began to rise. "You're a fake."

"Please, brother," the barkeep whispered. "Keep him quiet."

"All right," said Ozymandias wearily. "I'll show you something that can't be prestidigitation." The couple adjoining had begun to sing again. "They need a tenor. All right; listen!"

And the sweetest, most ineffably Irish tenor ever heard joined in on the duet. The singers didn't worry about the source; they simply accepted the new voice gladly and were spurred on to their very best, with the result that the bar knew the finest harmony it had heard since the night the Glee Club was suspended en masse.

Wolf looked impressed, but shook his head. "That's not magic, either. That's ventriloquism."

"As a matter of strict fact, that was a street singer

who was killed in the Easter Rebellion. Fine fellow, too; never heard a better voice unless it was that night in Darjeeling when . . ."

"Fake!" said Wolfe Wolf loudly and belligerently.

Ozymandias once more contemplated that long index finger. He looked at the professor's dark brows that met in a straight line over his nose. He picked his companion's limpish hand off the bar and scrutinized the palm. The growth of hair was not marked, but it was perceptible.

The magician chortled. "And you sneer at magic!"

"Whasso funny about me sneering at magic?"

Ozymandias lowered his voice. "Because, my fine furry friend, you are a werewolf."

The Irish martyr had begun "Rose of Tralee" and the two mortals were joining in valiantly.

"I'm what?"

"A werewolf."

"But there isn't any such thing. Any fool knows that."

"Fools," said Ozymandias, "know a great deal which the wise do not. There are werewolves. There always have been, and quite probably always will be." He spoke as calmly and assuredly as though he were mentioning that the earth was round. "And there are three infallible physical signs; the meeting eyebrows, the long index finger, the hairy palms. You have all three. And even your name is an indication. Family names do not come from nowhere. Every Smith has an ancestor somewhere who was a Smith. Every Fisher comes from a family that once fished. And your name is Wolf."

The statement was so quiet, so plausible, that Wolf faltered. "But a werewolf is a man that changes into a wolf. I've never done that. Honest I haven't."

"A mammal," said Ozymandias, "is an animal that bears its young alive and suckles them. A virgin is nonetheless a mammal. Because you have never changed does not make you any the less a werewolf."

"But a werewolf . . ." Suddenly Wolf's eyes lit up.

"A werewolf! But that's even better than a G-man! Now I can show Gloria!"

"What on earth do you mean, colleague?"

Wolf was climbing down from his stool. The intense excitement of this brilliant new idea seemed to have sobered him. He grabbed the little man by the sleeve. "Come on. We're going to find a nice quiet place. And you're going to prove you're a magician."

"But how?"

"You're going to show me how to change!"

Ozymandias finished his gin and tonic, and with it drowned his last regretful hesitation. "Colleague," he announced, "you're on!"

Professor Oscar Fearing, standing behind the curiously carved lectern of the Temple of the Dark Truth, concluded the reading of the prayer with mumbling sonority. "And on this night of all nights, in the name of the black light that glows in the darkness, we give thanks!" He closed the parchment-bound book and faced the small congregation, calling out with fierce intensity, "Who wishes to give his thanks to the Lower Lord?"

A cushioned dowager rose. "I give thanks!" she shrilled excitedly. "My Ming Choy was sick, even unto death. I took of her blood and offered it to the Lower Lord, and he had mercy and restored her to me!"

Behind the altar an electrician checked his switches and spat disgustedly. "Bugs! Every last one of 'em!"

The man who was struggling into a grotesque and horrible costume paused and shrugged. "They pay good money. What's it to us if they're bugs?"

A tall, thin, old man had risen uncertainly to his feet. "I give thanks!" he cried. "I give thanks to the Lower Lord that I have finished my great work. My protective screen against magnetic bombs is a tried and proven success, to the glory of our country and science and the Lord."

"Crackpot," the electrician muttered.

The man in costume peered around the altar. "Crackpot, hell! That's Chiswick from the physics department. Think of a man like that falling for this stuff! And listen to him: He's even telling about the government's plans for installation. You know, I'll bet you one of these fifth columnists could pick up something around here."

There was silence in the Temple when the congregation had finished its thanksgiving. Professor Fearing leaned over the lectern and spoke quietly and impressively. "As you know, brothers in Darkness, tonight is May Eve, the 30th of April, the night consecrated by the Church to that martyr missionary St. Walpurgis, and by us to other and deeper purposes. It is on this night, and this night only, that we may directly give our thanks to the Lower Lord himself. Not in wanton orgy and obscenity, as the Middle Ages misconceived his desires, but in praise and in deep, dark joy that issues forth from Blackness."

"Hold your hats, boys," said the man in the costume. "Here I go again."

"Eka!" Fearing thundered *"Dva tri chatur! Pancha! Shas sapta! Ashta nava dasha ekadasha!"* He paused. There was always the danger that at this moment some scholar in this university town might recognize that the invocation, though perfect Sanskrit, consisted solely of the numbers from one to eleven. But no one stirred, and he launched forth in more apposite Latin: *"Per vota nostra ipse nunc surgat nobis dicatus Baal Zebub!"*

"Baal Zebub!" the congregation chorused.

"Cue," said the electrician, and pulled a switch.

The lights flickered and went out. Lightning played across the sanctuary. Suddenly out of the darkness came a sharp bark, a yelp of pain, and a long-drawn howl of triumph.

A blue light now began to glow dimly. In the faint reflection of this, the electrician was amazed to see his costumed friend at his side, nursing his bleeding hand.

"What the . . ." the electrician whispered.

"Hanged if I know. I go out there on cue. all ready to make my terrifying appearance, and what happens? Great big dog up and nips my hand. Why didn't they tell me they'd switched the script?"

In the glow of the blue light the congregation reverently contemplated the plump little man with the fringe of beard and the splendid gray wolf that stood beside him. "Hail, O Lower Lord!" resounded the chorus, drowning out one spinster's murmur of "But my *dear*, I *swear* he was *much* handsomer last year."

"Colleagues!" said Ozymandias the Great, and there was utter silence, a dread hush awaiting the momentous words of the Lower Lord. Ozymandias took one step forward, placed his tongue carefully between his lips, uttered the ripest, juiciest raspberry of his career, and vanished, wolf and all.

Wolfe Wolf opened his eyes and shut them again hastily. He had never expected the quiet and sedate Berkeley Inn to install centrifugal rooms. It wasn't fair. He lay in darkness, waiting for the whirling to stop and trying to reconstruct the past night.

He remembered the bar all right, and the zombies. And the bartender. Very sympathetic chap that, up until he suddenly changed into a little man with a fringe of beard. That was where things began getting strange. There was something about a cigarette and an Irish tenor and a werewolf. Fantastic idea, that. Any fool knows . . .

Wolf sat up suddenly. He *was* the werewolf. He threw back the bedclothes and stared down at his legs. Then he sighed relief. They were long legs. They were hairy enough. They were brown from much tennis. But they were indisputably human.

He got up, resolutely stifling his qualms, and began to pick up the clothing that was scattered nonchalantly about the floor. A crew of gnomes was excavating his skull, but he hoped they might go away if he didn't pay too much attention to them. One thing was certain; he was going to be good from now on. Gloria or no Gloria, heartbreak or no heartbreak, drowning your sorrows wasn't good enough. If you felt like this and could imagine you'd been a werewolf . . .

But why should he have imagined it in such detail? So many fragmentary memories seemed to come back as he dressed. Going up Strawberry Canyon with the fringed beard, finding a desolate and isolated spot for magic, learning the words . . . He could even remember the words. The word that changed you and the one that changed you back.

Had he made up those words, too, in his drunken imaginings? And had he made up what he could only barely recall—the wonderful, magical freedom of changing, the single sharp pang of alteration and then the boundless happiness of being lithe and fleet and free?

He surveyed himself in the mirror. He looked exactly what he was, save for the unwonted wrinkles in his conservative single-breasted gray suit: a quiet academician, a little better built, a little more impulsive, a little more romantic than most, perhaps, but still just that—Professor Wolf.

The rest was nonsense. But there was, that impulsive side of him suggested, only one way of proving the fact. And that was to say The Word.

"All right," said Wolfe Wolf to his reflection. "I'll show you." And he said it.

The pang was sharper and stronger than he'd remembered. Alcohol numbs you to pain. It tore him for a moment with an anguish like the descriptions of childbirth. Then it was gone, and he flexed his limbs in happy amazement. But he was not a lithe, fleet, free beast. He was a helplessly trapped wolf, irrevocably entangled in a conservative, single-breasted gray suit.

He tried to rise and walk, but the long sleeves and legs tripped him over flat on his muzzle. He kicked with his paws, trying to tear his way out, and then stopped. Werewolf or no werewolf, he was likewise still Professor Wolf, and this suit had cost thirty-five dollars. There must be some cheaper way of securing freedom than tearing the suit to shreds.

He used several good, round, Low German expletives. This was a complication that wasn't in any of the werewolf legends he'd ever read. There, people just—boom!—became wolves or—bang!—became men again. When they were men, they wore clothes; when they were wolves, they wore fur. Just like Hyperman becoming Bark Lent again on top of the Empire State Building and finding his street clothes right there. Most misleading. He began to remember now how Ozymandias the Great had made him strip before teaching him the words . . .

The words! That was it. All he had to do was say the word that changed you back—*Absarka!*—and he'd be a man again, comfortably fitted inside his suit. Then he could strip and start all over again. You see? Reason solves all. ''*Absarka!*'' he said.

Or thought he said. He went through all the proper mental processes for saying *Absarka!* but all that came out of his muzzle was a sort of clicking whine. And he was still a conservatively dressed and helpless wolf.

This was worse than the clothes problem. If he could be released only by saying *Absarka!* and if, being a wolf, he could say nothing, why, there he was, Indefinitely. He could go find Ozzy and ask—but how could a wolf wrapped up in a gray suit get safely out of a hotel and set out hunting for an unknown address?

He was trapped. He was lost. He was . . .

''*Absarka!*''

Professor Wolfe Wolf stood up in his grievously rumpled gray suit and beamed on the beard-fringed face of Ozymandias the Great.

''You see, colleague,'' the little magician explained, ''I figured you'd want to try it again as soon as you got up, and I knew darned well you'd have your troubles. Thought I'd come over and straighten things out for you.''

Wolf lit a cigarette in silence and handed the pack

to Ozymandias. "When you came in just now," he said at last, "what did you see?"

"You as a wolf."

"Then it really . . . I actually . . ."

"Sure. You're a full-fledged werewolf, all right."

Wolf sat down on the rumpled bed. "I guess," he ventured slowly, "I've got to believe it. And if I believe that . . . But it means I've got to believe everything I've always scorned. I've got to believe in gods and devils and hells and . . ."

"You needn't be so pluralistic. But there is a God." Ozymandias said this as calmly and convincingly as he had stated last night that there were werewolves.

"And if there's a God, then I've got a soul?"

"Sure."

"And if I'm a werewolf . . . Hey!"

"What's the trouble, colleague?"

"All right, Ozzy. You know everything. Tell me this: Am I damned?"

"For what? Just for being a werewolf? Shucks, no; let me explain. There's two kinds of werewolves. There's the cursed kind that can't help themselves, that just go turning into wolves without any say in the matter; and there's the voluntary kind like you. Now most of the voluntary kind are damned, sure, because they're wicked men who lust for blood and eat innocent people. But they aren't damnably wicked because they're werewolves; they became werewolves because they are damnably wicked. Now you changed yourself just for the fun of it and because it looked like a good way to impress a gal; that's an innocent enough motive, and being a werewolf doesn't make it any less so. Werewolves don't have to be monsters; it's just that we only hear about the ones that are."

"But how can I be voluntary when you told me I was a werewolf before ever I changed?"

"Not everybody can change. It's like being able to roll your tongue or wiggle your ears. You can, or you can't; and that's that. And, like those abilities, there's probably a genetic factor involved, though nobody's done any serious research on it. You were a werewolf *in posse;* now you're one *in esse.* "

"Then it's all right? I can be a werewolf just for having fun and it's safe?"

"Absolutely."

Wolf chortled. "Will I show Gloria! Dull and unglamorous, indeed! Anybody can marry an actor or a G-man; but a werewolf . . ."

"Your children probably will be, too," said Ozymandias cheerfully.

Wolf shut his eyes dreamily, then opened them with a start. "You know what?"

"What?"

"I haven't got a hangover any more! This is marvelous. That is . . . Why, this is practical. At last the perfect hangover cure. Shuffle yourself into a wolf and back and . . . Oh, that reminds me. How do I get back?"

"Absarka."

"I know. But when I'm a wolf I can't say it."

"That," said Ozymandias sadly, "is the curse of being a white magician. You keep having to use the second-best form of spells, because the best would be black. Sure, a black-magic werebeast can turn himself back whenever he wants to. I remember in Darjeeling . . ."

"But how about me?"

"That's the trouble. You have to have somebody to say *Absarka!* for you. That's what I did last night, or do you remember? After we broke up the party at your friend's Temple . . . Tell you what. I'm retired now, and I've got enough to live on modestly because I can always magic up a little . . . Are you going to take up werewolfing seriously?"

"For a while, anyway. Till I get Gloria."

"Then why shouldn't I come and live here in your hotel? Then I'll always be handy to *Absarka* you. After you get the girl, you can teach her."

Wolf extended his hand. "Noble of you. Shake." And then his eye caught his wrist watch. "I've missed two classes this morning. Werewolfing's all very well, but a man's got to work for his living.''

"Most men.'' Ozymandias calmly reached his hand into the air and plucked a coin. He looked at it ruefully; it was a gold moidore. "Hang these spirits; I simply cannot explain to them about gold being illegal.''

"From Los Angeles,'' Wolf thought, with the habitual contempt of the northern Californian, as he surveyed the careless sport coat and the bright-yellow shirt of his visitor.

This young man rose politely as the professor entered the office. His green eyes gleamed cordially and his red hair glowed in the spring sunlight. "Professor Wolf?'' he asked.

Wolf glanced impatiently at his desk. "Yes.''

"O'Breen's the name. I'd like to talk to you a minute.''

"My office hours are from three to four Tuesdays and Thursdays. I'm afraid I'm rather busy now.''

"This isn't faculty business. And it's important.'' The young man's attitude was affable and casual, but he managed none the less to convey a sense of urgency that piqued Wolf's curiosity. The all-important letter to Gloria had waited while he took two classes; it could wait another five minutes.

"Very well, Mr. O'Breen.''

"And alone, if you please.''

Wolf himself hadn't noticed that Emily was in the room. He now turned to the secretary and said, "All right. If you don't mind, Emily . . .''

Emily shrugged and went out.

"Now, sir. What is this important and secret business?''

"Just a question or two. To start with, how well do you know Gloria Garton?''

Wolf paused. You could hardly say, "Young man, I am about to repropose to her in view of my becoming a werewolf.'' Instead he simply said—the truth if not the whole truth—"She was a pupil of mine a few years ago."

"I said *do*, not *did*. How well do you know her now?"

"And why should I bother to answer such a question?"

The young man handed over a card. Wolf read:

FERGUS O'BREEN

PRIVATE INQUIRY AGENT

Licensed by the State of California

Wolf smiled. "And what does this mean? Divorce evidence? Isn't that the usual field of private inquiry agents?"

"Miss Garton isn't married, as you probably know very well. I'm just asking you if you've been in touch with her much lately?"

"And I'm simply asking why you should want to know?"

O'Breen rose and began to pace around the office. "We don't seem to be getting very far, do we? I'm to take it that you refuse to state the nature of your relations with Gloria Garton?"

"I see no reason why I should do otherwise." Wolf was beginning to be annoyed.

To his surprise, the detective relaxed into a broad grin. "O.K. Let it ride. Tell me about your department: How long have the various faculty members been here?"

"Instructors and all?"

"Just the professors."

"I've been here for seven years. All the others at least a good ten, probably more. If you want exact figures, you can probably get them from the dean, unless, as I hope"—Wolf smiled cordially—"he throws you out flat on your red pate."

O'Breen laughed. "Professor, I think we could get

on. One more question, and you can do some pate-tossing yourself. Are you an American citizen?''

"Of course."

"And the rest of the department?"

"All of them. And now would you have the common decency to give me some explanation of this fantastic farrago of questions?"

"No," said O'Breen casually. "Good-bye, professor," His alert, green eyes had been roaming about the room, sharply noticing everything. Now, as he left, they rested on Wolf's long index finger, moved up to his heavy meeting eyebrows, and returned to the finger. There was a suspicion of a startled realization in those eyes as he left the office.

But that was nonsense, Wolf told himself. A private detective, no matter how shrewd his eyes, no matter how apparently meaningless his inquiries, would surely be the last man on earth to notice the signs of lycanthropy.

Funny. Werewolf was a word you could accept. You could say, "I am a werewolf," and it was all right. But say "I am a lycanthrope," and your flesh crawled. Odd. Possibly material for a paper on the influence of etymology on connotation for one of the learned periodicals.

But, hell! Wolfe Wolf was no longer primarily a scholar. He was a werewolf now, a white-magic werewolf, a werewolf-for-fun; and fun he was going to have. He lit his pipe, stared at the blank paper on his desk, and tried desperately to draft a letter to Gloria. It should hint at just enough to fascinate her and hold her interest until he could go south when the term ended and reveal to her the whole wonderful new truth. It . . .

Professor Oscar Fearing grunted his ponderous way into the office. "Good afternoon, Wolf. Hard at it, my boy?"

"Afternoon," Wolf replied distractedly, and continued to stare at the paper.

"Great events coming, eh? Are you looking forward to seeing the glorious Gloria?"

Wolf started. "How . . . What do you mean?"

Fearing handed him a folded newspaper. "You hadn't heard?"

Wolf read with growing amazement and delight:

GLORIA GARTON TO ARRIVE FRIDAY
Local Girl Returns to Berkeley

As part of the most spectacular talent hunt since the search for Scarlett O'Hara, Gloria Garton, glamorous Metropolis starlet, will visit Berkeley Friday.

Friday afternoon at the Campus Theater, Berkeley canines will have their chance to compete in the nation-wide quest for a dog to play Tookah the wolf dog in the great Metropolis epic, *Fangs of the Forest,* and Gloria Garton herself will be present at the auditions.

"I owe so much to Berkeley," Miss Garton said. "It will mean so much to me to see the campus and the city again." Miss Garton has the starring human role in *Fangs of the Forest.*

Miss Garton was a student at the University of California when she received her first chance in films. She is a member of Mask and Dagger, honorary dramatic society, and Rho Rho Rho Sorority.

Wolfe Wolf glowed. This was perfect. No need now to wait till term was over. He could see Gloria now and claim her in all his wolfish vigor. Friday—today was Wednesday—that gave him two nights to practice and perfect the technique of werewolfry. And then . . .

He noticed the dejected look on the older professor's face, and a small remorse smote him. "How did things go last night, Oscar?" he asked sympathetically. "How were your big Walpurgis night services?"

Fearing regarded him oddly. "You know that now? Yesterday April 30th meant nothing to you."

"I got curious and looked it up. But how did it go?"

"Well enough," Fearing lied feebly. "Do you know, Wolf," he demanded after a moment's silence, "what is the real curse of every man interested in the occult?"

"No. What?"

"That true power is never enough. Enough for yourself, perhaps, but never enough for others. So that no matter what your true abilities, you must forge on beyond them into charlatanry to convince the others. Look at St. Germain. Look at Francis Stuart. Look at Cagliostro. But the worst tragedy is the next stage; when you realize that your powers were greater than you supposed and that the charlatanry was needless. When you realize that you have no notion of the extent of your powers. Then . . ."

"Then, Oscar?"

"Then, my boy, you are a badly frightened man."

Wolf wanted to say something consoling. He wanted to say, "Look, Oscar. It was just me. Go back to your half-hearted charlatanry and be happy." But he couldn't do that. Only Ozzy could know the truth of that splendid gray wolf. Only Ozzy and Gloria.

The moon was bright on that hidden spot in the canyon. The night was still. And Wolfe Wolf had a severe case of stage fright. Now that it came to the real thing—for this morning's clothes-complicated fiasco hardly counted and last night he could not truly remember—he was afraid to plunge cleanly into wolfdom and anxious to stall and talk as long as possible.

"Do you think," he asked the magician nervously, "that I could teach Gloria to change, too?"

Ozymandias pondered. "Maybe, colleague. It'd depend. She might have the natural ability, and she might not. And, of course, there's no telling what she might change into."

"You mean she wouldn't necessarily be a wolf?"

"Of course not. The people who can change, change into all sorts of things. And every folk knows best the kind that most interests it. We've got an English and Central European tradition; so we know mostly about werewolves. But take Scandinavia, and you'll hear chiefly about werebears, only they call 'em berserkers. And Orientals, now, they're apt to know about weretigers. Trouble is, we've thought so much about were-*wolves* that that's all we know the signs for; I wouldn't know how to spot a weretiger just offhand."

"Then there's no telling what might happen if I taught her The Word?"

"Not the least. Of course, there's some werethings that just aren't much use being. Take like being a wereant. You change and somebody steps on you and that's that. Or like a fellow I knew once in Madagascar. Taught him The Word, and know what? Hanged if he wasn't a werediplodocus. Shattered the whole house into little pieces when he changed and almost trampled me under hoof before I could say *Absarka!* He decided not to make a career of it. Or then there was that time in Darjeeling . . . But, look colleague, are you going to stand around here naked all night?"

"No," said Wolf. "I'm going to change now. You'll take my clothes back to the hotel?"

"Sure. They'll be there for you. And I've put a very small spell on the night clerk, just enough for him not to notice wolves wandering in. Oh, and by the way— anything missing from your room?"

"Not that I noticed. Why?"

"Because I thought I saw somebody come out of it this afternoon. Couldn't be sure, but I think he came from there. Young fella with red hair and Hollywood clothes."

Wolfe Wolf frowned. That didn't make sense. Pointless questions from a detective were bad enough, but searching your hotel room . . . But what were detectives to a full-fledged werewolf? He grinned, nodded a friendly good-bye to Ozymandias the Great, and said The Word.

The pain wasn't so sharp as this morning, though still quite bad enough. But it passed almost at once, and his whole body filled with a sense of limitless freedom. He lifted his snout and sniffed deep at the keen freshness of this night air. A whole new realm of pleasure opened up for him through this acute new nose alone. He wagged his tail amicably at Ozzy and set up off the canyon on a long, easy lope.

For hours loping was enough—simply and purely enjoying one's wolfness was the finest pleasure one could ask. Wolf left the canyon and turned up into the hills, past the Big C and on into noble wildness that seemed far remote from all campus civilization. His brave new legs were stanch and tireless, his wind seemingly inexhaustible. Every turning brought fresh and vivid scents of soil and leaves and air, and life was shimmering and beautiful.

But a few hours of this, and Wolf realized that he was lonely. All this grand exhilaration was very well, but if his mate Gloria were loping by his side . . . And what fun was it to be something as splendid as a wolf if no one admired you? He began to want people, and he turned back to the city.

Berkeley goes to bed early. The streets were deserted. Here and there a light burned in a rooming house where some solid grind was plodding on his almost due term paper. Wolf had done that himself. He couldn't laugh in this shape, but his tail twitched with amusement at the thought.

He paused along the tree-lined street. There was a fresh human scent here, though the street seemed empty. Then he heard a soft whimpering, and trotted off toward the noise.

Behind the shrubbery fronting an apartment house sat a disconsolate two-year-old, shivering in his sun-suit and obviously lost for hours on hours. Wolf put a paw on the child's shoulder and shook him gently.

The boy looked around and was not in the least afraid. "He'o," he said brightening up.

Wolf growled a cordial greeting, and wagged his tail and pawed at the ground to indicate that he'd take the lost infant wherever it wanted to go.

The child stood up and wiped away its tears with a dirty fist which left wide, black smudges. "Tootoo-tootoo!" he said.

Games, thought Wolf. He wants to play choo-choo. He took the child by the sleeve and tugged gently.

"Tootootootoo!" the boy repeated firmly. "Die way."

The sound of a railway whistle, to be sure, does die away; but this seemed a poetic expression for such a toddler, Wolf thought, and then abruptly would have snapped his fingers if he'd had them. The child was saying "2222 Dwight Way," having been carefully brought up to tell its address when lost. Wolf glanced up at the street sign. Bowditch and Hillegas—2222 Dwight would be just a couple of blocks.

Wolf tried to nod his head, but the muscles didn't seem to work that way. Instead he wagged his tail in what he hoped indicated comprehension, and started off leading the child.

The infant beamed and said, "Nice woof-woof."

For an instant Wolf felt like a spy suddenly addressed by his right name, then realized that if some say "bow-wow" others might well say "woof-woof."

He led the child for two blocks without event. It felt good, having an innocent human being put his whole life and trust in your charge like this. There was something about children; he hoped Gloria felt the same. He wondered what would happen if he could teach this confiding infant The Word. It would be swell to have a pup that would . . .

He paused. His nose twitched and the hair on the back of his neck rose. Ahead of them stood a dog, a huge mongrel, seemingly a mixture of St. Bernard and Husky. But the growl that issued from his throat indicated that carrying brandy kegs or rushing serum was not for him. He was a bandit, an outlaw, an enemy of man and dog. And they had to pass him.

Wolf had no desire to fight. He was as big as this monster and certainly, with his human brain, much cleverer; but scars from a dog fight would not look well on the human body of Professor Wolf, and there was, moreover, the danger of hurting the toddler in the fracas. It would be wiser to cross the street. But before he could steer the child that way, the mongrel brute had charged at them, yapping and snarling.

Wolf placed himself in front of the boy, poised and ready to leap in defense. The scar problem was secondary to the fact that this baby had trusted him. He was ready to face this cur and teach him a lesson, at whatever cost to his own human body. But halfway to him the huge dog stopped. His growls died away to a piteous whimper. His great flanks trembled in the moonlight. His tail curled craven between his legs. And abruptly he turned and fled.

The child crowed delightedly. "Bad woof-woof go way." He put his little arms around Wolf's neck, *"Nice woof-woof."* Then he straightened up and said insistently, "Tootootootoo. Die way," and Wolf led on, his strong wolf's heart pounding as it had never pounded at the embrace of a woman.

"Tootootootoo" was a small frame house set back from the street in a large yard. The lights were still on, and even from the sidewalk Wolf could hear a woman's shrill voice.

"—since five o'clock this afternoon, and you've got to find him, officer. You simply must. We've hunted all over the neighborhood and—"

Wolf stood up against the wall on his hindlegs and rang the doorbell with his front right paw.

"Oh! Maybe that's somebody now. The neighbors said they'd . . . Come, officer, and let's see . . . Oh!"

At the same moment Wolf barked politely, the toddler yelled "Mamma!" and his thin and worn-looking young mother let out a scream half delight at finding her child and half terror of this large, gray canine shape that loomed behind him. She snatched up the infant protectively and turned to the large man in uniform. "Officer! Look! That big dreadful thing! It stole my Robby!"

"No," Robby protested firmly. "Nice woof-woof."

The officer laughed. "The lad's probably right, ma'am. It *is* a nice woof-woof. Found your boy wandering around and helped him home. You haven't maybe got a bone for him?"

"Let that big nasty brute into my home? Never! Come on, Robby."

"Want my nice woof-woof."

"I'll woof-woof you, staying out till all hours and giving your father and me the fright of our lives. Just wait till your father sees you, young man; he'll . . . Oh, good night, officer!" And she shut the door on the yowls of Robby.

The policeman patted Wolf's head. "Never mind about the bone, Rover. She didn't so much as offer me a glass of beer, either. My, you're a husky specimen, aren't you, boy? Look almost like a wolf. Who do you belong to, and what you are doing wandering about alone? Huh?" He turned on his flash and bent over to look at the nonexistent collar.

He straightened up and whistled. "No license. Rover, that's bad. You know what I ought to do? I ought to turn you in. If you weren't a hero that just got cheated out of his bone, I'd . . . I ought to do it, anyway. Laws are laws, even for heroes. Come on, Rover. We're going for a walk."

Wolf thought quickly. The pound was the last place on earth he wanted to wind up. Even Ozzy would never think of looking for him there. Nobody'd claim him, nobody'd say *Absarka!* and in the end a dose of chloroform . . . He wrenched loose from the officer's grasp on his hair, and with one prodigious leap cleared the yard, landed on the sidewalk, and started up the street. But the instant he was out of the officer's sight he stopped dead and slipped behind a hedge.

He scented the policeman's approach even before he heard it. The man was running with the lumbering haste of two hundred pounds. But opposite the hedge he, too, stopped. For a moment Wolf wondered if his ruse had failed; but the officer had paused only to scratch his head and mutter, "Say! There's something screwy here. *Who rang that doorbell?* The kid couldn't reach it, and the dog . . . Oh, well," he concluded. "Nuts," and seemed to find in that monosyllabic summation the solution to all his problems.

As his footsteps and smell died away, Wolf became aware of another scent. He had only just identified it as cat when someone said, "You're were, aren't you?"

Wolf started up, lips drawn back and muscles tense. There was nothing human in sight, but someone had spoken to him. Unthinkingly, he tried to say, "Where are you?" but all that came out was a growl.

"Right behind you. Here in the shadows. You can scent me, can't you?"

"But you're a cat," Wolf thought in his snarls. "And you're talking."

"Of course. But I'm not talking human language. It's just your brain that takes it that way. If you had your human body, you'd just think I was going *meowrr*. But you are were, aren't you?"

"How do you . . . Why did you think so?"

"Because you didn't try to jump me, as any normal dog would have. And besides, unless Confucius taught me all wrong, you're a wolf, not a dog; and we don't have wolves around here unless they're were."

"How do you know all this? Are you . . ."

"Oh, no. I'm just a cat. But I used to live next door to a werechow named Confucius. He taught me things."

Wolf was amazed. "You mean he was a man who changed to chow and stayed that way? Lived as a pet?"

"Certainly. This was back at the worst of the Depression. He said a dog was more apt to be fed and looked after than a man. I thought it was a smart idea."

"But how terrible! Could a man so debase himself as . . ."

"Men don't debase themselves. They debase each other. That's the way of most weres. Some change to keep from being debased, others to do a little more effective debasing. Which are you?"

"Why, you see, I . . ."

"*Sh!* Look. This is going to be fun. Holdup."

Wolf peered around the hedge. A well-dressed, middle-aged man was waking along briskly, apparently enjoying a night constitutional. Behind him moved a thin, silent figure. Even as Wolf watched, the figure caught up with him and whispered harshly, "Up, with 'em, buddy!"

The quiet pomposity of the stroller melted away. He was ashen and aspen, as the figure slipped a hand around into his breast pocket and removed an impressive wallet.

And what, thought Wolf, was the good of his fine, vigorous body if it merely crouched behind hedges as a spectator? In one fine bound, to the shocked amazement of the were-wise cat, he had crossed the hedge and landed with his forepaws full in the figure's face. It went over backward with him on top and then there was a loud noise, a flash of light, and a frightful sharp smell. For a moment Wolf felt an acute pang in his shoulder, like the jab of a long needle, and then the pain was gone.

But his momentary recoil had been enough to let the figure get to its feet. "Missed you, huh?" it muttered. "Let's see how you like a slug in the belly, you interfering . . ." and he applied an epithet which would have been purely literal description if Wolf had not been were.

There were three quick shots in succession even as Wolf sprang. For a second he experienced the most acute stomach-ache of his life. Then he landed again. The figure's head hit the concrete sidewalk and he was still.

Lights were leaping into brightness everywhere.

Among all the confused noises, Wolf could hear the shrill complaints of Robby's mother, and among all the compounded smells, he could distinguish scent of the policeman who wanted to impound him. That meant getting out, and quick.

The city meant trouble, Wolf decided as he loped off. He could endure loneliness while he practiced his wolfry, until he had Gloria. Though just as a precaution he must arrange with Ozzy about a plausible-looking collar, and . . .

The most astounding realization yet suddenly struck him! He had received four bullets, three of them square in the stomach, and he hadn't a wound to show for it! Being a werewolf certainly offered its practical advantages. Think what a criminal could do with such bullet-proofing. Or . . . But no. He was a werewolf for fun, and that was that.

But even for a werewolf, being shot, though relatively painless, is tiring. A great deal of nervous energy is absorbed in the magical and instantaneous knitting of those wounds. And when Wolfe Wolf reached the peace and calm of the uncivilized hills, he no longer felt like reveling in freedom. Instead he stretched out to his full length, nuzzled his head down between his forepaws, and slept.

"Now the essence of magic," said Heliophagus of Smyrna, "is deceit; and that deceit is of two kinds. By magic, the magician deceives others; but magic deceives the magician himself."

So far the lycanthropic magic of Wolfe Wolf had worked smoothly and pleasantly, but now it was to show him the second trickery that lurks behind every magic trick. And the first step was that he slept.

He woke in confusion. His dreams had been human—and of Gloria—despite the body in which he dreamed them, and it took several full minutes for him to reconstruct just how he happened to be in that body. For a moment the dream, even that episode in which he and Gloria had been eating blueberry waffles on a roller coaster, seemed more sanely plausible than the reality.

But he readjusted quickly, and glanced up at the sky. The sun looked as though it had been up at least an hour, which meant that the time was somewhere between six and seven. Today was Thursday, which meant that he was saddled with an eight-o'clock class. That left plenty of time to change back, shave, dress, breakfast and resume the normal life of Professor Wolf, which was, after all, important if he intended to support a wife.

He tried, as he trotted through the streets, to look as tame and unwolflike as possible, and apparently succeeded. No one paid him any mind save children, who wanted to play, and dogs, who began by snarling and ended by cowering away terrified. His friend the cat might be curiously tolerant of weres, but not so dogs.

He trotted up the steps of the Berkeley Inn confidently. The clerk was under a slight spell and would not notice wolves. There was nothing to do but rouse Ozzy, be *absarka'd,* and . . .

"Hey! Where you going? Get out of here! Shoo!"

It was the clerk, a stanch and brawny young man, who straddled the stairway and vigorously waved him off.

"No dogs in here! Go on now. Scoot!"

Quite obviously this man was under no spell, and equally obviously there was no way of getting up that staircase short of using a wolf's strength to tear the clerk apart. For a second Wolf hesitated. He had to get changed back. It would be a pity to use his powers to injure another human being—if only he had not slept and arrived before this unmagicked day clerk came on duty—but necessity knows no . . .

Then the solution hit him. Wolf turned and loped off just as the clerk hurled an ash tray at him. Bullets may be relatively painless, but even a werewolf's rump, he learned promptly, is sensitive to flying glass.

The solution was foolproof. The only trouble was

that it meant an hour's wait, and he was hungry. He found himself even displaying a certain shocking interest in the plump occupant of a baby carriage. You do get different appetites with a different body. He could understand how some originally well-intentioned werewolves might in time become monsters. But he was stronger in will, and much smarter. His stomach could hold out until this plan worked.

The janitor had already opened the front door of Wheeler Hall, but the building was deserted. Wolf had no trouble reaching the second floor unnoticed or finding his classroom. He had a little more trouble holding the chalk between his teeth and a slight tendency to gag on the dust; but by balancing his forepaws on the eraser trough, he could manage quite nicely. It took three springs to catch the ring of the chart in his teeth, but once that was pulled down there was nothing to do but crouch under the desk and pray that he would not starve quite to death.

The students of German 31B, as they assembled reluctantly for their eight o'clock, were a little puzzled at being confronted by a chart dealing with the influence of the gold standard on world economy, but they decided simply that the janitor had been forgetful.

The wolf under the desk listened unseen to their gathering murmurs, overheard that cute blonde in the front row make dates with three different men for the same night, and finally decided that enough had assembled to make his chances plausible. He slipped out from under the desk far enough to reach the ring of the chart, tugged at it, and let go.

The chart flew up with a rolling crash. The students broke off their chatter, looked up at the blackboard, and beheld in a huge and shaky scrawl the mysterious letters

ABSARKA

It worked. With enough people, it was an almost mathematical certainty that one of them in his puzzle-

ment—for the race of subtitle readers, though handi-
capped by the talkies, still exists—would read the
mysterious word aloud. It was the much-bedated
blonde who did it.

"*Absarka,*" she said wonderingly.

And there was Professor Wolfe Wolf, beaming cordially at his class.

The only flaw was this: He had forgotten that he was
only a werewolf, and not Hyperman. His clothes were
still at the Berkeley Inn, and here on the lecture platform he was stark naked.

Two of his best pupils screamed and one fainted.
The blonde only giggled appreciatively.

Emily was incredulous but pitying.
Professor Fearing was sympathetic but reserved.
The chairman of the department was cool.
The dean of letters was chilly.
The president of the university was frigid.
Wolfe Wolf was unemployed.

And Heliophagus of Smyrna was right. "The essence of magic is deceit."

"But what can I do?" Wolf moaned into his zombie
glass. "I'm stuck. I'm stymied. Gloria arrives in
Berkeley tomorrow, and here I am—nothing. Nothing
but a futile, worthless werewolf. You can't support a
wife on that. You can't raise a family. You can't . . .
you can't even propose . . . I want another. Sure you
won't have one?"

Ozymandias the Great shook his round, fringed
head. "The last time I took two drinks I started all
this. I've got to behave if I want to stop it. But you're
an able-bodied, strapping, young man; surely, colleague, you can get work?"

"Where? All I'm trained for is academic work, and
this scandal has put the kibosh on that forever. What
university is going to hire a man who showed up naked
in front of his class without even the excuse of being
drunk? And supposing I try something else, I'd have

to give references, say something about what I'd been doing with my thirty-odd years. And once these references were checked . . . Ozzy, I'm a lost man.''

"Never despair, colleague. I've learned that magic gets you into some tight squeezes, but there's always a way of getting out. Now take that time in Darjeeling . . .''

"But what can I do? I'll wind up like Confucius the werechow and live off charity, if you'll find me somebody who wants a pet wolf.''

"You know,'' Ozymandias reflected, "you may have something there, colleague.''

"Nuts! That was a gag. I can at least retain my self-respect, even if I go on relief doing it. And I'll bet they don't like naked men on relief, either.''

"No. I don't mean just being a pet wolf. But look at it this way: What are your assets? You have only two outstanding abilities. One of them is to teach German, and that is now completely out.''

"Check.''

"And the other is to change yourself into a wolf. All right, colleague. There must be some commercial possibilities in that. Let's look into them.''

"Nonsense.''

"Not quite. For every merchandise there's a market. The trick is to find it. And you, colleague, are going to be the first practical commercial werewolf on record.''

"I could . . . They say Ripley's Odditorium pays good money. Supposing I changed six times a day regular for delighted audiences?''

Ozymandias shook his head sorrowfully. "It's no good. People don't want to see real magic. It makes 'em uncomfortable—starts 'em wondering what else might be loose in the world. They've got to feel sure it's all done with mirrors. I know. I had to quit vaudeville because I wasn't smart enough at faking it; all I could do was the real thing.''

"I could be a Seeing Eye dog, maybe?''

"They have to be female.''

"When I'm changed I can understand animal language. Maybe I could be a dog trainer and . . . No, that's out. I forgot; they're scared to death of me."

But Ozymandias' pale-blue eyes had lit up at the suggestion. "Colleague, you're warm. Oh, are you warm! Tell me: Why did you say your fabulous Gloria was coming to Berkeley?"

"Publicity for a talent hunt."

"For what?"

"A dog to star in *Fangs of the Forest.*"

"And what kind of a dog?"

"A . . ." Wolf's eyes widened and his jaw sagged. "A wolf dog," he said softly.

And the two men looked at each other with a wild surmise—silent, beside a bar in Berkeley.

"It's all the fault of that Disney dog," the trainer complained. "Pluto does anything. Everything. So our poor mutts are expected to do likewise. Listen to that dope! 'The dog should come into the room, give one paw to the baby, indicate that he recognizes the hero in his Eskimo disguise, go over to the table, find the bone, and clap his paws gleefully!' Now who's got a set of signals to cover stuff like that? Pluto!" he snorted.

Gloria Garton said, "Oh." By that one sound she managed to convey that she sympathized deeply, that the trainer was a nice-looking young man whom she'd just as soon see again, and that no dog star was going to steal *Fangs of the Forest* from her. She adjusted her skirt slightly, leaned back, and made the plain wooden chair on the bare theater stage seem more than ever like a throne.

"All right." The man in the violet beret waved away the last unsuccessful applicant and read from a card: "Dog: Wopsy. Owner: Mrs. Channing Galbraith. Trainer: Luther Newby. Bring it in."

An assistant scurried offstage, and there was a sound of whines and whimpers as a door opened.

"What's got into those dogs today?" the man in the

violet beret demanded. "They all seem scared to death and beyond."

"I think," said Fergus O'Breen, "that it's that big gray wolf dog. Somehow, the others just don't like him."

Gloria Garton lowered her bepurpled lids and cast a queenly stare of suspicion on the young detective. There was nothing wrong with his being there. His sister was head of publicity for Metropolis, and he'd handled several confidential cases for the studio, even one for her, that time her chauffeur had decided to try his hand at blackmail. Fergus O'Breen was a Metropolis fixture; but still it bothered her.

The assistant brought in Mrs. Galbraith's Wopsy. The man in the violet beret took one look and screamed. The scream bounced back from every wall of the theater in the ensuing minute of silence. At last he found words. "A wolf dog! Tookah is the greatest role ever written for a wolf dog! And what do they bring us! A terrier yet! So if we wanted a terrier we could cast Asta!"

"But if you'd only let us show you . . ." Wopsy's tall young trainer started to protest.

"Get out!" the man in the violet beret shrieked. "Get out before I lose my temper!"

Wopsy and her trainer slunk off.

"In El Paso," the casting director lamented, "they bring me a Mexican hairless. In St. Louis it's a Pekinese yet! And if I do find a wolf dog, it sits in a corner and waits for somebody to bring in a sled to pull."

"Maybe," said Fergus, "you should try a real wolf."

"Wolf, *schmolf!*" He picked up the next card. "Dog: Yoggoth. Owner and trainer: Mr. O. Z. Manders. Bring it in."

The whining noise offstage ceased as Yoggoth was brought out to be tested. The man in the violet beret hardly glanced at the fringe-bearded owner and trainer. He had eyes only for that splendid gray wolf. "If you can only act . . ." he prayed, with the same fervor with which many a man has thought, "If you could only cook . . ."

He pulled the beret to an even more unlikely angle and snapped, "All right, Mr. Manders. The dog should come into the room, give one paw to the baby, indicate that he recognizes the hero in his Eskimo disguise, go over to the table, find the bone, and clap his paws joyfully. Baby here, here, here, table here. Got that?"

Mr. Manders looked at his wolf dog and repeated, "Got that?"

Yoggoth wagged his tail.

"Very well, colleague," said Mr. Manders. "Do it." Yoggoth did it.

The violet beret sailed into the flies, on the wings of its owner's triumphal scream of joy. "He did it!" he kept burbling. "He did it!"

"Of course, colleague," said Mr. Manders calmly.

The trainer who hated Pluto had a face as blank as a vampire's mirror. Fergus O'Breen was speechless with wonderment. Even Gloria Garton permitted surprise and interest to cross her regal mask.

"You mean he can do anything?" gurgled the man who used to have a violet beret.

"Anything," said Mr. Manders.

"Can he . . . Let's see, in the dance-hall sequence—can he knock a man down, roll him over, and frisk his back pocket?"

Even before Mr. Manders could say "Of course," Yoggoth had demonstrated, using Fergus O'Breen as a convenient dummy.

"Peace!" the casting director sighed. "Peace— Charley!" he yelled to his assistant. "Send 'em all away. No more try-outs. We've found Tookah! It's wonderful."

The trainer stepped up to Mr. Manders. "It's more than that, sir. It's positively superhuman. I'll swear I couldn't detect the slightest signal, and for such complicated operations, too. Tell me, Mr. Manders, what system do you use?"

Mr. Manders made a Hoopleish *kaff-kaff* noise. "Professional secret, you understand, young man. I'm planning on opening a school when I retire, but obviously until then . . ."

"Of course, sir. I understand. But I've never seen anything like it in all my born days."

"I wonder," Fergus O'Breen observed from the floor, "if your marvel dog can get off of people, too?"

Mr. Manders stifled a grin. "Of course! Yoggoth!"

Fergus picked himself up and dusted from his clothes the grime of the stage, which is the most clinging grime on earth. "I'd swear," he muttered, "that beast of yours enjoyed that."

"No hard feelings, I trust, Mr . . ."

"O'Breen. None at all. In fact, I'd suggest a little celebration in honor of this great event. I know you can't buy a drink this near the campus, so I brought along a bottle just in case."

"Oh," said Gloria Garton, implying that carousals were ordinarily beneath her, that this, however, was a special occasion, and that possibly there was something to be said for the green-eyed detective, after all.

This was all too easy, Wolfe Wolf-Yoggoth kept thinking. There was a catch to it somewhere. This was certainly the ideal solution to the problem of how to earn money as a werewolf. Bring an understanding of human speech and instructions into a fine animal body, and you are the answer to a director's prayer. It was perfect as long as it lasted; and if *Fangs of the Forest* was a smash hit, there were bound to be other Yoggoth pictures. Look at Rin-tin-tin. But it was too easy . . .

His ears caught a familiar "Oh" and his attention reverted to Gloria. This "Oh" had meant that she really shouldn't have another drink, but since liquor didn't affect her any way and this was a special occasion, she might as well.

She was even more beautiful than he had remembered. Her golden hair was shoulder-length now, and flowed with such rippling perfection that it was all he could do to keep from reaching out a paw to it. Her body had ripened, too, was even more warm and promising than his memories of her. And in his new shape he found her greatest charm in something he had not been able to appreciate fully as a human being, the deep, heady scent of her flesh.

"To *Fangs of the Forest!*" Fergus O'Breen was toasting. "And may that pretty-boy hero of yours get a worse mauling than I did."

Wolf-Yoggoth grinned to himself. That had been fun. That'd teach the detective to go crawling around hotel rooms.

"And while we're celebrating, colleagues," said Ozymandias the Great, "why should we neglect our star? Here, Yoggoth." And he held out the bottle.

"He drinks yet!" the casting director exclaimed delightedly.

"Sure. He was weaned on it."

Wolf took a sizable gulp. It felt good. Warm and rich—almost the way Gloria smelled.

"But how about you, Mr. Manders?" the detective insisted for the fifth time. "It's your celebration really. The poor beast won't get the four-figure checks from Metropolis. And you've taken only one drink."

"Never take two, colleague. I know my danger point. Two drinks in me and things start happening."

"More should happen yet than training miracle dogs? Go on, O'Breen. Make him drink. We should see what happens."

Fergus took another long drink himself. "Go on. There's another bottle in the car, and I've gone far enough to be resolved not to leave here sober. And I don't want sober companions, either." His green eyes were already beginning to glow with a new wildness.

"No, thank you, colleague."

Gloria Garton left her throne, walked over to the plump man, and stood close, her soft hand resting on his arm. "Oh," she said, implying that dogs were dogs, but still that the party was inevitably in her honor and his refusal to drink was a personal insult.

Ozymandias the Great looked at Gloria, sighed, shrugged, resigned himself to fate, and drank.

"Have you trained many dogs?" the casting director asked.

"Sorry, colleague. This is my first."

"All the more wonderful! But what's your profession otherwise?"

"Well, you see, I'm a magician."

"Oh," said Gloria Garton, implying delight, and went so far as to add, "I have a friend who does black magic."

"I'm afraid, ma'am, mine's simply white. That's tricky enough. With the black you're in for some real dangers."

"Hold on!" Fergus interposed. "You mean really a magician? Not just presti . . . sleight of hand?"

"Of course, colleague."

"Good theater," said the casting director. "Never let 'em see the mirrors."

"Uh-huh," Fergus nodded. "But look, Mr. Manders. What can you do, for instance?"

"Well, I can change . . ."

Yoggoth barked loudly.

"Oh, no," Ozymandias covered hastily, "that's really a little beyond me. But I can . . ."

"Can you do the Indian rope trick?" Gloria asked languidly. "My friend says that's terribly hard."

"Hard? Why, ma'am, there's nothing to it. I can remember that time in Darjeeling . . ."

Fergus took another long drink. "I," he announced defiantly, "want to see the Indian rope trick. I have met people who've met people who've met people who've seen it, but that's as close as I ever get. And I don't believe it."

"But, colleague, it's so simple."

"I don't believe it."

Ozymandias the Great drew himself up to his full lack of height. "Colleague, you are about to see it!" Yoggoth tugged warningly at his coat tails. "Leave me alone, Wolf. An aspersion has been cast!"

Fergus returned from the wings dragging a soiled length of rope. "This do?"

"Admirably."

"What goes?" the casting director demanded.

"Shh!" said Gloria. "Oh . . ."

She beamed worshipfully on Ozymandias, whose chest swelled to the point of threatening the security of his buttons. "Ladies and gentlemen!" he announced, in the manner of one prepared to fill a vast amphitheater with his voice. "You are about to behold Ozymandias the Great in—The Indian Rope Trick! Of course," he added conversationally, "I haven't got a small boy to chop into mincemeat, unless perhaps one of you . . . No? Well, we'll try it without. Not quite so impressive, though. And will you stop yapping, Wolf?"

"I thought his name was Yogi," said Fergus.

"Yoggoth. But since he's part wolf on his mother's side . . . Now quiet, all of you!"

He had been coiling the rope as he spoke. Now he placed the coil in the center of the stage, where it lurked like a threatening rattler. He stood beside it and deftly, professionally, went through a series of passes and mumblings so rapidly that even the superhumanly sharp eyes and ears of Wolf-Yoggoth could not follow them.

The end of the rope detached itself from the coil, reared in the air, turned for a moment like a head uncertain where to strike, then shot straight up until all the rope was uncoiled. The lower end rested a good inch above the stage.

Gloria gasped. The casting director drank hurriedly. Fergus, for some reason, stared curiously at the wolf.

"And now, ladies and gentlemen—oh, hang it, I do wish I had a boy to carve—Ozymandias the Great will ascend this rope into that land which only the users of the rope may know. Onward and upward! Be right back," he added reassuringly to Wolf.

His plump hands grasped the rope above his head and gave a little jerk. His knees swung up and clasped about the hempen pillar. And up he went, like a monkey on a stick, up and up and up—

—until suddenly he was gone.

Just gone. That was all there was to it. Gloria was beyond even saying "Oh." The casting director sat his beautiful flannels down on the filthy floor and gaped. Fergus swore softly and melodiously. And Wolf felt a premonitory prickling in his spine.

The stage door opened, admitting two men in denim pants and work shirts. "Hey!" said the first. "Where do you think you are?"

"We're from Metropolis Pictures," the casting director started to explain, scrambling to his feet.

"I don't care if you're from Washington, we gotta clear this stage. There's movies here tonight. Come on, Joe, help me get 'em out. And that pooch, too."

"You can't, Fred," said Joe reverently, and pointed. His voice sank to an awed whisper. "That's Gloria Garton . . ."

"So it is. Hi, Miss Garton, wasn't that last one of yours a stinkeroo!"

"Your public, darling," Fergus murmured.

"Come on!" Fred shouted. "Out of here. We gotta clean up. And you, Joe! Strike that rope!"

Before Fergus could move, before Wolf could leap to the rescue, the efficient stage hand had struck the rope and was coiling it up.

Wolf stared up into the flies. There was nothing up there. Nothing at all. Some place beyond the end of that rope was the only man on earth he could trust to say *Absarka!* for him; and the way down was cut off forever.

Wolfe Wolf sprawled on the floor of Gloria Garton's boudoir and watched that vision of volupty change into her most fetching negligee.

The situation was perfect. It was the fulfillment of his dearest dreams. The only flaw was that he was still in a wolf's body.

Gloria turned, leaned over, and chucked him under the snout. "Wuzzum a cute wolf dog, wuzzum?"

Wolf could not restrain a snarl.

"Doesn't um like Gloria to talk baby talk? Um was a naughty wolf, yes, um was."

It was torture. Here you are in your best beloved's hotel room, all her beauty revealed to your hungry eyes, and she talks baby talk to you! Wolf had been happy at first when Gloria suggested that she might take over the care of her co-star pending the reappearance of his trainer—for none of them was quite willing to admit that "Mr. O. Z. Manders" might truly and definitely have vanished—but he was beginning to realize that the situation might bring on more torment than pleasure.

"Wolves are funny," Gloria observed. She was more talkative when alone, with no need to be cryptically fascinating. "I knew a Wolf once, only that was his name. He was a man. And he was a funny one."

Wolf felt his heart beating fast under his gray fur. To hear his own name on Gloria's warm lips— But before she could go on to tell her pet how funny Wolf was, her maid rapped on the door.

"A Mr. O'Breen to see you, madam."

"Tell him to go 'way."

"He says it's important, and he does look, madam, as though he might make trouble."

"Oh, all right." Gloria rose and wrapped her negligee more respectably about her. "Come on, Yog— No, that's a silly name. I'm going to call you Wolfie. That's cute. Come on, Wolfie, and protect me from the big, bad detective."

Fergus O'Breen was pacing the sitting room with a certain vicious deliberateness in his strides. He broke off and stood still as Gloria and the wolf entered.

"So?" he observed tersely. "Reinforcements?"

"Will I need them?" Gloria cooed.

"Look, light of my love life." The glint in the green eyes was cold and deadly. "You've been playing games, and whatever their nature, there's one thing they're not. And that's cricket.''

Gloria gave him her slow, languid smile. ''You're amusing, Fergus.''

''Thanks. I doubt, however, if your activities are.''

''You're still a little boy playing cops and robbers. And what boogyman are you after now?''

''Ha-ha,'' said Fergus politely. ''And you know the answer to that question better than I do. That's why I'm here.''

Wolf was puzzled. This conversation meant nothing to him. And yet he sensed a tension of danger in the air as clearly as though he could smell it.

''Go on,'' Gloria snapped impatiently. ''And remember how dearly Metropolis Pictures will thank you for annoying one of its best box-office attractions.''

''Some things, my sweet, are more important than pictures, though you mightn't think it where you come from. One of them is a certain federation of forty-eight units. Another is an abstract concept called democracy.''

''And so?''

''And so I want to ask you one question: Why did you come to Berkeley?''

''For publicity on *Fangs*, of course. It was your sister's idea.''

''You've gone temperamental and turned down better ones. Why leap at this?''

''You don't haunt publicity stunts yourself, Fergus. Why are you here?''

Fergus was pacing again. ''And why was your first act in Berkeley a visit to the office of the German department?''

''Isn't that natural enough? I used to be a student here.''

''Majoring in dramatics, and you didn't go near the Little Theater. Why the German department?'' He paused and stood straight in front of her, fixing her with his green gaze.

Gloria assumed the attitude of a captured queen defying the barbarian conqueror. "Very well. If you must know—I went to the German department to see the man I love."

Wolf held his breath, and tried to keep his tail from thrashing.

"Yes," she went on impassionedly, "you strip the last veil from me, and force me to confess to you what he alone should have heard first. This man proposed to me by mail. I foolishly rejected his proposal. But I thought and thought—and at last I knew. When I came to Berkeley I had to see him . . ."

"And did you?"

"The little mouse of a secretary told me he wasn't there. But I shall see him yet. And when I do . . ."

Fergus bowed stiffly. "My congratulations to you both, my sweet. And the name of this more than fortunate gentleman?"

"Professor Wolfe Wolf."

"Who is doubtless the individual referred to in this?" He whipped a piece of paper from his sport coat and thrust it at Gloria. She paled and was silent. But Wolfe Wolf did not wait for her reply. He did not care. He knew the solution to his problem now, and he was streaking unobserved for her boudoir.

Gloria Garton entered the boudoir a minute later, a shaken and wretched woman. She unstoppered one of the delicate perfume bottles on her dresser and poured herself a stiff drink of whiskey. Then her eyebrows lifted in surprise as she stared at her mirror. Scrawlingly lettered across the glass in her own deep-crimson lipstick was the mysterious word

ABSARKA

Frowning, she said it aloud. *"Absarka . . ."*

From behind a screen stepped Professor Wolfe Wolf, incongruously wrapped in one of Gloria's lushest dressing robes. "Gloria dearest . . ." he cried.

"Wolf!" she exclaimed. "What on earth are you doing here in my room?"

"I love you. I've always loved you since you couldn't tell a strong from a weak verb. And now that I know that you love me . . ."

"This is terrible. Please get out of here!"

"Gloria . . ."

"Get out of here, or I'll sick my dog on you. Wolfie—Here, nice Wolfie!"

"I'm sorry, Gloria. But Wolfie won't answer you."

"Oh, you beast! Have you hurt Wolfie? Have you . . ."

"I wouldn't touch a hair on his pelt. Because, you see, Gloria darling, I am Wolfie."

"What on earth do you—" Gloria stared around the room. It was undeniable that there was no trace of the presence of a wolf dog. And here was a man dressed only in one of her robes and no sign of his own clothes. And after that funny little man and the rope . . .

"You thought I was drab and dull," Wolf went on. "You thought I'd sunk into an academic rut. You'd sooner have an actor or a G-man. But I, Gloria, am something more exciting than you've ever dreamed of. There's not another soul on earth I'd tell this to; but I, Gloria, am a werewolf."

Gloria gasped. "That isn't possible! But it all fits in. What I heard about you on the campus, and your friend with the funny beard and how he vanished, and, of course, it explains how you did tricks that any real dog couldn't possibly do . . ."

"Don't you believe me, darling?"

Gloria rose from the dresser chair and went into his arms. "I believe you, dear. And it's wonderful! I'll bet there's not another woman in all Hollywood that was ever married to a werewolf!"

"Then you will . . ."

"But of course, dear. We can work it out beautifully. We'll hire a stooge to be your trainer on the lot. You can work daytimes, and come home at night and I'll say *Absarka!* for you. It'll be perfect."

"Gloria . . ." Wolf murmured with tender reverence.

"One thing, dear. Just a little thing. Would you do Gloria a favor?"

"Anything!"

"Show me how you change. Change for me now. Then I'll *Absarka* you back right away.

Wolf said The Word. He was in such ecstatic bliss that he hardly felt the pang this time. He capered about the room with all the litheness of his fine wolfish legs, and ended up before Gloria, wagging his tail and looking for approval.

Gloria patted his head. "Good boy, Wolfie. And now, darling, you can just stay that way."

Wolf let out a yelp of amazement.

"You heard me, Wolfie. You're staying that way. You didn't happen to believe any of that guff I was feeding the detective, did you? Love you? I should waste my time! But this way you can be very useful to me. With your trainer gone, I can take charge of you and pick up an extra thousand a week or so. I won't mind that. And Professor Wolfe Wolf will have vanished forever, which fits right in with my plans."

Wolf snarled.

"Now don't try to get nasty, Wolfie darling. Um wouldn't threaten ums darling Gloria, would ums? Remember what I can do for you. I'm the only person who can turn you into a man again. You wouldn't dare teach anyone else that. You wouldn't dare let people know what you really are. An ignorant person would kill you. A smart one would have you locked up as a lunatic."

Wolf still advanced threateningly.

"Oh, no. You can't hurt me. Because all I'd have to do would be to say the word on the mirror. Then you wouldn't be a dangerous wolf any more. You'd just be a man here in my room, and I'd scream. And after what happened on the campus yesterday, how long do you think you'd stay out of the madhouse?"

Wolf backed away and let his tail droop.

"You see, Wolfie darling? Gloria has ums just where she wants ums. And ums is going to be a good boy."

There was a rap on the boudoir door, and Gloria called, "Come in."

"A gentleman to see you, madam," the maid announced. "A Professor Fearing."

Gloria smiled her best cruel and queenly smile. "Come along, Wolfie. This may interest you."

Professor Oscar Fearing, overflowing one of the graceful chairs of the sitting room, beamed benevolently as Gloria and the wolf entered. "Ah, my dear! A new pet. Touching."

"And what a pet, Oscar. Wait till you hear."

Professor Fearing buffed his pince-nez against his sleeve. "And wait, my dear, until you hear all that I have learned. Chiswick has perfected his protective screen against magnetic bombs, and the official trial is set for next week. And Farnsworth has all but completed his researches on a new process for obtaining osmium. Gas warfare may start any day, and the power that can command a plentiful supply of . . ."

"Fine, Oscar," Gloria broke in. "But we can go over all this later. We've got other worries right now."

"What do you mean, my dear?"

"Have you run onto a red-headed young Irishman in a yellow shirt?"

"No, I . . . Why, yes. I did see such an individual leaving the office yesterday. I believe he had been to see Wolf."

"He's on to us. He's a detective from Los Angeles, and he's tracking us down. Some place he got hold of a scrap of record that should have been destroyed. He knows I'm in it, and he knows I'm tied up with somebody here in the German department."

Professor Fearing scrutinized his pince-nez, approved of their cleanness, and set them on his nose. "Not so much excitement, my dear. No hysteria. Let us approach this calmly. Does he know about the Temple of the Dark Truth?"

"Not yet. Nor about you. He just knows it's somebody in the department."

"Then what could be simpler? You have heard of the strange conduct of Wolfe Wolf?"

"Have I?" Gloria laughed harshly.

"Everyone knows of Wolf's infatuation with you. Throw the blame onto him. It should be easy to clear yourself and make you appear an innocent tool. Direct all attention to him and the organization will be safe. The Temple of the Dark Truth can go its mystic way and extract even more invaluable information from weary scientists who need the emotional release of a false religion."

"That's what I've tried to do. I gave O'Breen a long song and dance about my devotion to Wolf, so obviously phony he'd be bound to think it was a cover-up for something else. And I think he bit. But the situation is trickier than you guess. Do you know where Wolfe Wolf is?"

"No one knows. After the president . . . ah . . . rebuked him, he seems to have vanished."

Gloria laughed again. "He's right here. In this room."

"My dear! Secret panels and such? You take your espionage too seriously. Where?"

"There!"

Professor Fearing gaped. "Are you serious?"

"As serious as you are about the future of Fascism. That is Wolfe Wolf."

Fearing approached the wolf incredulously and extended his hand.

"He might bite," Gloria warned him a second too late.

Fearing stared at his bleeding hand. "That, at least," he observed, "is undeniably true." And he raised his foot to deliver a sharp kick.

"No, Oscar! Don't! Leave him alone. And you'll have to take my word for it—it's way too complicated. But the wolf is Wolfe Wolf, and I've got him completely under control. He's absolutely in our hands.

We'll switch suspicion to him, and I'll keep him this
way while Fergus and his friends the G-men go off
hotfoot on his trail.''

"My dear!" Fearing ejaculated. "You're mad.
You're more hopelessly mad than the devout members
of the Temple." He took off his pince-nez and stared
again at the wolf. "And yet Tuesday night . . . Tell
me one thing: From whom did you get this . . . this
wolf dog?"

"From a funny plump little man with a fringy
beard."

Fearing gasped. Obviously he remembered the furor
in the Temple, and the wolf and the fringe-beard.
"Very well, my dear. I believe you. Don't ask me
why, but I believe you. And now . . ."

"Now it's all set, isn't it? We keep him here helpless, and we use him to . . ."

"The wolf as scapegoat. Yes. Very pretty."

"Oh! One thing . . ." She was suddenly frightened.

Wolfe Wolf was considering the possibilities of a
sudden attack on Fearing. He could probably get
out of the room before Gloria could say *Absarka!*
And after that? Whom could he trust to restore
him? Especially if G-men were to be set on his
trail . . .

"What is it?" Fearing asked.

"That secretary. That little mouse in the department
office. She knows it was you I asked for, not Wolf.
Fergus can't have talked to her yet, because he swallowed my story; but he will. He's thorough."

"Hm-m-m. Then, in that case . . ."

"Yes, Oscar?"

"She must be attended to." Professor Oscar Fearing beamed genially and reached for the phone.

Wolf acted instantly, on inspiration and impulse. His
teeth were strong, quite strong enough to jerk the
phone cord from the wall. That took only a second,
and in the next second he was out of the room and

into the hall before Gloria could open her mouth to speak that word that would convert him from a powerful and dangerous wolf to a futile man.

There were shrill screams and a shout or two of "Mad dog!" as he dashed through the lobby, but he paid no heed to them. The main thing was to reach Emily's house before she could be "attended to." Her evidence was essential. That could swing the balance, show Fergus and his G-men where the true guilt lay. And, besides, he admitted to himself, Emily was a nice kid . . .

His rate of collision was about one point six six per block, and the curses heaped upon him, if theologically valid, would have been more than enough to damn him forever. But he was making time, and that was all that counted. He dashed through traffic signals, cut into the path of trucks, swerved from under street cars, and once even leaped over a stalled car which obstructed him. Everything was going fine, he was halfway there, when two hundred pounds of human flesh landed on him in a flying tackle.

He looked up through the brilliant lighting effects of smashing his head on the sidewalk and saw his old Nemesis, the policeman who had been cheated of his beer.

"So, Rover!" said that officer. "Got you at last, did I? Now we'll see if you'll wear a proper license tag. Didn't know I used to play football, did you?"

The officer's grip on his hair was painfully tight. A gleeful crowd was gathering and heckling the policeman with fantastic advice.

"Get along, boys," he admonished. "This is a private matter between me and Rover here. Come on," and he tugged even harder.

Wolf left a large tuft of fur and skin in the officer's grasp and felt the blood ooze out of the bare patch on his neck. He heard an oath and a pistol shot simultaneously, and felt the needlelike sting drive through his shoulder. The awestruck crowd thawed before him.

Two more bullets hied after him, but he was gone, leaving the most dazed policeman in Berkeley.

"I hit him," the officer kept muttering blankly. "I hit the . . .''

Wolfe Wolf coursed along Dwight Way. Two more blocks and he'd be at the little bungalow that Emily shared with a teaching assistant in something or other. That telephone gag had stopped Fearing only momentarily; the orders would have been given by now, the henchmen would be on their way. But he was almost there . . .

"He'o!" a child's light voice called to him. "Nice woof-woof came back!"

Across the street was the modest frame dwelling of Robby and his shrewish mother. The child had been playing on the sidewalk. Now he saw his idol and deliverer and started across the street at a lurching toddle. "Nice woof-woof!" he kept calling. "Wait for Robby!"

Wolf kept on. This was no time for playing games with even the most delightful of cubs. And then he saw the car. It was an ancient jalopy, plastered with wisecracks even older than itself; and the high-school youth driving was obviously showing his girl friend how it could make time on this deserted residential street. The girl was a cute dish, and who could be bothered watching out for children?

Robby was directly in front of the car. Wolf leaped straight as a bullet. His trajectory carried him so close to the car that he could feel the heat of the radiator on his flank. His forepaws struck Robby and thrust him out of danger. They fell to the ground together, just as the car ground over the last of Wolf's caudal vertebrae.

The cute dish screamed. "Homer! Did we hit them?"

Homer said nothing, and the jalopy zoomed on.

Robby's screams were louder. "You hurt me! You hurt me! *Baaaaad* woof-woof!"

His mother appeared on the porch and joined in

with her own howls of rage. The cacophony was terrific. Wolf let out one wailing yelp of his own, to make it perfect and to lament his crushed tail, and dashed on. This was no time to clear up misunderstandings.

But the two delays had been enough. Robby and the policeman had proved the perfect unwitting tools of Oscar Fearing. As Wolf approached Emily's little bungalow, he saw a gray sedan drive off. In the rear was a small, slim girl, and she was struggling.

Even a werewolf's lithe speed cannot equal a motor car. After a block of pursuit, Wolf gave up and sat back in his haunches panting. It felt funny, he thought even in that tense moment, not to be able to sweat, to have to open your mouth and stick out your tongue and . . .

"Trouble?" inquired a solicitous voice.

This time Wolf recognized the cat. "Heavens, yes," he assented wholeheartedly. "More than you ever dreamed of."

"Food shortage?" he cat asked. "But that toddler back there is nice and plump."

"Shut up," Wolf snarled.

"Sorry; I was just judging from what Confucius told me about werewolves. You don't mean to tell me that you're an altruistic were?"

"I guess I am. I know werewolves are supposed to go around slaughtering, but right now I've got to save a life."

"You expect me to believe that?"

"It's the truth."

"Ah," the cat reflected philosophically. "Truth is a dark and deceitful thing."

Wolfe Wolf was on his feet. "Thanks," he barked. "You've done it."

"Done what?"

"See you later." And Wolf was off at top speed for the Temple of the Dark Truth.

That was the best chance. That was Fearing's headquarters. The odds were at least even that when it wasn't being used for services it was the hang-out of his ring, especially since the consulate had been closed in San Francisco. Again the wild running and leaping, the narrow escapes; and where Wolf had not taken these too seriously before, he knew now that he might be immune to bullets, but certainly not to being run over. His tail still stung and ached tormentingly. But he had to get there. He had to clear his own reputation, he kept reminding himself; but what he really thought was, *I have to save Emily.*

A block from the Temple he heard the crackle of gunfire. Pistol shots and, he'd swear, machine guns, too. He couldn't figure what it meant, but he pressed on. Then a bright yellow roadster passed him and a vivid flash came from its window. Instinctively he ducked. You might be immune to bullets, but you still didn't just stand still for them.

The roadster was gone and he was about to follow when a glint of bright metal caught his eye. The bullet which had missed him had hit a brick wall and ricocheted back onto the sidewalk. It glittered there in front of him—pure silver.

This, he realized abruptly, meant the end of his immunity. Fearing had believed Gloria's story, and with his smattering of occult lore he had known the successful counterweapon. A bullet, from now on, might mean no more needle sting, but instant death.

And so Wolfe Wolf went straight on.

He approached the Temple cautiously, lurking behind shrubbery. And he was not the only lurker. Before the Temple, crouching in the shelter of a car every window of which was shattered, were Fergus O'Breen and a moonfaced giant. Each held an automatic, and they were taking pot shots at the steeple.

Wolf's keen, lupine hearing could catch their words even above the firing. "Gabe's around back," Moonface was explaining. "But it's no use. Know what that steeple is? It's a revolving machine-gun turret. They've been ready for something like this. Only two men in there, far as we can tell, but that turret covers all the approaches.''

''Only two?'' Fergus muttered.

''And the girl. They brought a girl here with them. If she's still alive.''

Fergus took careful aim at the steeple, fired, and ducked back behind the car as a bullet missed him by millimeters. ''Missed him again! By all the kings that ever ruled Tara, Moon, there's got to be a way in there. How about tear gas?''

Moon snorted. ''Think you can reach the firing gap in that armored turret at this angle?''

''That girl . . .'' said Fergus.

Wolf waited no longer. As he sprang forward, the gunner noticed him and shifted his fire. It was like a needle shower in which all the spray is solid steel. Wolf's nerves ached with the pain of reknitting. But at least machine guns apparently didn't fire silver.

The front door was locked, but the force of his drive carried him through and added a throbbing ache in his shoulder to his other discomforts. The lower-floor guard, a pasty-faced individual with a jutting Adam's apple, sprang up, pistol in hand. Behind him, in the midst of the litter of the cult, ceremonial robes, incense burners, curious books, even a Ouija board, lay Emily.

Pasty-face fired. The bullets struck Wolf full in the chest and for an instant he expected death. But this, too, was lead, and he jumped forward. It was not his usual powerful leap. His strength was almost spent by now. He needed to lie on cool earth and let his nerves knit. And this spring was only enough to grapple with his foe, not to throw him.

The man reversed his useless automatic and brought its butt thudding down on the beast's skull. Wolf reeled back, lost his balance, and fell to the floor. For a moment he could not rise. The temptation was so strong just to lie there and . . .

The girl moved. Her bound hands grasped a corner of the Ouija board. Somehow, she stumbled to her rope-tied feet and raised her arms. Just as Pasty-face rushed for the prostrate wolf, she brought the heavy board down.

Wolf was on his feet now. There was an instant of temptation. His eyes fixed themselves to the jut of that Adam's apple, and his long tongue licked his jowls. Then he heard the machine-gun fire from the turret, and tore himself from Pasty-face's unconscious form.

Ladders are hard on a wolf, almost impossible. But if you use your jaws to grasp the rung above you and pull up, it can be done. He was halfway up the ladder when the gunner heard him. The firing stopped, and Wolf heard a rich German oath in what he automatically recognized as an East Prussian dialect with possible Lithuanian influences. Then he saw the man himself, a broken-nosed blond, staring down the ladder well.

The other man's bullets had been lead. So this must be the one with the silver. But it was too late to turn back now. Wolf bit the next rung and hauled up as the bullet struck his snout and stung through. The blond's eyes widened as he fired again and Wolf climbed another round. After the third shot he withdrew precipitately from the opening.

Shots still sounded from below, but the gunner did not return them. He stood frozen against the wall of the turret watching in horror as the wolf emerged from the well. Wolf halted and tried to get his breath. He was dead with fatigue and stress, but this man must be vanquished.

The blond raised his pistol, sighted carefully, and fired once more. He stood for one terrible instant, gazing at this deathless wolf and knowing from his grandmother's stories what it must be. Then deliberately he clamped his teeth on the muzzle of the automatic and fired again.

Wolf had not yet eaten in his wolf's body, but food

must have been transferred from the human stomach to the lupine. There was at least enough for him to be extensively sick.

Getting down the ladder was impossible. He jumped. He had never heard anything about a wolf's landing on his feet, but it seemed to work. He dragged his weary and bruised body along to where Emily sat by the still unconscious Pasty-face, his discarded pistol in her hand. She wavered as the wolf approached her, as though uncertain yet as to whether he was friend or foe.

Time was short. With the machine gun dead, Fergus and his companions would be invading the Temple at any minute. Wolf hurriedly nosed about and found the planchette of the Ouija board. He pushed the heart-shaped bit of wood onto the board and began to shove it around with his paw.

Emily watched, intent and puzzled. "A," she said aloud. "B—S——"

Wolf finished the word and edged around so that he stood directly beside one of the ceremonial robes. "Are you trying to say something?" Emily frowned.

Wolf wagged his tail in vehement affirmation and began again.

"A—" Emily repeated. "B—S—A—R——"

He could already hear approaching footsteps.

"—K—A— What on earth does that mean? *Absarka . . .*"

Ex-professor Wolfe Wolf hastily wrapped his naked human body in the cloak of the Dark Truth. Before either he or Emily knew quite what was happening, he had folded her in his arms, kissed her in a most thorough expression of gratitude, and fainted.

Even Wolf's human nose could tell, when he awakened, that he was in a hospital. His body was still limp and exhausted. The bare patch on his neck, where the policeman had pulled out the hair, still stung, and there was a lump where the butt of the automatic had con-

nected. His tail, or where his tail had been, sent
twinges through him if he moved. But the sheets were
cool and he was at rest and Emily was safe.

"I don't know how you got in there, Mr. Wolf, or
what you did; but I want you to know you've done your
country a signal service." It was the moonfaced giant
speaking.

Fergus O'Breen was sitting beside the bed, too.
"Congratulations, Wolf. And I don't know if the doctor would approve, but here."

Wolfe Wolf drank the whiskey gratefully and looked
a question at the huge man.

"This is Moon Lafferty," said Fergus. "F.B.I. man.
He's been helping me track down this ring of spies
ever since I first got wind of them."

"You got them—all?" Wolf asked.

"Picked up Fearing and Garton at the hotel," Lafferty rumbled.

"But how . . . I thought . . ."

"You thought we were out for you?" Fergus answered. "That was Garton's idea, but I didn't quite
tumble. You see, I'd already talked to your secretary.
I knew it was Fearing she'd wanted to see. And when
I asked around about Fearing, and learned of the Temple and the defense researches of some of its members, the whole picture cleared up."

"Wonderful work, Mr. Wolf," said Lafferty.
"Any time we can do anything for you . . . And how
you got into that machine-gun turret . . . Well,
O'Breen, I'll see you later. Got to check up on the
rest of this round-up. Pleasant convalescence to you,
Wolf."

Fergus waited until the G-man had left the room.
Then he leaned over the bed and asked confidentially,
"How about it, Wolf? Going back to your acting ca-
reer?"

Wolf gasped. "What acting career?"

"Still going to play Tookah? If Metropolis makes
Fangs with Miss Garton in a Federal prison."

Wolf fumbled for words. "What sort of non-sense . . ."

"Come on, Wolf. It's pretty clear I know that much. Might as well tell me the whole story."

Still dazed, Wolf told it. "But how did you know it?" he concluded.

Fergus grinned. "Look, Dorothy Sayers said some place that in a detective story the supernatural may be introduced only to be dispelled. Sure, that's swell. Only in real life there come times when it won't be dispelled. And this was one. There was too much. There were your eyebrows and fingers, there were the obviously real magical powers of your friend, there were the tricks which no dog could possibly do without signals, there was the way the other dogs whimpered and cringed . . . I'm pretty hard-headed, Wolf, but I'm Irish. I'll string along only so far with the materialistic, but too much coincidence is too much."

"Fearing believed it, too," Wolf reflected. "But one thing that worries me—if they used a silver bullet on me once, why were all the rest of them lead? Why was I safe from then on?"

"Well," said Fergus, "I'll tell you. Because it wasn't 'they' who fired the silver bullet. You see, Wolf, up till the last minute I thought you were on 'their' side. I, somehow, didn't associate good will with a werewolf. So I got a mold from a gunsmith and paid a visit to a jeweler and . . . I'm glad I missed," he added sincerely.

"*You're* glad!"

"But look. Previous question stands. Are you going back to acting? Because if not, I've got a suggestion."

"Which is?"

"You say you fretted about how to be a practical, commercial werewolf. All right. You're strong and fast. You can terrify people even to committing suicide. You can overhear conversations that no human being could get in on. You're invulnerable to bullets. Can you tell me better qualifications for a G-man?''

Wolf goggled. ''Me? A G-man?''

''Moon's been telling me how badly they need new men. They've changed the qualifications lately so that your language knowledge'll do instead of the law or accounting they used to require. And, after what you did today, there won't be any trouble about a little academic scandal in your past. Moon's pretty sold on you.''

Wolf was speechless. Only three days ago he had been in torment because he was not an actor or a G-man. Now . . .

''Think it over,'' said Fergus.

''I will. Indeed I will. Oh, and one other thing. Has there been any trace of Ozzy?''

''Nary a sign.''

'':I like that man. I've got to try to find him and . . .''

''If he's the magician I think he is, he's staying up there only because he decided he likes it.''

''I don't know. Magic's tricky. Heaven knows I've learned that. I'm going to do all I can for that fringe-bearded old colleague.''

''Wish you luck. Shall I send in your other guest?''

''Who's that?''

''Your secretary. Here on business, no doubt.''

Fergus disappeared discreetly as he admitted Emily. She walked over to the bed and took Wolfe's hand. His eyes drank in her quiet, charming simplicity, and his mind wondered what freak of belated adolescence had made him succumb to the blatant glamour of Gloria.

They were silent for a long time. Then at once they both said, ''How can I thank you? You saved my life.''

Wolf laughed. ''Let's not argue. Let's say we saved our life.''

'':You mean that?'' Emily asked gravely.

Wolf pressed her hand. "Aren't you tired of being an office wife?"

In the bazaar of Darjeeling, Chulundra Lingasuta stared at his rope in numb amazement. Young Ali had climbed up only five minutes ago, but now as he descended he was a hundred pounds heavier and wore a curious fringe of beard.

NO NEWS TODAY

by Cleve Cartmill

Some of you will be disappointed because this editorial completely fills today's issue of the *Argus*. But I feel it is more important than news, this article. And some of the stores may be annoyed because there is no room for their ads, but a newspaper's first duty is to its readers.

You will not see me any more, so I take this means to impress on your minds one fact:

Dr. Evan Scot is not a son of Satan.

You must believe that. I am going to give you the reasons, and you will see. Then, when I finish, and after Mother Grace has run off enough copies for our subscribers, we will clean up the press, have a couple of drinks, and step through the door into the black emptiness which has been there for three days, blotting all lights, waiting for us.

I'll tell you about that blackness in due time. First, I want to explain that the rumor about Dr. Scot would never have been started if Mother Grace had attended to his job.

That was last week, the day after graduation exercises at the high school. Mother Grace came into my office from the composing room and flung several sheets of copy on my desk.

"I'll s-set no copy for a s-son of Satan," he said. He stutters a little when he is excited.

I put my feet down and looked at the copy. It was an account of the exercises, and included a few excerpts from Dr. Scot's commencement address. I then looked at Mother Grace.

He was a pink ball of indignation, his white hair almost standing out straight, his blue eyes flickering, and his round chin outthrust like a shelf.

I didn't say anything. I simply went out to the composing room and took a look at the jug of whiskey that caused Judith to name him "Mother." She said he cradled it like a lost child on Saturday nights. The jug was untouched, as it had been for the last month, since Mother went on the wagon because of the research which engaged his free time.

Back in my office, I frowned down at him. "What's it all about, Mother?"

"Evan Scot is the spawn of Lucifer. I'm damned if I'll set any type that's got his name in it."

"Dr. Scot is one of our most prominent citizens."

"That's what I mean, Buck."

"You're not making sense. Explain yourself."

"I don't dare, Buck. I like you. Just edit Scot's name out of the story and we'll forget the matter."

"We can't leave Scot's name out of the story. He was one of the highlights. The school board would be on our necks. So would Judith. She'd want to know why we messed up her copy. What would you tell her?"

"I wouldn't tell her anything, Buck. Same as I won't tell you."

I didn't want to fire him. He's a good printer. He's been all over the world several times, has worked in every State in the Union, and he treats a linotype like a younger brother. He had settled here in my shop two years ago, and was as much a part of the place as the weathered "Job Printing" sign over the door. No, I didn't want to fire him, but I had to have some kind of discipline.

"Set the story as it is," I said.

"S-set it yourself. I'm q-quitting."

He took off his apron, put on his coat, and stamped out with a thirsty gleam in his eye.

Many of you know what that little man did. He got drunk and started the rumor about Dr. Scot. I don't

think anybody paid any attention to him except Ralph
Lake, but we took care of Ralph last night. I'm sure
he doesn't believe it any longer, and he'll never see
this editorial.

While Mother was getting drunk, I knew nothing
about it, of course. I was busy setting type. I'm not
too good at it, as you will remember. That was the
issue which carried Henry Longernin's name mis-
spelled six ways, and in which the PTA story did not
appear. That was the issue which carried so many short
paragraphs of odd facts about different parts of the
world. Such paragraphs are kept standing on galleys
in any print shop to use as filler, and I was too slow
on the linotype to set all the local copy Judith had
turned in, so I threw in several columns of filler.

When I was making up the pages, I was reminded
of the predicament another country editor got into
when he ran short of filler one day. His paper was full,
except for a couple of inches in one lower corner of
his front page. He was one of those crusading, bitter
cusses that gave so much color to early American fron-
tiers, and he set up a paragraph by hand in large type
so that it would fill the hole. The paragraph: "A local
banker and another rat fought with their fists last night
at the corner of First and Main until a gentleman who
was asleep in the gutter woke up and asked them to
be more quiet." All three of the men referred to took
a poke at the editor next day, and it is said that the
practice of keeping filler on hand started at that time.

At any rate, I had plenty, and when I had run off
the edition on the flatbed press I went home to bed. I
didn't know what had happened to Mother, and I knew
I would need another printer.

I got some inkling of Mother's activities the next
morning when Dr. Evan Scot stalked into my office.
He gave me a nod of cold recognition, and refused to
take a chair.

"I have come to demand an apology, Mr. Buck."

This was not the hearty, pompous Dr. Scot I knew.
He had an icy purpose in his eyes, and his chubby

hands were rigid. I picked up a copy of the *Argus*, and skimmed through the commencement story which I had set.

"Are you misquoted, doctor? Name spelled wrong?"

He waved an impatient white hand. "I don't know, I haven't even glanced at your paper. An employee of yours, I am told, a man named Grace, has slandered me."

"He's no longer an employee of mine."

Dr. Scot inclined his head in a fractional bow. "Very well, I shall take the matter up with the—ah, proper authorities. Sorry to have disturbed you, Mr. Buck."

As he turned to go, feet scuffed across the reception room, and Mother Grace came to the door, stood swaying a little on widespread legs. He was drunk.

"Your evilness," he saluted Dr. Scot.

The doctor gave Mother an aloof examination, eyes lit by a remote curiosity as they touched on Mother's puffed face, tousled white hair, wrinkled clothes, and stubbly beard.

"You talk too much," Dr. Scot said.

"But with authority, sir," Mother replied.

"What authority?"

"The very highest, I suspect. The 'Sabbaticon.' "

"What is that?"

Mother Grace leered crookedly. "Don't play innocent, prince."

Dr. Scot's reaction to this was what caused me to agree with Mother Grace until Satan's public-relations counsel set us straight on the matter. Dr. Scot was angry. You could see a muscle twitch under one jowl, and his ample shoulders lifted a fraction. But his anger was cold. Thoughtful is perhaps a better term. He held his gaze steady on Mother Grace for a full ten seconds. Then:

"You talk too much," he repeated, and thrust through the door.

* * *

Mother Grace stared after him for a few seconds, then came inside unsteadily and dropped into a chair.

"Buck, I want to talk to you."

"You'd better. What goes on, Mother? Are you serious in this talk about Dr. Scot?"

"Deadly, Buck. And I've got a notion that it *is* deadly, too. I don't think I'll be around much longer. But before I disappear, I'd like to get some information out to the public."

"Disappear to where?"

"Who knows? Where did the others disappear to? The ones who walked through their doors and were never seen again? I don't know where they went, but I think I know why. Do you want to hear about it?"

"If it's entertaining, and brief."

"It may be dangerous, Buck."

"Nonsense. You're still drunk."

Mother looked at me with a still, unwavering earnestness. "Yes, I am, a little. Otherwise I'd be afraid to tell you. But I can't keep it bottled up any longer. Wait."

He went into the composing room, and I could hear him rummaging in the little cubbyhole where he slept. He came back with a peculiar book and several pages of manuscript in his careful handwriting. He tossed the book on my desk.

"That's the 'Sabbaticon,' Buck."

It seemed to be of leather. The cover was a heavy sort of calf, with no inscription or decoration, and the pages were of a thin, almost transparent leather, with a texture like heavy crêpe. These pages were closely covered with symbols which were strange to me. I had never seen a language with characters remotely similar.

I laid the book aside. "Well?"

"That's the handbook for the Sons of Satan."

"Let's have it from the beginning, Mother. You're still not making sense."

He began to talk, and after a few minutes I went

through the reception room and locked the front door. I didn't want us to be interrupted.

He said that, according to this all-leather book, a world-wide society, called the Sons of Satan, had been formed early in the history of civilization. The title of the group is accurate, he said; they are physical offspring of the devil, conceived in unions at Sabbats, gatherings of worshipers of evil.

"Where did you get this book?" I asked.

Mother Grace gave me a bleak look. "It belonged to my mother, Buck."

"Good heavens. What does that mean?"

"I don't know. I don't want to know. She died when I was born, and my uncle who raised and educated me gave it to me among other effects she had left. I've spent my life trying to translate it. The language isn't Latin, Greek, Sanskrit, or any other known today. I finished the translation a couple of weeks ago."

"How do you know your translation is correct?"

"I . . . I feel it, Buck. Here's the meat of it, the rules of operation." He handed me part of his translation.

I won't reproduce it here. There isn't space, nor time, perhaps. We're a little rushed for time. We're getting hungry, and we are determined not to suffer. We are just going to step through the door into that dead-black void.

But the rules. The Sons of Satan are supposed to be men of comfortable means. No more. Not wealthy, but the kind we common work-a-day folk admire. The men who are active in community affairs, the kind who are pointed out as local examples for children to follow.

They are not many, these Sons of Satan; only enough to provide a flavor of moderate success everywhere.

Their opinions are respected, but of course, divided. Thus they attract followers to both sides of any question. This stirs up conflict that is highly desirable from their point of view. Their principal advice to youth is, roughly: "Work. Earn your bread by the sweat of your brow. Keep your nose to the grindstone. Fame and success can be yours only if you are diligent.''

"Making a virtue of a curse on mankind," Mother Grace commented on this.

"Diligence is a virtue," I said. "Men do succeed by constant effort."

"How many?" Mother Grace jeered. "What percentage of those who slave away their lives ever attain to comfort? I'll tell you. Only enough to promote envy, dissatisfaction, and uneasiness. It's in there. Read on."

I see that in describing the text of the "Sabbaticon" I have written in the present indicative. "They are," I have said of the Sons of Satan. I want to make it clear that I don't believe they exist. You must not believe it, either.

I finished. I looked at Mother Grace. "I don't believe it."

He picked up the leather book and opened it to the last page. "It's easy to check. All I have to do is read a paragraph aloud. If my translation is correct, we'll have the old boy himself here in the office."

"Don't be idiotic."

"Want me to try? Want me to summon up the Prince of Darkness? I've been afraid to try before."

"Your translation may be correct, but the whole book is probably a prehistoric fairy tale."

"By whom, Buck? By whom?"

"How should I know?" The uneasy feeling I'd had while reading his translation began to wear off, and I managed a grin. "Go ahead. Give him a call. We'll get an exclusive interview."

Mother Grace stacked the sheets of his translation neatly on one corner of my desk, pushed his chair to one side, and knelt. Despite his rumpled condition and appearance of hard wear, he had a curious dignity.

"I hope we know what I'm doing," he said softly, and began to chant in a monotone.

He had hardly said two words, or phrases, or whatever, of that scrambled language before we had a visitor.

He appeared in the connecting doorway to the reception room. Appeared suddenly, silently, without any traditional puffs of smoke or smell of brimstone. He was young, and aside from his somewhat peculiar ears and odd black costume, he was not very different from the rest of us.

He broke into Mother Grace's chant. "You talk too much." He pointed a long, dark finger at the "Sabbaticon," said, "You have no right to that," and the book vanished. "Or that," he said, and the translation was gone.

"Shut up!" he said as Mother Grace opened his mouth as if to ask a question. "Listen to me, both of you. I am going to leave you here. Any time you like, just step out of a door, or window, and you'll receive detailed attention."

He seemed about to leave. "May I ask a question?"

He flicked an impatient look at me. "What do you want?"

"You mentioned detailed attention. What does that mean?"

"You'll see."

"Are you Satan himself?" Mother Grace asked.

"Certainly not," the creature snapped. "He has better matters to occupy him. I'm his public-relations counsel."

"B-but the invocation," Mother stuttered. "It was s-supposed to call up the d-devil."

The creature looked at Mother Grace long and thoughtfully. "So that's what you were doing? I—see. I'll be back," he said, and vanished.

Mother Grace got up off his knees. He was trembling. But no more than I was. The full impact of the event had just hit me. We looked at each other and worked our mouths in an effort to speak, but couldn't make a sound. Mother Grace staggered to the door.

Something brought him up short. Nothing physical, but something he saw. He looked fixedly toward the street for some time. He found his voice, or at least a ghost of it.

"C-come here, B-Buck."

That was when I saw the darkness.

I couldn't see through the windows or the glass on the door. I could hear traffic sounds in the street as usual, but I couldn't see anything. The word "ARGUS" on the big window was clearly outlined on the deeper black beyond.

I didn't feel that somebody had painted the windows. I felt that the dark had existence, beyond the windows and the door. I felt that it had—well, entity. I feel that way now, while I'm writing this.

I had a bad time getting out the words: "Open the door, Mother, open the door."

He went to the door, unlocked it, yanked it open. He shrank back, and I, even though I was across the room, took a backward step.

We couldn't see through the open door.

It's hard to tell about that darkness. If I try, I'll make it sound ridiculous. So I'd better not try. Just take my word for it, it wasn't at all ridiculous.

Somebody called from outside: "Hello, Buck. Hello, Mother."

We each lifted a hand. As we did so, Judith stepped through that black nothingness, her hair an almost blinding brightness against the background, and the white silhouette of her dress was like a cutout pattern.

We stood for a moment, Mother examining the floor, I trying to see some flicker of movement in traffic I could hear outside, Judith examining both of us. I knew suddenly I had to know what would happen if I stepped outside. I had to know if we had been tricked. I took a pencil from my pocket.

"Here," I said to Judith. "Toss this through the door."

She frowned. "Games?"

"Just throw it."

She did so, and I heard it fall on the walk. It hit that

curtain of blackness and, for me, vanished. "Now bring it to me, please."

"I'm no water spaniel," she said. "Fetch it yourself."

"I mean it, Judith. This is no gag."

She shook a puzzled head and stepped into nothing. She came back and gave me the pencil. I threw it.

I didn't hear it fall.

Judith blinked. "You ought to go on the stage, Buck. I saw it, then I didn't. Nice illusion."

"Little thing I picked up," I said.

"From your tone, I'd say you dug it up."

"What did you see, chicken?"

"See? I know enough about that sort of thing to know I didn't *see* anything. I thought, though, I saw a pencil fly barely through the door and—*f-f-ft*. It wasn't there any more. How did you do it?"

"It's a secret." To Mother Grace, who was staring at the door, I said, "Let's go to work."

He ambled into the composing room. I flung another look at the door and started after him.

"Buck," Judith said softly, "wait a minute."

She looked unhappy, puzzled. "What is it, kid?"

"It's about Ralph, Buck. And what Mother Grace told him last night."

"Come in my office." When we were in there, and I couldn't see the blackness, "Tell," I said.

"Well, Mother got stiff as a butler last night and gave Ralph a lot of guff about how we're being tricked by some crazy devil's club, he calls it. He was so convincing that Ralph believes it. So Ralph wants to ring wedding bells, even though we're broke. The hell with work, Ralph said, with that and everything else. There's no point to working, he said, if it's all a hoax. I don't know quite what to do with him. We still haven't paid his dental bill."

What could I tell her? At that time, I believed Mother's story. "Bring him in tomorrow, Judith. We'll have Mother issue a denial, or something. We'll figure out something. And you can have today off."

"Thanks, Buck," she said. "I've a couple of stories to write first."

"Leave your notes. I'll write 'em. I'm expecting a visitor for an important conference."

She gave me a sheaf of typed stationery. "These are the speeches for the Club Moderne tonight. Quote as liberally as you like. Here are the scores on the baseball game yesterday, and police notes. One drunk, two vags. Nothing ever happens in this town. See you tomorrow."

I went out to talk to Mother Grace.

Now I want all of you *Argus* subscribers to understand that it is difficult for me to relate and interpret events from this point in my narrative to the present. I am going to be honest with you. Please believe me. But I am going to tell what I think is essential to a correct analysis, and no more. There are certain facts I must leave unrelated, for I feel that they would confuse the issue.

Newspaper reporters learn early in their training to "slant" a story. By the twist of a phrase, by the deletion of contributing factors, they learn to make even a factual account of events in motion to mean something that is not wholly—or something that is more than—the truth. I am going to do that here, but only in order to be what I think is more honest. I want this last testament to be read and remembered as the truth.

One of the facts I am going to eliminate from consideration is the story Mother Grace had set on the linotype while I was talking about Ralph Lake with Judith. I leave it out because it simply can't be true; I don't dare let you believe it.

When I came into the composing room, Mother added the last slug of type to the galley on his machine and took a proof. He handed it to me without comment. I read it, and I believed it—at the time.

"These are verbatim quotations from the 'Sabbaticon'?" asked.

"I'll swear to it," Mother Grace said. "I've been

so close to that devilish book that I know it, word for word. I'll never forget it."

I read it again. Then I followed Mother's glance to the little window high in the wall above the press. The darkness was there, too, a kind of polarized darkness which allowed light to come into the building, but prevented us from seeing out.

"I want to compare our reactions, Mother. Do you see a sort of blackness?"

"Yeah, Buck. That pencil, too. Even the hairs in my eyebrows prickled."

"Maybe we can't get a paper out."

"I thought about that, Buck. But let's try. We've got to let the world know."

"Yes. We've got to let the world know. But look, if there's only one in every hundred thousand who is a Son of Satan, how could they be tracked? It would be like the seventeenth century witch hunts. Thousands of innocents would be killed."

"There's a sign, Buck."

He told me the sign, and I am not telling it here, because, as I say, it would confuse the issue. And I no longer believe it.

And I ask you to believe my first statement: Dr. Evan Scot is not a Son of Satan. I ask you to take it on faith. You must believe me, as you will see. I am not going to tell you the sign so that you can look for it on him. I don't want you to become confused.

"Look, Mother," I said as soon as I got my voice working again. "If I can't throw a pencil through the door, it stands to reason we can't get an issue of the paper outside. But let's don't shoot our whole load on an experiment. Let's put out the regular edition, with none of this in it. A trial balloon, so to speak. If that goes out, then we can shoot this tomorrow."

"That's sense, Buck."

"Another thing. Our—ah, visitor said he'd be back. When, do you think?"

"How the hell should I know?"

"You know more about his kind than I. You had the book, didn't you?"

That hurt him, and I hadn't meant it to. He jerked, as if I'd hit him with a lead pig, then looked at me steadily.

"Buck, if you think I'm one of the Sons that got away, and I'll admit possession of the book might indicate it, I'd rather you'd kill me here. Or I'll step out the door. I mean that, Buck. If you think there's something wrong about my ancestry, if you can't trust me to the limit, I'd rather get out. I want people to have this information. want to help, but if you're afraid of me, I'll walk out into whatever that is waiting."

I put my hand on his shoulder. "Let's get to work, pal."

That edition went out, but as you know, you didn't get a paper the next day, or yesterday. The press broke down. There was nothing unusual about it. It does that occasionally. We did not feel that supernatural forces had stopped us, because we could see a gear that had crystallized. It wasn't even dramatic, crawling around in grease and printer's ink.

But we didn't have time to talk to Judith and Ralph, and they said they'd come back later.

They did. Last night. So did the creature who had arrived while Mother Grace was chanting the paragraph from the "Sabbaticon." We had just finished repairing the press, cleaned ourselves up, and were having a drink, when he was suddenly there again, in the composing room with us.

His strange ears were fairly quivering. "I've got a million things to do," he said, "and you pull a stupid trick like that, Grace. Shut up! Listen to me, both of you. As a result of flapping your mouth, a special reception is being prepared for you. Not only that, but I'll be forced to throw the Wall around half the houses in this town if the rumors you set in motion are accepted as facts. Fools! As if I weren't busy enough, you try to overwork me further."

There seemed nothing to be gained by being afraid of him, or nice to him, so I said, "You're the fool. Why did you leave that copy of the book where anybody could get it?"

"Shut up!" he snapped. "I didn't do it. It was before my time. It wouldn't have happened if I'd had anything to do with it."

"But it happened, and it wasn't our fault. Why should we suffer?"

"Because I say you shall."

"So you're afraid to let the truth become known? You don't think you could cope with people if they realize that most of our eternal verities are vicious jokes to keep us unhappy forever?"

"Who said anything about truth, fool?"

"Your actions admit it. You don't have to say it."

"I didn't say that the truth was in that book. I tell you this: the Wall is not around this building necessarily because you have discovered a truth, but because you believe it to be true. The same will be done to anyone else who believes as you." He turned to Mother Grace, who was staring at the little window high in the wall above the press. "Have you told this story in detail to anyone besides this idiot?"

Mother Grace was slow in bringing his eyes back into focus, and before he could say anything, a pounding rattled the locked front door, and Judith yelled:

"Oh, Buck! Let us in!"

Mother Grace answered the question. "No. I didn't tell anybody."

"Who's out there?" our visitor snapped.

"A couple of my employees, here for a conference."

"Keep them in the front. I don't want them to see me. I'm busy enough as it is."

"I'll be right back."

I told Judith and Ralph to stay in the reception room and went back. I wanted the answer to one more question.

"Look," I said. "You won't admit the truth of

Mother's story, you won't deny it. Answer me this: Is the 'Sabbaticon' itself a hoax? Was it planted just to increase the sum total of unhappiness?''

He smiled. "That would be an amusing refinement. If it had been planted, if people believed it, and if every man would then look on his neighbor with a suspicion of diabolic origin—yes, that would be pretty. I'll file that away for future reference.''

"Then it isn't true?''

"Oh, I didn't say that," he said quickly. "I didn't say anything.''

"I say the 'Sabbaticon' was the hoax, then. I say that its story of the Sons of Satan was untrue. I am going to tell the readers of my paper that, if I may.''

"Surely," he agreed. "If you can make them believe it, I won't need to use the Wall on this town. I'll welcome anything to avoid that on top of my other duties.''

"What about us?" Mother Grace asked. "Wh-what if w-we change our b-belief? Will we get free?''

"No. Oh, if you changed your belief, yes. But you can't. You believe it too deeply. Now, I've wasted too much time here already. I don't care what you do, but if you clear up the mess this fool started, your reception won't be quite so—ah, special, when you step into the Wall.''

He was suddenly gone, and my first sensation was regret that he had never turned his back to us once. I can't tell you whether he had a tail or not.

But I can clear up his one definite misstatement. I have said several times that I do not believe the "Sabbaticon" was a true record. Once I had penetrated the hoax, I didn't believe any more in the Sons of Satan. My disbelief was so strong that the first thing I did was to tear up the proofs of the quotations Mother Grace had set—the quotations I did not include in this—and threw the type into the linotype pot.

We convinced Ralph Lake. He finally believed that Mother Grace's story was a phase of D.T.'s. How we did it is not important. Those of you who know the big, stubborn prizefighter will realize what a job we had. But he believed us, and so shall you.

Mother Grace and I also gave all our money to Judith and Ralph, and drew checks for our bank balances, and got their promise to catch the early-morning train to Kansas City, where they will be married. I mention this here, so that the bank will honor the checks when they come in.

*   *   *

The asterisks indicate an interruption. Dr. Evan Scot came in as I sat at my typewriter finishing this editorial. I don't have time to begin this over again from the beginning. Mother Grace and I are too hungry. He has been taking the sheets from me as I finish them, to set in type. This is the twenty-first sheet. I am sure you will forgive me for having used up all these words to try to prove something that was proved so dramatically a moment ago.

Mother Grace and Dr. Scot got into an argument. Dr. Scot wanted an apology. Mother Grace refused. I stepped between them to stop the fight. Mother Grace dared Dr. Scot to take off his shirt.

Mother Grace was so angry he was crying. "You d-don't dare take it off—you don't dare, you son of Lucifer!"

Dr. Scot gave him a cold but puzzled look, and stripped slowly and deliberately to the waist. Mother Grace looked at Dr. Scot's back, and his shoulders slumped.

"I apologize, doc," he said. "I w-was wrong. Damn it!" he shouted, and went back into the composing room.

Dr. Scot got back into his clothes, nodded a cool good-by to me, and stepped into the Wall. I could hear his steps on the sidewalk, but I couldn't see him, nor could I see street lamps, or star shine, through that curtain.

We are going to step into it as soon as we run this

edition off the press, but I am glad there is no danger to you.

Provided—that you don't believe in the Sons of Satan. I don't. I say it again, I don't. You must not. *Must* not.

The Wall will be around your house if you do.

THE NIGHT TRAIN
TO LOST VALLEY

by August Derleth

Something about city lights in the dusk takes me back
to the old days when I was "on the road." A traveling
salesman for harnesses and leather goods—"drummers," we were called then—certainly prosaic enough
just past the turn of the century. A curious thing, too,
for lights were not too much a part of that hill-country
route in New Hampshire. Brighton to Hempfield to
Dark Rock to Gale's Corners—and at last to Lost Valley, on a little country train running out of Brighton
on the spur to Lost Valley and back, the train I had to
take to make Lost Valley and work back down to
Brighton. And unique it was, surely, in more ways
than one—old-fashioned locomotive, coal car, and sel-
dom more than one coach with a baggage car.

I took the night train because there was no other. It
went up in the evening out of Brighton, and it came
back next morning. Strange, rugged country. Strange
people, too—uncommonly dark, and in many ways
primitive—not backward, exactly, I would never have
called them that, but given to certain old ways not
frequently encountered even in the first decade of the
century, when vestiges of the 1890s still lingered in
widely scattered areas of the country. But beautiful
country, for all its strangeness: that could not be gain-
said. Dark, brooding country, much wooded, with
startling vistas opening up before one's eyes on the
morning trip down out of Lost Valley.

I used to wonder why the spur had been run to Lost
Valley, unless the town had given greater promise when
the railroad was put through—a promise clearly never

fulfilled, for it was small, its houses clustered close
together, with many trees, even in its main street. The
dusty roads, too, wound in and out among the trees.
But, being in the heart of agricultural country, however sparsely settled, it supported a large harness shop,
so that it was important to get into Lost Valley for the
seasonal order.

The train used to wait on a siding in Brighton, steam
up, ready to pull away. Sometimes, when people went
down to Concord for an inauguration or for just a
shopping trip, the single coach had to expand to two,
and both were filled; but usually there were few people to make the trip all the way up to Lost Valley—
about seventy miles or thereabouts, and quite often,
considering the relatively few times I made the trip, I
was the only passenger—sharing the train with the
conductor, the brakeman, the engineer, and a fireman,
with all of whom I grew quite friendly in the course
of time, since the train's personnel did not change
much in a decade.

The conductor, Jem Watkins, was an old fellow, lean
and a little bent, with a sharp, wry humor which fitted
in somehow with his small bright eyes and his thin
goatee. I knew him better than the others, for often on
the twenty-odd miles between Gale's Corners and Lost
Valley, he came in and sat to talk. The brakeman did
this too, on those occasions when I was the sole passenger. A tall, saturnine individual named Toby Colter, he never had much to say, but he could become
enthusiastic about the weather, and he seemed to have
an inexhaustible store of anecdotes concerning the
weather in the vicinity of Lost Valley. Abner Pringle,
the engineer, and Sib Whately, the fireman, I knew
less well. I had a hailing knowledge of them, so to
speak, and little more, but they were always friendly.
They were all four hill-country men, all, in fact, from
Lost Valley or its vicinity, and they were filled with
the lore of that country.

Strange lore—strange with the strangeness of alli-
ance to old things, to old customs long since forgotten.

To what extent they were forgotten in Lost Valley I have since had more than one occasion to wonder, though there is not much doubt but that I would never have thought of any kinship at all between the town and the old customs if it had not been for my last trip to Lost Valley. It is always of that last trip and what happened that night that I come to think, finally, perplexed, unsure, and filled with a kind of amazed wonder still. Everything else—the trip up and back, the long talks with Jem Watkins and Toby Colter, the people of the town, the big orders placed in Lost Valley, even to a large extent the wild beauty of the scenery—ultimately falls into the general pattern of reminiscence, but not the last trip to Lost Valley.

Yet, vivid as it is, there is always an element of doubt. Did it, after all, really happen? Or was it a dream? For it had the quality of a dream, beyond question, and it had the hazy aftereffect of a dream. Things sometimes happen to a man which are so far out of the ordinary that he tends inevitably to discredit his senses. Conversely, dreams of such realism sometimes take place that a man deliberately seeks some supporting evidence to convince himself of their reality. Dream or reality, it does not matter. Something happened that night in Lost Valley, something of which the train and the men on it and I myself were an integral part, something which left in memory an abiding wonder and a chaotic confusion, and which might have had a meaning of which I have never cared—or dared—to think.

I knew it was to be my last trip, since I was going into office work; so that the event was in itself unusual. And then, too, the train—for once in the decade I had taken it—set out ahead of time. It was unprecedented, and if I had not been at the station in Brighton fully half an hour early, I would have missed the train and would have had to go to Lost Valley on the following day. I have often wondered whether what happened to me that night would have taken place the following night.

The early starting of the train was only the beginning of the curious events of that night. For one thing, when I waved at Abner Pringle, on my way past the locomotive to the single coach, I was startled to see an expression of almost ludicrous consternation upon his usually placid features, and he returned my wave with halfhearted reluctance. His reaction was so unexpected that before I had gone ten steps, I was convinced that I had imagined it. But I had not, for at sight of me, Jem Watkins likewise looked by turns unpleasantly surprised and dismayed.

"Mr. Wilson," he said in an uncertain voice.

"You don't look glad to see me, and that's a fact, Jem," I said.

"You're makin' the trip—tonight?"

I had climbed into the coach by this time, Jem Watkins after me, with his conductor's cap in one hand and the other scratching his head.

"I'm late this year, I know it," I said. "But I'm making the trip." I looked at him, and he at me; I could not get away from the conviction that I was the last person Jem Watkins expected or wanted to see. "But if you don't want to take me, Jem, why, say so."

Jem swallowed. The adam's apple of that scrawny neck moved up and down. "Couldn't you go up tomorrow?"

"Tonight," I said. "I'll tell you something. It's my last trip."

"Your last trip?" he echoed in a weak voice. "You mean—you're stayin' with us up there?"

"Well, no, not exactly. I've been transferred to the office. You'll have a new man hereafter, and I hope you'll treat him as nice as you always treated me."

Strangely, it seemed that the conductor was slightly mollified at the news that this was to be my last trip; I had thought, perhaps in some vanity, that he might regret it. Yet he was not wholly pleased, and perhaps nothing would have pleased him but that I descend and leave him and his train go along up to Lost Valley without me. Perhaps in other circumstances I might have done so, despite my feeling at a loss to account for my reception; but now, with promotion just ahead, I did not want to waste a minute in getting over with my last tasks as a salesman. So I settled myself, and tried to appear unconcerned about the curious way in which Jem Watkins stood there in the aisle of the coach, turning his hat in his hands, this way and that, and not knowing just what to say.

"The people up there are pretty busy this time of year," he said finally. "I don't know whether it wouldn't be best to send in by mail for your order from Mr. Darby."

"And miss saying goodbye to him?" I said. "Mr. Darby wouldn't like that."

Jem Watkins retreated, baffled, after a hurried look at his watch, and in a few moments the train pulled out of the station, just four minutes short of half an hour ahead of time. Since I was the only passenger, I knew Jem would be back; we had hardly gone two miles beyond Brighton, when he came walking into the car, and Toby Colter was with him, both of them looking uneasy and grim.

"We talked it over," said Jem slowly, while Toby nodded portentously, "and we kind of figured you might like to stay in Gale's Corners tonight and come in to Lost Valley in the morning."

I laughed at this; it seemed so ingenuous. "Come now, Jem, it's to Lost Valley I'm going, and no other place. Gale's Corners in the morning, remember? We've done it twice a year for ten years, and you've never thought of changing before."

"But this year you're late, Mr. Wilson," said Toby.

"That I am. And if I don't hurry now, I won't be back in Boston by the second. Let me see, it's April thirtieth today, and I've got to run into Gainesville before I head back to Boston. I can just make it."

"You won't see Mr. Darby tonight," said Jem.

"Why not?"

"Because he won't be there, that's why."

"Well, then I'll see him in the morning." But I

thought with regret that I would not be sitting around that old-fashioned stove in the harness shop spending the evening in the kind of trivial talk which is the very stuff of life in country places.

Jem took my ticket and punched it, and Toby, after a baffled glance at me, left the car. Jem seemed resigned now. He sat looking out to the fleeting landscape; the last of the sun was drawing off the land, and out of the east, in the pockets among the hills, a blue and purple haze that was twilight was gathering. We were perhaps ten miles out of Brighton and already drawing near to Hempfield. And by that time I was filled with the strangeness of this ride—with everything about it, from the unexpected early start to the conductor's incredible attitude.

The country through which we were traveling was one of increasing wildness, and at this hour especially beautiful, for the last sunlight still tipped the hilltops, and the darkness of dusk welled up from the valleys, while the sky overhead was a soft blue of unparalleled clarity, against which the few small cirrus clouds were a startling white. It was that hour of the day during which the face of heaven and of earth changed with singular rapidity, so that in a few moments the clouds which had been white, were peach, and in a few more, crimson on the under side and old rose on top, and soon lavender, while the blue of the sky became dark overhead, and changed to aquamarine and amethyst above the lemon and turquoise of the afterglow. The train moved into the west, and I watched the ever-changing world outside the coach with a pleasure all the deeper and more appreciative for the knowledge that perhaps I would never again be viewing this particular scene.

The route to Lost Valley went steadily into hill country, and up to just beyond Gale's Corners by four miles or thereabouts, the railroad was an almost imperceptible up-grade; then, sixteen miles or so this side of Lost Valley, the down-grade began, though it was not the equivalent of the previous up-grade, so that clearly Lost Valley lay in a little pocket of the higher hills beyond Gale's Corners. We stopped briefly in Hempfield, apparently for the debouching of mail, and went on again without further interruption. I had made an effort to look out of the window to notice whether the station agent at Hempfield was at all surprised at the train's early arrival, but if he was, he did not show it. The conductor had leaned out of the window and passed the time of the evening with him, opining that it would be a clear night, and then again resumed his seat opposite me, from which he glanced at me with a kind of helpless dubiousness from time to time.

His unnatural uncommunicativeness troubled me eventually. "Jem," I said, "how has old Mrs. Perkins been? She was quite sick last time I was up."

"Oh, she's dead, Mr. Wilson," said Jem, nodding his head lugubriously. "Died in February."

"Too bad. And how's that crippled baby of Beales'?"

"Poorly, Mr. Wilson, poorly." He gave me a curious look just then, a very curious look, and for a moment I had the idea that he was about to say something; but evidently he thought better of it, for he did not speak, except to say, "Poorly," again.

"I'm sorry not to see Mr. Darby tonight," I went on. "I enjoy sitting around that stove with the old-timers who come in."

Jem said nothing.

"What would he be doing tonight?"

"Why, round about this time he finishes his winter work, as you'd ought to know, Mr. Wilson, and he's pretty busy tottin' up his books and gettin' things in order."

"That's so," I said, "but I've seen him at that earlier in April than this, and he never closed up shop for it then."

"Mr. Darby's gittin' old," said Jem, with unexpected vehemence.

Those were his last words until we were past Gale's

Corners, and then he spoke only in answer to my perplexed comment that none of the station agents along the route had shown any surprise at the train's being almost three-quarters of an hour early, for it had accelerated its speed considerably since leaving Brighton.

"We're usually ahead of time this time of year," said Jem. And once more there was that curious, baffled glance—as if he thought I knew something I was not telling and wished that I would say it and clear the air.

Soon then we came into sight of Lost Valley—or what, in the gathering darkness, I knew to be Lost Valley: a cluster of lights, not many, for there were not more than thirty buildings in the hamlet, and it existed not so much because of the people who lived within its limits as it did because of those people back in the hills who did their trading there. Then we drew up at the station, and there was old Henry Pursley bent over the telegraph key with the yellow light of his lamp-lit room streaming out to the station platform: a cozy scene and one of pleasant warmth.

But I had no sooner stepped down from the train into the light than he looked up and saw me; and instead of the customary greeting I expected, his jaw dropped, and he sat staring at me, and then, accusingly, it seemed, at Jem. Only then did he greet me, soberly, and, coming out, spoke in a low voice to Jem, which sounded as if he were berating Jem for forgetting something. I went up along the street away from the station and seeing that Darby's Harness Shop was indeed dark, I crossed over to the one two-story house in town, that of the widowed Mrs. Emerson and her daughter, Angeline, where I was accustomed to staying. And there, too, I was greeted with the same consternation and surprise, and for a moment it seemed that for once the door of the house would be closed against me, but then Angeline, a tall dark girl with black eyes and a flamelike mark under one ear, opened the door and invited me in.

"You're late this spring, Mr. Wilson," she said.

I admitted it. "But it's my last trip," I explained, and told them why.

Mrs. Emerson looked at me shrewdly, "You've not eaten, Mr. Wilson. You look dissatisfied."

I felt dissatisfied and would have gone on to tell them why, if it were not that I felt they, too, would say nothing to me, for, after all, I was an outsider, and in all small towns, even in less secluded places, a man from "outside" does not gain the confidence of villagers for years, sometimes as many as twenty or more. I admitted that I had not eaten.

"Then you'll have to eat, Mr. Wilson."

"I wouldn't think of troubling you, thank you, Mrs. Emerson."

Mrs. Emerson, however, would hear of nothing but that Angeline must at once prepare food, and she herself brought me a bitter-tasting tea which, she said, she had brewed of bergamotte and mint; and it did have a minty aroma, though it tasted more bitter than minty, and I took the opportunity, when the women were both out of the sitting room for a moment, of pouring the brew into a pot containing a large fern, prayerfully hoping that no harm would come to the fern. I had drunk enough, in any case, to leave an unpleasant taste in my mouth, about which I complained to Mrs. Emerson as soon as she appeared, whereupon she immediately produced a piece of old-fashioned sweet chocolate.

"I thought might be you wouldn't care for it too much, but it's good for you just the same. But this'll take the taste of it away."

So it did. And the meal itself, which was a good and ample one, did more—it made me realize that, what with all this rushing about of the day in Brighton and on the way there, I was tired. The hour was nine o'clock, and, while it was by no means late, it was to bed I wanted to go. Thereupon, with all the customary show of hospitality I had come to expect of my hostesses in the years past, I was shown to my room.

Once abed, I fell asleep with unusual alacrity.

From that point on, I cannot be sure that what happened was reality. It may have been dream. But there were subsequently certain disquieting factors, which, pieced together, pointed to conclusions wholly outside my small world—though I had never before realized how small the world was. What happened may have been a powerful, transcendent dream. It may not.

It began with my waking. I woke suddenly with a headache and the taste of Mrs. Emerson's bitter tea strong and hot in my mouth. Intending to go for water, I got up, put on my trousers, shoes, and shirt, and went downstairs, feeling my way in the dark. Before I reached the bottom of the stairs, I was aware of a commotion outside the house, and, pausing to look out, I saw an extraordinary movement of people in the direction of the railroad station, and then, peering up the street, I saw that the train—the night train to Lost Valley on which I had come—was standing, steam up, at the station. But, most strange of all, the people I saw were clad in conical hats and black cloaks; some of them carried torches, and some did not.

I turned and struck a match, and by its light I saw that a trunk under the stair had been thrown open, clothing taken out, and everything left as it was, as if someone had been in great haste to get away. Among the pieces there was a black cloak and a conical hat, which I divined to be the property of the late Mr. Emerson. I stood for a moment looking down at them; then the match went out.

What was it out there in the streets? Where were all these people going? Men, women, and children—it seemed as if the entire population of Lost Valley was deserting the town.

I reached down in the dark and touched the black cloak. I lifted it and set it in my shoulders, drawing it tight around my neck; it swathed me from neck to toe. I took up the conical hat and put it on and saw that it provided a kind of masking fold for the face as well.

Then, acting on an extraordinary impulse, I opened the door and went out to join the thronging people.

All were going to the train, and all were boarding the train. But the train was headed away from the only direction it could take out of Lost Valley, and it stood not quite at the station, but a little beyond it, and beyond the turntable where it customarily turned around to make the morning trip down to Brighton. The coach was not lit, but the light from the firebox and the glare of a half dozen torches held by men mounted on the locomotive made a weird illumination in a night dark save for the locomotive's headlight pointed to the woods ahead. And, looking in that direction, I was startled to see what must have been newly laid, but not new tracks, leading away into the dark hills beyond Lost Valley.

So much I saw before mounting into the unlit coach, which was crowded with silent people. Then nothing more. No light flared in the crowded coach. No one spoke. The silence was unbelievable, no human voice was heard save once the cry of a baby I could not see. Nor was the coach alone filled; so was the baggage car, and so, too, was the coal car. People clung to the train, from the locomotive to the rear platform—a great, silent throng, the entire population of Lost Valley, bent on a mission in the dead of night, for the hour surely approached midnight judging by the stars overhead, and the position of the gibbous moon which hung yellow low in the eastern sky. There was an extraordinary feeling of excitement, of tension, and of wonder in the coach, and I too began to feel it in the increased beating of my pulse, and in a kind of apprehensive exhilaration caught from my hooded and cloaked companions.

Without bell or whistle-sound, the train set out, drawing away from the deserted village into the dark hills. I tried to estimate how far we went—I thought not farther than seven miles. But we passed under arched trees of great age, through glens and narrow valleys, past murmurous brooks, past mourning whippoorwills and owls, into a veritable kingdom of night, before the train slowed to a stop, and at once everyone aboard began to get out, still wordless and tense. But this time the torchbearers took the lead, and certain others pushed up to be right behind them, while others waited patiently to fall into line, and I myself, fearful least some regular order be imposed upon the throng, waited until last, and then fell into step beside another hooded man, who, I felt sure, could be none other than Abner Pringle, for only he had such girth and height.

They did not go far, but, coming suddenly to an open space, the torchbearers alone went forward and ranged themselves below a strange stone image—or was it an image? The light flickered so and danced upon the stone there in the wood, I could not be sure; yet it seemed to be an image, and presently all were prostrate on the ground before the stone, and there remained, myself among them, until those who had walked directly behind the torchbearers rose and began a slow, rhythmic dancing, while another of them walked directly to the foot of the stone and began to chant in a voice I felt sure was Mr. Darby's. Latin, by the sound of it—but not pure Latin, for mixed with it was a gibberish I could not understand. Nor could I hear enough of the Latin to know what it was that was being said. A calling upon God, certainly. But what God? No Christian God in this place, for no Christian hand had touched the curious stone and the altarlike approach to it. If indeed it were an altar. Some hand had cut away the trees there, and someone had kept the grass down in that place. And there was something about the "fruits of the earth" and something more about "Ahriman" and something about the "Gift" (or "gifts") to come.

Then suddenly, a blue flame shone before the stone, and at sight of it the prostrate ones rose to their feet and began a wild dance to music coming from somewhere—a piping of fluted notes, which burst forth into the dark night like the startled voices of the forest's habitants themselves—music which grew wilder and wilder, as the dancers did, also—and I, too, for I was seized by a compulsion I could not struggle against, and I danced among them, sometimes alone, sometimes with someone—once, I am sure, with Angeline, in a wild, sensuous rout. The music mounted to a powerful crescendo, and on every side people screamed and chanted strange unintelligible words, and the dancing became more and more abandoned, until, as abruptly as it had begun, the music stopped.

At this instant, the celebrant before the stone stepped forward, bent and took up something there, tore away its covering, raised it high, whirling it thrice around his head, and dashed it to the stone, where its cry was stilled. What was it? What manner of creature had been sacrificed there? It seemed unfurred, unfeathered, too. White and unclothed. *A baby?*

A great sigh rose up. Then silence. The blue flame at the stone flickered, turned to green, to red, and began to subside.

The torchbearers started to file away from the stone, and the hooded celebrants waited to fall in line after them, though the master of the ceremony had been joined by two others, and all three were now bent about the base of the stone, while the others made their silent way back to the waiting train.

There we waited, again in unbroken silence, until all were once more on board, clinging to all sides of the train, filling every space. Then the train started up again, backing down to Lost Valley from which it had come away an hour or more before. How long I could not say. Time seemed to have no meaning in this eldritch night, but the moon was far higher than it had been. Two hours perhaps. Though it seemed incredible that we had been away so long.

I had wisely taken my place near to the door of the coach, so that I could make my escape quickly, get back to the house, remove my cloak and hood, and be in my room before Mrs. Emerson and Angeline returned. So I slipped away from the train and lost my-

self in the shadows. When the door opened and closed
for the two women, I was once again in bed.

But had I ever left that bed?

I woke up tired, true. But I woke up to Lost Valley
as I had always known it. When had my dream begun?

At the breakfast table, Mrs. Emerson asked whether
the tea had agreed with me.

I told her it did not.

"Nor with me, either. It gave me a headache," she
said. "And such a taste!"

"Well, nobody caught *me* drinking it," said Angeline.

I went over to the harness shop, and there was August Darby, just as hale and hearty as ever, just as
friendly. A jovial fellow, fat-cheeked, Teutonic in his
looks, with a full moustache and merry eyes.

"Heard you were in town last night. Man, why
didn't you come to the house? I was there. Worked on
my books till one o'clock," he said. His smile was
fresh, guileless, innocent. "But today—I'm tired. I'm
getting old."

He had a large order for me, and he made it larger
before I left, after he found out he might not see me
again.

I made a point of walking in the vicnity of the railroad station.

There were no tracks leading to the woods beyond
the town. Nothing. There was no sign that any tracks
had ever been there. The train was turned and waiting,
and, seeing me go by, Jem Watkins called out, "Hey
there, Mr. Wilson—you nearly ready?"

"Just about," I said.

I turned and went back into the village and stopped
at Beales' house. I knocked on the door and Mrs. Beale
came to answer, with her husband standing not far
behind. Strange! He looked as if he had been crying.
Red-eyed, bitter-mouthed. He stood a moment, and
then was gone, backing away somewhere out of my
sight.

"Hello, Mrs. Beale. How's the baby?"

She looked at me with a most extraordinary expression in her eyes. She glanced down, and I did, too. She was carrying folded baby clothes.

"Not well," she said. "Not well at all, Mr. Wilson. I'm afraid it won't be long."

"May I see her?"

She looked at me for a long moment. "I'm afraid not, Mr. Wilson. She's sleeping. It's been a hard time getting her to sleep."

"I'm sorry," I said.

I bade her goodbye and stepped away. But not before I had seen what she had been about when I knocked. Folding and wrapping baby clothes, a lot of them, and putting them away—not in a bureau—but in a trunk there in the front room.

I went over to the station and got into the train. From the window I took a last look at Lost Valley. When you come into a town as most drummers do, you take the town for granted, and sometimes you never notice things which other travelers might see at once. Like, for instance, churches. In ten years' time I had never noticed it—but now I did. There was no church of any kind in Lost Valley.

Anyone would say that is a small point—and it is. How many small points does it take to make a big one, I wonder? I ask myself how long it would take to lay seven miles of track, and I know it couldn't be done in a night. No, not in two nights. But then, it needn't be done in that time, not at all. Track could have been laid there for years, and all that needed to be done was perhaps a quarter of a mile from the station to just past the woods' edge out of sight. And afterwards, it could be taken up again, as easily, and stored away once more.

And in backward places like Lost Valley—little towns no one ever sees except such casual travelers like myself, and then but briefly, overnight—there are all kinds of primitive survivals, I understand. Perhaps even witchcraft or more ancient lore which has to do

with human sacrifice to some dark alien god to pro-
pitiate him and thus assure the earth's fertility. Nobody
knows what happens in such places. But most of them,
unlike Lost Valley, have at least one church.

I remembered afterward that April thirtieth was
Walpurgis Eve. And everyone along the Brighton-Lost
Valley line seemed to understand that on that day the
train set out earlier than its scheduled time. Could they
know why? Not likely. For that matter, did I? I could
not say with any sureness that I did.

Where does a dream begin? Where does it end? For
that matter, what about reality? That too begins and
ends. Plainly, on the way, back, Jem Watkins and Toby
Colter, for all their chattering talk, were tired. I could
not imagine Jem's goatlike capering by torchlight. Nor
Toby's clumsiness either. And Mr. Darby! Who else
had a voice like him? None that I knew—but then, I
did not know everyone in Lost Valley. Darby and Mrs.
Emerson tired, too. But he had been up late working
on his accounts, and she had spent a sleepless night
because of bitter tea. Or had they?

Whose dream had I been in? Mine—or theirs?

Perhaps I would never have doubted that it was a
dream had it not been for that visit I paid to the Beales.
Even the sight of the baby clothes being folded and
put away, set against that vivid memory of what had
been flung in sacrifice against that silent stone thing
in the woods, would not alone have given me the doubt
I had. But on the way down, while Jem obligingly, as
always, held the train at the stations, on the spur to
Brighton, while I got out and got my orders from the
local harness shops, I thought about it, and at last,
getting back on the train at Hempfield for the final job
to Brighton, I spoke about Beales' baby.

"I meant to call and see Beales' baby," I began.

Jem cut me off, loquaciously. "Good thing you
didn't, Mr. Wilson. That poor little thing died in the
night. You'd like to've upset them."

But at Beales' it had been sleeping less than two
hours ago. Here in the sunny coach the baby in Jem's

words was dead in the night. Was this, after all, the same dark train which played its part in some ancient woodland rite? A country train—worn locomotive, coal-car, baggage car, and creaking coach, making its run once daily up to Lost Valley, and once daily back. And in the night did it always rest quietly at the station at Lost Valley? Or did it, once a year, on Walpurgis Eve, make a secret sally into darkness?

I bade the train goodbye at Brighton. I said goodbye to Jem and Toby, Abner and Sib, who shook my hand as if I had been a lifelong friend. But somehow, I was never quite fully able to say goodbye to Lost Valley. It stayed just out of sight on the perimeter of consciousness, ready to reappear in the mind's eye at a moment's urging, at any casual thing that stirred memory. Like a country train on a little spur. Or masquerades and hooded things. Or city lights in the dusk.

I heard about Lost Valley indirectly once after that. It was at a Cambridge party—one of those gatherings which include a wide variety of people. I was passing a little group on my way to the punchbowl, when I heard Lost Valley mentioned. I turned. I recognized the speaker: Jeffrey Kinnan, a brilliant young Harvard man, a sociologist, and I listened.

"Genetically, Lost Valley is most interesting. Apparently there has been inbreeding there for generations. We should soon find an increasing number of degenerates in that vicinity. In genetics. . . ."

I walked away. Genetics indeed! Something that was old before Mendel was a mote in the cosmos. I could have spoken, too, but how could I be sure? Was it a dream or not? Certainly, wrapped up in his genetics, Kinnan would have called it a nightmare.

THE SACRIFICE
by Perceval Gibbon

"I do not think," said the Vrouw Grobelaar, looking at me with a hard unwinking eye, "that idle men should have pretty wives. Though Katje will lose that poppy red-and-white when she begins to grow fat. Still—"

Katje made an observation.

"Her mother," pursued the Vrouw Grobelaar, still holding me fixed, "spent seventeen years in one room, because she could not go through the door; and when she died they took the roof off and hoisted her out like a bullock from a well. But as I was saying, it is not well that idle men—those with leisure for their little-nesses, like schoolmasters, and doctors and Predi-kants—should have pretty wives, or they tend to waste themselves. A man with real work and money matters and the governing of cattle and land and Kafirs to fill his day, for such a one it is very well. Her prettiness is an interval, like the drink he takes in the noonday. But for an idle man it becomes the air he breathes. He is all-dependent on it, and it is a small and breakable thing.

"Look how men have been wrecked upon a morsel of pink-and-white, how strong brains have scattered like seed from a burst pod for a trifle of hunger in a pair of eyes. I remember many such cases which would make you stare for the foolishness of men and the worthlessness of some women. There was the Heer Mostert, Predikant at Dopfontein, who fell to blasphemy and witchcraft when his wife Paula was sick and muttered emptily among her pillows."

The old lady shifted in her wide chair and took her eyes from me at last.

"She was pretty, if you like," she said. "A tall girl, with a small red mouth, and hair that swathed her head like coils of bronze. The Predikant, who had more fire in him than a minister should have, and more fulness of blood than is good for any man, spent the half of his life in the joy of being near to her. She was full in the face and slow with a sleek languor, but on his coming there was to see a quickness of welcome spread itself in her. She would flush warmly, and her eyes would cry to him. Their love glowed between them; they were children together in that mighty bond. So when a spring that came down with chill rains smote Paula with a fever, and laid her weakly on her bed, the Predikant was a widower already, and walked with a face white and hard, drawn suddenly into new lines of pain and fear.

"Women are strange in sickness. Some are infants, greatly needing caresses and the neighbourhood of one tender and familiar. Others grow bitter, with an unwonted spite and temper, venting their ill-ease on all about them. But after the first, Paula was neither of these. The sense of things left her, and she lay on her bed with wide eyes that saw nothing and spoke brokenly about babies. For she had none. The doctor, a man of much brisk kindness, whose face was grown to a cheerful shape, frowned as he bent above her and questioned her heart and pulse. Paula was very ill, and as he looked up he saw the Predikant, tall and still, standing at the foot of the bed, gazing on the girl's face that gave no gaze back; and there was little he could say.

" 'Speak to her,' he told him.

"The Predikant kneeled down beside her, and took her hand, that pinched and plucked upon the quilt, into his.

" 'Paula!' he said gently. 'Wife!' and oh! the yearning that shivered nakedly in his voice.

" 'Little hands,' moaned Paula weakly—'little

hands beating on my breasts. Little weak hands; oh,
so little and weak!'

"The Predikant bowed his head, and the doctor saw
his shoulders bunch in a spasm of grief.

" 'Paula!' he called again. 'Paula, dear. It is I—
John. Don't you know John, Paula? Won't you answer
me, dear?'

"With eyes shut tight, he lifted a face of passionate
prayer.

" 'Say daddy!' said Paula, crooning faintly. 'Say
daddy.'

"The doctor passed his arm across the Predikant.

" 'Come away,' he said gently. 'This does no good.
Come away, now. There is plenty of hope.'

"He led him outside, rocking like a sightless man.
When he sat down on the edge of the stoep, he stared
straight before him for a little while, fingering a button
on his coat till it broke off. Then he flung it from him
and laughed—laughed a long quiet laugh that had no
tincture of wildness.

" 'Look here,' said the doctor, 'unless you go and
lie down, you'll not be fit to help me with Paula when
I need you. Lie down or work, whichever you please.
But one or the other, my man.'

" 'Suppose,' said the Predikant quietly—'suppose I
go and pray?'

" 'That'll do capitally,' answered the doctor. 'But
pray hard, mind. It might even do some good. There's
nothing certain in these cases.'

" 'I have just been thinking that,' said the Predikant, turning to him with a face full of doubt. 'But we
can try everything, at any rate.'

" 'We will, too,' said the doctor cheerfully; and
then the Predikant passed to his room to pour out the
soul that was in him in prayer for the life of Paula.

"It was a great battle the doctor fought in the dark
room in which she lay. When late that night the Predikant, his face dull white in the ominous gloom, came
again to the rail at the foot of the bed, his hand fell

on something soft that hung there. It was Paula's long bronze hair they had cut off for coolness to her head.

"The doctor did not wait for the question.

" 'There will be a crisis before day,' he said.

" 'What does that mean?' asked the other. The doctor explained that Paula would rise, as it were, to the crest of a steep hill, whence she would go down to life or death as God should please.

" 'But what can we do?' demanded the Predikant.

" 'Very little,' replied the doctor. 'Beyond the care I am giving her now, the thing is out of our hands. We can only look on and hope. There is always hope.'

" 'And always hopes betrayed,' said the Predikant. 'But is she worse now than she was this afternoon when she babbled of the little hands?'

" 'Yes,' answered the doctor.

" 'But I prayed,' said the Predikant, with a faint note of argument and question.

" 'Quite right, too,' replied the doctor. 'Go and pray again,' he suggested.

"The Predikant shook his head. 'It is wasting time,' he whispered, and turned to tiptoe out. But at the door he turned and crept back again.

" 'It is my wife, you see,' he said mildly—'my wife, so if one thing fails we must try another. You see?'

"The doctor nodded soothingly, and the Predikant crept out again.

"The doctor sat beside the bed and watched the sick woman, and heard her weak murmur of children born in the dreams of fever. It was a still night, cool, and hung with a white glory of stars, and the point at which life and death should meet and choose drew quickly near. There was this and that to do, small offices that a woman should serve; but the doctor had ordered the women away and did them himself. He was a large man, who continually fell off when he mounted a horse, but in a sick-room he was extraordinarily deft, and trod velvet-footed. So in the business of leading Paula to the point where God would relieve him time went fast, and presently he knew the minute was at hand.

"He was sitting, intent and strung, when he heard from the garden outside the house a bell tinkle lightly. He frowned, for it was no time for noises; but it tinkled again and yet again, louder and more insistent, while a change grew visibly on the face of the sick woman, and he knew that the issue was stirring in the womb of circumstance. Then, brazenly, the bell rang out, and with an oath on his breath he rose and slipped soundlessly from the room.

"When he reached the garden all was still, and he loosed his malediction upon the night air. But even as he turned to go back the bell fluttered near at hand, and he dived among the bushes to silence it. He nearly fell over one that kneeled between two big shrubs and wagged a little ram bell.

" 'What in hell is this?' demanded the doctor fiercely, seizing the bell.

" 'It is me,' answered a voice, and the Predikant rose to his feet. 'Be careful where you tread. There are things lying about your feet you had better not touch. Has it done her any good?'

" 'You stricken fool,' cried the doctor, 'do you know no better than to go rattling your blasted bells about the place tonight? You're mad, my man—mad and inconvenient.'

" 'But is she better?' persisted the Predikant.

" 'I'll tell you in ten minutes,' replied the doctor. 'But if you make any more noise you'll kill her, mind that.'

"The Predikant went with him to the stoep, and stayed there while the doctor returned to the bedside. At the end of an interval he was out again, and took the husband by the arm.

" 'It's over,' he said. 'She's doing finely. Sleeping like a child. You can thank God now, Mynheer Mostert.'

The Predikant stared at him dumbly.

" 'Thank God, did you say?' he asked at last.

" 'And me,' answered the doctor, smiling.

" 'I do thank you,' answered the Predikant. 'I do thank you from my heart, doctor. But for the rest—'

"And here, with a voice as even as one who speaks on the traffic of every day, with a calm face, he poured forth an awful, a soul-wracking blasphemy.

" 'Here!' cried the doctor, startled. 'Draw the line somewhere, Predikant. That sort of thing won't do at all, you know.'

" 'Now let me see my wife,' said the Predikant; and after a while, when he had warned him very solemnly on the need for silence, the doctor took him in and showed him Paula, thin and shorn, sleeping with level breath. The Predikant looked on her with parted lips and clenched hands, and when he was outside again, he turned to the doctor.

" 'I value my soul,' he said simply. 'But it is worth it.'

" 'I haven't a notion what you are gibbering about,' answered the doctor, who had a glass in his hand. 'But there's long sleep and a dream-killer in this tumbler, and you've to drink it.'

" 'I need nothing,' said the Predikant, but at the doctor's urgency he drank the dose, and was soon in his bed and sleeping.

"Next day, when he was let in to Paula's bedside, she smiled and murmured at him, and nodded weakly when he spoke. The doctor warned him about noise.

" 'We've won her back,' he explained, 'and she's going to do well. But she has had a hard time, and there's no denying she is very weak and ill. So if you go back to your bell-ringing or any of those games you'll undo everything. She's to be kept quiet, do you hear?'

" 'I hear,' answered the Predikant. 'There shall be stillness. Not that it matters for all your words, but there shall be stillness.'

" 'I warn you,' retorted the doctor seriously, 'that it matters very much. You're off your axle, my friend, and I shall have to doctor you. But if I hear of any foolishness, Predikant or no Predikant, I'll have you locked up as sure as your name's Mostert.'

"He left him there, and started through the garden to his cart that stood in the road. On his way he stubbed his foot against something that lay on the earth—a great metal cup. He picked it up.

" 'I am not a heathen,' he said, as he brought it to the Predikant, 'and therefore a Communion cup is no more to me than a sardine-tin, when it is out of its place. I don't want to know what you were doing out here the other night, my friend; but you had better put this back in the Kerk before somebody misses it.'

"The Predikant took it from him, but said nothing.

" 'And look here,' went on the doctor, 'it was my skill and knowledge that saved your wife. Nothing else. Good-day.'

"As he drove off, he saw the Predikant still standing on the stoep, the great cup, stained here and there with earth, in his hand.

"From that hour Paula mended swiftly. Even the doctor was surprised at the manner in which health sped back to her, and the young roses returned to her cheeks.

" 'There's more than medicine in this,' he said one day. 'Do you know what it is, Predikant?'

" 'Yes,' said the Predikant.

" 'You do, eh! Well, it's clean young blood, my friend, and nothing else,' answered the doctor, watching him with a slight frown of shrewdness.

"The Predikant said nothing. For days there had been a kind of gloom on him, lit by a savage satisfaction in the betterment of his wife. His manner was like a midnight, in which a veld-fire glows far off. He had grown thinner, and his face was lean and grey, while in his eyes smouldered a spark that had no relation to joy or triumph.

" 'Clean young blood,' repeated the doctor. 'No miracles, if you please.' He thought, you see, he had divined the Predikant's secret. 'I'm a man of science,' he went on, 'and when I come across a miracle I'll shut up shop.'

"Paula, from her pillows, heard them with a little wonder, and she was not slow to see the trouble and change in her husband's haunted face. So that night, when he came to say good-night to her, she drew his hand down to her breast, and searched for the seed of his woe.

" 'You look so thin and ill, my dear,' she said gently. 'You have worried too much over me. You have paid too great a price for your wife.'

"She felt him tremble between her arms.

" 'A great one,' he answered, 'but not too great.'

" 'Not?' she smiled restfully, as he lifted his face from her bosom and looked into her eyes.

" 'Never too great a price for you,' he said. 'Never that.'

" 'My love!' she answered, and for a while they were silent together.

"Then she stirred. 'Do you know, John,' she said, 'that you and I have not prayed together since first this sickness took me? Shall we thank God together, now that He has willed to leave us our companionship for yet a space?'

" 'No!' he said quietly.

" 'Dear!' She was surprised. 'I was asking you to thank God with me.'

"He nodded, 'I heard you, but it serves no purpose. God forgot us, Paula.'

"His eyes were like coals gleaming hotly. 'I prayed,' he cried, 'and yet you slipped farther from me and nearer the grave. I strewed my soul in supplication, and there was talk of winding-sheets. And then, in the keen hour of decision, when you tilted in the balance, I sought elsewhere for aid; and while I defiled all holiness, ere yet I had finished the business, comes to me that doctor and tells me all is well. What think you of that, Paula?'

"She had heard him with no breaking of the little smile that lay on her lips—the little all-forgiving smile

that is the heritage of mothers,—and now that he was
done she smiled still.

" 'I remember the old tales,' she answered. 'How
does the witch call the devil, John? Water in the Communion cup, bread and blood and earth—is that it? and
two circles—two, is it?'

" 'Three,' he corrected.

" 'Ah, yes; three.' She laughed soothingly. 'You
poor muddled boy,' she murmured. 'Do you prize me
so much, John? Poor John. You must let me be wise
for both of us, John. I am not afraid of the devil, at
all events.'

" 'Nor I,' he answered, 'so long as you are well.'

" 'But I am getting well now,' she answered. 'And
I do want you to pray with me, dear. Put your head
down, dear, and let me whisper to you.'

"She soothed him gently and sweetly, buttressing
his weakness with her love. How can I know what she
said or what he answered? She wrought upon him with
the kind arts God gives a woman to pay her for being
a woman, and soon she had softened something of the
miserable madness that possessed him, and he kneeled
beside the bed, sobbing rendingly, and prayed. Her
hand lay on his head, and after a while, when the violence had passed by, he was taken with a serene
peace.

"He bade her good-night, tenderly.

" 'Good-night,' she answered, 'and, John—I would
that I could give you half of what you would have given
for me.'

"As he went out at the door he saw her face smiling
at him, with a great warmth of love and pity transfig-
uring it.

"Next morning, when the doctor came, he stayed
near an hour in her room, and then came to the Predikant.

" 'Just tell me,' he said to him,—'just tell me
straight and short, what you did to your wife last
night.'

"The Predikant told him in a few words what had

passed between them, while the doctor watched him and curled his lip.

" 'Exactly,' he said, when the Predikant had done. 'Quite what I should have guarded against in you. Now you may go to your wife as quickly as you like. She is dying!'

"It was so. She died in his arms in half an hour, with the little smile of baffled motherhood yet on her lips."

Katje clenched her hands and looked out to the veld in silence.

YOUNG GOODMAN BROWN

by Nathaniel Hawthorne

Young Goodman Brown came forth at sunset into the street at Salem village; but put his head back, after crossing the threshold, to exchange a parting kiss with his young wife. And Faith, as the wife was aptly named, thrust her own pretty head into the street, letting the wind play with the pink ribbons of her cap while she called to Goodman Brown.

"Dearest heart," whispered she, softly and rather sadly, when her lips were close to his ear, "prithee put off your journey until sunrise and sleep in your own bed to-night. A lone woman is troubled with such dreams and such thoughts that she's afeared of herself sometimes. Pray tarry with me this night, dear husband, of all nights in the year."

"My love and my Faith," replied young Goodman Brown, "of all nights in the year, this one night must I tarry away from thee. My journey, as thou callest it, forth and back again, must needs be done 'twixt now and sunrise. What, my sweet, pretty wife, dost thou doubt me already, and we but three months married?"

"Then God bless you!" said Faith, with the pink ribbons; "and may you find all well when you come back."

"Amen!" cried Goodman Brown. "Say thy prayers, dear Faith, and go to bed at dusk, and no harm will come to thee."

So they parted; and the young man pursued his way until, being about to turn the corner by the meeting-house, he looked back and saw the head of Faith still peeping after him with a melancholy air, in spite of her pink ribbons.

"Poor little Faith!" he thought, for his heart smote him. "What a wretch am I to leave her on such an errand! She talks of dreams, too. Methought as she spoke there was trouble in her face, as if a dream had warned her what work is to be done to-night. But no, no; it would kill her to think it. Well, she's a blessed angel on earth; and after this one night I'll cling to her skirts and follow her to heaven."

With this excellent resolve for the future, Goodman Brown felt himself justified in making more haste on his present evil purpose. He had taken a dreary road, darkened by all the gloomiest trees of the forest, which barely stood aside to let the narrow path creep through, and closed immediately behind. It was all as lonely as could be; and there is this peculiarity in such a solitude, that the traveller knows not who may be concealed by the innumerable trunks and thick boughs overhead; so that with lonely footsteps he may yet be passing through an unseen multitude.

"There may be a devilish Indian behind every tree," said Goodman Brown to himself; and he glanced fearfully behind him as he added, "What if the devil himself should be at my very elbow!"

His head being turned back, he passed a crook of the road, and, looking forward again, beheld the figure of a man, in a grave and decent attire, seated at the foot of an old tree. He arose at Goodman Brown's approach and walked onward side by side with him.

"You are late, Goodman Brown," said he. "The clock of the Old South was striking as I came through Boston, and that is full fifteen minutes agone."

"Faith kept me back a while," replied the young man, with a tremor in his voice, caused by the sudden appearance of his companion, though not wholly unexpected.

It was now deep dusk in the forest, and deepest in that part of it where these two were journeying. As nearly as could be discerned, the second traveller was

about fifty years old, apparently in the same rank of
life as Goodman Brown, and bearing a considerable
resemblance to him, though perhaps more in expression than features. Still they might have been taken for
father and son. And yet, though the elder person was
as simply clad as the younger, and as simple in manner
too, he had an indescribable air of one who knew the
world, and who would not have felt abashed at the
governor's dinner table or in King William's court,
were it possible that his affairs should call him thither.
But the only thing about him that could be fixed upon
as remarkable was his staff, which bore the likeness
of a great black snake, so curiously wrought that it
might almost be seen to twist and wriggle itself like a
living serpent. This, of course, must have been an oc-
ular deception, assisted by the uncertain light.

"Come, Goodman Brown," cried his fellow-
traveller, "this is a dull pace for the beginning of a
journey. Take my staff, if you are so soon weary."

"Friend," said the other, exchanging his slow pace
for a full stop, "having kept covenant by meeting thee
here, it is my purpose now to return whence I came.
I have scruples touching the matter thou wot'st of."

"Sayest thou so?" replied he of the serpent, smiling
apart. "Let us walk on, nevertheless, reasoning as we
go; and if I convince thee not thou shalt turn back.
We are but a little way in the forest yet."

"Too far! too far!" exclaimed the goodman, uncon-
sciously resuming his walk. "My father never went
into the woods on such an errand, nor his father before
him. We have been a race of honest men and good
Christians since the days of the martyrs; and shall I
be the first of the name of Brown that ever took this
path and kept"—

"Such company, thou wouldst say," observed the
elder person, interpreting his pause. "Well said,
Goodman Brown! I have been as well acquainted with
your family as with ever a one among the Puritans;
and that's no trifle to say. I helped your grandfather,
the constable, when he lashed the Quaker woman so

smartly through the streets of Salem; and it was I that brought your father a pitch-pine knot, kindled at my own hearth, to set fire to an Indian village, in King Philip's war. They were my good friends, both; and many a pleasant walk have we had along this path, and returned merrily after midnight. I would fain be friends with you for their sake.''

"If it be as thou sayest,'' replied Goodman Brown, "I marvel they never spoke of these matters; or, verily, I marvel not, seeing that the least rumor of the sort would have driven them from New England. We are a people of prayer, and good works to boot, and abide no such wickedness.''

"Wickedness or not," said the traveller with the twisted staff, "I have a very general acquaintance here in New England. The deacons of many a church have drunk the communion wine with me; the selectmen of divers towns make me their chairman; and a majority of the Great and General Court are firm supporters of my interest. The governor and I, too—But these are state secrets.''

"Can this be so?" cried Goodman Brown, with a stare of amazement at his undisturbed companion. "Howbeit, I have nothing to do with the governor and council; they have their own ways, and are no rule for a simple husbandman like me. But, were I to go on with thee, how should I meet the eye of that good old man, our minister, at Salem village? Oh, his voice would make me tremble both Sabbath day and lecture day.''

Thus far the elder traveller had listened with due gravity; but now burst into a fit of irresponsible mirth, shaking himself so violently that his snakelike staff actually seemed to wriggle in sympathy.

"Ha! ha! ha!" shouted he again and again; then composing himself, "Well, go on, Goodman Brown, go on; but, prithee, don't kill me with laughing.''

"Well, then, to end the matter at once," said Goodman Brown, considerably nettled, "there is my wife,

Faith. It would break her dear little heart; and I'd rather break my own.''

''Nay, if that be the case,'' answered the other, ''e'en go thy ways, Goodman Brown. I would not for twenty old women like the one hobbling before us that Faith should come to any harm.''

As he spoke he pointed his staff at a female figure on the path, in whom Goodman Brown recognized a very pious and exemplary dame, who had taught him his catechism in youth, and was still his moral and spiritual adviser, jointly with the minister and Deacon Gookin.

''A marvel, truly, that Goody Cloyse should be so far in the wilderness at nightfall,'' said he. ''But with your leave, friend, I shall take a cut through the woods until we have left this Christian woman behind. Being a stranger to you, she might ask whom I was consorting with and whither I was going.''

''Be it so,'' said his fellow-traveller. ''Betake you to the woods, and let me keep the path.''

Accordingly the young man turned aside, but took care to watch his companion, who advanced softly along the road until he had come within a staff's length of the old dame. She, meanwhile, was making the best of her way, with singular speed for so aged a woman, and mumbling some indistinct words—a prayer, doubtless—as she went. The traveller put forth his staff and touched her withered neck with what seemed the serpent's tail.

''The devil!'' screamed the pious old lady.

''Then Goody Cloyse knows her old friend?'' observed the traveller, confronting her and leaning on his writhing stick.

''Ah, forsooth, and is it your worship indeed?'' cried the good dame. ''Yea, truly is it, and in the very image of my old gossip, Goodman Brown, the grandfather of the silly fellow that now is. But—would your worship believe it?—my broomstick hath strangely disappeared, stolen, as I suspect, by that unhanged witch, Goody Cory, and that, too, when I was all anointed with the juice of smallage, and cinquefoil, and wolf's bane''—

"Mingled with fine wheat and the fat of a newborn babe,'' said the shape of old Goodman Brown.

"Ah, your worship knows the recipe,'' cried the old lady, cackling aloud. "So, as I was saying, being all ready for the meeting, and no horse to ride on, I made up my mind to foot it; for they tell me there is a nice young man to be taken into communion to-night. But now your good worship will lend me your arm, and we shall be there in a twinkling.''

"That can hardly be,'' answered her friend. "I may not spare you my arm, Goody Cloyse; but here is my staff, if you will.''

So saying, he threw it down at her feet, where, perhaps, it assumed life, being one of the rods which its owner had formerly lent to the Egyptian magi. Of this fact, however, Goodman Brown could not take cognizance. He had cast up his eyes in astonishment, and, looking down again, beheld neither Goody Cloyse nor the serpentine staff, but this fellow-traveller alone, who waited for him as calmly as if nothing had happened.

"That old woman taught me my catechism,'' said the young man; and there was a world of meaning in this simple comment.

They continued to walk onward, while the elder traveller exhorted his companion to make good speed and persevere in the path, discoursing so aptly that his arguments seemed rather to spring up in the bosom of his auditor than to be suggested by himself. As they went, he plucked a branch of maple to serve for a walking stick, and began to strip it of the twigs and little boughs, which were wet with evening dew. The moment his fingers touched them they became strangely withered and dried up as with a week's sunshine. Thus the pair proceeded, at a good free pace, until suddenly, in a gloomy hollow of the road, Goodman Brown sat himself down on the stump of a tree and refused to go any farther.

"Friend,'' said he, stubbornly, "my mind is made

up. Not another step will I budge on this errand. What if a wretched old woman do choose to go to the devil when I thought she was going to heaven; is that any reason why I should quit my dear Faith and go after her?''

''You will think better of this by and by,'' said his acquaintance, composedly. ''Sit here and rest yourself a while; and when you feel like moving again, there is my staff to help you along.''

Without more words, he threw his companion the maple stick, and was as speedily out of sight as if he had vanished into the deepening gloom. The young man sat a few moments by the roadside, applauding himself greatly, and thinking with how clear a conscience he should meet the minister in his morning walk, nor shrink from the eye of good old Deacon Gookin. And what calm sleep would be his that very night, which was to have been spent so wickedly, but so purely and sweetly now, in the arms of Faith! Amidst these pleasant and praiseworthy meditations, Goodman Brown heard the tramp of horses along the road, and deemed it advisable to conceal himself within the verge of the forest, conscious of the guilty purpose that had brought him thither, though now so happily turned from it.

On came the hoof tramps and the voices of the riders, two grave old voices, conversing soberly as they drew near. These mingled sounds appeared to pass along the road, within a few yards of the young man's hiding-place; but, owing doubtless to the depth of the gloom at that particular spot, neither the travellers nor their steeds were visible. Though their figures brushed the small boughs by the wayside, it could not be seen that they intercepted, even for a moment, the faint gleam from the strip of bright sky athwart which they must have passed. Goodman Brown alternately crouched and stood on tiptoe, pulling aside the branches and thrusting forth his head as far as he durst without discerning so much as a shadow. It vexed him the more, because he could have sworn, were such a thing possible, that he recognized the voices of the minister and Deacon Gookin, jogging along quietly, as they were wont to do, when bound to some ordination of ecclesiastical council. While yet within hearing, one of the riders stopped to pluck a switch.

"Of the two, reverend sir," said the voice like the deacon's, "I had rather miss an ordination dinner than to-night's meeting. They tell me that some of our company are to be here from Falmouth and beyond, and others from Connecticut and Rhode Island, besides several of the Indian powwows, who, after their fashion, know almost as much deviltry as the best of us. Moreover, there is a goodly young woman to be taken into communion."

"Mightly well, Deacon Gookin!" replied the solemn old tones of the minister. "Spur up, or we shall be late. Nothing can be done, you know, until I get on the ground."

The hoofs clattered again; and the voices, talking so strangely in the empty air, passed on through the forest, where no church had ever been gathered or solitary Christian prayed. Whither, then, could these holy men be journeying so deep into the heathen wilderness? Young Goodman Brown caught hold of a tree for support, being ready to sink down on the ground, faint and overburdened with the heavy sickness of his heart. He looked up to the sky, doubting whether there really was a heaven above him. Yet there was the blue arch, and the stars brightening in it.

"With heaven above and Faith below, I will yet stand firm against the devil!" cried Goodman Brown.

While he still gazed upward into the deep arch of the firmament and had lifted his hands to pray, a cloud, though no wind was stirring, hurried across the zenith and hid the brightening stars. The blue sky was still visible, except directly overhead, where this black mass of cloud was sweeping swiftly northward. Aloft in the air, as if from the depths of the cloud, came a confused and doubtful sound of voices. Once the listener fancied that he could distinguish the accents of

towns-people of his own, men and women, both pious
and ungodly, many of whom he had met at the communion table, and had seen others rioting at the tav-
ern. The next moment, so indistinct were the sounds,
he doubted whether he had heard aught but the murmur of the old forest, whispering without a wind. Then
came a stronger swell of those familiar tones, heard
daily in the sunshine at Salem village, but never until
now from a cloud of night. There was one voice, of a
young woman, uttering lamentations, yet with an uncertain sorrow, and entreating for some favor, which,
perhaps, it would grieve her to obtain; and all the unseen multitude, both saints and sinners, seemed to en-
courage her onward.

"Faith!" shouted Goodman Brown, in a voice of
agony and desperation; and the echoes of the forest
mocked him, crying, "Faith! Faith!" as if bewildered
wretches were seeking her all through the wilderness.

The cry of grief, rage, and terror was yet piercing
the night, when the unhappy husband held his breath
for a response. There was a scream, drowned immediately in a louder murmur of voices, fading into far-
off laughter, as the dark cloud swept away, leaving the
clear and silent sky above Goodman Brown. But
something fluttered lightly down through the air and
caught on the branch of a tree. The young man seized
it, and beheld a pink ribbon.

"My Faith is gone!" cried he, after one stupefied
moment. "There is no good on earth; and sin is but a
name. Come, devil; for to thee is this world given."

And, maddened with despair, so that he laughed
loud and long, did Goodman Brown grasp his staff and
set forth again, at such a rate that he seemed to fly
along the forest path rather than to walk or run. The
road grew wilder and drearier and more faintly traced,
and vanished at length, leaving him in the heart of the
dark wilderness still rushing onward with the instinct
that guides mortal man to evil. The whole forest was
peopled with frightful sounds—the creaking of the
trees, the howling of wild beasts, and the yell of In-

dians; while sometimes the wind tolled like a distant church bell, and sometimes gave a broad roar around the traveller, as if all Nature were laughing him to scorn. But he was himself the chief horror of the scene, and shrank not from its other horrors.

"Ha! ha! ha!" roared Goodman Brown when the wind laughed at him. "Let us hear which will laugh loudest. Think not to frighten me with your deviltry. Come witch, come wizard, come Indian powwow, come devil himself, and here comes Goodman Brown. You may as well fear him as he fear you."

In truth, all through the haunted forest there could be nothing more frightful than the figure of Goodman Brown. On he flew among the black pines, brandishing his staff with frenzied gestures, now giving vent to an inspiration of horrid blasphemy, and now shouting forth such laughter as set all the echoes of the forest laughing like demons around him. The fiend in his own shape is less hideous than when he rages in the breast of man. Thus sped the demoniac on his course, until, quivering among the trees, he saw a red light before him, as when the felled trunks and branches of a clearing have been set on fire, and throw up their lurid blaze against the sky, at the hour of midnight. He paused, in a lull of the tempest that had driven him onward, and heard the swell of what seemed a hymn, rolling solemnly from a distance with the weight of many voices. He knew the tune; it was a familiar one in the choir of the village meeting-house. The verse died heavily away, and was lengthened by a chorus, not of human voices, but of all the sounds of the benighted wilderness pealing in awful harmony together. Goodman Brown cried out, and his cry was lost to his own ear by its unison with the cry of the desert.

In the interval of silence he stole forward until the light glared full upon his eyes. At one extremity of an open space, hemmed in by the dark wall of the forest, arose a rock, bearing some rude, natural resemblance either to an altar or a pulpit, and surrounded by four

blazing pines, their tops aflame, their stems untouched, like candles at an evening meeting. The mass
of foliage that had overgrown the summit of the rock
was all on fire, blazing high into the night and fitfully
illuminating the whole field. Each pendent twig and
leafy festoon was in a blaze. As the red light arose
and fell, a numerous congregation alternately shone
forth, then disappeared in shadow, and again grew, as
it were, out of the darkness, peopling the heart of the
solitary woods at once.

"A grave and dark-clad company," quoth Goodman
Brown.

In truth they were such. Among them, quivering to
and fro between gloom and splendor, appeared faces
that would be seen next day at the council board of the
province, and others which, Sabbath after Sabbath,
looked devoutly heavenward, and benignantly over the
crowded pews, from the holiest pulpits in the land.
Some affirm that the lady of the governor was there.
At least there were high dames well known to her, and
wives of honored husbands, and widows, a great multitude, and ancient maidens, all of excellent repute,
and fair young girls, who trembled lest their mothers
should espy them. Either the sudden gleams of light
flashing over the obscure field bedazzled Goodman
Brown, or he recognized a score of the church members of Salem village famous for their especial sanc-
tity. Good old Deacon Gookin had arrived, and waited
at the skirts of that venerable saint, his revered pastor.
But irreverently consorting with these grave, reputa-
ble, and pious people, these elders of the church, these
chaste dames and dewy virgins, there were men of
dissolute lives and women of spotted fame, wretches
given over to all mean and filthy vice, and suspected
even of horrid crimes. It was strange to see that the
good shrank not from the wicked, nor were the sinners
abashed by the saints. Scattered also among their pale-
faced enemies were the Indian priests, or powwows,
who had often scared their native forest with more hid-

eous incantations than any known to English witch-craft.

"But where is Faith?" thought Goodman Brown; and as hope came into his heart, he trembled.

Another verse of the hymn arose, a slow and mournful strain, such as the pious love, but joined to words which expressed all that our nature can conceive of sin, and darkly hinted at far more. Unfathomable to mere mortals is the lore of fiends. Verse after verse was sung; and still the chorus of the desert swelled between like the deepest tone of a mighty organ; and with the final peal of that dreadful anthem there came a sound, as if the roaring wind, the rushing streams, the howling beasts, and every other voice of the unconcerted wilderness were mingling and according with the voice of guilty man in homage to the prince of all. The four blazing pines threw up a loftier flame, and obscurely discovered shapes and visages of horror on the smoke wreaths above the impious assembly. At the same moment the fire on the rock shot redly forth, and formed a glowing arch above its base, where now appeared a figure. With reverence be it spoken, the figure bore no slight similitude, both in garb and manner, to some grave divine of the New England churches.

"Bring forth the converts!" cried a voice that echoed through the field and rolled into the forest.

At the word, Goodman Brown stepped forth from the shadow of the trees and approached the congregation, with whom he felt a loathful brotherhood by the sympathy of all that was wicked in his heart. He could have well-nigh sworn that the shape of his own dead father beckoned him to advance, looking downward from a smoke wreath, while a woman, with dim features of despair, threw out her hand to warn him back. Was it his mother? But he had no power to retreat one step, nor to resist, even in thought, when the minister and good old Deacon Gookin seized his arms and led him to the blazing rock. Thither came also the slender form of a veiled female, led between Goody

Cloyse, that pious teacher of the catechism, and Martha Carrier, who had received the devil's promise to be queen of hell. A rampant hag was she. And there stood the proselytes beneath the canopy of fire.

"Welcome, my children," said the dark figure, "to the communion of your race. Ye have found thus young your nature and your destiny. My children, look behind you!"

They turned; and flashing forth, as it were, in a sheet of flame, the fiend worshippers were seen; the smile of welcome gleamed darkly on every visage.

"There," resumed the sable form, "are all whom ye have reverenced from youth. Ye deemed them holier than yourselves, and shrank from your own sin, contrasting it with their lives of righteousness and prayerful aspirations heavenward. Yet here are they all in my worshipping assembly. This night it shall be granted you to know their secret deeds: how hoary-bearded elders of the church have whispered wanton words to the young maids of their households; how many a woman, eager for widows' weeds, has given her husband a drink at bedtime and let him sleep his last sleep in her bosom; how beardless youths have made haste to inherit their fathers' wealth; and how fair damsels—blush not, sweet ones—have dug little graves in the garden, and bidden to me, the sole guest, to an infant's funeral. By the sympathy of your human hearts for sin ye shall scent out all the places—whether in church, bed-chamber, street, field, or forest—where crime has been committed, and shall exult to behold the whole earth one stain of guilt, one mightly blood spot. Far more than this. It shall be yours to penetrate, in every bosom, the deep mystery of sin, the fountain of all wicked arts, and which inexhaustibly supplies more evil impulses than human power—than my power at its utmost—can make manifest in deeds. And now, my children, look upon each other."

They did so; and, by the blaze of the hell-kindled torches, the wretched man beheld his Faith, and the wife her husband, trembling before that unhallowed altar.

"Lo, there ye stand, my children," said the figure, in a deep and solemn tone, almost sad with its despairing awfulness, as if his once angelic nature could yet mourn for our miserable race. "Depending upon one another's hearts, ye had still hoped that virtue were not all a dream. Now are ye undeceived. Evil is the nature of mankind. Evil must be your only happiness. Welcome again, my children, to the communion of your race."

"Welcome," repeated the fiend worshippers, in one cry of despair and triumph.

And there they stood, the only pair, as it seemed, who were yet hesitating on the verge of wickedness in this dark world. A basin was hollowed, naturally, in the rock. Did it contain water, reddened by the lurid light? or was it blood? or, perchance, a liquid flame? Herein did the shape of evil dip his hand and prepare to lay the mark of baptism upon their foreheads, that they might be partakers of the mystery of sin, more conscious of the secret guilt of others, both in deed and thought, than they could now be of their own. The husband cast one look at his pale wife, and Faith at him. What polluted wretches would the next glance show them to each other, shuddering alike at what they disclosed and what they saw!

"Faith! Faith!" cried the husband, "look up to heaven, and resist the wicked one."

Whether Faith obeyed he knew not. Hardly had he spoken when he found himself amid calm night and solitude, listening to a roar of the wind which died heavily away through the forest. He staggered against the rock, and felt it chill and damp; while a hanging twig, that had been all on fire, besprinkled his cheek with the coldest dew.

The next morning young Goodman Brown came slowly into the street of Salem village, staring around him like a bewildered man. The good old minister was taking a walk along the graveyard to get an appetite for breakfast and meditate his sermon, and bestowed a blessing, as he passed, on Goodman Brown. He shrank from the venerable saint as if to avoid an anathema. Old Deacon Gookin was at domestic worship, and the holy words of his prayer were heard through the open window. "What God doth the wizard pray to?" quoth Goodman Brown. Goody Cloyse, that excellent old Christian, stood in the early sunshine at her own lattice, catechizing a little girl who had brought her a pint of morning's milk. Goodman Brown snatched away the child as from the grasp of the fiend himself. Turning the corner by the meeting-house, he spied the head of Faith, with the pink ribbons, gazing anxiously forth, and bursting into such joy at sight of him that she skipped along the street and almost kissed her husband before the whole village. But Goodman Brown looked sternly and sadly into her face, and passed on without a greeting.

Had Goodman Brown fallen asleep in the forest and only dreamed a wild dream of a witch-meeting?

Be it so if you will; but, alas! it was a dream of evil omen for young Goodman Brown. A stern, a sad, a darkly meditative, a distrustful, if not a desperate man did he become from the night of that fearful dream. On the Sabbath day, when the congregation were singing a holy psalm, he could not listen because an anthem of sin rushed loudly upon his ear and drowned all the blessed strain. When the minister spoke from the pulpit with power and fervid eloquence, and, with his hand on the open Bible, of the sacred truths of our religion, and of saint-like lives and triumphant deaths, and of future bliss or misery unutterable, then did Goodman Brown turn pale, dreading lest the room should thunder down upon the gray blasphemer and his hearers. Often, awaking suddenly at midnight, he shrank from the bosom of Faith; and at morning or eventide, when the family knelt down at prayer, he scowled and muttered to himself, and gazed sternly at his wife, and turned away. And when he had lived long, and was borne to his grave a hoary corpse, followed by Faith, an aged woman, and children and grandchildren, a goodly procession, besides neighbors not a few, they carved no hopeful verse upon his tombstone, for his dying hour was gloom.

THE VICAR OF HELL
by Edward D. Hoch

Considering the fact that Sir Francis Bryan was, during his lifetime, one of the most notorious men in the British Isles, it is unusual that he should have become one of the forgotten men of history, overlooked by virtually every modern encyclopedia and text book.

Since my business is publishing, it was this fact, more than any other, that took me to England that winter on a strange quest. And before my long search was ended I was to find my very life threatened by a murder that took place over four hundred years ago. . . .

The first thing I heard, as I left the big four-motored plane at London airport, was a small portable radio playing one of Gershwin's old tunes, "A Foggy Day." It was indeed a foggy day in London town, and for a time there'd been some doubt about our ability to land the plane. They told me such fog was common in London during the winter months, and I guess that was supposed to settle any complaints I might have voiced.

Actually, it had just turned December by the calendar; but in a city like London, where the annual mean temperature was only around 51 degrees, anything past the middle of November could be considered winter.

Had I been planning a sight-seeing visit to the tightly sprawling city on the Thames, I'm sure I'd have picked a better month than December. But this was a business trip; and though the whole thing had been my idea in the first place, I hadn't much choice over the time of the year.

And so there I was, in London in the middle of a

mild fog, bound for a meeting with a girl bearing the unusual name of Rain Richards.

I'd first seen the name at the bottom of a letter sent to our London office, and forwarded to me in New York. Since I was a married man approaching the age of forty, I had not even considered the fact that Miss Rain Richards might be young and beautiful and intelligent. But she was all three of these—and much more besides—as I realized the moment she'd opened the thick oak door of her house in the London suburbs.

She was tall and slim, with the stature of a fashion model, and yet there was something about her that hinted at a darkness beneath the surface. "I've been expecting you," she said after I'd introduced myself. "Please come in."

She led me down a narrow, dusky hall into a large room that might have been a study. Three walls were hung with a variety of small arms—guns, revolvers and automatics of all types. I judged there to be close to a hundred of them in the collection.

"Yours?" I motioned toward the walls, never dreaming that they were.

"Yes," she surprised me by saying. "Shooting is a hobby with me."

"Interesting. Now, about this matter, Miss Richards. . . ."

"You can call me Rain."

"That really is your name? I could hardly believe it when I saw the letter."

"I was born in India during the monsoon," she said, by way of explanation. "I guess my folks had a sense of humor or something."

From the looks of her, I would have guessed her age to be about twenty-seven, but it was hard to tell. I might have been five years off in either direction. She lit a cigarette as she talked, and casually blew smoke out her nostrils. "But you don't want to hear about me, of course. You've come about my letter."

"That's correct. You were quite right in saying that

we'd be interested in this book you mention. Suppose you tell me a little more about it.''

She relaxed deep into the chair and began to talk, with a soft toneless voice that flowed through the room like a glistening stream.

"You've heard of Sir Francis Bryan? Good! Very few people have, you know. I myself first became interested in Bryan while I was at your Columbia University. One day I came across a line in Milton which refers to him as the 'Vicar of Hell,' and that started me searching. It was a hard, long job, because most modern historians seem to have completely forgotten Bryan. But I finally found a few facts.''

She paused long enough to take another draw on her cigarette, and then continued. "Bryan lived during the first half of the sixteenth century, and he was a friend and advisor to Henry VIII. He was also a cousin of the ill-fated Anne Boleyn, and when she was put on trial, which resulted in her execution, death in 1536, he deserted her in order to remain in Henry's good graces. This deed caused Thomas Cromwell to refer to him in a letter as 'the Vicar of Hell,' a name that stuck with him until his death—though some historians credit Henry with first calling him that.''

"But what about this unsolved murder you mentioned in your letter?" I asked her.

"Oh yes. Well, in 1548, James Butler—an Irishman and the Ninth Earl of Ormonde—was poisoned while visiting here in London. Because they feared that his widow might marry an enemy of the crown, and thus strengthen his land-holdings, certain highly placed persons persuaded Francis Bryan, himself a widower, to woo and marry her—for the good of the country. Bryan succeeded in this last duty for his country, and he moved to Ireland to take over his new lands. However, he lived only two years, and died mysteriously in 1550.''

"So you have two mysterious deaths on your hands— James Butler and Bryan himself.''

"Yes," she continued, in an earnest voice that he was beginning to like. "Now my researches have turned up further information, unknown thus far to any of the historians. Sometime during the 17th century, about a hundred years after these deaths, there was published a large volume which claimed to give a somewhat shocking solution to these deaths. The book was immediately suppressed by the government, and all copies were seized and destroyed."

"Then what makes you think you can turn up a copy, three hundred years later?"

She rose from the chair and began striding back and forth across the room, her long legs moving quickly beneath the tight folds of her skirt. "Two weeks ago I received a letter from a man who'd heard of my quest. He offered to obtain a copy of the suppressed book for ten thousand pounds."

I relaxed and felt for my own American cigarettes. "So that's why you contacted a book publisher. You expect us to put up . . . What? Around $30,000? Put up around $30,000 for a book that might not even exist!"

"No; I simply want you to go with me to see this man. He refused even to see me unless I brought someone along who could offer that kind of money. Actually, ten thousand pounds isn't very much for a book that may have been written by another Boswell."

I sighed, and puffed on the cigarette. "I suppose not," I admitted. "At least it's worth talking to this fellow." Actually since I'd crossed the ocean on this mission already, I had no intention of going back empty-handed. But there was no reason for letting Rain Richards know that—at least not yet.

"Good," she said; "let me call him."

She placed a call to a number in the Kensington Gardens section of London, "At least that's where he told me he was located," and waited until a man's voice answered. "Hello? Mister Hugo Carrier? This is Rain Richards. I have an interested party over from

the States. Can we get together sometime tonight? Oh
. . . well, how about first thing in the morning?
Fine. . . . Let me jot down the address. . . . Good,
we'll see you around ten in the morning.''

She hung up and turned back to me. ''He can't see
us until ten in the morning; will that be all right with
you?''

''Guess it'll have to be. I'll stop by here for you
around nine-thirty.''

''Fine,'' she replied, the hint of a smile lingering
on her face. ''Till then. . . .''

I left her in the doorway and walked back toward
my hotel. With the coming of night, the fog seemed
even thicker, but I found Waterloo Bridge after nearly
an hour of walking and hailed a cab for the remaining
distance.

Back in my hotel room, I found myself preoccupied
with the memory of the girl named Rain. I took out a
book and started to read, but it didn't help. I found
myself comparing her with my wife, Shelly, and presently I took out my wallet and gazed at the photo of
Shelly—the one I'd taken at the beach some three years
ago.

Finally, unable to settle the troubled thoughts of my
own mind, I climbed into bed and dropped off into a
sound sleep. . . .

The morning dawned, bright and sunny, with only
a slight mist to remind me of the fog of the night
before. It was almost like a morning in New York,
when the canyons of Manhattan seem like valleys for
the flowering river of mist.

Now that I realized just how far Rain lived from the
center of London, I took a cab the entire distance. She
met me at the door, looking as young and cool as I
remembered her. ''Come in,'' she greeted me. ''I'm
just doing a little shooting downstairs. You may watch,
if you like.''

I followed her to the basement, where I found a
sandbagged area, with targets on the far wall, that ap-

parently served as her shooting gallery. On a shelf in front of her were a number of hand guns, and I recognized a U.S. Army .45 and .25 pocket automatic, and several foreign pistols.

"This is my favorite," she said, choosing a tiny weapon from the shelf. "A .41 caliber Derringer. Watch!"

She brought the gun up to eye level with a single sweeping motion that my eye could hardly follow. There was a deafening roar as both of its twin barrels spouted flame, and I could see the bull's eye of one of the targets fly away at the bullets' impact.

"You're quite a shot."

"I had to be. I was in Burma when the Japanese invaded; they killed my folks."

"I'm sorry. . . ."

"I'm over it now," she said. "I'm back in jolly old England, where everybody's respectable; and the war seems a long ways back. I suppose I'm lucky that my family had money back here, so I can devote myself to foolish projects like searching for lost manuscripts, and such."

As she spoke, she traded the Derringer for a tiny Colt .25 automatic and let go with five quick shots at another target. We walked over to examine it together. Four of the bullets had circled the bull's eye; the fifth was off to one side.

"That should have been in the center," she complained. "Well, what say we go to see Mister Carrier? It's nearly ten now."

I agreed and she put away the guns. "Have to clean them later—that's one part of it I don't like. Here, I'll take the Derringer with me; never can tell when it'll come in handy."

She dropped it into her purse and I raised my eyebrows lightly. "Do you have a permit for that?"

"The bobbies don't carry guns around here. Somebody has to have one, or there's no telling what would happen."

I shrugged and followed her out. The trip to Hugo

Carrier's tiny flat on the other side of London was
made in a swift little MG with Rain at the wheel. It
was my first ride in one of them, but it seemed to
handle well under her command.

Presently we came to a halt before a run-down block
of apartments off Bayswater Road. "This is the address he gave me; he's on the second floor."

We climbed the shadowy stairs to the first landing,
and in the dim light of a single naked bulb read the
names on the door. "Here it is," I said. "Hugo Carrier."

I knocked at the door and waited, but no one came.
I knocked again.

"It's only five minutes after ten," Rain said. "He
must be here."

"Maybe he's still asleep." I tried the knob of the
door, more as a reflex action than for any other reason.
It swung open at my touch, and in that instant I already
knew what we would find inside.

But I was unprepared for the horror that met our
eyes. For there, pinned to the opposite wall of the
room, was the body of a man. His arms were spread
in a cross, and the hands pinned to the wall with long
arrows through each palm. A third arrow protruded
from the man's chest.

Behind me, Rain Richards screamed. . . .

2

The room seemed filled with the quiet men from
Scotland Yard, popping their flashbulbs and dusting
for fingerprints. We told our story for the tenth time
to the inspector, who seemed to be in charge.

"You hadn't previously met this man, Miss Richards?" he wanted to know.

"No," she shook her head. "I'd only talked to him
on the phone."

"And have you any knowledge of this mark on the
floor?" He was pointing to something that Rain and I
had missed in the first shock of our discovery. It was

a sort of pentagram, in a circle, drawn in red on the floor in front of Carrier's body. There was no doubt that the design had been drawn with the dead man's blood. . . .

They took us down to the yards for further questioning, but they seemed to be getting nowhere. Presently we were introduced to still another questioner, an Inspector Ashly.

As soon as I heard the name, something clicked in my mind, like the tumblers of a safe. "Ashly! Inspector Ashly!" I exclaimed. "Simon Ark told me about you once."

Ashly's face became alert at the mention of that name. "You know Simon Ark?"

"Very well; I met him years ago back in the States. He told me of the odd happening at Devonshire a few years back."

Ashly was interested now. "I sometimes thought it was all a bad dream; I doubted, somehow, that the man ever really existed. It's certainly a relief to talk to someone else who knows him."

Ashly was a short man with a deep, booming voice, and I well remember Simon Ark's tale of their adventures together in the snows of Devonshire. He was much as Simon had described him, and in that moment I knew that the odd murder of Hugo Carrier was another case that called for Simon's special talents.

"But did you know that Simon Ark was in England?" I asked him.

"No! Where is he?"

"I have no idea, but he left New York over a month ago. If we could find him, I'm sure he could help us on this case."

Inspector Ashly frowned. "He's not a detective, though. And there hardly seem to be any supernatural elements in this case. . . ."

"I wouldn't be too sure," I replied. "You've probably heard that a pentagram was drawn in blood on the floor of the room. Isn't that an old symbol of witchcraft and satanism?"

Ashly struck the table with his fist. "I believe you're right. And if so, we can build up a newspaper story that's sure to attract Simon Ark if he's anywhere around."

After that, we left the buildings of New Scotland Yard, and walked through the chill December air toward Westminster Abbey. Whitehall was buzzing with midday activity, and before we'd gone two blocks there was already a newsboy shouting about the "weird murder in Kensington."

We walked on, aimlessly, until at last Rain asked, "Who is this Simon Ark you both seemed to know, anyway? Is he a detective?"

"No," I replied, searching for the right words to explain the fantastic story. "He's perhaps the wisest man in the world, a man with a past that may date back to the beginning of the Christian era. He's been searching the world for a long time, perhaps for centuries, in hopes of meeting the devil in combat."

"But . . . are you trying to kid me? Is he some sort of crazy man, or what?"

A double-decked bus rumbled by us, and we turned west on Victoria Street. Behind us, Big Ben was just tolling the hour of one o'clock.

"Whatever he is, he's not crazy," I told her. "Actually, the Comte de Saint-Germain claimed to have lived for four thousand years, and it's possible that he did. And the German physician, Paracelsus, is once supposed to have fought bodily with Satan. Certainly Simon Ark's story is no more fantastic than theirs."

"But who is he? Where did he come from?"

"That's something nobody knows. My own guess is that he was once a Coptic priest, back in the early centuries after Christ; but he never says much about it. He told me once, though, that he knew Saint Augustine, personally—which would make him well over 1500 years old."

Rain laughed at that and gripped my arm with hers.

"I was beginning to think you were serious, but you're just having some fun with me."

"Believe me, I *am* serious."

"Well, then you'll have to show me this man and let me judge for myself. I saw many unusual things in India, but never a man who claimed to be over 1500 years old."

A breeze somewhat cooler than the rest hit us then, and she pushed closer to me. "Let's get inside somewhere, out of this confounded cold air."

"What we should be doing is trying to find that book Carrier had for us," I told her. "If the book was the cause of his murder, it must be certainly worth having."

She was excited now, with the hint of intrigue in the air. "You mean that you really think there might be a connection between the book and his murder?"

"It's certainly possible; we should have searched the place for it."

"Oh, the police would have found it if it were there," she replied. "It's a folio, you know. Hardly the thing you hide behind a picture or anything."

"It does seem odd, though, that if all the copies were destroyed three hundred years ago, Carrier should come up with one now. Maybe the whole thing was a swindle of some sort."

"I doubt that," she said. "He seemed only interested in receiving payment for the book."

We'd reached Victoria Station by this time, and we decided to hail a cab for the long trip back to Rain's place, rather than return for the MG. Even the taxi trip across London was slow at this time of day, and it was nearly two when we reached her house.

"Let me bring in the mail," she said. "Not that there's ever. . ." She paused and ripped open an envelope that had been addressed in a quick, almost illegible scrawl.

"Look!" she exclaimed, "It's from Carrier."

"What? Let me see that!" I took it away from her

shaking hands and read: *I may not be alive tomorrow when you come. If they get me first, I will at least have cheated them of their secret. The book you seek is titled 'The Worship Of Satan,' and together with accounts of diverse crimes of the 16th and 17th centuries, it also includes the forbidden rituals of devil worship. The only copy still in existence in London is in an ancient dwelling at 65 Crashaw Place, behind the* Blue Pig Pub. *You will find a room there which was once a priest's hole, during the Elizabethan persecution of the Catholics. The book is in this room, though to insure payment of the agreed sum, I cannot tell you more as to its location. I sincerely hope that my fears will prove groundless. Hugo Carrier.''*

She had been reading it over my shoulder, and she said, ''What's all this about devil worship? What has that got to do with Sir Francis Bryan?''

''I don't know, Rain; I don't know. I just hope that we succeed in contacting Simon Ark.''

''Maybe you were right about this all being some sort of gigantic swindle.''

I frowned and shook my head. ''He sounds like an educated man, which doesn't mean he might not have been planning a swindle—but the fact of his murder seems to bear out his honesty. In fact, he's one of those men I sort of wish I'd met during his life.''

She lit a cigarette and dropped the letter on a table. ''Are you sorta glad you met me?''

I raised my eyebrows to look at her, but she'd already gone into the kitchen in search of drinks for us. I ignored the question and said, ''We should probably go to this place he mentions and look around. We might be able to turn up the book.''

She returned with two tall frosted glasses. ''I'm beginning to think it's not worth all the trouble. After all, we might end up with arrows in us, too.''

''It's certainly a weird business,'' I agreed as I sipped my drink. ''Say, these are pretty good. What's in them?''

"A secret love potion," she murmured with a grin; "let's have a little music."

"I'm a married man, you know," I told her, trying unsuccessfully to keep it sounding light.

She came to me then, with the radio behind her playing something soft by Mantovani, and the clatter of passing traffic drifting in from the street. And it was as I'd feared it would be since I first met her.

I tried to think about Shelly, and our little house in Westchester; but gradually the memories faded from my brain, and I was a man of flesh and desire. . . .

Later, too long later, as night drifted slowly in from the east, we left the house and started out for the address in Crashaw Place. In the night's already deepening shadows, an occasional bird glided down from above, and it might have been a bat or a gull. I only knew it was a moving, living creature up there in the dark, and maybe I wished I was up there too.

"It's not too far," Rain told me, in a voice that made even a casual remark into a hint of intimacy. "We can follow the river all the way."

The Thames was winding on its never-ending journey to the sea, and as we followed along its banks, the whole of London seemed to sleep, even at this early hour. It was as if we were alone in the city, alone without the cluster of crowds and the rumble of civilization.

I paused a moment to light a cigarette, and it was then I saw two men moving in on us. "Rain!" I shouted. "Look out!"

She whirled quickly and a blow from the first man's blackjack caught her on the shoulder. I hurled myself at him, and we went down in a heap. I tried to see where our second attacker was, but the first one was keeping me busy.

Finally I broke free and grabbed up Rain's hand. "Come on," I managed to shout, dragging her with me down a flight of stone steps that led to the water's edge.

I could feel them behind us as we hurtled down the stairs, and at the bottom step I felt strong fingers of steel tear at my throat. I lost my grip on Rain and went tumbling backwards, the hulking attacker on top of me. I struggled to free myself from those murderous fingers, but already I saw one hand leave my throat and come up with a glistening knife.

"Die, damn you," the raspy voice squeaked, and in that instant I thought I had reached the end of everything. But suddenly a roar split the air and his face seemed to fly apart before me. His dying grip relaxed on my neck, and I saw the little smoking Derringer in Rain's steady hand.

"I didn't want to kill him," she sobbed; "but there was no time for a good shot."

"Don't worry. Where's the other one now?"

"Up there!" She pointed to the top of the steps, where the second assassin stood outlined against the dark sky.

"Duck! He's got a gun!" I pulled her down just as the man fired.

"It's a .45," she told me between gasps. "And my gun is empty."

I glanced fearfully at the dim river a few feet away. "Can you swim?"

"A little, but we'd never make it to the water."

"We'll have to try, Come on." He saw us the instant we made our move, and I saw his gun hand move around for a second shot at us.

Then suddenly he seemed to falter, and for the first time I saw the dim figure in the darkness behind him. The .45 slipped from his hand and clattered to the concrete below; then he followed it, diving over in a graceful arc that thudded his body against the very edge of the bank and then hurled it into the black river.

We stood rooted to the spot, looking up at the dim figure who moved down the steps toward us. And then I recognized the tall, heavy-set features of Simon Ark. . . .

3

"Simon! You certainly arrived just in time. How did you ever find us?"

He smiled slightly, as he always did, and replied, "There are ways. I see you already disposed of one of them."

We looked down at the bloody face of the man Rain's bullets had killed. "Luckily for me," I said. "This is Rain Richards, a most unusual girl, and a crack shot with a pistol."

Simon Ark grunted a greeting and bent to examine the body. "Do you think this is connected in any way with the death of Hugo Carrier last night?" he asked us.

"I don't know," I replied, "but Rain received a letter from Carrier this noon. He told us of a pub where something was hidden, and we were on our way there now."

"Hidden," he repeated, suddenly interested. "What is it you seek?"

"A book," I told him. "A book called 'The Worship Of Satan,' written during the 17th century, but banned by the government, which destroyed all copies. The book supposedly gives the solution to the 1548 murder of Sir James Butler and the mysterious death two years later of Sir Francis Bryan."

"Sir Francis Bryan," Simon Ark muttered. "The Vicar of Hell. . . ."

"You've heard of him," Rain said, sounding surprised.

"I've heard of him. . . ."

Simon Ark was the same as when I'd last seen him, back in the States a few months earlier. He still had the mysterious quality about him that sometimes made you wonder at the things he said. In that moment, I felt certain he'd known Francis Bryan personally, somehow in the dark past.

"Your old friend Inspector Ashly is working on the case," I told him.

"I saw his name in the papers; he's a brilliant man. I'll call him now and tell him what happened here. Then we can be on our way to this pub you mentioned."

"You're coming with us?" Rain asked.

"Certainly. 'The Worship Of Satan' is a most unusual book. If there is a copy still remaining, I would like to see it."

We had climbed the steps from the river now, and in the distance I could see a police car, apparently called by some alert neighbor, bearing down upon us.

"Simon, do you really think this devil worship business is tied in with Carrier's murder?"

He gazed out across the river, as if looking at something far away which only he could see, and then he answered. "In the year 1100, King William the Second was slain by an arrow in the New Forest. His death was part of a human sacrifice of a cult of devil worshippers. Today they still worship, and kill, in much the same way."

His words sent a chill through me, and I put my arm around Rain's slim shoulders. Then the police joined us, and Simon spoke quickly to them, in that old manner of his which could somehow convince anyone of anything. He wrote a brief message to Chief Inspector Ashly and then we departed.

"I believe this pub should be our first stop," he said. "Do you know the way?"

Rain nodded and led us down a dark alley, away from the river. "I feel better now with you two strong men to protect me," she said.

"I doubt if they'll bother us further," Simon Ark comforted her. "They must have learned from Hugo Carrier that he'd sent you the letter."

A slight mist was beginning to gather in the streets, and I suspected we were in for more fog. "Doesn't the fog ever lift around here?" I mumbled.

"This is the season for it," Simon Ark said. "London has been foggy in December for as long as I can remember. The Fall is the worst time for it."

* * *

Presently, we reached Crashaw Place and ahead of us we could make out the weather-beaten sign of the *Blue Pig,* "By Appointment To His Majesty King George V." It was a run-down place that might have looked better thirty years earlier, under George's reign. Now it was badly in need of a paint job, and I couldn't help thinking that a bit of good old American neon would have pepped up the swaying sign.

Inside, a few obviously regular customers lined the bar, and turned as we entered, in mild expectation of seeing some of their nightly drinking companions. Rain was the only girl in the place, but none of them seemed to mind. We ordered three beers because that seemed to be the thing everyone was drinking, and carried them to a table.

Presently, when Simon Ark was certain he'd identified a stout, balding gentleman as the owner, he rose and walked over to him. "Pardon me, sir, but I'm a visitor in your country. . . ."

"Oh," the stout man said. "Well, we're always happy to entertain foreigners at the Blue Pig, sir. My name is George Kerrigan. I'm the owner of this here place."

"Very pleased to meet you, Mr. Kerrigan. I'm Simon Ark, and these are my friends. We've been told that the rear of this building dates back to the 17th century, and we're very anxious to examine it further."

"Glad to be of service," Kerrigan smiled at us. "Yes, sir, this here's just about the only old building like it still standing. You know, there was that God-awful fire back in 1666, and it just about burned down the whole damned town." He spoke as if he'd witnessed it personally, with just the right degree of awe.

"We understand," Simon Ark continued, "that you even have a room where Catholic priests hid during the persecutions."

"That we have, sir—or at least them's the stories

what goes with the old place. Come on back this way and I'll show you."

We followed him down a musty corridor which led into the rear of the pub. Here, in a house that was obviously much older than the front, he paused to un-lock a door and throw it open before us. "Haven't been in here myself in a good many months," he told us. "Wait a minute while I get some candles."

"No electricity?" Rain asked, somewhat startled.

"Not in this room, miss; we never use it, so we never bothered to wire it."

He returned in a moment with a multi-branched candlestick held high, and led us into the room. It was no more, really, than an enclosed space some twenty feet square, without windows, and with only the one door through which we'd entered. An ancient, musty smell hung over the place, suggesting that even the air we were now breathing might have been several hun-dred years old. The walls were covered with a fantastic blaze of colored wallpaper, which even now was just beginning to fade. The only bit of furniture in the room was a huge old carved table, some ten feet long, which stood against the opposite wall. Its top had been cov-ered with newspapers, apparently to preserve the fin-ish.

Kerrigan was busy telling us the history of the room, from its priesthole days through the reigns of various kings and queens, but I noticed that Simon Ark was far more concerned with the ancient table. He brushed aside the dusty newspapers, which I noticed were some four weeks old, and smiled slightly when he came upon a shallow drawer in the table's side. But the smile faded when he found the drawer empty.

I, meanwhile, had strolled over to one of the walls and was trying to decipher some patterns from the faded rainbows of color. But the paper seemed to be designed without any purpose, a weird reminder of 17th century England.

Simon Ark was on his knees, examining the bottom

of the long table now; but if Kerrigan thought this odd, he made no comment. He had trapped Rain in a corner and was continuing his brief history of England. "You know, miss, George III himself once visited this very pub, near the end of his reign. Of course there are those who say he was crazy at the time, but he was certainly a friendly one. My great-grandfather used to tell me about those days when I was very small. . . ."

"Pardon me," Simon Ark interrupted, resuming an upright position. "But if this room was once a hiding place for priests, I'm sure it has more than one exit. Suppose you show us the secret way out."

Kerrigan never blinked an eye, but simply led us to one of the room's corners as if he'd intended to show it to us all along. "Here it is," he said, and gave a yank to an almost-invisible metal ring set flush with the floor. A well-oiled trap door rose out of the floor and we peered down into the darkness below.

"It simply leads to the cellar," Kerrigan explained. "I don't even store anything down there any more. Too many rats." He lowered the candles a bit so we could see that the cellar was truly empty.

"Well, thank you very much for the tour," Simon told him. "I think that's about all we wanted to see."

He relocked the room behind us and led the way back to the pub's main room. "Have a beer on me before you go," he told us. "And stop by again some time."

"Thanks," Rain replied. "We will."

Soon afterwards, we departed and headed back through the gathering fog to Rain's house. When we were a safe distance away from the *Blue Pig,* I asked Simon, "What do you think about it? Any idea where the book might be hidden?"

"I have ideas about many things," he told us; "I even have ideas about the odd-looking stains on that tabletop."

"Stains?" I wondered. "I didn't notice any."

Simon Ark grunted. "In any event, we have much more here than simply the mystery of the Vicar of

Hell. Although certainly the death of Carrier suggests that the missing book is involved.''

By the time we reached Rain's place, the fog had closed in completely, and visibility was down to some fifty yards. We followed her in, on her invitation to make some coffee, and settled down around the fireplace.

I tossed a couple of logs on, and before long the room was alive with the glow of leaping flames. Simon Ark settled back in his chair, closed his eyes, and began to talk.

"Although most history books merely imply that the one-eyed Sir Francis Bryan earned the title of 'Vicar of Hell' by deserting his cousin, Anne Boleyn, when she needed him most, it seems probably there were further reasons. And in a period when witch cults and black magic were running wild throughout England, perhaps it is not too fantastic to suspect that Bryan himself was involved in one of these cults. Certainly that, more than anything else, would have earned him the odd title.''

Rain arrived with the steaming coffee and passed it to us. "But what about the murder of James Butler in 1548? And Bryan's own mysterious death two years later?''

"There are two possible solutions which immediately present themselves. Bryan himself could have poisoned James Butler in order to marry his wife, Joan. Then, when Joan discovered this, she herself killed her husband's murderer.''

Rain sipped her coffee and lit a cigarette. "And I suppose you'll say the other possibility is that Joan killed both of her husbands.''

Simon Ark smiled and nodded. "I admit that was my thought.'' And then, half to himself, he added, "I only regret that I never had the honor of meeting the Vicar of Hell. . . .''

Rain shot me a glance at that, but I was used to such remarks from Simon's lips. I ignored it and asked instead, "Do you really think this book, 'The Worship Of Satan,' has something in it about Bryan?"

"Very possible, or else there would have been no reason for the government to ban it at the time; books on devil worship and the like were quite common. From the size of it, I would say it must also have included several large illustrations."

We talked further on the subject, but presently, as midnight drew near, Simon Ark departed, promising to call us in the morning. "It might be a good idea to get some sleep," he cautioned me. "Tomorrow might be a long day."

"Why?"

"Because there will be a full moon tomorrow night," he said, and then he was gone, into the fog."

I came back into Rain's living room, puzzling over these words. I looked at a calendar and saw that there would indeed be a full moon on the following night. "What do you suppose he meant by that?" Rain asked me.

"I don't know. But let's forget about all that for now." I walked over and sat next to her on the couch.

"Should we forget about your wife back in New York, too?"

I didn't answer her.

Instead, my hand went out and found hers, and I drew her close to me in the flickering light from the fireplace. . . .

4

Simon Ark was at my hotel room before noon on the following morning, and I was surprised to see that Inspector Ashly was with him. "Good morning," I greeted them. "What's up?"

"Everything, from what Simon's been telling me," Ashly said. "You fellows must have had a pretty busy night, shooting up would-be killers and such."

"We're lucky we're even alive," I said; "Simon arrived just in time last night."

"He told me. He also had me check on the two dead men, and I find they both frequented the *Blue Pig* pub.''

"That figures," I said, lighting a before-breakfast cigarette. "There's something funny about that place."

Simon Ark chuckled. "The understatement of the year, certainly. If you had been a little more observant, I'm sure you would have come to the same conclusions that I did about the *Blue Pig,* and its mysterious back room."

"And just what are your conclusions?" I asked, aware that he'd already outlined his ideas to Inspector Ashly.

"I'm convinced that a Black Mass, and various other ceremonies of Satanism, are being carried on at the *Blue Pig,* in that very room. And I'm further convinced that there's another meeting of the group being held this evening."

"I'll admit that I suspected something funny, but I think now you're going a little overboard, aren't you, Simon?"

"He's got me convinced," Ashly boomed out in that deep voice which still amazed me. "Wait until you've heard the whole thing."

I settled back and sighed. "OK, Simon. Go ahead and convince me."

"Well," he began, "the arrow murder of Hugo Carrier hinted at some sort of ritual crime; and, as I already told you, this type of slaying has been used before by devil worshippers. The attack on you and Rain proved that Carrier's murder was caused by his knowledge of the book, 'The Worship Of Satan.' The people who killed him did so because they feared he would reveal the location of the book. Therefore the book itself, or its location, or both, are dangerous to them."

"All right so far," I admitted. "But why does that make it the *Blue Pig?*''

"First, the men who attacked you were from the *Blue Pig.* Second, Carrier gave that as the location of the book. Third, George Kerrigan lied to us when we visited him last night.''

"Lied? About what?''

''He said he never stored things in the cellar, yet the secret trap-door was well-oiled. And he said he hadn't been in the room in months, yet the newspapers covering the table were four weeks old.''

''So I'll agree he lied. But why does it have to be devil worship? Maybe he just runs a card game in that room.''

Simon Ark closed his eyes once more. ''Those were bloodstains on the table top,'' he said very quietly. ''It was used as an altar, for animal—or perhaps human—sacrifices. . . .''

The three of us were silent for a moment. It was hard for me to believe that such a thing could happen in twentieth century London. And yet I knew, from past experiences with Simon Ark, that there were things happening every day beyond human knowledge. It was sometimes as if a vast alternate world of evil were operating all the time, giving us an occasional glimpse into its horrible scenes.

''But why?'' I asked. ''Why, of all places, should they choose an ancient pub like the *Blue Pig?*''

''Because it was once a hiding place for priests, a place where actual Mass was celebrated, the next best thing to a church. And because it later became the resting place of the only existing copy of 'The Worship Of Satan.' ''

''Horrible. . . .'' Inspector Ashly muttered. ''Now tell us how you're so certain they'll meet again tonight.''

''Many strange things happen when the moon is full. Cults of devil worshippers do not necessarily, or always, meet at the time of the full moon; but when I noticed that the newspapers covering the table were just four weeks old—dated on the first day of last month's full moon—I guessed this was the time of their previous meeting. Thus, since there is another full moon beginning tonight, I believe we'll find them there again.''

Ashly rose to his feet. "My men will be ready to close in whenever you give the word, Simon. I know from the last time we met that your theories are usually correct.''

I lit another cigarette and began to think about the breakfast I was missing. "Since when is it against the law to carry on religious rites in a private dwelling?'' I asked.

Ashly bristled slightly at my question. "This isn't a religion; and you seem to have forgotten the poor devil they left pinned to the wall with three arrows in him.''

"I guess I did for a moment,'' I admitted, feeling slightly subdued. "So—what's our plan of action?''

"The Inspector and his men will surround the place, early in the evening, and await my signal to move in,'' Simon Ark explained. "I will be in the basement, under that trap door, and you can join me if you wish.''

"I wouldn't miss it,'' I told him. "If you're going to find Satan himself in that room, I want to be along, too.''

Ashly sighed. "I believe you two are crazy to risk discovery like that, but I know better than to try arguing with Simon here.''

"It might be best,'' Simon said, "if you could get a gun from somewhere, though. Could you borrow one from Rain?''

"Sure could.''

"Don't let me hear anything about this,'' Ashly muttered. "In London, even the police have a difficult time getting permission to carry guns.''

"Well, you'd better have them tonight,'' Simon Ark told him. "These people are very close to insanity, all of them; when cornered, they might do anything.''

After that, they left me; and then I was alone with my thoughts of the night to come. And my thoughts of Rain and of my own house in Westchester, and of Shelly who waited there for me. For the first time I wondered if I would ever go back to her. . . .

* * *

The cab carried me through Picadilly Circus, past the neon signs now darkened in the light of day where Gordon's Gin and Wrigley's Gum fought each other for the customer's attention. And presently I was back at Rain's place in the suburbs. "Hello, again," she greeted me at the door. "Have a good night's sleep?"

"Fine." I quickly outlined the details of Simon Ark's revelations. "How's chances of borrowing a gun till tomorrow?"

"Sure," she said, leading me to a cabinet. "Which one do you want?"

"I used a .45 in the Military Police. That's the only one I'm sure of, so I'd better take one of those."

She handed me the heavy automatic, together with an empty clip and a box of bullets. I shoved seven of them into the clip and then rammed it into the butt. "Thanks a lot, Rain. I'll have it back in the morning."

"Let me come with you," she said then. "I'll go crazy sitting home here, thinking about it."

"Sorry; that's out of the question. Ashly's even worried with Simon and I on the scene. But I'll call you as soon as it's over."

"Is that a promise?"

"That's a promise." I kissed her lightly on the lips and then went out into the street, the automatic hanging heavy in my topcoat pocket.

I took time out to cable the New York office that I expected to obtain the missing book that evening, and close the deal. Then I went to a middle-class bar in downtown London and spent the rest of the afternoon trying to think about nothing at all.

When I got back to the hotel I found an air mail letter from Shelly awaiting me. I tossed it on the bed without opening it.

I wondered, for just a second, if possibly I was going to the *Blue Pig* that night in some subconscious hope that death would solve my problem for me.

Because now I was convinced that I loved Rain Richards. . . .

The basement of the *Blue Pig Pub* was a surprisingly easy place to enter, and it took Simon and me only a few moments to locate the door to the old cellar and place ourselves beneath the trap door.

I took the .45 from my pocket, and jacked a bullet into the chamber; after that we waited.

And waited. . . .

Presently, when my wrist watch glowed 11:30, and I had just about given up hope, we heard some movement in the room above. At almost the same instant we caught the sound of people entering through the basement, as we had come.

We took shelter behind some musty packing cases, and watched several men and a few women entering the room through the trap door. Finally, when the sounds from above told us the ceremony had begun, we resumed our post beneath the door.

Simon Ark edged it up a fraction of an inch, and through the opening I saw a scene I'll never forget. There, behind the long table, stood the white-robed figure of George Kerrigan, his arms outstretched toward the ceiling. On either end of the table burned dozens of long black candles, sending their dancing flames over the kneeling figures of some twenty men and women who nearly filled the small room.

The brightly colored wallpaper had been covered in spots by hanging pictures of basilisks and other mythical monsters, and behind Kerrigan I saw a statue of Jupiter, the ancient god. "Like the one the pagans erected on Calvary, after Christ's death," Simon Ark whispered. "We are in the midst of evil here."

"What are we waiting for, then?" I asked; "let's go!"

"Be patient. There is still more to be seen."

The kneeling figures above were swaying back and forth now, as if under the influence of some narcotic. And a low murmuring chant was slowly building up among them.

"It's horrible," I said, half to myself.

Simon Ark let the trap door fall into place and he said, very quietly, "Perhaps, though, the evil up there is no greater than the evil in your own heart."

"What?" I muttered. "What do you mean?"

"Who is to say that the sin of adultery is any less serious than the sin of devil worship?" he asked, quietly. "Certainly they are both works of Satan."

"Are you crazy, Simon? Why pick a time like this to give me a lecture on morality?"

"It is as good a time as any, my old friend. I came here searching for the devil, and perhaps I have found him in the least likely of all places—inside of you!"

The chanting from above had grown louder, and it pounded at my eardrums as I listened to Simon's words. "No. . . ." I mumbled. "No. . . ."

"Leave this woman, and go home to Shelly, before it is too late."

"I. . . ."

Suddenly, the chanting above turned to shouting, and there was a rush of movement. I lifted the trap door again and saw a startling sight. "It's Rain! They've got Rain!"

Simon Ark was at my side; and he, too, saw the struggling girl in the grip of two strong men. "She must have sneaked in, and Kerrigan recognized her. The little fool!"

And I saw that the white-robed Kerrigan had already produced his deadly bow and arrows. His right hand was drawing back on the bow string and the trembling arrow was pointing through the flickering stillness at Rain's struggling body.

I waited no longer. While my left hand slammed up on the trap door, my right was already bringing the heavy .45 into firing position.

George Kerrigan half-turned toward me, and the look of utter surprise was spreading over his face when my bullet tore into his shoulder.

After that, it was chaos. . . .

* * *

I came out of it with a bloody nose and a torn sleeve, thanks mostly to the prompt arrival of Inspector Ashly and his men. My bullet had completely shattered Kerrigan's shoulder, and he was unconscious by the time the ambulance arrived. His followers were quickly rounded up and led away, and soon only Simon and Ashly and Rain and I remained in the room.

"That bow and arrow should be enough to convict them of Carrier's murder," Ashly said. "I only hope the newspapers don't get ahold of this devil worship angle, or I fear they'll have you stripped nude and about to be sacrificed on the altar, Miss Richards. These reporters are great at building up a sensational story."

"I'm just happy to be alive," Rain answered. "Right now I don't care what they say about me. When I saw that arrow pointing at my chest, all I could remember was poor Carrier pinned to the wall."

"You owe your life to your friends here," Ashly told her.

"I know. Now I just wish Simon would tell us where the book is hidden so we could all go home."

"That's right, Simon," I agreed. "Where is this elusive copy of 'The Worship Of Satan'?"

He sighed, and motioned around the room, now brightly lit by several portable police spotlights. "Right where it's always been, my friends; it should have been obvious to you from the beginning. After all, why was it necessary to kill Carrier to keep him from telling its location? Why didn't they simply move it to a new hiding place?"

"That's right," I agreed. "Why didn't they move it?"

"Because they couldn't; because it was the one part of this room that could not easily be disposed of or transported to another place."

We looked around at the long table, and at the pictures, and at the statue, but we saw nothing.

"Where?" Rain asked simply.

Simon Ark closed his eyes. "During the 17th Century, when a book was banned by a government censor, it was not always burned. If the book was a large one, like a folio, the pages were damasked into wallpaper. . . ."

"Wallpaper!"

"Certainly. The text was blotted out by overprinting with a heavy design in bright colors, and it was used for wallpaper. Here," he motioned around the room at the multi-colored walls, "here is the last remaining copy of 'The Worship Of Satan,' and with it is the final secret of the Vicar of Hell. . . ."

After that, much later, I walked with Rain Richards through the mist of a cold London morning. . . .

"I'll get the University Laboratory to work on that wallpaper right away," she said, "but it'll still be months before the original printing is readable."

"I know," I said, "but somehow it isn't as important as it was a few days ago. Whether Bryan was a murderer himself, or whether he was merely the second victim of his murderous wife, is something that need not concern us, really. The punishment for the crimes has been meted out long ago by a much higher court than ours."

"I suppose so," she agreed reluctantly. "It's only too bad that it had to cause so much trouble and death."

We walked further in silence, and then I said, "You know, it's all over between us. . . ."

"Yes, I know. . . ."

"Simon Ark talked to me tonight, while we waited in the basement."

"He's quite a man, isn't he?"

"Yes, I suppose he is."

"Remember me to your wife."

"Yes," I said, but we both knew that I never would. "Goodbye. . . ."

"Goodbye, Rain. . . ."

I watched her as she walked away into the morning mist. I watched her until she was out of sight and then I went back to my hotel room.

The air mail letter from Shelly was still on the bed; I tore it open, and settled down in a chair to read it . . .

THE WORDS OF GURU
by C. M. Kornbluth

Yesterday, when I was going to meet Guru in the woods a man stopped me and said: "Child, what are you doing out at one in the morning? Does your mother know where you are? How old are you, walking around this late?"

I looked at him, and saw that he was white-haired, so I laughed. Old men never see; in fact men hardly see at all. Sometimes young women see part, but men rarely ever see at all. "I'm twelve on my next birthday," I said. And then, because I would not let him live to tell people, I said, "and I'm out this late to see Guru."

"Guru?" he asked. "Who is Guru? Some foreigner, I suppose? Bad business mixing with foreigners, young fellow. Who is Guru?"

So I told him who Guru was, and just as he began talking about cheap magazines and fairy tales I said one of the words that Guru taught me and he stopped talking. Because he was an old and his joints were stiff he didn't crumple up but fell in one piece, hitting his head on the stone. Then I went on.

Even though I'm going to be only twelve on my next birthday I know many things that old people don't. And I remember things that other boys can't. I remember being born out of darkness, and I remember the noises that people made about me. Then when I was two months old I began to understand that the noises meant things like the things that were going on inside my head. I found out that I could make the noises too, and everybody was very much surprised. "Talking!"

they said, again and again. "And so very young!
Clara, what do you make of it?" Clara was my mother.

And Clara would say: "I'm sure I don't know. There
never was any genius in my family, and I'm sure there
was none in Joe's." Joe was my father.

Once Clara showed me a man I had never seen before, and told me that he was a reporter—that he wrote
things in newspapers. The reporter tried to talk to me
as if I were an ordinary baby; I didn't even answer
him, but just kept looking at him until his eyes fell and
he went away. Later Clara scolded me and read me a
little piece in the reporter's newspaper that was supposed to be funny—about the reporter asking me very
complicated questions and me answering with baby
noises. It was not true, of course. I didn't say a word
to the reporter, and he didn't ask me even one of the
questions.

I heard her read the little piece, but while I listened
I was watching the slug crawling on the wall. When
Clara was finished I asked her: "What is that gray
thing?"

She looked where I pointed, but couldn't see it.
"What grey thing, Peter?" she asked. I had her call
me by my whole name, Peter, instead of anything silly
like Petey. "What gray thing?"

"It's as big as your hand, Clara, but soft. I don't
think it has any bones at all. It's crawling up, but I
don't see any face on the topwards side. And there
aren't any legs."

I think she was worried, but she tried to baby me
by putting her hand on the wall and trying to find out
where it was. I called out whether she was right or left
of the thing. Finally she put her hand right through the
slug. And then I realized that she really couldn't see
it, and didn't believe it was there. I stopped talking
about it then and only asked her a few days later:
"Clara, what do you call a thing which one person
can see and another person can't?"

"An illusion, Peter," she said. "If that's what you
mean." I said nothing, but let her put me to bed as

usual, but when she turned out the light and went away I waited a little while and then called out softly. "Illusion! Illusion!"

At once Guru came for the first time. He bowed, the way he always has since, and said: "I have been waiting."

"I didn't know that was the way to call you," I said.

"Whenever you want me I will be ready. I will teach you, Peter—if you want to learn. Do you know what I will teach you?"

"If you will teach me about the gray thing on the wall," I said, "I will listen. And if you will teach me about real things and unreal things I will listen."

"These things," he said thoughtfully, "very few wish to learn. And there are some things that nobody ever wished to learn. And there are some things that I will not teach."

Then I said: "The things nobody has ever wished to learn I will learn. And I will even learn the things you do not wish to teach."

He smiled mockingly. "A master has come," he said, half-laughing. "A master of Guru."

That was how I learned his name. And that night he taught me a word which would do little things, like spoiling food.

From that day to the time I saw him last night he has not changed at all, though now I am as tall as he is. His skin is still as dry and shiny as ever it was, and his face is still bony, crowned by a head of very coarse, black hair.

When I was ten years old I went to bed one night only long enough to make Joe and Clara suppose I was fast asleep. I left in my place something which appears when you say one of the words of Guru and went down the drainpipe outside my window. It always was easy to climb down and up, ever since I was eight years old.

I met Guru in Inwood Hill Park. "You're late," he said.

"Not too late," I answered. "I know it's never too late for one of these things."

"How do you know?" he asked sharply. "This is your first."

"And maybe my last," I replied. "I don't like the idea of it. If I have nothing more to learn from my second than my first I shan't go to another."

"You don't know," he said. "You don't know what it's like—the voices, and the bodies slick with unguent, leaping flames; mind-filling ritual! You can have no idea at all until you've taken part."

"We'll see," I said. "Can we leave from here?"

"Yes," he said. Then he taught me the word I would need to know, and we both said it together.

The place we were in next was lit with red lights, and I think that the walls were of rock. Though of course there was no real seeing there, and so the lights only seemed to be red, and it was not real rock.

As we were going to the fire one of them stopped us. "Who's with you?" she asked, calling Guru by another name. I did not know that he was also the person bearing that name, for it was a very powerful one.

He cast a hasty, sidewise glance at me and then said: "This is Peter of whom I have often told you."

She looked at me then and smiled, stretching out her oily arms. "Ah," she said, softly, like the cats when they talk at night to me. "Ah, this is Peter. Will you come to me when I call you, Peter? And sometimes call for me—in the dark—when you are alone?"

"Don't do that!" said Guru, angrily pushing past her. "He's very young—you might spoil him for his work."

She screeched at our backs: "Guru and his pupil— fine pair! Boy, he's no more real than I am—you're the only real thing here!"

"Don't listen to her," said Guru. "She's wild and raving. They're always tight-strung when this time comes around."

We came near the fires then, and sat down on rocks.

They were killing animals and birds and doing things with their bodies. The blood was being collected in a basin of stone, which passed through the crowd. The one to my left handed it to me. "Drink," she said, grinning to show me her fine, white teeth. I swallowed twice from it and passed it to Guru.

When the bowl had passed all around we took off our clothes. Some, like Guru, did not wear them, but many did. The one to my left sat closer to me, breathing heavily at my face. I moved away. "Tell her to stop, Guru," I said. "This isn't part of it, I know."

Guru spoke to her sharply in their own language, and she changed her seat, snarling.

Then we all began to chant, clapping our hands and beating our thighs. One of them rose slowly and circled about the fires in a slow pace, her eyes rolling wildly. She worked her jaws and flung her arms about so sharply that I could hear the elbows crack. Still shuffling her feet against the rock floor she bent her body backwards down to her feet. Her belly muscles were bands nearly standing out from her skin, and the oil rolled down her body and legs. As the palms of her hands touched the ground, she collapsed in a twitching heap and began to set up a thin wailing noise against the steady chant and hand beat that the rest of us were keeping up. Another of them did the same as the first, and we chanted louder for her and still louder for the third. Then, while we still beat our hands and thighs, one of them took up the third, laid her across the altar, and made her ready with a stone knife. The fire's light gleamed off the chipped edge of obsidian. As her blood drained down the groove, cut as a gutter into the rock of the altar, we stopped our chant and the fires were snuffed out.

But still we could see what was going on, for these things were, of course, not happening at all—only seeming to happen, really, just as all the people and things there only seemed to be what they were. Only I was real. That must be why they desired me so.

As the last of the fires died Guru excitedly whispered: "The Presence!" He was deeply moved.

From the pool of blood from the third dancer's body there issued the Presence. It was the tallest one there, and when it spoke its voice was deeper, and when it commanded its commands were obeyed.

"Let blood!" it commanded, and we gashed ourselves with flints. It smiled and showed teeth bigger and sharper and whiter than any of the others.

"Make water!" it commanded, and we all spat on each other. It flapped its wings and rolled its eyes, which were bigger and redder than any of the others.

"Pass flame!" it commanded, and we breathed smoke and fire on our limbs. It stamped its feet, let blue flames roar from its mouth, and they were bigger and wilder than any of the others.

Then it returned to the pool of blood and we lit the fires again. Guru was staring straight before him; I tugged his arm. He bowed as though we were meeting for the first time that night.

"What are you thinking of?" I asked. "We shall go now."

"Yes," he said heavily. "Now we shall go." Then we said the word that had brought us there.

The first man I killed was Brother Paul, at the school where I went to learn the things that Guru did not teach me.

It was less than a year ago, but it seems like a very long time. I have killed so many times since then.

"You're a very bright boy, Peter," said the brother.

"Thank you, brother."

"But there are things about you that I don't understand. Normally I'd ask your parents but—I feel that they don't understand either. You were an infant prodigy, weren't you?"

"Yes, brother."

"There's nothing very unusual about that—glands, I'm told. You know what glands are?"

Then I was alarmed. I had heard of them, but I was not certain whether they were the short, thick green men who wear only metal or the things with many legs with whom I talked in the woods.

"How did you find out?" I asked him.

"But Peter! You look positively frightened, lad! I don't know a thing about them myself, but Father Frederick does. He has whole books about them, though I sometimes doubt whether he believes them himself."

"They aren't good books, brother," I said. "They ought to be burned."

"That's a savage thought, my son. But to return to your own problem—"

I could not let him go any further knowing what he did about me. I said one of the words Guru taught me and he looked at first very surprised and then seemed to be in great pain. He dropped across his desk and I felt his wrist to make sure, for I had not used that word before. But he was dead.

There was a heavy step outside and I made myself invisible. Stout Father Frederick entered, and I nearly killed him too with the word, but I knew that would be very curious. I decided to wait, and went through the door as Father Frederick bent over the dead monk. He thought he was asleep.

I went down the corridor to the book-lined office of the stout priest and, working quickly, piled all his books in the center of the room and lit them with my breath. Then I went down to the schoolyard and made myself visible again when there was nobody looking. It was very easy. I killed a man I passed on the street the next day.

There was a girl named Mary who lived near us. She was fourteen then, and I desired her as those in the Cavern out of Time and Space had desired me.

So when I saw Guru and he had bowed, I told him of it, and he looked at me in great surprise. "You are growing older, Peter," he said.

"I am, Guru. And there will come a time when your words will not be strong enough for me."

He laughed. "Come, Peter," he said. "Follow me

if you wish. There is something that is going to be done—'' He licked his thin, purple lips and said: ''I have told you what it will be like.''

''I shall come,'' I said. ''Teach me the word.'' So he taught me the word and we said it together.

The place we were in next was not like any of the other places I had been to before with Guru. It was No-place. Always before there had been the seeming passage of time and matter, but here there was not even that. Here Guru and the others cast off their forms and were what they were, and No-place was the only place where they could do this.

It was not like the Cavern, for the Cavern had been out of Time and Space, and this place was not enough of a place even for that. It was No-place.

What happened there does not bear telling, but I was made known to certain ones who never departed from there. All came to them as they existed. They had not color or the seeming of color, or any seeming of shape.

There I learned that eventually I would join with them; that I had been selected as the one of my planet who was to dwell without being forever in that No-place.

Guru and I left, having said the word.

''Well?'' demanded Guru, staring me in the eye.

''I am willing,'' I said. ''But teach me one word now—''

''Ah,'' he said grinning. ''The girl?''

''Yes,'' I said. ''The word that will mean much to her.''

Still grinning, he taught me the word.

Mary, who had been fourteen is now fifteen and what they call incurably mad.

Last night I saw Guru again and for the last time. He bowed as I approached him. ''Peter,'' he said warmly.

''Teach me the word,'' said I.

''It is not too late.''

''Teach me the word.''

"You can withdraw—with what you master you can master also this world. Gold without reckoning, sardonyx and gems, Peter! Rich crushed velvet—stiff, scraping, embroidered tapestries!"

"Teach me the word."

"Think, Peter, of the house you could build. It could be of white marble, and every slab centered by a winking ruby. Its gate could be of beaten gold within and without and it could be built about one slender tower of carven ivory, rising mile after mile into the turquoise sky. You could see the clouds float underneath your eyes."

"Teach me the word."

"Your tongue could crush the grapes that taste like melted silver. You could hear always the song of the bulbul and the lark that sounds like the dawn star made musical. Spikenard that will bloom a thousand thousand years could be ever in your nostrils. Your hands could feel the down of purple Himalayan swans that is softer than a sunset cloud."

"Teach me the word."

"You could have women whose skin would be from the black of ebony to the white of snow. You could have women who would be as hard as flints or as soft as a sunset cloud."

"Teach me the word."

Guru grinned and said the word.

Now, I do not know whether I will say that word, which was the last Guru taught me, today or tomorrow or until a year has passed.

It is a word that will explode this planet like a stick of dynamite in a rotten apple.

THE POWER

by Murray Leinster

Memorandum from Professor Charles, Latin Department, Haverford University, to Professor McFarland, the same faculty:

Dear Professor McFarland:
In a recent batch of fifteenth-century Latin documents from abroad, we found three which seem to fit together. Our interest is in the Latin of the period, but their contents seem to bear upon your line. I send them to you with a free translation. Would you let me know your reaction?

Charles.

To Johannus Hartmannus, Licentiate in Philosophy,
Living at the house of the goldsmith Grote,
Lane of the Dyed Flee,
Leyden, the Low Countries:

Friend Johannus:
I write this from the Goth's Head Inn, in Padua, the second day after Michaelmas, Anno Domini 1482. I write in haste because a worthy Hollander here journeys homeward and has promised to carry mails for me. He is an amiable lout, but ignorant. Do not speak to him of mysteries. He knows nothing. Less than nothing. Thank him, give him to drink, and speak of me as a pious and worthy student. Then forget him.

I leave Padua tomorrow for the realization of all my hopes and yours. This time I am sure. I came here to purchase perfumes and mandragora and the other necessities for an Operation of the utmost imaginable importance, which I will conduct five nights hence upon a certain hilltop near the village of Montevecchio. I have found a Word and a Name of incalculable power, which in the place that I know of must open to me knowledge of all mysteries. When you read this, I shall possess powers at which Hermes Trismegistos only guessed, and which Albertus Magnus could speak of only by hearsay. I have been deceived before, but this time I am sure. I have seen proofs!

I tremble with agitation as I write to you. I will be brief. I came upon these proofs and the Word and the Name in the village of Montevecchio. I rode into the village at nightfall, disconsolate because I had wasted a month searching for a learned man of whom I had heard great things. Then I found him—and he was but a silly antiquary with no knowledge of mysteries! So riding upon my way I came to Montevecchio, and there they told me of a man dying even then because he had worked wonders. He had entered the village on foot only the day before. He was clad in rich garments, yet he spoke like a peasant. At first he was mild and humble, but he paid for food and wine with a gold piece, and villagers fawned upon him and asked for alms. He flung them a handful of gold pieces and when the news spread the whole village went mad with greed. They clustered about him, shrieking pleas, and thronging ever the more urgently as he strove to satisfy them. It is said that he grew frightened and would have fled because of their thrusting against him. But they plucked at his garments, screaming of their poverty, until suddenly his rich clothing vanished in the twinkling of an eye and he was but another ragged peasant like themselves and the purse from which he had scattered gold became a mere coarse bag filled with ashes.

This had happened but the day before my arrival, and the man was yet alive, though barely so because the villagers had cried witchcraft and beset him with flails and stones and then dragged him to the village priest to be exorcised.

I saw the man and spoke to him, Johannus, by representing myself to the priest as a pious student of the snares Satan has set in the form of witchcraft. He barely breathed, what with broken bones and pitchfork wounds. He was a native of the district, who until now had seemed a simple ordinary soul. To secure my intercession with the priest to shrive him ere he died, the man told me all. And it was much!

Upon this certain hillside where I shall perform the Operation five nights hence, he had dozed at midday. Then a Power appeared to him and offered to instruct him in mysteries. The peasant was stupid. He asked for riches instead. So the Power gave him rich garments and a purse which would never empty so long— said the Power—as it came not near a certain metal which destroys all things of mystery. And the Power warned that this was payment that he might send a learned man to learn what he had offered the peasant, because he saw that peasants had no understanding. Thereupon I told the peasant that I would go and greet this Power and fulfill his desires, and he told me the Name and the Word which would call him, and also the Place, begging me to intercede for him with the priest.

The priest showed me a single gold piece which remained of that which the peasant had distributed. It was of the age of Antonius Pius, yet bright and new as if fresh minted. It had the weight and feel of true gold. But the priest, wryly, laid upon it the crucifix he wears upon a small iron chain about his waist. Instantly it vanished, leaving behind a speck of glowing coal which cooled and was a morsel of ash.

This I saw, Johannus! So I came speedily here to Padua, to purchase perfumes and mandragora and the other necessities for an Operation to pay great honor to this Power whom I shall call up five nights hence. He offered wisdom to the peasant, who desired only gold. But I desire wisdom more than gold, and surely I am learned concerning mysteries and Powers! I do not know any but yourself who surpasses me in true knowledge of secret things. And when you read this, Johannus, I shall surpass even you! But it may be that I will gain knowledge so that I can transport myself by a mystery to your attic, and there inform you myself, in advance of this letter, of the results of this surpassing good fortune which causes me to shake with agitation whenever I think of it.

> Your friend Carolus,
> at the Goth's Head Inn in Padua.

. . . fortunate, perhaps, that an opportunity has come to send a second missive to you, through a crippled man-at-arms who has been discharged from a mercenary band and travels homeward to sit in the sun henceforth. I have given him one gold piece and promised that you would give him another on receipt of this message. You will keep that promise or not, as pleases you, but there is at least the value of a gold piece in a bit of parchment with strange symbols upon it which I enclose for you.

Item: I am in daily communication with the Power of which I wrote you, and daily learn great mysteries.

Item: Already I perform marvels such as men have never before accomplished by means of certain sigils or talismans the Power has prepared for me.

Item: Resolutely the Power refuses to yield to me the Names or the incantations by which these things are done so that I can prepare such sigils for myself. Instead, he instructs me in divers subjects which have no bearing on the accomplishment of wonders, to my bitter impatience which I yet dissemble.

Item: Within this packet there is a bit of parchment. Go to a remote place and there tear it and throw it upon the ground. Instantly, all about you, there will appear a fair garden with marvelous fruits, statuary, and pavilion. You may use this garden as you will, save that if any person enter it, or you yourself, carrying a sword or dagger or any object however small made of iron, the said garden will disappear immediately and nevermore return.

This you may verify when you please. For the rest, I am like a prisoner trembling at the very door of Paradise, barred from entering beyond the antechamber by the fact of the Power withholding from me the true essentials of mystery, and granting me only crumbs—which, however, are greater marvels than any known certainly to have been practiced before. For example, the parchment I send you. This art I have proven many times. I have in my script many such sigils, made for me by the power at my entreaty. But when I have secretly taken other parchments and copied upon them the very symbols to the utmost exactitude, they are valueless. There are words or formulas to be spoken over them or—I think more likely—a greater sigil which gives the parchments their magic property. I begin to make a plan—a very daring plan—to acquire even this sigil.

But you will wish to know of the Operation and its results. I returned to Montevecchio from Padua, reaching it in three days. The peasant who had worked wonders was dead, the villagers having grown more fearful and beat out his brains with hammers. This pleased me, because I had feared he would tell another the Word and Name he had told me. I spoke to the priest and told him that I had been to Padua and secured advice from high dignitaries concerning the wonder-working, and had been sent back with special commands to seek out and exorcise the foul fiend who had taught the peasant such marvels.

The next day—the priest himself aiding me!—I took up to the hilltop the perfumes and wax tapers and other things needed for the Operation. The priest trembled, but he would have remained had I not sent him away. And night fell, and I drew the magic circle and the pentacle, with the Signs in their proper places. And when the new moon rose, I lighted the perfumes and the fine candles and began the Operation. I have had many failures, as you know, but this time I knew confidence and perfect certainty. When it came time to use the Name and the Word I called them both loudly, thrice, and waited.

Upon this hilltop there are many greyish stones. At the third calling of the Name, one of the stones shivered and was not. Then a voice said dryly:

"Ah! So that is the reason for this stinking stuff! My messenger sent you here?"

There was a shadow where the stone had been and I could not see clearly. But I bowed low in that direction:

"Most Potent Power," I said, my voice trembling because the Operation was a success, "a peasant working wonders told me that you desired speech with a learned man. Beside your Potency I am ignorant indeed, but I have given my whole life to the study of mysteries. Therefore I have come to offer worship or such other compact as you may desire in exchange for wisdom."

There was a stirring in the shadow, and the Power came forth. His appearance was that of a creature not more than an ell and a half in height, and his expression in the moonlight was that of sardonic impatience. The fragrant smoke seemed to cling about him, to make a cloudiness close about his form.

"I think" said the dry voice, "that you are as great a fool as the peasant I spoke to. What do you think I am?"

"A Prince of Celestial race, your Potency," I said, my voice shaking.

There was a pause. The Power said as if wearily:

"Men! Fools forever! Oh, man, I am simply the last of a number of my kind who traveled in a fleet from another star. This small planet of yours has a core of the accursed metal, which is fatal to the devices of my race. A few of our ships came too close. Others strove to aid them, and shared their fate. Many, many years since, we descended from the skies and could never rise again. Now I alone am left."

Speaking of the world as a planet was an absurdity, of course. The planets are wanderers among the stars,

traveling in their cycles and epicycles as explained by
Ptolemy a thousand years since. But I saw at once that
he would test me. So I grew bold and said:

"Lord, I am not fearful. It is not needful to cozen
me. Do I not know of those who were cast out of
Heaven for rebellion? Shall I write the name of your
leader?"

He said "Eh?" for all the world like an elderly man.
So, smiling, I wrote on the earth the true name of Him
whom the vulgar call Lucifer. He regarded the mark-
ings on the earth and said:

"Bah! It is meaningless. More of your legendary!
Look you, man, soon I shall die. For more years than
you are like to believe I have hid from your race and
its accursed metal. I have watched men, and despised
them. But—I die. And it is not good that knowledge
should perish. It is my desire to impart to men the
knowledge which else would die with me. It can do
no harm to my own kind, and may bring the race of
men to some degree of civilization in the course of
ages."

I bowed to the earth before him. I was aflame with
eagerness.

"Most Potent One," I said joyfully. "I am to be
trusted. I will guard your secrets fully. Not one jot nor
tittle shall ever be divulged!"

Again his voice was annoyed and dry.

"I desire that this knowledge be spread so that all
may learn. But—" Then he made a sound which I do
not understand, save that it seemed to be derisive—
"What I have to say may serve, even garbled and
twisted. And I do not think you will keep secrets in-
violate. Have your pen and parchment?"

"Nay, Lord!"

"You will come again, then, prepared to write what
I shall tell you."

But he remained, regarding me. He asked me questions, and I answered eagerly. Presently he spoke in a
meditative voice, and I listened eagerly. His speech
bore an odd similarity to that of a lonely man who

dwelt much on the past but soon I realized that he
spoke in ciphers, in allegory, from which now and
again the truth peered out. As one who speaks for the
sake of remembering, he spoke of the home of his race
upon what he said was a fair planet so far distant that
to speak of leagues and even the span of continents
would be useless to convey the distance. He told of
cities in which his fellows dwelt—here, of course, I
understood his meaning perfectly—and told of great
fleets of flying things rising from those cities to go to
other fair cities, and of music which was in the very
air so that any person, anywhere upon the planet, could
hear sweet sounds or wise discourse at will. In this
matter there was no metaphor, because the perpetual
sweet sounds in Heaven are matters of common
knowledge. But he added a metaphor immediately after, because he smiled at me and observed that the
music was not created by a mystery, but by waves like
those of light, only longer. And this was plainly a cipher, because light is an impalpable fluid without
length and surely without waves!

Then he spoke of flying through the emptiness of
the empyrean, which again is not clear, because all
can see that the heavens are fairly crowded with stars,
and he spoke of many suns and other worlds, some
frozen and some merely barren rock. The obscurity of
such things is patent. And he spoke of drawing near
to this world which is ours, and of an error made as if
it were in mathematics—instead of in rebellion—so that
they drew close to Earth as Icarus to the sun. Then
again he spoke in metaphors, because he referred to
engines, which are things to cast stones against walls,
and in a larger sense for grinding corn and pumping
water. But he spoke of engines growing hot because
of the accursed metal in the core of Earth, and of the
inability of his kind to resist Earth's pull—more metaphor—and then he spoke of a screaming descent from
the skies. And all of this, plainly, is a metaphorical
account of the casting of the Rebels out of Heaven,

and an acknowledgment that he is one of the said Rebels.

When he paused, I begged humbly that he would show me a mystery and of his grace give me protection in case my converse with him became known.

"What happened to my messenger?" asked the Power.

I told him, and he listened without stirring. I was careful to tell him exactly, because of course he would know that—as all else—by his powers of mystery, and the question was but another test. Indeed, I felt sure that the messenger and all that had taken place had been contrived by him to bring me, a learned student of mysteries, to converse with him in this place.

"Men!" he said bitterly at last. Then he added coldly. "Nay! I can give you no protection. My kind is without protection upon this earth. If you would learn what I can teach you, you must risk the fury of your fellow countrymen."

But then, abruptly, he wrote upon parchment and pressed the parchment to some object at his side. He threw it upon the ground.

"If men beset you," he said scornfully, "tear this parchment and cast it from you. If you have none of the accursed metal about you, it may distract them while you flee. But a dagger will cause it all to come to naught!"

Then he walked away. He vanished. And I stood shivering for a very long time before I remembered me of the formula given by Apollonius of Tyana for the dismissal of evil spirits. I ventured from the magic circle. No evil befell me. I picked up the parchment and examined it in the moonlight. The symbols upon it were meaningless, even to one like myself who has studied all that is known of mysteries. I returned to the village, pondering.

I have told you so much at length, because you will observe that this Power did not speak with the pride or the menace of which most authors on mysteries and

Operations speak. It is often said that an adept must conduct himself with great firmness during an Operation, lest the Powers he has called up overawe him. Yet this Power spoke wearily, with irony, like one approaching death. And he had spoken of death, also. Which was of course a test and a deception, because are not the Principalities and Powers of Darkness immortal? He had some design it was not his will that I should know. So I saw that I must walk warily in this priceless opportunity.

In the village I told the priest that I had had encounter with a foul fiend, who begged that I not exorcise him, promising to reveal certain hidden treasures once belonging to the Church, which he could not touch or reveal to evil men because they were holy, but could describe the location of to me. And I procured parchment, and pens, and ink, and the next day I went alone to the hilltop. It was empty, and I made sure I was unwatched and—leaving my dagger behind me—I tore the parchment and flung it to the ground.

As it touched, there appeared such a treasure of gold and jewels as truly would have driven any man mad with greed. There were bags and chests and boxes filled with gold and precious stones, which had burst with the weight and spilled out upon the ground. There were gems glittering in the late sunlight, and rings and necklaces set with brilliants, and such monstrous hoards of golden coins of every antique pattern . . .

Johannus, even I went almost mad! I leaped forward like one dreaming to plunge my hands into the gold. Slavering, I filled my garments with rubies and ropes of pearls, and stuffed my scrip with gold pieces, laughing crazily to myself. I rolled in the riches. I wallowed in them, flinging the golden coins into the air and letting them fall upon me. I laughed and sang to myself.

Then I heard a sound. On the instant I was filled with terror for the treasure. I leaped to my dagger and snarled, ready to defend my riches to the death.

Then a dry voice said: "Truly you care naught for riches!"

It was savage mockery. The Power stood regarding me. I saw him clearly now, yet not clearly because there was a cloudiness which clung closely to his body. He was, as I said, an ell and a half in height, and from his forehead there protruded knobby feelers which were not horns but had somewhat the look save for bulbs upon their ends. His head was large and—But I will not attempt to describe him, because he could assume any of a thousand forms, no doubt, so what does it matter?

Then I grew terrified because I had no Circle or Pentacle to protect me. But the Power made no menacing move.

"It is real, that riches," he said dryly. "It has color and weight and the feel of substance. But your dagger will destroy it all."

Didyas of Corinth has said that treasure of mystery must be fixed by a special Operation before it becomes permanent and free of the power of Those who brought it. They can transmute it back to leaves or other rubbish, if it be not fixed.

"Touch it with your dagger," said the Power.

I obeyed, sweating in fear. And as the metal iron touched a great piled heap of gold, there was a sudden shifting and then a little flare about me. And the treasure—all, to the veriest crumb of a seed-pearl!—vanished before my eyes. The bit of parchment reappeared, smoking. It turned to ashes. My dagger scorched my fingers. It had grown hot.

"Ah, yes," said the Power, nodding. "The force-field has energy. When the iron absorbs it, there is heat." Then he looked at me in a not unfriendly way. "You have brought pens and parchment," he said, "and at least you did not use the sigil to astonish your fellows. Also you had the good sense to make no more perfumish stinks. It may be that there is a grain of wisdom in you. I will bear with you yet a while. Be seated and take parchment and pen—Stay! Let us be comfortable. Sheathe your dagger, or better, cast it from you."

I put it in my bosom. And it was as if he thought, and touched something at his side, and instantly there was a fair pavilion about us, with soft cushions and a gently playing fountain.

"Sit," said the Power. "I learned that men like such things as this from a man I once befriended. He had been wounded and stripped by robbers, so that he had not so much as a scrap of accursed metal about him, and I could aid him. I learned to speak the language men use nowadays from him. But to the end he believed me an evil spirit and tried valorously to hate me."

My hands shook with my agitation that the treasure had departed from me. Truly it was a treasure of such riches as no King has ever possessed, Johannus! My very soul lusted after that treasure! The golden coins alone would fill your attic solidly, but the floor would break under their weight, and the jewels would fill hogsheads. Ah, Johannus! That treasure!

"What I will have you write," said the Power, "at first will mean little. I shall give facts and theories first, because they are easiest to remember. Then I will give the applications of the theories. Then you men will have the beginning of such civilization as can exist in the neighborhood of the accursed metal."

"Your Potency!" I begged abjectly. "You will give me another sigil of treasure?"

"Write!" he commanded.

I wrote. And, Johannus, I cannot tell you myself what it is that I wrote. He spoke words, and they were in such obscure cipher that they have no meaning as I con them over. Hark you to this, and seek wisdom for the performance of mysteries in it! "The civilization of my race is based upon fields of force which have the property of acting in all essentials as substance. A lodestone is surrounded by a field of force which is invisible and impalpable. But the fields used by my people for dwellings, tools, vehicles, and even ma-

chinery are perceptible to the senses and act physically
as solids. More, we are able to form these fields in
latent fashions; and to fix them to organic objects as
permanent fields which require no energy for their
maintenance, just as magnetic fields require no energy
supply to continue. Our fields, too, may be projected
as three-dimensional solids which assume any desired
form and have every property of substance except
chemical affinity.''

Johannus! Is it not unbelievable that words could
be put together, dealing with mysteries, which are so
devoid of any clue to their true mystic meaning? I
write and I write in desperate hope that he will eventually give me the key, but my brain reels at the difficulty of extracting the directions for Operations
which such ciphers must conceal! I give you another
instance: ''When a force-field generator has been
built as above, it will be found that the pulsatory
fields which are consciousness serve perfectly as con-
trols. One has but to visualize the object desired, turn
on the generator's auxiliary control, and the generator will pattern its output upon the pulsatory
consciousness-field . . .''

Upon this first day of writing, the Power spoke for
hours, and I wrote until my hand ached. From time to
time, resting, I read back to him the words that I had
written. He listened, satisfied.

''Lord!'' I said shakily. ''Mighty Lord! Your Potency! These mysteries you bid me write—they are beyond comprehension!''

But he said scornfully:

''Write! Some will be clear to someone. And I
will explain it little by little until even you can
comprehend the beginning.'' Then he added. ''You
grow weary. You wish a toy. Well! I will make you
a sigil which will make again that treasure you played
with. I will add a sigil which will make a boat for
you, with an engine drawing power from the sea
to carry you wheresoever you wish without need
of wind or tide. I will make others so you may create

a palace where you will, and fair gardens as you please . . .''

These things he has done, Johannus. It seems to amuse him to write upon scraps of parchment, and think, and then press them against his side before he lays them upon the ground for me to pick up. He has explained amusedly that the wonder in the sigil is complete, yet latent, and is released by the tearing of the parchment, but absorbed and destroyed by iron. In such fashion he speaks in ciphers, but otherwise sometimes he jests!

It is strange to think of it, that I have come little by little to accept this Power as a person. It is not in accord with the laws of mystery. I feel that he is lonely. He seems to find satisfaction in speech with me. Yet he is a Power, one of the Rebels who was flung to earth from Heaven! He speaks of that only in vague, metaphorical terms, as if he had come from another world like *the* world, save much larger. He refers to himself as a voyager of space, and speaks of his race with affection, and of Heaven—at any rate the city from which he comes, because there must be many great cities there—with a strange and prideful affection. If it were not for his powers, which are of mystery, I would find it possible to believe that he was a lonely member of a strange race, exiled forever in a strange place, and grown friendly with a man because of his loneliness. But how could there be such as he and not a Power? How could there be another world?

This strange converse has now gone on for ten days or more. I have filled sheets upon sheets of parchment with writing. The same metaphors occur again and again. ''Force-fields''—a term without literal meaning—occurs often. There are other metaphors such as ''coils'' and ''primary'' and ''secondary'' which are placed in context with mention of wires of copper metal. There are careful descriptions, as if in the plainest of language, of sheets of dissimilar metals which are to be placed in acid, and other descriptions

of plates of similar metal which are to be separated by
layers of air or wax of certain thicknesses, with the
plates of certain areas! And there is an explanation of
the means by which he lives. "I, being accustomed
to an atmosphere much more dense than that on
Earth, am forced to keep about myself a field of force
which maintains an air density near that of my home
planet for my breathing. This field is transparent, but
because it must shift constantly to change and refresh
the air I breathe, it causes a certain cloudiness of
outline next my body. It is maintained by the generator I wear at my side, which at the same time pro-
vides energy for such other force-field artifacts as I
may find convenient."—Ah, Johannus! I grow mad
with impatience! Did I not anticipate that he would
some day give me the key to this metaphorical speech,
so that from it may be extracted the Names and the
Words which cause his wonders, I would give over in
despair.

Yet he has grown genial with me. He has given me
such sigils as I have asked him, and I have tried them
many times. The sigil which will make you a fair garden is one of many. He says that he desires to give to
man the knowledge he possesses, and then bids we
write ciphered speech without meaning, such as: "The
drive of a ship for flight beyond the speed of light is
adapted from the simple drive generator already described simply by altering its constants so that it cannot generate in normal space and must create an
abnormal space by tension. The process is—" Or
else—I choose at random, Johannus—"The accursed
metal, iron, must be eliminated not only from all cir-
cuits but from nearness to apparatus using high-
frequency oscillations, since it absorbs their energy
and prevents the functioning . . ."

I am like a man trembling upon the threshold of
Paradise, yet unable to enter because the key is with-
held. "Speed of light!" What could it mean in metaphor? In common parlance, as well speak of the speed
of weather or of granite! Daily I beg him for the key

to his speech. Yet even now, in the sigils he makes for me, is greater power than any man has ever known before!

But it is not enough. The Power speaks as if he were lonely beyond compare; the last member of a strange race upon earth; as if he took a strange, companion-like pleasure in merely talking to me. When I beg him for a Name or a Word which would give me power beyond such as he doles out in sigils, he is amused and calls me fool, yet kindly. And he speaks more of his metaphorical speech about forces of nature and fields of force—and gives me a sigil which should I use it will create a palace with walls of gold and pillars of emerald! And then he amusedly reminds me that one greedy looter with an axe or hoe of iron would cause it to vanish utterly!

I go almost mad, Johannus! But there is certainly wisdom unutterable to be had from him. Gradually, cautiously, I have come to act as if we were merely friends, of different race and he vastly the wiser, but friends rather than Prince and subject. Yet I remember the warnings of the most authoritative authors that one must be ever on guard against Powers called up in an Operation.

I have a plan. It is dangerous, I well know, but I grow desperate. To stand quivering upon the threshold of such wisdom and power as no man has ever dreamed of before, and then be denied . . .

The mercenary who will carry this to you, leaves tomorrow. He is a cripple, and may be months upon the way. All will be decided ere you receive this. I know you wish me well.

Was there ever a student of mystery in so saddening a predicament, with all knowledge in his grasp yet not quite his?

Your friend
Carolus

Written in the very bad inn in Montevecchio.

Johannus! A courier goes to Ghent for My Lord of Brabant and I have opportunity to send you mail. I think I go mad, Johannus! I have power such as no man ever possessed before, and I am fevered with bitterness. Hear me!

For three weeks I did repair daily to the hilltop beyond Montevecchio and take down the ciphered speech of which I wrote you. My scrip was stuffed with sigils, but I had not one word of Power or Name of Authority. The Power grew mocking, yet it seemed sadly mocking. He insisted that his words held no cipher and needed but to be read. Some of them he phrased over and over again until they were but instructions for putting bits of metal together, mechanicwise. Then he made me follow those instructions. But there was no Word, no Name—nothing save bits of metal put together cunningly. And how could inanimate metal, not imbued with power of mystery by Names or Words or incantations, have power to work mystery?

At long last I become convinced that he would never reveal the wisdom he had promised. And I had come to such familiarity with this Power that I could dare to rebel, and even to believe that I had chance of success. There was the cloudiness about his form, which was maintained by a sigil he wore at his side and called a "generator." Were that cloudiness destroyed, he could not live, or so he had told me. It was for that reason that he, in person, dared not touch anything of iron. This was the basis of my plan.

I feigned illness, and said that I would rest at a peasant's thatched hut, no longer inhabited, at the foot of the hill on which the Power lived. There was surely no nail of iron in so crude a dwelling. If he felt for me the affection he protested, he would grant me leave to be absent in my illness. If his affection was great, he might even come and speak to me there. I would be alone in the hope that his friendship might go so far.

Strange words for a man to use to a Power! But I had talked daily with him for three weeks. I lay groan-

ing in the hut, alone. On the second day he came. I
affected great rejoicing, and made shift to light a fire
from a taper I had kept burning. He thought it a mark
of honor, but it was actually a signal. And then, as he
talked to me in what he thought my illness, there came
a cry from without the hut. It was the village priest, a
simple man but very brave in his fashion. On the signal of smoke from the peasant's hut, he had crept near
and drawn all about it an iron chain that he had muffled with cloth so that it would make no sound. And
now he stood before the hut door with his crucifix
unpraised, chanting exorcisms. A very brave man, that
priest, because I had pictured the Power as a foul fiend
indeed.

The Power turned and looked at me, and I held my
dagger firmly.

"I hold the accursed metal," I told him fiercely.
"There is a ring of it about this house. Tell me now,
quickly, the Words and the Names which make the
sigils operate! Tell me the secret of the cipher you had
me write! Do this and I will slay this priest and draw
away the chain and you may go hence unharmed. But
be quick, or—"

The Power cast a sigil upon the ground. When the
parchment struck earth, there was an instant's cloudiness as if some dread thing had begun to form.
But then the parchment smoked and turned to ash.
The ring of iron about the hut had destroyed its power when it was used. The Power knew that I spoke
truth.

"Ah!" said the Power dryly. "Men! And I thought
one was my friend!" He put his hand to his side. "To
be sure! I should have known. Iron rings me about.
My engine heats . . ."

He looked at me. I held up the dagger, fiercely unyielding.

"The Names!" I cried. "The Words! Give me
power of my own and I will slay the priest!"

"I tried," said the Power quietly, "to give you
wisdom. And you will stab me with the accursed

metal if I do not tell you things which do not exist. But you need not. I cannot live long in a ring of iron. My engine will burn out; my force-field will fail. I will stifle in the thin air which is dense enough for you. Will not that satisfy you? Must you stab me, also?''

I sprang from my pallet of straw to threaten him more fiercely. It was madness, was it not? But I was mad, Johannus!

"Forbear," said the Power. "I could kill you now, with me! But I thought you my friend. I will go out and see your priest. I would prefer to die at his hand. He is perhaps only a fool."

He walked steadily toward the doorway. As he stepped over the iron chain, I thought I saw a wisp of smoke begin, but he touched the thing at his side. The cloudiness about his person vanished. There was a puffing sound, and his garments jerked as if in a gust of wind. He staggered. But he went on, and touched his side again and the cloudiness returned and he walked more strongly. He did not try to turn aside. He walked directly toward the priest, and even I could see that he walked with a bitter dignity.

And—I saw the priest's eyes grow wide with horror. Because he saw the Power for the first time, and the Power was an ell and a half high, with a large head and knobbed feelers projecting from his forehead, and the priest knew instantly that he was not of any race of men but was a Power and one of those Rebels who were flung out from Heaven.

I heard the Power speak to the priest, with dignity. I did not hear what he said. I raged in my disappointment. But the priest did not waver. As the Power moved toward him, the priest moved toward the Power. His face was filled with horror, but it was resolute. He reached forward with the crucifix he wore always attached to an iron chain about his waist. He thrust it to touch the Power, crying, *"In nomine Patri—"*

Then there was smoke. It came from a spot at the Power's side where was the engine to which he touched the sigils he had made, to imbue them with the power of mystery. And then—

I was blinded. There was a flare of monstrous, bluish light, like a lightning-stroke from Heaven. After, there was a ball of fierce yellow flame which gave off a cloud of black smoke. There was a monstrous, outraged bellow of thunder.

Then there was nothing save the priest standing there, his face ashen, his eyes resolute, his eyebrows singed, chanting psalms in a shaking voice.

I have come to Venice. My scrip is filled with sigils with which I can work wonders. No men can work such wonders as I can. But I use them not. I labor daily, nightly, hourly, minute by minute, trying to find the key to the cipher which will yield the wisdom the Power possessed and desired to give to men. Ah, Johannus! I have those sigils and I can work wonders, but when I have used them they will be gone and I shall be powerless. I had such a chance at wisdom as never man possessed before, and it is gone! Yet I shall spend years—aye!—all the rest of my life, seeking the true meaning of what the Power spoke! I am the only man in all the world who ever spoke daily, for weeks on end, with a Prince of Powers of Darkness, and was accepted by him as a friend to such a degree as to encompass his own destruction. It must be true that I have wisdom written down! But how shall I find instructions for mystery in such metaphors as—to choose a fragment by chance—"plates of two dissimilar metals, immersed in an acid, generate a force for which men have not yet a name, yet which is the basis of true civilization. Such plates . . ."

I grow mad with disappointment, Johannus! Why did he not speak clearly? Yet I will find out the secret . . .

* * *

Memorandum from Peter McFarland, Physics Department, Haverford University, to Professor Charles, Latin, the same faculty:

Dear Professor Charles:
My reaction is, Damnation! Where is the rest of this stuff?

McFarland.

THE STRANGER FROM KURDISTAN

by E. Hoffmann Price

"You claim that demonolatry went out of existence at the end of the Middle Ages, that devil-worship is extinct? . . . No, I do not speak of the Yezidis of Kurdistan, who claim that the Evil One is as worthy of worship as God, since, by virtue of the duality of all things, good could not exist without its antithesis, evil; I speak rather of a devil-worship that exists today, in this Twentieth Century, in civilized, Christian Europe; secret, hidden, yet nevertheless quite real; a worship based upon a sacrilegious perversion of the ritual of the church. . . . How do I know? That is aside from the question; suffice it to say that I know that which I know."

So high was the tower of Semaxii that it seemed to caress the very stars; so deep-seated were its foundations that there was more of its great bulk beneath the ground than there was above. Bathed in moonlight was its crest; swathed in sevenfold veils of darkness was its ponderous base. Old as the pyramids was this great pile of granite which took its name from the ruined city, of equal antiquity, sprawled at its base.

A dark form approached, advancing swiftly through the gloom-drenched ruins, a darkness among the shadows, a phantom that moved with sinister certitude.

Suddenly the shadow halted, and its immobility became a part of the surrounding darkness. Other and lesser forms passed, slinking silently to the cavernous entrance of Semaxii, there vanishing in its obscure depths. And all were unaware of the form that had regarded them from its vantage-point.

A cloud parted. A ray of moonlight fought its way through the Cimmerian shadows, dissolving all save one, the darkest; and this darkest one it revealed as the tall form of a man wrapped in a black cape, and wearing a high silk hat.

Another rift in the clouds; more light, which now disclosed the features as well as the form of the shadowy stranger; haughty features with a nose like the beak of a bird of prey; the cold, pitiless eye of an Aztec idol; thin lips drooping in the shadow of a cynical smile; a man relentless and magnificent in defeat.

"The fools have all assembled to pay tribute to their folly; seventy-seven of them who will tonight adore their lord and master . . . and with what rites?—. . . It is long since I have witnessed . . ."

He paused in his reflections to count the strokes of a bell whose sound crept softly across the wastelands.

"Little of my last night remains; however, let me waste it well."

So saying, he gathered his cape about him, and swiftly strode to the entrance of the tower.

"Halt!" snapped a voice from the gateway.

The ray of an electric-torch bit the darkness and fell full upon the stranger's face.

"Halt, and give the sign."

"Who am I to give, or you to receive?" answered the stranger, as if intoning an incantation or reciting a fixed formula.

"Pass on."

And thus the stranger passed the outer guard of the shrine of demonolatry, the holy of holies where Satan received the homage of his vassals. Past the outer guard was the stranger, but far from the sanctuary wherein the Black Mass was celebrated, wherein the Lord of the World was worshipt with blasphemous rites.

A hundred steps of icy granite, winding like the coils of a vast earthworm, led to the foundations of the tower. And at intervals, sheeted and hooded warders halted the stranger and demanded sign and password; and each in turn, as he received a sign, shrank and dropped his gaze before the eye of the stranger.

Presently he found himself before a door guarded by two masked figures garbed in vermilion. Again there was an exchange of signs, after which the two vermilion figures bowed low as the door opened to admit him to the vaulted sanctuary where the Devil was that night to be invoked.

The stranger doffed his high hat, then after a courtly bow to the assemblage, strode up the aisle and seated himself on one of the brazen stools that were placed, row after row, like the pews of a chapel. Once seated, he gazed about him, taking stock of his surroundings.

The black altar before him, with its crucifix bearing a hideously caricatured Christ, received but a passing glance; nor was any more attention accorded to the walls and vaulted ceiling whose obscene carvings leered at him through the acrid, smoke-laden air. Not yet, apparently, did he note the acolyte who was trimming the black candles at the altar, nor did he seem to wonder that the floor beneath his feet was sprinkled with powdered cinnabar. It was the company itself that he studied, observing with interest the old and young, male and female, the seventy-seven who had assembled to adore Satan, their lord and master.

In the main, the seventy-seven were persons of wealth and distinction, who, having tried and found wanting every field of human endeavor and achievement, had sought thrills in the mediaeval rites of devil-worship; rakes whose jaded appetites sought satiation in the orgies that followed the celebration of the Black Mass; atheists who, deeming passive atheism an inadequate form of rebellion, found expression in a ritual whose sacrilege satisfied their iconoclastic desires.

Attendants bearing trays made their way among the seventy-seven, offering them glasses of wine and small amber-colored pastils. These last the worshipers either swallowed or else dissolved in their wine and drank.

The stranger turned to the initiate who occupied the stool at his side.

"Tell me, brother, the nature of the rites to be celebrated here tonight."

The initiate eyed him narrowly as he sipped his wine.

"What do you mean?"

"Why," began the stranger blandly, "I am a foreigner, and I fancied that the ritual here may be different from what it is in my native land. I must confess," he continued, "that I am puzzled to see an altar and a crucifix in this shrine devoted to the worship of the Evil One."

The initiate stared at him in amazement.

"It must be a curious rite that you witnessed. Do you not know that we have a priest who celebrates the mass, and then——"

"A priest?" interrupted the stranger. "The mass? Why——"

"Surely; if not a priest, if not a mass, how could the arch-enemy become incarnate in the bread which we, the worshipers of Satan defile and pollute as a tribute to our lord and master? Surely you must be a foreigner from some heathen land not to know that only an ordained priest of the church can cause the miracle of transubstantiation to take place. But tell me, who are you?"

"You would be amazed," replied the stranger, smiling enigmatically, "if you knew who I am."

Then, before the initiate could continue his queries, a gong sounded, thinly, rather as the hiss of a serpent than as the clang of bronze; a panel of the vault opened, admitting the vermilion-robed, misshapen bulk of the priest. Following were nine acolytes, likewise robed in vermilion, and bearing censers fuming with an overpoweringly heavy incense. As they marched slowly down the aisle, they raised their voices in a shrill chant. The seventy-seven sank to their knees, heads bowed.

The high priest halted before the altar, bowed solemnly, then, with the customary gestures and phrases, went through the ritual of the mass, the kneeling acolytes making the responses in Latin. He then descended to the bottom step of the altar and began his invocation to Satan.

"Oriflamme of Iniquity, thou who guidest our steps and givest us strength to endure and courage to resist, receive our petitions and accept our praise; Lord of the World, hear the prayers of thy servants; Father of Pride, defend us against the hypocrisies of the favorites of God! Master, thy faithful servants implore thee to bless their iniquities which destroy soul and conscience alike; power, glory and riches they beg of thee, King of the Disinherited, Son who battles with the inexorable Father: all this we ask of thee, and more, Master of Deceptions, Rewarder of Crime, Lord of Luxurious Vice and Monumental Sin, Satan thee whom we adore, just and logical god!"

The high priest rose, faced the altar and crucifix bearing its life-sized mockery of a caricatured Christ, and cried out in his blasphemies: "And thou, thou in my office as priest I compel to descend into this host, to become incarnate in this bread, Jesus, filcher of homage, thief of affection! Harken! From the day that the virgin gave thee birth thou hast failed in thy promises; the ages have wept in awaiting thee, mute and fugitive god! Thou wert to redeem mankind, and thou hast failed; thou wert to appear in glory, and thou liest asleep; thou who wert to intercede for us with the Father, hast failed in thy mission, lest thy eternal slumber be disturbed! Thou hast forgotten the poor to whom thou hast preached! Thou who hast dared punish by virtue of unheard-of laws, we would hammer upon thy nails, bear down upon thy crown of thorns, draw blood anew from thy dry wounds! And this we can do, and this we *will* do, in violating the repose of thy body, profaner of magnificent vice, glutton enamored of gluttony, accused Nazarene, idle king, sluggish god!''

''Amen,'' came the hoarse response of the seventy-seven through the stifling, incense-laden air.

The priest, having once more ascended the altar steps, turned and with his left hand blessed the worshipers of Satan. Then, facing the Crucified One, in a solemn but mocking tone he pronounced, *''Hoc est enim corpus meum.''*

At these words the seventy-seven, crazed as much by the drugged wine and ambur-hued pastils as by the sacrilegious madness of the ceremony, groveled upon the floor, howling and moaning, overcome by a demoniac frenzy. The priest seized the consecrated bread, spat upon it, subjected it to unmentionable indignities, tore it to pieces which he offered to the worshipers of Satan, who crept forward to receive this mockery of a communion.

The first of that mad group of devil-worshipers rose to his knees and was about to receive his portion when there came interruption.

''Fools, cease this mockery!''

It was the stranger's voice, a voice whose note of command, ringing through that vaulted chapel like the clear, cold peal of destruction, silenced the frenzied devotees, so that not a breath was audible. The acolytes stood transfixed at the altar. The high priest alone retained command of himself; but even he was momentarily abashed, shrinking before the flaming, fierce eye of the stranger.

Yet the priest quickly recovered himself.

''Who are you,'' he snarled, ''to interrupt the sacrifice?''

The seventy-seven, though still speechless, had recovered from the complete paralysis that their faculties had suffered. They saw the stranger confronting the high priest on the altar steps; they heard his voice, in reply, rich, sonorous, majestic:

''You, the high priest of Satan, and ask me who I am? I am Ahriman, whom the Persians feared; I am

Malik Taus, the white peacock whom men worship in far-off Kurdistan; I am Lucifer, the morning star; I am that Satan whom you invoked. Behold, I have returned in mortal form to meet and defy my adversary.''

He pointed to the crucifix, then continued, ''And a worthy adversary he is. Nor think that yonder simulacrum is the Christ I have sworn to overthrow. Fools! Besotted beasts, think you that it is serving me to deride a foe who has held me at bay these countless ages? Think you to serve me by this mummery? This very mass which you have celebrated, though in derision and in defiance of him, acknowledges his divinity; and though in mockery, you have nevertheless accepted him in taking this bread as his body. Is this serving me, your lord and master?''

''Impostor!'' shrieked the high priest, his face distorted with rage; ''impostor, you claim to be Satan?''

That high-pitched scream stirred the seventy-seven from their inertia, aroused them again to their frenzy. Gibbering and howling, they leapt to their feet and closed in on the stranger.

But at that instant a cloak of elemental fire, the red, blinding flame of a thousand suns, enshrouded Satan's form, and from it rang that same clear, cold voice, ''Fools! Madmen! I disown and utterly deny you!''

Once again in the ruins at the foot of the Tower of Semaxii was the dark stranger, Satan as he had revealed himself to his followers. He seemed to be alone, yet he was speaking, as if with someone facing him.

''Nazarene,'' he said, ''on that day wherein I challenged you to meet me with weapons and ground of your own choosing to do battle for possession of the world, I was foolish and knew not whereof I spoke.''

He paused, lowered his eyes for a moment, as if to rest them from the strain of gazing at an awful and intolerable radiance, then continued: ''You they crucified; me they would have torn to pieces, their

Lord and master; both of us they have denied. I wonder whose folly is the greater, yours in seeking to redeem mankind, or mine in striving to make it my own.''

And with these words Satan turned, his head bowed, and turning, disappeared among the ruins.

THE GLOBE OF MEMORIES
by Seabury Quinn

Montagu gazed affectionately on his latest acquisition. Poking through the maze of "antique shoppes" that line Third Avenue where it bounds Murray Hill on the east, he had come upon the little sphere of crystal, and his heart warmed to it at first glance. There was a vacancy on the third shelf of his glass-window and the little, faintly iridescent globe would fill it admirably—fill it as though made to order.

He set the vitric orb upon his desk and gazed into its limpid depths. It was something like three inches in diameter, crystalline and faintly cloudy at once, and in its center stood a tiny house with grouping, battlemented towers and a castellated roof. From the barbicans there sloped a series of green terraces, all fashioned out of frail, bright glass, and in the background, almost microscopically small, showed the spires and roofs of a walled town.

"Clever people, these Chinese or French or Czechs or whoever made this thing," grinned Montagu as he raised the glass sphere level with his eyes and watched the play of sunlight through its lucid depths. "They must—I say!" he broke off wonderingly and blinked perplexedly. With the movement of his hand some sort of sediment in the liquid filling of the globe had been disturbed, and a vague obscurity began to shroud the tiny castle from his gaze. It was not quite like the limy white of stirred-up sediment, however; rather, it resembled slowly drifting smoke or thickening whorls of gathering fog.

He shook his head to clear his eyes. That must be

it. Gazing in the crystal held against the light had dazzled him. He closed his eyes against the baffling mist which swirled inside the ball, and secure in knowing every inch of the study floor, stepped toward the table to replace the little sphere. One, two steps he had taken when an unfamiliar sound beneath his feet forced both eyes open suddenly.

He was not treading on the well-worn Hamadan which carpeted his study floor; he was walking on a graveled path and his feet were stockingless and shod with sandals of rough rawhide.

"This is amaz—great Scott!" he muttered. His gait was hampered by the folds of something like a heavy gown which flapped against his shins. It was rough, coarse stuff, an indeterminate, slate-gray in color, and enveloped him from neck to ankles. Hanging from his throat across his breast and nearly to his garment's hem was a sort of apron of rough serge, and under this about his waist was bound a girdle of coarse hempen cord with knotted ends that struck against his knees at every step. Dependent from the girdle was a strand of heavy skull-shaped beads strung on an iron chain and arranged in series, groups of ten beads, each about the size of a small marble, being separated from one another by knobs the size of a shelled hazelnut. At the end was a bead of walnut's size with a brass-and-wooden crucifix hung from it.

"Good Lord!" gasped Montagu, "this is a mediæval Friar's costume! What—" Involuntarily, he raised his hand to brush his hair back—a gesture he was wont to make when puzzled—and the sharp cry of dismay he gave was tragic. His hair grew thickly down about his temples, and its natural curl had caused him some bad moments as a schoolboy. Now, as he passed his hand across his head, his fingers touched smooth scalp, a head from which the hair was shaven in a circle as though marked off by a skull-cap, then shaved before the ears and upward from the nape of the neck till only a thin line of close-cropped hair was left to band his head, as though a wreath of stubble had been laid upon an utterly bald scalp.

"If this is a dream," he told himself, "it's a most unpleasant one. I must—"

Through the fog which filled the air a figure loomed before him, a figure clad in a long gown. He could not tell at first if it were man or woman, but as the shape advanced he saw it was a man who wore his hair cut in a bob that reached down to the bottoms of his ears, and was dressed in a loose robe of some woolen stuff of somber bottle-green. Beneath the gown he wore red stockings which reached up his legs like tights; long, pointed shoes were on his feet; a peak-crowned cap trimmed with a heron's feather sat upon his straight black hair. His skin was very dark and his eyes so large and black and deep-set that they looked like oval pits of darkness set beneath his overhanging brows.

"*Dominus tecum,* Fra Albertus," he greeted with a cold, unpleasant smile.

"*Pax tecum,*" answered Montagu, not realizing till the gesture was complete that he had raised his right hand and described a cross with it.

"What made me do that?" he demanded of himself as he stepped along the gravel path. "It was the proper thing to do, of course, but how did I know—" his voice trailed off in silent wonder as he looked before him.

The mists had cleared, and he was coming to a castle, its walls and battlements in sharp relief against the fresh blue sky. He recognized it instantly. Point for point and line for line, it was the castle of the glass globe, enlarged a hundred thousand times, but faithful in its reproduction. Across a valley, clearly outlined in the sunlight, rose the walls and spires and red-tiled roofs of a small town.

Terraces of close-clipped grass stretched from the castle walls to a small river. Luminously green in the rays of the declining sun, the upper levels reached to the wide moat; the lower banks were mottled with deep shadow where the shade of ancient trees was cast. A company of young men in bright costumes played at quoits upon the green, and as he passed they ceased their sport and greeted him respectfully, though without cordiality. *"Dominus vobiscum,"* he murmured as he raised his hand in that familiar-unfamiliar sign and continued straight across the drawbridge which gave entry to the castle gate.

A dozen halberdiers in brazen helmets and cuirasses and tall boots of Spanish leather lounged in the guardroom. Czechs these; light-eyed, yellow-bearded Dalmatian mercenaries faithful to their bread and salt, and to nothing else beneath the dome of heaven. Their leader greeted Montagu with neither friendship nor hostility.

"Thou'rt expected, Fra Alberto," he announced. "Go thou to the chapel; I'll send a varlet to inform the lady Fulvia of thy coming."

Montagu was aware the guardsman did not speak in English, yet what the language was he had no idea. At any rate, he had no difficulty in understanding.

"Wilt send one with me to the chapel?" he returned, and as he spoke he realized he used the same strange tongue the captain of the guard employed. "Mine eyes are dazzled from the sun."

The warder eyed him sharply, then turned to a subordinate who lounged upon a bench.

"Get thee to the chapel wi' Messer Cheat-the-Devil," he commanded. "His eyes are holden wi' the dark."

None too cheerfully the fellow rose, slipped his sword into its bawdric loop and led the way along the corridor.

It was cold as a sealed tomb inside the castle. Here and there the stone walls ran with clammy sweat where the moisture in the heated air had been congealed on them. At intervals, though not with any sort of regularity, the stones were hung with Flemish tapestries. Here and there stone lamps like little basins protruded from the walls, and in them floated burning wicks, but the principle illumination came from swinging lamps with shades of bright Venetian glass which splashed down little pools of red or violet or green upon the gray floor-tiles.

The chapel was a sanctuary of cool twilight. A few stray sunbeams slanted through the intricately carved mullions of the narrow windows and wrought net-like figures on the floor, bringing into bright relief the glowing colors of the Isphahan carpets which were spread upon the stones. A tapestry depicting the Nativity hung across one wall; from the groined and carved ceiling hung a sanctus lamp of hammered silver and bright ruby glass which cast a ruddy glow upon the marble altar with its cloth of fair white linen and its cross of beaten brass. Opposite the altar was the entrance to the vesting-room where stoles of crimson and bright yellow and a set of vestments for the acolytes were hung. Beside the door stood the confessional, carved of age-discolored oak. Instinctively, Montagu swung back its gate and shut himself inside, and as he did so caught the rustle of a woman's garments.

He could see her indistinctly through the lattice, a tall and slender figure cloaked in somber black, a white veil bound about her head and gathered loosely round her face. This much he saw, but whether she were dark or fair, young, old, or middle-aged, he could not tell.

"Bless me, father, for I have sinned," came a faint, soft voice, and as he leant his cheek against the grille he felt the stirring of soft breath against his ear and caught the faintly tantalizing aroma of flower-essence that clung about her garments.

Mechanically, unwittingly, but perfectly, he made the proper responses, asked the proper searching questions, and marveled as he did so. Born and reared a Unitarian, son and grandson of devoted members of that informal faith, he knew by instinct every nuance of the roman rubric! The confession was a short one, and in less than fifteen minutes Montagu had murmured his *absolvo te,* and his penitent departed silently as she had come.

Slowly he rose from the padded cushion where he knelt, let himself out from the confessional and stood a moment by the chapel door. He had no idea what his next move was; perhaps he could retrace his steps and find the castle entrance—

"Ho, Messer Dodge-the-Evil-One," a loud voice greeted, "Her ladyship commands thy presence in her bower. She'll have thee break thy fast with her. Fair gospel, eh, my friend? A monk hath never so much of prayer that he can forget his belly, meseemeth."

"Cease thy prating, varlet; lead me to her ladyship," Montagu's tone was sharp with quick resentment.

" 'Varlet?' This to me, thou shave-pate?' cried the soldier. "By'r Lady, if 'twere not for that long robe o' thine—" Half jocosely, half angrily, he thrust his halberd-head at Montagu.

Next instant he was sprawling on the floor, for Montagu had snatched the pike-staff from his hand and dealt him such a blow that had not the fellow's skull been guarded by a morion he would have been knocked senseless.

"Now, by the seven thousand holy virgins of Cologne, monk or no monk, I'll have the gizzard out of thee for that!" the guardsman roared, springing to his feet and dragging at his sword.

It was Fra Albertus he attacked, but it was Albert Montagu, captain, O.R.C., expert with the bayonet and three times medal winner with the foil and saber, who opposed him. Steel of sword and steel of halberd struck together with a clash; the guardsman beat and hammered with his blade, while Montagu advanced against him steadily, never letting him have peace, constantly menacing him with his halberd's point. Awkwardly the soldier parried a quick thrust, then lunged out madly. It was the opening Montagu had waited. With a quick riposte he drove his longer weapon underneath the guardsman's blade, then, checking his arm in mid-thrust, brought the wide head of his halberd up, driving its flat against his adversary's forearm with such force that the sword fell clattering from the fellow's nerveless fingers, leaving him unweaponed and defenseless while the pike blade shone with deadly menace in his eyes.

A lightly-clapping sound, as though soft palms were struck together, broke the pregnant silence, and a cool, imperious voice commanded: "Give him absolution and the *coup de grace*, Sir Monk. Meseems that he expects it. So do I."

Montagu whirled at the words, a hot flush mounting to his cheeks. There was more than gentle irony intended, he was sure. The speaker really wished to see him kill his unarmed adversary.

Framed in the roseate patch of light cast by a swinging lamp she stood before him like a portrait from some mediæval romance. Tall, willowy, aloof and proud as Lucifer's half-sister she appeared, but so beautiful that he was fairly breathless at the sight of her.

She wore a wide-sleeved overmantle of deep violet, trimmed about the edges with the regal ermine, and under it a narrow gown of cloth of gold. Her hair was smoothly parted in the middle, and its cloven tide flowed down across her shoulders in two heavy plaits which reached her knees and were laced with strands of pearls. Upon her head, less aureate than the smooth bright hair it covered, was a little cap of golden net sewn thick with seed-pearls. Upon her narrow feet were pointed shoes of creamy leather threaded with gold bullion, appliqued with violet silk and tipped with incrustations of small sapphires. Her face was pale as Parian marble, save for the scarlet line of pomegranate-red lips, eyes of the clear blue of summer skies; serene and lovely, an arrogant, narrow chin, long, tapering brows and nostrils slim with hauteur. The youthfulness of her slight body shone resplendent through the golden tissue of her gown like a pale, hot flame that shines through polished ivory.

"Lay on, Sir Friar," she bade him while her narrow nostrils flared the faintest bit with pleased anticipation. "That was a shrewdly smitten blow. I wait the finish."

Albert shrugged his shoulders in annoyance. "Here, fellow, take thy tools, and be more cautious ere ye seek another quarrel," he admonished as he flung the halberd at the guardsman's feet.

"You wished converse with me, my lady?" he asked the girl with a cold, formal bow.

"Now, by'r Lady, it doth seem to me thou'rt grown in courtesy," she answered as her cool eyes swept appraisingly over his bare, sandaled feet, his gown of sackcloth and his shaven head. " 'Twill mend my mood to break my fast with thee today."

Silently she turned upon her soft-soled shoes and led the way along the corridor.

The room to which she led him occupied a portion of the tower looking out across the valley. Almost circular in shape, it was a fairly large apartment having divans at the walls strewn with silk cushions of bright colors. The few articles of furniture, scant but of decided elegance, were oriental in design, as was the bronze lamp hanging from the ceiling.

She struck a silver gong and almost instantly a serving-wench appeared with a wooden salver piled with food. In silver dishes there were pigeons stewed in wine, a loaf of white bread graced a platter, and from a silver pitcher curled the fragrant steam of hot, spiced wine. Two small goat-horns, framed in silver strands and exquisitely inlaid, served as goblets, and for dessert were comfits made of marchpane. There were neither forks nor spoons, but two small daggers, razor-sharp, lay on the tray, and with these they dismembered the stewed pigeons, thrusting the pieces into their mouths and pausing between mouthfuls to immerse their fingers in a ewer of warm, perfumed water and wipe them on the napkins of white linen.

As they ate she studied him with black-fringed, curious eyes.

"Methinks thou'rt somewhat different, Fra Alberto," she observed at length, and as Montagu looked up he caught the flicker of a dimple shadowed in her cheek.

In a polished silver mirror he beheld a picture, but it was not one he recognized. The face was like his own, but the gleaming white of hairless skull, accentuated by the narrow fringe of close-cropped hair which circled round his skull, gave it a wholly alien appearance. The collar of a coarse gown came high about his neck, and at the back there showed the swelling of the cowl which hung between his shoulders.

"Aye, different," he repeated, turning from the vision of that shaven-pated head. "I am surely not the man I was this morning."

"Man?" she echoed with a touch of acid irony. "Are monks, then, men? Had thought that they were a third sex, neither male nor female, like those bees that make no honey."

Montagu could feel his cheeks grow warm. This chit, this little mediæval savage, who could probably not write her name! An angry retort mounted to his lips, and:

"What thinkest thou concerning me, *ma donna?*" he heard himself replying. She studied him a moment, her virginally blue eyes taking inventory of him from his sandaled feet to tonsured head, and she seemed to find the survey faintly entertaining, for again there was a hint of smile upon her mobile lips, the merest hint of dimples deepening in her cheeks.

"Sith thou hast asked, methinks thou'rt more a man than monk," she answered. "I saw thy strife with Husar by the chapel door, and for a moment I did pray that he would spit thee, but when I saw how manfully thou fought, my prayers were all for thee. By Agnes' eyes, that was a shrewdly given blow wherewith thou didst unsword the villain!"

"But why should you have prayed he'd run me through?" asked Montagu.

Defiance mixed with pride showed in her pale, patrician face. "Those twenty *aves* and two *paters* said

whilst kneeling bare-kneed on the gravel of the pleasaunce walk did not engender Christian charity.''

Montagu looked at her in amazement. "Twenty *aves*
. . . kneeling bare-kneed on the gravel?'' he repeated
slowly. "When—"

His question died as he looked in her face. Half
wonderingly, half fearfully, she gazed at him, her lips
a little parted, something like a frightened recognition
dawning in her eyes. One slim hand fluttered to her
throat and he saw the signet cut in amethyst gleam on
her forefinger.

"Thy eyes—thy voice—they are not—" she began,
but stopped abruptly as a shadow fell athwart the
threshold.

Smiling bleakly, the man whom he had met as he
approached the castle stood at gaze, and it seemed to
Montagu there was a light of mocking mirth in his
dark eyes.

"How now, my lord Antonio?" asked the lady Fulvia. "You come unbidden to my bower—"

"If thou canst entertain one man at meat, meseems
thou hast scant right to take offense when thy affianced
waits on thee," he answered with a bow.

"We are not yet affianced," she returned, "and I
entertain no men within my bower. Knowest well that
Fra Alberto is my ghostly counsellor; I must hold converse with him for my soul's sake."

The man's deep eyes regarded her ironically, but he
made no answer. Instead, he turned to Montagu and
scrutinized him narrowly. "I hear thou hast distinction
as a man of arms, as well as one of God, Fra 'berto,"
he said slowly. "A very paragon of manly strength,
though somewhat lacking in the manly beauty that ap-
peals to ladies' hearts." He fixed his speculative gaze
upon the tonsure which disfigured Albert's head; then
with another bitter smile: "Still, a young and stalwart
monk is better than no man at all, I wis—"

"Antonio!" Flaming-cheeked, the lady Fulvia faced
him, her small hands clenched until the nails bit deep
into her palms.

"You swine!" Despite the handicap of clinging cassock, Albert crossed the room in two strides and seized the fellow by the shoulders. "Apologize to Lady Fulvia, or—"

Her scream gave warning of his peril, and he glanced down just in time to see Antonio's hand drag at the poniard at his belt.

Quickly loosening the grip of his right hand, he pushed out with his left, spun the other half-way round, slipped his disengaged hand underneath his arm, clasped his neck in a half-nelson and wrenched with all his might.

Beneath the unexpected pressure, Antonio turned a somersault, pitched headlong to the floor and sprawled upon the carpet.

"Santo Dio!" He roused to his knees, eyes bright with fear. "No man art thou, but a dev—"

The smash of Albert's fist against his mouth broke off his words.

"Crave pardon of the lady Fulvia, or I'll beat thee to a posset!" he warned, "Hold up thy hands, thou dog; hold up thy hands in prayer and name thyself the foul liar that thou art!"

"Nay, nay, Fra 'berto, do not strike again!" the girl besought as Montagu drew back his fist. "Antonio is truly penitent; he spoke in thoughtlessness, and did not mean his words."

"I spake in thoughtlessness, and am truly penitent," the man repeated through blanched lips. "Prithee, sweet cousin, bid him let me go in peace!"

"Begone in peace," she answered almost listlessly.

Antonio crept trembling toward the door, but at the sill he turned and bent his thumbs across his palms, encircling them with the second and third fingers, holding the first and little fingers straight. Thus clasped, he thrust his hands at Montagu.

"Aroint thee, Satanas!" he gasped. "Thou canst not harm me—"

Albert took a forward step, and the door slammed between them.

Turning, he faced the girl, who stood up straight before him, hands clasped before her, as if in prayer.

"Art feared of me—Fulvia?" he asked softly, dropping the ceremonial title from her name.

She was afraid, terribly afraid, he saw. Her face had gone chalk-white and her vivid lips were almost gray, but her eyes were wide and steady, a little pleading, a little questioning.

"I—in sooth, I know not whether thou art sprite or devil," she replied through lips she strove to keep from trembling. "Say, wilt thou do me harm?"

"Of course not," he returned. "Why should I harm you?"

"Are not all devils—"

"What makes you sure that I'm a devil?" he broke in. "Antonio is evil, you know that. He affronted thee, and I chastised him for it. Did not the good Saint George defend the innocent against the wicked; did not Michael hurl rebellious angels out of heaven?"

"Soothly," she nodded as a trace of color crept back in her cheeks, "and Saint Martin was a soldier and a mighty man of war—"

"Well, then," he laughed, "you see you have no need to fear. I never harmed a woman in my life. Indeed," he added, warming to the subject of his magnanimity, "if it did not bite me first, I never harmed a fly!"

"But—but you gave me twenty *aves* and two *paters*—said upon my bare knees on the pleasaunce gravel, too—because I did befriend a little dog mine uncle's pages plagued. You said that Christians may not show a kindness to a soulless animal."

"I *did?*"

"Nay, marry, thou didst not!" she answered positively. "Fra Alberto gave that penance, but *thou'rt not—Fra—Alberto!*"

Once more her lips were trembling, and he could see small shivers shake her slender frame, but she made no move to flee from him, and the frightened look in her blue eyes was half a plea, half invitation.

"Who thinkest thou I am?"

"A devil, certes, but a good and kindly devil who never harmed a woman or a fly—unless belike the fly hight Hursar or Antonio."

Frank and trusting as a child, she laid her hand in his and led him to the narrow lancet-window which looked out across the valley toward the city.

"They make high carnival in town tonight," she smiled invitingly across her shoulder. "Surely, none could think amiss of it if the lady Fulvia were to travel to the city in company with Fra Alberto, her confessor. The prioress of the convent of Saint Agnes is my kinswoman. I fain would visit her the night, and—if I tarried at the fair awhile, or lost my way amid the booths of mountebanks and conjurers"—for a breath she hesitated, then—"if a gentlewoman is not safe accompanied by a holy friar, certes, virtue has gone out of Christendom. Wilt come with me, Fra—Fra Diavolo?"

The carnival was in full flower. Night was turned to day by strings of colored lanterns stretched from house to house across the streets. A pandemonium of pleasure, an orgy of jollity reigned. Reed pipes skirled, drums beat, tambourines clashed musically. A hundred booths displayed a hundred marvels. Apes danced to elfin music in the torchlight, conjurers and prestidigitators showed a skill which seemed inspired by the Evil One. Musk, attar, cinnamon and myrrh, frankincense and aloes were offered by a hundred swartfaced hawkers. Jongleurs and fire-eaters, rope-dancers and tumblers showed the marvels of their callings. A barber-chirurgeon drew teeth to the accompaniment of his victims' howls and the mingled jeers and applause of the crowd.

His cowl drawn close about his head, a black eye-mask across his face, Albert shuffled through the laughing, jostling throng. At his side, arm linked in his, walked the lady Fulvia with a violet domino cloaked about her shoulders. She wore her hood drawn forward, and a mascaron of gold-hued tissue hid her

features from such revelers as dared impudently to peer
beneath the shadow of her capuch. More than once,
attracted by the offerings of the fakirs, Albert would
have made a purchase, but each time was a forcible
reminder that friars' cassocks have no pockets, nor
friars wherewithal to fill them even if they had.

At the intersection of two streets a crowd was gathered where a young girl, white and supple as a fresh-
peeled willow withe in sateen trunks and silver
breastlets, performed contortionistic feats. "San Marco,
she hath ne'er a bone within her corse!" an idler swore
as the little maid set hands and elbows on the floor,
then raised her feet above her head and brought them
slowly forward. "God's wounds!" another answered as
the girl crossed supple legs above her shoulders and
swung her feet before her laughing face; "methinks she
is the very daughter of the snake that tempted Mother
Eve!"

An ancient hag in flaunting colored rags and tar-
nished metal ornaments came sidling through the
crowd and crept to Fulvia's side. Beneath her bell-
crowned hat and headkerchief of gaudy cotton cloth
her face was deeply bitten with the sun and with an
intricate crisscross of wrinkles, but her eyes were
shrewd and bright and bird-like. "Ah, pretty mistress," she besought in a shrill piping tone, "let me
read your palm, let the gipsy tell the fortune that awaits
you. Love and joy and length of days are surely yours,
for you tread among the great folk. Yes," she added,
advancing till she clawed at Fulvia's cloak, "you tread
among the great folk, mistress, and surely the poor
man is servant to the rich, the borrower servant to the
lender."

He could see the smile that curved the girl's lips
underneath her mask, and wondered at its wistfulness
as she laid her hand within the hag's dry claws and
answered softly: "Nay, old mother, has it not been
written that whatsoever a man soweth, that shall he
also reap?"

"Ah-hee!" the aged beldame wheezed, "thou

speakest rightly, mistress, for the watchers of the dead e'en now are numbering the tale, and some there are that dwell in mighty places who eftsoons shall hear the tolling of the passing bell.''

She dropped the girl's white hand and hobbled off into the crowd, and in a moment her quaint head-dress vanished in the tide of parti-colored dominos.

"Mad?" Albert asked. "Meseemeth that her words lacked sense—''

Fulvia was drawing him away, the insistent pressure of her arm in his leading him farther and farther from the close-packed lighted street. "Nay," she returned, and he could feel her tremble with excitement, or, perhaps, with fear, "there was a might of meaning in her words for those who understand.''

They had left the milling, laughing crowd, and were standing at the stairhead of a landing where the darkened river crept between the blank-walled houses, its surface shining and unruffled as a sheet of tautly-stretched black satin.

"I must leave thee for a time, Fra 'berto," she said softly. "There are those with whom I must hold converse, and they have small liking for thy cloth.''

"My cloth?" he echoed questioningly; then, with sudden understanding: "See here, you know that I'm no friar. You said I was a devil—yourself did name me Fra Diavolo. Why not take me with you?''

She considered him for a moment, then impulsively put out her hands. "I had forgotten, Fra—Diavolo," she answered softly. "Thy cappuccio obscured thy face, and I did not see thine eyes. Come, we have need of men of valor.''

Turning toward the river she emitted a low, sailing call, and in a moment called twice more. Presently, they heard a softly-splashing sound as a boat with muffled oars came toward them from the shadows. The rower glanced up challengingly at sight of Albert's hood and cassock, but a low word from the girl appeased him. " 'Tis but a mask," she whispered. "He will serve us faithfully.''

"Whither go we?" Albert asked as their little boat slipped silently between the ranks of houses.

For a moment she made no reply; then, irrelevantly, "Dost see my shoon?" she queried, stretching out her slender, high-arched feet for his inspection.

They were the same shoes she had worn when he first saw her, heelless, pointed, light-cream colored, sewn with golden threads and appliqued with violet silk, tipped with incrustations of small sapphires. Glove-tight, they clung to her small feet, bringing into charming definition delicately arched instep and the outline of the slender toes that lay uncrowded like the fingers of a shapely hand.

"They are made of human skin," she told him; then, as though in explanation: "My uncle gave them to me."

"Human skin? Good Lord—"

"Nay, not so; a fouly evil one, I ween."

"What mean ye?" Albert asked. She had crossed her knees, rested an elbow on the uppermost, and leant her chin upon a small clenched fist, staring out upon the murky waters with troubled, thought-filled eyes. At length:

"Mine uncle's farmers and villeins groan beneath a yoke of tyrany more sore than any which the wicked Pharaoh pressed upon the Hebrew children," she said softly, almost musingly. "They reap the increment of little that they sow, the impost-gatherer despoils their barns, drives off their cattle, even takes the fowls from their door-step and the eggs from out the nest. Their daughters are made things of sport for men at arms, their children cry for bread, and if they ask for justice—" She raised her foot again, that he might better see the shoe encasing it.

" 'Twas at lambing-time that Salvatore dared to lead the peasants to the castle for petition of redress. Mine uncle's stewards had gone through the farms and garnered in the young of sheep and goat, taking the dams of those too young to graze, and when the peasants raised their protest they were answered with the lash.

"Salvatore talked not of revolt; he believed the word of Holy Writ that the servant should be subject to his master. He only asked that of their flocks' increase the farmers retain a quarter-part, rendering to my uncle three in four. With him came his mother and his wife, his sons and daughters, and a babe still at the breast.

"Mine uncle met them at the drawbridge head, surrounded by his guard. When Salvatore had completed his petition the Dalmatian butchers rushed upon him, and made captives of them all. His wife and mother and his little children—e'en the suckling babe—they drowned before him in the waters of the moat. His sons' heads they struck off and fixed upon their pikes. His daughters—*santis-sima, Maria!* 'twould have been far better had they shared their brothers' fate. The girls were four, mine uncle's guard hath half a hundred men. 'Twas very piteous to hear them scream with torment of lust-riven flesh.

"Next morning after matins they did sound the tocsin, and when the farmers were come from all the country round, mine uncle bade them watch and see what fate befell a rebel. Thereafter they dragged Salvatore forth, and in sight of all the people flayed him quick. 'Twas Hursar did the butcher's work, Hursar whom thou hast worsted in the fence today. Dost marvel that I bade thee slay him?

"Of Salvatore's skin they made a binding for the missal wherefrom thou readest—Fra Alberto reads the office of the Holy Mass in chapel. Moreover, they did fashion gloves thereof, to delight mine uncle when he rides amain upon the hunt. Also they made of it these shoon which mine uncle gave to me."

"But—the things are loathsome; I'd not wear them!" Albert blazed.

"Thou would'st, didst thou regard them as I do," she answered softly.

"Lord! You don't mean you *want* to wear 'em?"

"Yes. Soothly."

He gazed at her in horrified amazement, and her

eyes were pleading, almost tender, as they met his look.

"Bethink thee," she leant forward and took up the crucifix that hung upon his rosary, "why do men revere this symbol of the gallows which our Lord was hanged upon?"

"As a memento of the sacrifice He made—I see! Forgive my lack of understanding! I had thought—"

"Many think as thou didst, Fra Diavolo. They say the lady Fulvia is cruel and pitiless; proud, cold and wanting in compassion."

The boat slipped silently along the darkened river; the whisper of its softly feathered oars and the muffled rhythm of the cloth-wrapped sweeps against their locks were all that broke the silence. Abruptly:

"Dost thou believe such things are right?" she asked. "Is it thy thought that one man, however high his birth, should have such power over others?"

"We hold these truths to be self-evident; that all men are created equal; that they are endowed by their Creator with certain inalienable rights; that among these are life, liberty and the pursuit of happiness," he quoted, and a thrill of pride of country mounted in him as he spoke.

Her blue eyes widened and a light like distant stars reflected in a quiet pool shone in them as she leant toward him.

"Say—say those words again!" she gasped. "Never have I heard their like. Not in all the writings of the fathers is such perfect gospel to be found! Teach me, dear devil, let me grave them on my heart: . . . all men are created equal . . . endowed by their Creator with the right of life and liberty! Whence come those tidings?"

"It is the profession of my people's faith," he answered. "Long years agone, when they threw off the yoke of tyranny, they took those words and others like them for the motto of their government."

"And in thy land do all men live by them?" she

asked. "Hath none the right to say them nay? Thy king—"

"We have no king. In my land all the people rule. Except for crime, no man's inherent right to name his rulers can be taken from him, and every man is safe in goods and person. Each man's house is unto him a castle, however lowly it may be, and so strong a castle is it that though the rain and wind may enter, the greatest in the land durst not step unbidden through the door."

"O, sweet devil, dear Fra Diavolo, take me with thee to that happy land of thine!" she begged. "Maugre it be hell, there would I bide for ever. Say thou wilt take me with thee when thou dost return!"

"I cannot, child," he answered sadly. "Not only space, but time divides us."

"Then promise thou wilt stay and help remake this doleful world into a model of that country whence thou comest."

"That I cannot promise, either," he replied. "I am not the master of my fate."

"But thou would'st stay here with me, an 'twere given thee to choose?" She leant toward him, and the perfume of her hair was in his nostrils, the flutter of her breath upon his cheek.

"Stay?" Albert answered gaspingly, while his lungs seemed fighting for air like those of a spent swimmer almost worsted by the tide. "Stay, my dear? If I might have the choice, I'd hold time still for ever; I'd let heaven beg for me while I clung to earth by nothing stronger than a kiss!"

The violet hood had slipped back from her lustrous hair, and in the faintly glowing moonlight it shone like gilded silver. Her eyelids drooped until the heavy lashes made twin arcs of shadow on her cheeks, and her lips were slightly parted as she leaned toward him and turned her face up for his kiss. There was that in the utterness of her surrender, the total yielding up of self, that almost frightened him. But she was in his arms, her mouth was answering his with rapturous av-

idness, and her uncoifed perfumed hair a golden maze
in which all hesitancy lost itself.

"My dear," he faltered, "my precious, my beloved . . ."

"Dear devil, sweetest devil; my adored Fra Diavolo!" she whispered crooningly as she laid her head
against his sackcloth-covered breast.

Their boat had beached upon a little shingle, and
the oarsman rose and pushed against the sloping gravel
with his sweep, holding the craft stationary. There was
a little stretch of water between boat and sand, and
Albert lifted Fulvia in his arms to bear her dry-shod
to the strand. The tide was cool as though it gushed
from mountain springs, and he shivered as he felt the
coldness of the water wavering round his sandaled feet.
The girl put up a hand and stroked his cheek.

"Art chilled, sweet devil?" she asked gently. "Then
drink and be anwarmed," and with a little sigh she
laid her lightly parted lips against his mouth.

Mist, faint as steam that simmers from a heating
pot, was rising from the river, and as they made their
way back from the beach they found themselves confronted by black darkness thickened with the drifting
fog. More than once his feet were tangled in invisible
obstructions, but the girl walked steadily ahead, her
hand in his to guide him through the murk. Straining
his eyes, Albert found that he could see a little way
around him, but except by glimpses anything ten feet
away was blotted out by swirling mists. At length they
paused before a rustling iron grille which Fulvia
opened with the surety of touch of an initiate, then led
him swiftly down a flagstone path. To right and left he
saw small huts of stone, some barred by gratings, some
blank-faced in the gloom. Leafless poplars reached
skeletons like stripped fishbones to the cloud-flecked
sky; here and there a moldering granite shaft stood
stark and lonely in a maze of briar-bushes.

"Where are we?" whispered Albert.

"The *campo santo*."

"The *campo santo*—cemetery?"

"Yea, 'tis here the watchers of the dead assemble."

They approached a mausoleum larger than the rest, and as they reached its steps a hoarse voice challenged through the fog-bound gloom, and Albert saw the glimmer of a pike-blade. "Is not the poor man servant to the rich, and the borrower servant to the lender?" asked the unseen sentry.

"Nay," answered Fulvia, "has it not been written that whatsoever a man soweth, that shall he also reap?"

The menacing steel withdrew into the clump of laurel bushes and they mounted the sepulchral stairs, pushed back the grille, and let themselves into a vaulted tomb. At the far end of the mortuary chamber was a well, down which there curved a stairway to the crypt-room underneath. Fulvia's soft-soled shoes whispered gently on the stones, but Albert's rawhide sandals seemed to wake a thousand echoes as he stumbled down the stairs.

About a flat-topped stone sarcophagus there grouped a little crowd, monstrous and misshapen-seeming as a crew of gnomes from Niflheim in the torchlight's smoky glare. As Fulvia and Albert entered, the leader of the group drummed on the coffin-top with a blanched thighbone and called:

"Have any cause to ask redress of injury?"

"I have," a masked form answered, rising from its seat beside the coffin.

"Who speaks?"

"Nicolo the farmerer, brother to the shepherd Salvatore."

"What dost thou charge?"

"Murder. Murder of my kinsman and his wife, his sons and suckling babe; defloration of his daughters, then their murder; all without just cause."

"Whom accusest thou?"

"Count Cristoforo di San Cologero, lord of the lands whereon my brother toiled, lord of the lands beyond the river, lord of the lands beyond the hills. Him I indict of murder, of him I ask redress of kinsman's blood, of women's tears, of maidens' ravished innocence!''

"Does any speak for Count Cristoforo di San Cologero?'' asked the chairman of the junta.

Slowly, rhythmically, without hurry, without undue delay, he beat upon the coffin-lid with the thigh-bone. A deep, reverberant blow: "Matthew?'' Another blow: "Mark?'' A third drum-beat: "Luke?''

Beat followed slow, deliberate beat, and after each the leader called the name of an Apostle. Finally, when twelve names, ending with Barnabas, had been called: "Judas Iscariot?''

"Yea!'' answered all the crowd in unison, and Albert heard the girl's clear treble mingle with the sullen voices of the men.

"Whence answers Judas for his client?''

"From hell, where they who shed the blood of innocents are prisoned.''

A pause which lasted while a man might count a hundred followed; then:

"Have ye reached a judgment, Watchers of the Dead?''

"Aye!''

"What is your judgment?''

"Let him die the death!''

"How shall he die it?''

"By the draft.''

"Who gives the potion?''

"I.'' muffled in her domino, her face hidden by the golden mask, Fulvia stepped forward and put forth her hand.

"Thou'lt not falter?'' asked the leader, while his eyes gleamed red in the torchlight through the peepholes of his mask. "He is of thy blood—''

"Abel's blood cried out for vengeance from the earth; Salvatore's and his wife's and children's asks for justice from the land, and none will answer it. Give me the phial. I will keep mine oath, and God do so to me, and more, if I should fail my promise!''

Light flashed upon a little flask as it changed hands, and Fulvia hid it in her draperies.

"Watchers of the Dead," began the leader, but a strident cry cut through his words.

"Fly, fly!" the hail resounded through the tomb. "They are upon us—*i signori di notte*—the night-watch!"

"Here, friend, thou'lt find it useful, an thou knowest how to use it!" rasped a rough voice as a sword was thrust into Albert's hand. "Guard well the lady Fulvia; we'll lure the varlets from the shore, and thou should'st reach thy boat without mishap."

The masked men swarmed out of the chamber, and in a moment they heard shouts and clash of metal mingled with oaths fierce as heavy blows.

Albert tucked his cassock-hem inside his hempen girdle, and, sword in hand, began to climb the stairs with Fulvia at his heels. The sounds of conflict had grown dim among the graves, and they raced toward the cemetery gate, dropping now and then behind a ruined tombstone when combatants drew near them.

At the river's rim their boat lay beached, the rower leaning forward in his seat as though asleep.

"Thanks be to San Giorgio, we have won through them!" breathed Fulvia as they hastened to the boat. "Come, Messer Devil, we shall soon be—*Santo Dio!*"

From behind the gunwales of the boat rose two armed men, while the oarsman leaped up from his seat, cast his cloak aside, and revealed himself an armored *bravo*.

Albert swung the girl behind him, and as the *bravi* charged he leaned down and seized a handful of fine gravel from the beach. Before the leading *bravo's* blade could clash with his, he flung the sandy grit with all his might in the fellow's face, and as he howled with pain, drove at him with his sword. The point struck flesh, glanced upward on the man's cheek-bone, then sank in half a foot as, slipping past the bony ridge, it pierced the eye and lodged itself within the brain.

Cold air, chill as currents from the beating wings of

death, fanned Albert's face as the second *bravo* struck
at him, but with a quick turn he dodged the flailing
blow, disengaged his blade and caught the other's
sword upon its edge.

The very force of his opponent's charge bore Albert
back, and he felt the breath go out of him as the brass
cuirass collided with his chest. Bending backward, he
struck out with all his force, bringing a left uppercut
in contact with the soldier's hairy chin. There was a
clicking as of castinets as the *bravo's* teeth snapped
shut, and with a grunt he toppled back unconscious
from the blow.

The third man was more wary. Refusing to accept
the opening Albert seemed to offer as he raised his
sword above his head, he advanced a gliding step or
two, retreated quickly out of reach, then poised on
guard, his sword held straight before him.

Albert made a feint, then a quick lunge, and as his
adversary parried in quarte sank back upon his heel,
executed a quick cut-over, and lunged straight at the
bravo's throat. The brazen gorget topping the cuirass
prevented his blade from running through the other's
neck, but the force with which he struck unsteadied
his opponent, and his point glanced upward, cut across
the jugular, and left a red spate in its wake.

"Make haste!" he cried, seizing both of Fulvia's
hands and swinging her across the little strip of water
to the waiting boat. He picked up the oars and fitted
them into the rowlocks.

The craft was clumsy, wide-beamed and flat-
bottomed, but once he had it out upon the stream it
answered readily enough as he pulled at the sweeps.

"Which way lies town?" he asked. "I know not my
directions. Thou must guide me.

Half an hour later they were clamoring at the pos-
tern of the convent of Saint Agnes. When at last the
sleepy portress answered their alarum she bestowed a
single scornful glance on them and slammed the
wicket.

"Get ye gone, ye vagabonds!" she shrilled. "San

Antonio's curse upon ye rakes and trulls who play such knavish tricks o' nights!''

Her sandals clattered echoes of her righteous indignation as she shuffled down the passage, nor could all their ringing bring her back again.

"So that's the hospitality of Holy Church?'' Albert asked sarcastically, but Fulvia laughed lightly.

"In good sadness, bold Sir Devil, meseems the reverent sister wardress had some cause for her suspicions,'' she assured him. "Look thou at me, and at thyself.''

Her domino was rent to tatters by the briary bushes of the graveyard, and wet with river water. From her hood her unbound hair hung about her face and on her shoulders like a golden cataract; mold and cobwebs from the tomb adorned her with a hundred dusty festoons.

Albert had an even more grotesque appearance. His cassock was tucked in his belt and kilted to his knees; through his hempen girdle was thrust a long, bare sword; upon his head, cocked at a rakish angle, sat a brazen morion he had appropriated from a fallen member of the watch.

Laughter kindled in their eyes and gurgled in their throats as they finished their inspection of each other, but the seriousness of their plight stopped Albert's mirth.

"What shall we do?''he asked. " 'Tis six leagues to the castle, and there is no conveyance. The city swarms with vagrants and cutpurses. We cannot linger in the streets.''

"There is a house I know, an old deserted villa,'' Fulvia replied, "but 'tis said the spirits of the damned dead walk there. Durst enter it?''

"Why not?'' he laughed. " 'Twill be a roof above our heads, and the rabble will keep off for fear of ghosts. As for us, 'tis from the living, not the dead, we need protection.''

Hand in hand they crept through the deserted street till they reached a wicket in a high, blank-faced stone wall. Fulvia pushed and pushed again, but the rusted gate refused to give, and it was not till Albert lent his strength to hers that they managed to bear back the grille.

The garden was a ghost of former glories. Rose bushes, overgrown and weedy, stretched out thorn-clawed arms to hold them back as they passed the broken trellises. The laurel arbor was an almost-submerged island in a rising tide of nettles; grass grew in the graveled paths; the marble statues toppled from their pedestals.

Stumbling through the weed-choked desert, they came at the last to the house door, low and iron-studded. Albert put his shoulder to it, and with a groan as if in protest at the violence, the portal swung back slowly, and a long, dark corridor gaped at them.

Step by cautious step they felt their way along the passageway till they reached a central hall. This was floored with black and white encaustic tiles, but here and there a slab was missing, and the orifices seemed to grin at them like tooth-holes gaping in the jawbones of a skull.

Through a window at the bend of the grand stairway came a pallid shaft of moonlight which stained the dark with a feeble luminance, giving half-seen articles of furniture a dim and ghastly outline more terribly suggestive than Cimmerian blackness.

The very house appeared resentful of their presence. Whispers seemed to follow and shadows flit behind them. Veiled eyes seemed on them constantly. Some-thing evil seemed to stand beside their elbows, watch-ing, invisible . . . waiting.

Albert drew his sword and folded his left arm around Fulvia's shoulders. "Don't let it get you down," he bade; then, as she turned questioning eyes on him: "Be not afraid.'Tis nothing but the dark which daunts us."

Above the stairway were the chambers, and in one of these they found a place for her to rest. It was high-vaulted in the Lombard-Gothic style; the walls were

hung with faded tapestries; medals, statuettes and am-
phoræae stood in dark-wood cabinets. Beneath a silken
canopy, supported by gilt figures carved in olive-wood,
loomed, dimly visible, a mighty bedstead.

With his folded sleeve he brushed the dust from
silken counterpane and pillows; then, as Fulvia sat
upon the piled mattress, he knelt before her and drew
off her shoes. Her feet were just as he had visioned
them, high-instepped, narrow-heeled, white as lilies
and embroidered with a dainty tracery of violet veins.
The nails were filbert-shaped and had the sheen of
nacre. Yielding to temptation past endurance, he
kissed the long straight toes that never had been bent
by rigid shoes, and laid his cheek against the soft, pink
soles.

"Could rest here till eternity is rolled up like a scroll
and feast my heart upon thy worship, sweetest devil,"
the girl whispered, "but thou are languished, and the
day holds much for thee." With a sigh she drew her
feet reluctantly within her robe and stowed her shoes
inside the wide sleeves of her overmantle, then held
her arms up to him. "One kiss, beloved devil, ere we
say good-night," she murmured.

In the chamber next to Fulvia's, Albert fought for
wakefulness. The empty house was charged with menace; he must stay awake to guard her . . . what was
that little bottle she received in the tomb . . . wonder
what the fellows in the trust department would say if
they could see him in this get-up. . . .

A wild, shrill scream, a cry that seemed more filled
with madness than with fright, ripped through the gos-
samer of dream that shrouded him. *Fulvia!*

Sleep-dazed, he stumbled toward the doorway of her
room and kicked the leather curtain from his path.

The chamber blazed with light. A dozen forms as
hideous as the figments of a nightmare gathered round
the girl, who crouched in panic on the floor. Several
of them flourished torches, and in their flare he saw
the sickening horror of them. Some were partly
masked, but where the vizards slipped away he saw

that they were skull-faced—fleshless. Some had lost a hand, and brandished rotting stumps of wrists aloft; one or two danced maniacally upon a single leg, and the air was filled with a foul stench that made his stomach retch.

"The pretty one has come to dwell with us!" they chanted with a skirl of hideous glee. "Clean flesh has come among us—sweet, clean woman-flesh!"

One of them reached out a putrefying stump of hand as if to stroke her cheek, and at the gesture Fulvia groveled on the floor as though she fain would press herself into the tiles, and her scream trailed off to soundlessness with very shrillness.

Here were the "spirits of the damned dead" who walked the ancient villa. Lepers!

Albert charged in silence, lips closed against the nauseating fetor of the room. His sword sheared through the first skull which it struck as though it were a rotten pumpkin, and he wrenched it loose while blood and mangled brains gushed out upon the foul wrappings of the leper's head. Swift as forked lightning, his lunging blade stabbed down two others of the girl's tormenters, and as a fourth one clawed at him with unclean, scale-flecked hands, he dashed the pommel of his weapon straight into the festering face and felt the rotting flesh give way like putrid fruit.

With skirling squeaks, more like the squealing of a rat than any sound from human throat, the ghastly crew dashed from the room, and Albert bent and took the swooning girl into his arms.

Sword poised before him, he marched through the darkened halls until he came upon the entrance they had forced. Kicking the door open he bore her to the laurel arbor and set her gently on the grass.

"Nay, sweetest devil, dearest Fra Diavolo, put me not from out thine arms, I do beseech thee," Fulvia moaned. "Hold me close, my love; clasp me in thy bosom as the husk may hold the fruit till tonight becomes tomorrow. Am terribly afraid."

Dawn was blushing in the east before she slept, and the convent bells had rung for tierce before she woke.

"Good morrow, Fra Diavolo," she smiled up in his eyes; then, suddenly remembering the horror of the night: "Oh, let us go, sweet fiend," she begged. "Am terrified of this unhallowed place. E'en with thee standing guard, it likes me not."

Hand in hand they left the ruined garden of the living dead. The gnomon on the castle sun-dial shadowed III before they reached the drawbridge head. The way across the valley and the heights had been a weary one, and Albert had been forced to carry Fulvia for much of it; for her soft-soled shoes were no protection on the rock-strewn roads, and she wearied quickly in the day's fierce heat. A cotter gave them bread and goat's milk for their noonday meal, and the last three leagues they traveled on a franklin's stoneboat. Everywhere, he noticed, farmerer and peasant, boor and villein greeted Lady Fulvia as though she were a saint come down from Paradise to walk amongst them, and though they looked on him with surly questioning at first, the fact that she was with him seemed to quiet all suspicion.

"There is bed room in the vestry, an thou carest to rest," she told him as they parted by the chapel door. "Sleep well, my sweet *diabolus*. Will see thee at the board."

He found a corded cot hid in an alcove of the vesting-room and a jug of water and a ewer on a bench. Cleansing himself as best he could with this, and wiping on a cotta for want of proper towel, he flung himself upon the bed and slept until a trembling page came tiptoeing to bid him to the banquet board.

A thousand candles made the vaulted banquet hall almost as bright as day, and on the long and narrow tables gleamed horn lanterns and copper lamps and tapers. Laurel branches had been massed about the great high table on the dais where the puissant Count Cristoforo di San Cologero sate in state before the bright-hued Flemish tapestry depicting Lazarus at the gate of Dives, and on the board a fair white cloth was spread; but on the common tables there was room for no such frivolous trappings, for already they were overheaped with food and dishes.

As Count Cristoforo entered, musicians in the minstrels' gallery made harmony with flageolet and hautboy, viol and drum, and as he took his seat a stream of waiters entered from the kitchen. Platters and bowls of larks and lampreys, capons and pheasants, ducks, geese and peacocks, carp, salmon, ox-heads and pig's-heads, calves'-brains, venison and pork, mutton and beef, came in endless order, and comfits, sweetmeats, marchpane, came between. Last of all came wines and possets, and in jugs of earthenware the stronger drinks that stole the wits away and loosed the tongues.

At the center of the table stood a great gilt dish of salt, and just above this they made room for Albert.

Men at arms and gentlemen, scribes and clerks, stewards and intendants with their womanfolk gathered at the common tables, and the noise of laughter, conversation and the gusty appetites they brought to their food was well-nigh deafening. Everyone, it seemed, clerk, guard, steward and lady, talked at the top of his ability. Listeners there were none.

At the table on the dais sate Count Cristoforo, Lady Fulvia, the lord Antonio and a sallow, dark-haired man whose somber fur-trimmed robe, no less than his demeanor of great gravity, labeled him a doctor learnèd in the law.

Christoforo was a mountain of a man. Great-paunched, with three chins folding on his throat beneath his bristling beard, his vein-encrusted cheeks hung down like the dewlaps of a hound, and his pudgy hands, braceleted with rings of fat, were large enough to close around a capon as an ordinary hand might compass a roast pigeon. He laughed much and talked loudly, making up by boisterous gayety for the reticence of his companions.

Fulvia was proud, cold, silent and aloof, eating with

a daintiness which showed small appetite for the rich food the servants brought. Not once did she vouchsafe a glance at her companions.

Antonio wolfed food greedily, but as he ate he never took his burning eyes from Fulvia's profile.

The lawman, as became his dignity, partook of food and drink in learnèd silence, but that he lacked in neither appetite nor thirst was proven by the nimbleness required of the page who served him.

When the feast had lasted some two hours, and the drinking, singing and unseemly jesting had become uproarious, Count Cristoforo rose and beat upon the table with his dagger-hilt.

"My friends," he roared as soon as something like a lull succeeded the wild hubbub, "we are gathered here tonight to drink success unto a union of two branches of our family. This night the lady Fulvia, my niece and ward, becomes affianced bride of Lord Antonio Giovanni di Verniatti, my well-belovèd heir and kinsman. Drink—drink to their bridal, and a long line of descendants to perpetuate our race!"

Fulvia's eyes were on him, cold as inlaid eyes of stone in a face of carven ivory, as he raised the chalice of chased silver brimming with red wine, and drained it at a draft.

He wiped his thick lips on his sleeve and held his cup out for replenishment. "And now a toast to the fair bride-elect, the fairest flower of all Tuscany—" he shouted, but stopped upon a hiccup, and a look of consternation spread across his bloated face. "San Michele!" he cried in a voice gone thin with terror— an absurdly small voice to come from such a barrel of a throat— "I am envenomed!"

He leaned against the table, both hands clasped across his bulging paunch, eyes bulging from his livid face. Great beads of sweat stood out upon his forehead and rolled down his hairy cheeks, his eyes shone with a glassy luster, and his yellow teeth protuded from his writhing lips. A cry, half bellow, half despairing groan, came from his gaping mouth, and he slipped

down to the floor, clutching at the air with distraught
fingers.

"Misericordia!" he shrieked. *"Misericordia, domine!"*

His cries were muted to low muttering groans, and
he sprawled face-downward on the rug-strewn floor,
fingers twitching "Fulvia!" he rolled upon one shoulder, and in his glazing eyes shone realization. "Thou
said'st that God would give me blood to drink when I
flayed Salvatore! Didst thou—didst thou give me—"
With a final tremor he lay still, eyes gazing sightlessly
up at the girl, jaw fallen, swollen, purpled tongue pro-
truding from his mouth.

"Seize that woman!" Like a whip-crack Lord
Antonio's words rang through the room.

Albert leaped up from his seat as a score of guards-
men sprang to do the new count's bidding.

Hursar, the Dalmation he had worsted yesterday,
stood in his path, and he struck out savagely, felt his
fist collide with the man's jaw and saw him stumble
back against the table. By the guardsman's clutching
hand there stood an earthen bowl of half-cooled mutton broth, and with an oath he siezed the vessel and
raised it overhead to hurl its scalding contents into
Albert's face.

Steam was streaming from the bowl. It rose in ever-
thickening clouds, spreading like a mist across the
flickering points of candlelight, blotting out the objects in the room.

Albert spread his hands to sweep the vapor from his
eyes, clutched out blindly, and touched—the edge of
his own pearwood kidney-desk.

Sunlight slanted through the windows with their
hangings of Calcutta print, picking up the muted reds
and blues and ochers of the antique Persian carpet,
bringing out the highlights in his mother's portrait,
framed above the mantel-piece. Five steps it took to
cross between the window and his desk; he had started
from the window when the mist had first seemed to
obscure his eyes as he looked into the little globe . . .

the globe? He glanced down at his hand. There it was, a little sphere of crystal, three inches in diameter; in its center stood a tiny house with grouping, battle-mented towers and a castellated roof. In the back-ground, almost microscopically small, showed the spires and roofs of a walled town.

"Fulvia!" he called. "Where are you, dear? I'm coming . . . they shan't take you . . ."

The mocking, wailing laughter of fire-apparatus si-rens bidding all and sundry clear the way, drifted through the opened windows from the street. Faint, but understandable, a newsboy's hail came through the summer afternoon: "Extry poiper! Read all about that big poison plot!"

He was home; home in New Rochelle. This was the Twentieth Century.

And Fulvia? Fulvia stood surrounded by her ene-mies, separated from him by three thousand miles of ocean and—*seven hundred years!*

"Nonsense, son, it was as plain a case of self-induced hypnosis as I've ever seen! Every favorable element was present—the bright, globular object to concentrate attention, the sun's rays focused by the crystal, the suggestion of a mediæaeval atmosphere by that castle in the ball—everything. Why, you need no further proof than that the whole forty hours com-passed by your dreams were crowded into the little time it took you to walk five steps." Doctor Bain-bridge, plump, florid and white-haired, drew the Rus-sian leather case from the upper left-hand pocket of his white waistcoat, snapped his oxford glasses open, adjusted them with care, and began to scribble a pre-scription.

"Here we are," he announced; "just a little iron, quinine and strychnin. Take it regularly three times every day, and you'll soon be fit again."

"I don't see how it could have been hypnosis, self-induced or otherwise," objected Albert. "Lord knows I've tried to capture it again. I've held the globe ex-actly as I did that afternoon, even timed myself, so the sun would be precisely in the same position, and looked and looked in it, but—nothing's happened. I've got to get back to her, Doctor. I must, I tell you! The memory of her face as those soldiers closed on her, that terrible smile with which Antonio regarded her— they drive me crazy!''

"Easy on, son," soothed the doctor. "I'm not particularly surprised you've not been able to repeat the auto-hypnotism. Things like that are generally accidents. You were ripe for it that afternoon, that's all.

"See here, let's say you're normally not allergic to milk, beef, eggs or beer—most people aren't. But if a proper combination of physical circumstances develops, so that you have what laymen call a bilious condition, any one of 'em will make you sick as a tinker's dog. I've seen you finish four old-fashioneds in a row and never bat an eye; yet you know there are times when a single Scotch and soda seems to go to your head like a stratosphere balloon. It's all a case of physical condition, boy. That afternoon last week you were tired, nervously or physically exhausted, or something you'd eaten for luncheon had failed to digest properly, thus keeping a greater supply of blood than normal in the region of the stomach and intestines and away from the brain—any one or all of a dozen different things might have contributed to put you into exactly the condition necessary for hypnosis to develop.

"Judging from your description, I'd say you suffered from a kind of nightmare under auto-hypnotic anesthesia.''

"But, Doctor," Albert argued, "it can't have been a dream. Dreams, whether we have 'em in sleep or hypnosis, are predicated on our waking knowledge, aren't they? I'm assistant trust officer at the Consolidated; it wouldn't be possible for me, with my background, to dream out the complexities of a television outfit, would it?''

"H'm; hardly," Doctor Bainbridge answered.

"Then," Albert flashed triumphantly, "I couldn't have dreamed this! I've never been to Italy; I knew nothing of Thirteenth Century costumes or customs; I never attended service in a Catholic church, and I surely never saw a leper; yet you tell me everything I described was photographically accurate. How could I possibly have dreamt these things for which I had no apperceptive basis? No, Doctor, it won't do. I'm convinced I've had a vision of the past, perhaps a flash of ancestral memory.

"Psychologists tell us we never really forget anything, that every experience an individual has, from earliest infancy, leaves a complete, detailed and indelible record on his mnemonic apparatus. Something that has happened—some word, some scene—is apparently completely erased from memory; then, years later, maybe, associational paths previously blocked or covered over are suddenly and swiftly cleared, and in an instant that forgotten memory stands out in complete and clear detail. That's so, isn't it?"

"Of course," said Doctor Bainbridge, "but we're talking of the individual, now—"

"Quite so, but if these seemingly impossible flashes of buried memories are observable in individuals, why should it not be possible—certainly, it's no more strain on our credulity to believe it!—that the ancestral experiences of every individual are engraved in detail on his memory, and just as his own experiences can be brought up from the file-rooms of the subconscious, if the proper associational combination can be found, so in a proper case, his ancestral memories may be evoked?

"Let's put it another way: Let's say we're in a rowboat, going down a high-banked, widening river. We're unfamiliar with the stream above the point where we started, the banks and windings shut it from our view. That's the situation of the average man; it was mine until the other day. Now, suppose an aviator comes along, and takes us on his plane. The moment we rise high enough, we have a view of all that portion of the stream we've traveled, and *all that went before,* as well. We're able to see over the barriers of banks and turns, we're in position to—''

"See that part we haven't traveled yet, as well," broke in the doctor with a laugh. "It's an ingenious theory, son, but it's too far-fetched. I know the arguments about ancestral memory, but I've yet to see a demonstration of 'em. Some of our super-physicists contend that since it's light that makes it possible for images to be recorded through the camera of the eye, every action that occurred since time began is photographed on the light-rays, just as if it were imprinted on a film. Then they go a step farther, and assert that once the light-rays bounce off our planet, they continue traveling through interstellar space eternally. According to their theory, then, if one possesses a powerful enough telescope, he only needs to train it off in space to witness the signing of the Declaration of Independence, the destruction of Pompeii and Herculaneum, or the Crucifixion. Ingenious, but nonsensical; utterly nonsensical. We've enough signs and wonders which are scientifically demonstrable without flying off on metaphysical tangents.

"What you need"—his manner dropped informal friendliness and became once more professional—"is more rest and exercise. That job of assistant trust officer in a bank as big as the Consolidated is too great a strain for any kid of thirty-two. Take six months' leave of absence. Get out in the air and think more about your golf and tennis scores and less about estates and wills and trusts. There'll be plenty of time for that when your liver begins to soften and your arteries get hard."

Every afternoon at three Albert stood before his study window with the little globe.

"Fulvia!" he would whisper hoarsely, "I'm trying to come back across the years to you. Help me, dear!"

Monday, Tuesday, Wednesday he strove in desperation to pass the fast-shut gate to yesterday; Thursday, Friday, Saturday he strained in agony against unyielding panels of a door that had no key.

Sunday afternoon it happened.

He had been gazing in the crystal for some twenty minutes when he saw it slowly change in color. Its limpid depths shaded to a bottle-green, then to an intense, opaque blackness, like a lump of polished carbon. An icy wind seemed to be blowing on him. He had that eery, half-numbed feeling which a restless sleeper knows when the pre-dawn cold comes through the opened windows and reaches for him through the blankets with chill fingers. Curiously, he felt light, intangible, imponderable, as though he were a wraith that drifted helpless in the shifting currents of the air.

All was dark about him, dark with the clammy dampness of a long-forgotten, fast-sealed tomb, or the blackness of an oubliette. When he put out his hands to right or left he touched cold, sweat-damped stone, his feet slid over dank, slick tiles; but, strangely, he did not appear to walk; rather, he seemed to float unhindered and unweighted through the gloom.

The clank of iron-shod feet came rattling down the corridor and he saw the bloody stain of torchlight in the darkness as a squad of pikemen bearing flambeaux marched at quick-step through the gloom. By the luminance they brought he could see that the passageway lacked width to let them by, and he shrank against the wall to give them room, but they never slackened step as they approached, nor, though their torchlight must have shone upon him, did any of them vouchsafe any notice of his presence.

"Tramp—tramp—tramp; thump—thump—thump," their armored feet beat on the stones. They were close enough to touch him, they had come abreast of him—they had passed.

They had marched right through him with no greater realization of his presence than if he had been air. And he—he put his hands up to his brow to hold his reeling wits in place—had felt no sense of contact as their bodies passed through his!

Beyond the turn of the black passageway a little rivulet of light flowed out beneath an iron-studded door.

He seized the ring-bolt at its lock in both his hands
and pulled with all his strength, but he might as well
have tugged at the masonry in which the door was set.
Three times he strove to draw the barrier back, then,
exhausted, leaned against it with a sigh of weariness.
It was as if the panels melted at his touch. Without
resistance he walked through the four-inch, iron-
strapped oak planks and found himself in a low chamber.

The room was hung with black; black carpet on the
floor, black tapestries upon the wall. On a dais stood
a long table with a covering of black. Behind the table
sat a row of seven men, all gowned and hooded in
black baize, their somber cloaks and masks seeming
to melt into the black background of the room. The
only spots of color were the shifting pools of bloody
light which flickered from the red-glass lamps upon
the table, and the violet and golden hues of Fulvia's
gown and mantle.

Erect and proud as Sophonisba before Scipio she
faced the masked inquisitors while one read her ac-
cusation from a parchment scroll:

"That the Lady Fulvia Maria Calvia di Gradenigo
did maliciously and wickedly, moved thereto by temptation of the Devil, administer to her kinsman and liege
lord, the might and right worshipful Count Cristoforo
di San Cologero, a poisoned draft distilled by witch-
ery, whereof the mighty and right worshipful Count
Cristoforo aforesaid did die in mortal agony.

"That the Lady Fulvia Maria Calvia di Gradenigo
aforesaid, not having the fear of God before her eyes,
did wickedly, sinfully and iniquitously consort, fore-
gather and cohabit with a demon incubus who had sac-
rilegiously and most impiously assumed the form and
habit of the good and holy Fra Albertus, her chaplain
and confessor . . ."

"What say ye to the crimination, Lady Fulvia?" the
clerk asked when the long list of her evil deeds had
been recited.

A door was lightly opened back of the black tapestry, and Antonio tiptoed softly to the central figure at the table and whispered earnestly into his ear.

The masked inquisitor listened silently, then nodded in assent.

"Lady Fulvia, my cousin and aforetime promised wife," Antonio turned from the hooded judge and smiled at her, "I have prayed this worshipful tribunal to have clemency, and am authorized to tell you that an thou wilt confess thy guilt and spare them the great pain of putting you to torture, thou shalt not suffer pain from either steel or iron, fire or hemp, neither shalt thou be imprisoned long, nor suffer banishment or immolation in a cloister. Dost consent?"

Fulvia raised a creamy shoulder in disdainful shrug. "Why, certes, sith I am condemned aforehand, what boots it if I make acknowledgment?" she answered.

"And when didst thou become aware this demon who assumed a holy form and habit was no man?" the president of the tribunal asked while the scratching of the clerk's quill pen was like the rasping of a file on iron as he wrote the deposition down.

"When I saw him overman the butcher Hursar at the chapel entry I was sure he was not Father Albertino," she replied; "then, when my cousin and affianced husband yonder did force himself into my bower and affront me with foul slanders, this seeming Fra Alberto bade him eat his words, and when he would not, overcame him with as little travail as he were an unbreeched lad."

"In sooth, he did what never natural man hath done," Antonio broke in sneeringly.

"Then, when we were beset by leprous outcasts, he fended me right and worthily, and—"

"And thou didst spend the nighttime in his company, alone?" the president asked. His voice was smooth and deep; kindly, reassuring in its tone.

"Yea—"

"And thou didst give him—"

"Naught by my lips and feet to kiss, I swear it."

"Thy *feet?*"

"Yea, he worshipped me—"

"Enough! Thou madest thyself a queen and goddess among devils! Hast added blasphemy to other crimes. Sign thy confession, harlot!"

The quill pen scratched as she laboriously spelt her name out on the sanded parchment.

"This is thy true and full confession, made of thy free will, without constraint or mental reservation?" asked the president.

"Thou sayest it."

A rustle of black draperies as the hooded arbiters arose and eyed her ominously through the peep-holes of their masks.

"Our sentence, then, is this," the deep voice of the president seemed to swell and fill the little, low-ceiled chamber till the very sable draperies fluttered with its force; "the judgment of this court is that the Lady Fulvia Maria Calvia di Gradenigo be exposed naked in the marketplace and stoned with stones until she dies. Thereafter her body shall be burnt to ashes and those cast in the river, that her sinful flesh may never find a resting-place where Christian dead are buried.

"Look to her, jailer!"

A sable tapestry was swept aside and a door creaked on its unoiled hinges. Half a dozen men at arms marched in and lined themselves each side of Fulvia.

They led her into the adjoining room, where the executioner, arrayed in scarlet hose and doublet, with a scarlet mask across his face, stood with two masked helpers.

They stripped her sumptuous garments off and clothed her in the short, coarse-linen shrift of the condemned. They fastened manacles upon her wrists and gyves upon her tender ankles; last of all they riveted an iron carcanet around her neck and latched an ell-long chain to it. Thus, chained and collared like a savage beast, she stood to wait their pleasure.

"By the belly of Saint Jude," swore Hursar, who was in command of the guards' squad, as Fulvia's creamy body shone with ivory luminance against the murky darkness of the dungeon, "there's a dainty morsel for a lusty man, albeit too frail for much endurance!"

"Hold thy peace, thou hell-born devil's spawn, or by the Mass thou'lt feel the nip of red-hot pincers!" cried the executioner; then, very gently as he took her collar-chain to lead her from the room: "Art ready, lady?"

Tethered by her neck-chain to a ring-bolt in the floor, Fulvia crouched upon the molding, verminous straw which strewed her dungeon. Her shackle was too short to permit her to sit upright, and the heavy bracelets and leg-irons bruised her tender flesh with each attempt at movement. "Ah, Fra Diavolo, dear, dear demon, where art thou now?" she sobbed. "Hast thou, too, deserted me in this dark hour?"

With a strain that seemed to wrench his soul asunder, Albert forced an answer: "I am here, belovèd."

His words were scarcely louder than the whisper of a breeze across a field of standing grain, but she heard them.

"Diabolus?" she called. "Art here, my love? I cannot see thee."

"I cannot see myself," he answered. "I seem discarnate."

"Art—art dead?" she asked. "Do devils die like mortals?"

"Nay, dearest, I am living," he replied, "but—" With an effort like the struggle of a sleeper to shake off the incumbrance of a nightmare, Albert thrust himself toward her. The air seemed almost solid; he had to battle with it as he might have struggled through the breakers when the surf was running high, but by sheer determination he forced himself across the dungeon's filthy floor. And as he fought he felt his strength increasing; by the time he reached her side he had attained a sort of visibility. Faint as a figure on a screen projected by a dull and flickering light he was, but still there was a tiny substance to his shadow, and

when he reached his hands to her she felt them on her
cheeks.

"Ah—ah," her breath came quickly between flut-
tering lips. "I feel thy touch, dear devil! Draw closer,
fold me in thine arms, hold my head against thy heart
and let me dream away that little that is left of life
encompassed by thy love!"

He crouched beside her on the stinking straw and
took her in his spectral arms.

She held her mouth up for his kiss, and though it
was no more than a mere breath of air upon her lips,
she shuddered with delight at it.

"Ah, love, dear love," she whispered, "when first
I brought thee to my bower and looked into thy gentle
eyes, my very heart took flight to thine, like a little
bird that to its nest returns at eventide." And she
twined her arms about him, very gently, lest they break
his shadow-shape, and kissed him on the mouth, the
cheek, the throat, the tonsured head.

And "sweetness of the honeycomb, delight of eyes
and fairest among women," he named her. "Rose of
gold, and tower of ivory, most beautiful of all God's
creatures," and other lover-like endearments he
breathed into her while he fought against the impo-
tency of his unsubstantialness and sought to strain her
to his bosom.

"Hear the singing of my heart, sweet devil," she
commanded, and held his head against the little breasts
that lifted her coarse-linen shrift. "Hearest thou the
tune it sings? Di-abo-lus, di-abo-lus; 'tis thy dear ap-
pellation which it beat since first I saw thee; 'tis thy
sweet name 'twill call tomorrow, when—when—" A
shudder stopped her words, for she was young, and
death was very dreadful.

And Albert kissed her hands, her brow, her neck,
her feet, and last of all her eager, yearning mouth.

"Art thou in hell?" she asked at length, when they
were surfeited with kisses. "Shall I join thee there
tomorrow?"

"Nay, love I do not bide in hell, at least not in the kind thou meanest."

"Where is thy dwelling, then?"

"In a land across the sea which takes its name from famed Atlantis, a land no one now living has yet dreamt of."

"Toward the sinking sun?"

"Yeah, westward; separated from thee by three thousand miles of ocean and a septuple of centuries.

"O, heaven! Time and space alike are barriers between us!" wailed Fulvia. "But love is stronger; love will lead us to each other. Promise thou wilt wait for me, dear devil!"

"Through time and through eternity I'll seek thee," he returned, "and never will I give my love to any other."

So, clasping mouth to mouth and heart to heart, they crouched there on the dungeon's fetid straw till daylight marked a little square of cross-barred luminance against the window.

A great stake had been set up on the execution platform in the marketplace, and to this they conducted her.

As the double file of men at arms tramped from the fortress with the prisoner in their midst the city folk and countrymen fell to their knees and a chant went up to heaven: *"Miserere mei, Domine*—have mercy upon me, O God, after Thy great goodness, according to the multitude of Thy mercies . . ."

The headsman, in red, sleeveless doublet, his face concealed by a red mask, struck the shackles from her hands and feet, but left the iron collar round her neck; for by the chain attached to this she must be tethered to the stake, like a bear chained to its post for baiting.

Kneeling on the stones as he removed the gyves, the fellow mumbled: "It is not I who does this thing to thee, my lady, but the orders of the great ones of the church and state. Prithee, forgive a humble man who does his bounden duty, and remember me when thou comest to thy happy place."

"Nay, dost not know that I am excommunicate?" she smiled upon him sadly. "What service could the prayers of such as I do thee?"

"Natheless, lady, I had rather have thy prayers than the orisons of fifty tonsured priests," he answered. "Sith Holy Mass may not be said for thy repose, the prayers of every humble home throughout the city and the countryside shall rise for thee tonight, and every night thereafter. Pray thou for us sinful men, my lady!"

"Why, then, good boor, I will," she promised. "If it so be that prayers are made in that place where I go, know that mine shall rise for thee."

He pressed the edge of her coarse shrift against his lips, then, since time crowded, took his iron shears and slit the cloth from hem to throat, and with a quick jerk freed her body from it.

She stood exposed before the people in her slender beauty, her slim and boyish thighs, her little breasts that hung like raindrops on a window-pane, and the virginally-low swelling rondure between.

"Take up the stones!" It was Antonio's voice that called the order, but from somewhere in the crowd a counter-order rang:

"He that is without sin among you, let him first cast a stone at her!"

A murmur of assent, low, but ominous and menacing as the rumble of approaching thunder, swelled among the throng, and several of the hardier pushed against the leveled pikes that framed the hollow square about the execution platform.

"Make haste!" Antonio bade. "The louse-bit rabble murmurs. Have done with it!"

Hursar and two others laid their halberds by and swaggered toward the platform.

Now that Death grinned in her eyes her valiant spirit quailed. "Help, Fra Diavolo, pity me!" she cried. "Succor me—"

The impact of a cobble on soft flesh smashed her plea half uttered. Possibly the fellow meant it for a mercy-stroke; more probably his pent-up spite propelled the missile as Hursar hurled a fist-sized stone into her stomach pit.

Her agony was dreadful to behold. Eyes glazed and starting from her face, mouth squared with ghastly pain, she doubled forward as the great stone struck her solar plexus, and her hands beat impotently against the air as she gasped and fought for breath.

The aim of Hursar's fellow was more merciful. Drawing back his hand he hurled a flint which caught her on the temple, cutting through the blue-veined flesh and smashing the thin bone. There was a rattle of the rust chain that held her to the stake, her knees bent flaccidly, and she hung unconscious and inert against the iron collar.

Thud followed thud as stone was hurled. The lovely arms lost shape as their fragile bones were broken by the battering cobblestones. The tapering legs were twisted lengths of formless flesh. In half an hour all was finished, and the sweet white body which was Fulvia had been flailed into a bloody, shapeless mass that bobbed and twitched and bounced grotesquely on its chain as men at arms and some few heartless townsmen tried their aim on it.

Albert struggled like a maniac against the obstacle of formlessness. He tried to shield her body with his own. The stones passed through him without hindrance, nor could he fell their passage. He sought to seize a fallen stone and hurl it at the grinning Hursar or the cold malevolent Antonio. The rubbles might have weighed a ton, for all his puny efforts counted. Strive as he would, he could not budge one from the ground.

At last, by a supreme effort, he managed to grasp one in his clutching fingers. Slowly, while he fought down torturing weariness, he raised it, poised it for the throw, hurled it straight at Hursar.

The force that he expended overbalanced him. He fell face-downward as he flung the missile, struck the ground and lay there panting, sick with effort and exhaustion.

Slowly, lethargically, his eyes opened. He was lying on his study floor. Beside him, smashed to fragments, was the little crystal globe of memories. The gateway to the past was closed irrevocably.

A year of lonely living had wrought great change in Albert Montagu. His curling hair was flecked with gray, at the temples it was white. His face showed lines of suffering, and his eyes were the eyes of one who watches by the corpse of happiness.

Nothing but the fact that he had known the bridegroom since they sported their first knickerbockers had induced him to forsake his hermit-like existence and attend the Trotter-Dorsay wedding. A hundred times he wished he had not come.

The ceremony had been held upon the lawn, and the bridesmaids had been coolly lovely in pale pastels.

Now he stood alone beside a garden hedge, wondering how soon he could depart in decency. The murmur of a girlish conversation did not tend to lessen his discomfort:

"That's Albert Mantagu. Stunning, isn't he, with that thin, stern face and prematurely gray hair? They say he had a disappointment in love and—"

"I saw him get a disappointment when he came," the other girl broke in. "Just as he was getting from his car his hat blew off, and the car behind ran over it. I'll bet he was mad! There's nothing quite as funny as a high hat when it's mashed—"

"Oh, look, there's Anne Bartholomew! Talk about your proud, cold, haughty queens! That girl's Mary Stuart and Medea rolled into one."

Idly, Albert looked across the lawn and felt a sudden tightening in his throat.

Tall, willowy, aloof and proud as Lucifer's half-sister she appeared, but so beautiful that he was fairly breathless at the sight of her. She wore a violet tunic coat of marquisette, and under it a daffodil-hued gown of airy organdy. Her hair was bright as new-strained honey, and her face as pale as Parian marble, save for the scarlet line of pomegranate-red mouth. Beneath long, tapering brows her eyes were clear and blue as August skies; the line of her narrow, arrogant chin was perfect as she turned her face for a moment. The youthfulness of her slight body shone resplendent through her garments, like a pale, hot flame that shines through polished ivory.

"Fulvia!" he choked, and in ten strides had crossed the lawn and stood before the girl.

Anne Bartholomew looked with cool, inquiring eyes at this young man who called her a strange name. Obviously, he was not one of those who had made too many visits to the punch bowl; quite as obviously, he was a gentleman.

"I'm sorry, I don't seem to know you. Have we met before?"

"Seven hundred years ago—"

Her slim, patrician brows arched slightly. He had been drinking, after all.

"Fulvia! You must—you can't say you've forgotten Diabolus—Fra Diavolo . . ."

"Fra Diavolo?" A small frown furrowed her smooth forehead. She hesitated for a moment, and in her eyes there came the look of one who seeks to capture a lost chord of music or a snatch of half-remembered verse. "Diabolus . . . I seem . . . a chapel . . ."

"And Hursar . . . and Antonio!" he added breathlessly.

"A carnival?" Still doubtful, she seemed groping through a buried treasure-house of memory.

"The meeting in the tomb . . . the fight with the *signori di notte* . . ."

"Wasn't there an old house, a deserted mansion?" Something like fear stirred in her calm eyes.

"And that ancient bedroom . . . your little feet . . ."

"A—a stake set up in the town square?" Mounting terror, recollection of a dream so dreadful that it chilled the summer sunshine, swept across her face, but:

"Remember that night in the dungeon, dear," he pleaded. "You said, 'Promise thou wilt wait for me, dear devil,' and—"

"You said, 'Through time and through eternity I'll seek thee, and never will I give my love to any other!' "

"Fulvia!"

"Sweet devil—dearest Fra Diavolo!"

Hand clasped in hand they faced each other, and in their eyes there shone reflection of the breaking dawn in Paradise.

"I say, Montagu, I've found something that belongs to you, and had it mended!" Mr. Trotter, bulging with officiousness and fairly fizzing with champagne, came up to them, a newly ironed silk hat extended in his pudgy, well-kept hand.

But Anne and Albert—Fulvia and Fra Diavolo—took no notice.

They had found something that belonged to them— and it was mended.

SCHOOL FOR THE UNSPEAKABLE

by Manly Wade Wellman

Bart Setwick dropped off the train at Carrington and stood for a moment on the station platform, an honest-faced, well-knit lad in tweeds. This little town and its famous school would be his home for the next eight months; but which way to the school? The sun had set, and he could barely see the shop signs across Carrington's modest main street. He hesitated, and a soft voice spoke at his very elbow:

"Are you for the school?"

Startled, Bart Setwick wheeled. In the gray twilight stood another youth, smiling thinly and waiting as if for an answer. The stranger was all of nineteen years old—that meant maturity to young Setwick, who was fifteen—and his pale face had shrewd lines to it. His tall, shambling body was clad in high-necked jersey and unfashionably tight trousers. Bart Setwick skimmed him with the quick, appraising eye of young America.

"I just got here," he replied. "My name's Setwick."

"Mine's Hoag." Out came a slender hand. Setwick took it and found it froggy-cold, with a suggestion of steel-wire muscles. "Glad to meet you. I came down on the chance someone would drop off the train. Let me give you a lift to the school."

Hoag turned away, felinely light for all his ungainliness, and led his new acquaintance around the corner of the little wooden railway station. Behind the structure, half hidden in its shadow, stood a shabby buggy with a lean bay horse in the shafts.

"Get in," invited Hoag, but Bart Setwick paused for a moment. His generation was not used to such vehicles. Hoag chuckled and said, "Oh, this is only a school wrinkle. We run to funny customs. Get in."

Setwick obeyed. "How about my trunk?"

"Leave it." The taller youth swung himself in beside Setwick and took the reins. "You'll not need it tonight."

He snapped his tongue and the bay horse stirred, drew them around and off down a bush-lined side road. Its hoofbeats were oddly muffled.

They turned a corner, another, and came into open country. The lights of Carrington, newly kindled against the night, hung behind like a constellation settled down to Earth. Setwick felt a hint of chill that did not seem to fit the September evening.

"How far is the school from town?" he asked.

"Four or five miles," Hoag replied in his hushed voice. "That was deliberate on the part of the founders—they wanted to make it hard for the students to get to town for larks. It forced us to dig up our own amusements." The pale face creased in a faint smile, as if this were a pleasantry. "There's just a few of the right sort on hand tonight. By the way, what did you get sent out for?"

Setwick frowned him mystification. "Why, to go to school. Dad sent me."

"But what for? Don't you know that this is a high-class prison prep? Half of us are lunkheads that need poking along, the other half are fellows who got in scandals somewhere else. Like me." Again Hoag smiled.

Setwick began to dislike his companion. They rolled a mile or so in silence before Hoag again asked a question:

"Do you go to church, Setwick?"

The new boy was afraid to appear priggish, and made a careless show with, "Not very often."

"Can you recite anything from the Bible?" Hoag's soft voice took on an anxious tinge.

"Not that I know of."

"Good," was the almost hearty response. "As I was saying, there's only a few of us at the school to-night—only three, to be exact. And we don't like Bible-quoters."

Setwick laughed, trying to appear sage and cynical. "Isn't Satan reputed to quote the Bible to his own——"

"What do you know about Satan?" interrupted Hoag. He turned full on Setwick, studying him with intent, dark eyes. Then as if answering his own question: "Little enough, I'll bet. Would you like to know about him?"

"Sure I would," replied Setwick, wondering what the joke would be.

"I'll teach you after a while," Hoag promised cryptically, and silence fell again.

Half a moon was well up as they came in sight of a dark jumble of buildings.

"Here we are," announced Hoag, and then, throwing back his head, he emitted a wild, wordless howl that made Setwick almost jump out of the buggy. "That's to let the others know we're coming," he explained. "Listen!"

Back came a seeming echo of the howl, shrill, faint and eery. The horse wavered in its muffled trot, and Hoag clucked it back into step. They turned in at a driveway well grown up in weeds, and two minutes more brought them up to the rear of the closest building. It was dim gray in the wash of moonbeams, with blank inky rectangles for windows. Nowhere was there a light, but as the buggy came to a halt Setwick saw a young head pop out of a window on the lower floor.

"Here already, Hoag?" came a high, reedy voice.

"Yes," answered the youth at the reins, "and I've brought a new man with me."

Thrilling a bit to hear himself called a man, Setwick alighted.

"His name's Setwick," went Hoag. "Meet Andoff, Setwick. A great friend of mine."

Andoff flourished a hand in greeting and scrambled out over the window-sill. He was chubby and squat and even paler than Hoag, with a low forehead beneath lank, wet-looking hair, and black eyes set wide apart in a fat, stupid-looking face. His shabby jacket was too tight for him, and beneath worn knickers his legs and feet were bare. He might have been an overgrown thirteen or an undeveloped eighteen.

"Felcher ought to be along in half a second," he volunteered.

"Entertain Setwick while I put up the buggy," Hoag directed him.

Andoff nodded, and Hoag gathered the lines in his hands, but paused for a final word.

"No funny business yet, Andoff," he cautioned seriously. "Setwick, don't let this lard-bladder rag you or tell you wild stories until I come back."

Andoff laughed shrilly. "No, no wild stories," he promised. "You'll do the talking, Hoag."

The buggy trundled away, and Andoff swung his fat, grinning face to the new arrival.

"Here comes Felcher," he announced. "Felcher, meet Setwick."

Another boy had bobbed up, it seemed, from nowhere. Setwick had not seen him come around the corner of the building, or slip out of a door or window. He was probably as old as Hoag, or older, but so small as to be almost a dwarf, and frail to boot. His most notable characteristic was his hairiness. A great mop covered his head, bushed over his neck and ears, and hung unkemptly to his bright, deepset eyes. His lips and cheeks were spread with a rank down, and a curly thatch peeped through the unbuttoned collar of his soiled white shirt. The hand he offered Setwick was almost simian in its shagginess and in the hardness of its palm. Too, it was cold and damp. Setwick remembered the same thing of Hoag's handclasp.

"We're the only ones here so far," Felcher remarked. His voice, surprizingly deep and strong for so small a creature, rang like a great bell.

"Isn't even the head-master here?" inquired Setwick, and at that the other two began to laugh uproariously, Andoff's fife-squeal rendering an obbligato to Felcher's bell-boom. Hoag, returning, asked what the fun was.

"Setwick asks," groaned Felcher, "why the head-master isn't here to welcome him."

More fife-laughter and bell-laughter.

"I doubt if Setwick would think the answer was funny," Hoag commented, and then chuckled softly himself.

Setwick, who had been well brought up, began to grow nettled.

"Tell me about it," he urged, in what he hoped was a bleak tone, "and I'll join your chorus of mirth."

Felcher and Andoff gazed at him with eyes strangely eager and yearning. Then they faced Hoag.

"Let's tell him," they both said at once, but Hoag shook his head.

"Not yet. One thing at a time. Let's have the song first."

They began to sing. The first verse of their offering was obscene, with no pretense of humor to redeem it. Setwick had never been squeamish, but he found himself definitely repelled. The second verse seemed less objectionable, but it hardly made sense:

> All they tried to here
> Now goes untaught.
> Ready, steady, each here,
> Knowledge we sought.
> What they called disaster
> Killed us not, O master!
> Rule us, we beseech here,
> Eye, hand and thought.

It was something like a hymn, Setwick decided; but before what altar would such hymns be sung? Hoag must have read that question in his mind.

"You mentioned Satan in the buggy on the way

out,'' he recalled, his knowing face hanging like a
mask in the half-dimness close to Setwick. ''Well, that
was a Satanist song.''

''It was? Who made it?''

''I did,'' Hoag informed him. ''How do you like
it?''

Setwick made no answer. He tried to sense mockery
in Hoag's voice, but could not find it. ''What,'' he
asked finally, ''does all this Satanist singing have to
do with the headmaster?''

''A lot,'' came back Felcher deeply, and ''A lot,''
squealed Andoff.

Hoag gazed from one of his friends to the others,
and for the first time he smiled broadly. It gave him a
toothy look.

''I believe,'' he ventured quietly but weightily, ''that
we might as well let Setwick in on the secret of our
little circle.''

Here it would begin, the new boy decided—the
school hazing of which he had heard and read so much.
He had anticipated such things with something of excitement, even eagerness, but now he wanted none of
them. He did not like his three companions, and he
did not like the way they approached whatever it was
they intended to do. He moved backward a pace or
two, as if to retreat.

Swift as darting birds, Hoag and Andoff closed in
at either elbow. Their chill hands clutched him and
suddenly he felt light-headed and sick. Things that had
been clear in the moonlight went hazy and distorted.

''Come on and sit down, Setwick,'' invited Hoag,
as though from a great distance. His voice did not
grow loud or harsh, but it embodied real menace. ''Sit
on that window-sill. Or would you like us to carry
you?''

At the moment Setwick wanted only to be free of
their touch, and so he walked unresistingly to the sill
and scrambled up on it. Behind him was the blackness
of an unknown chamber, and at his knees gathered the

three who seemed so eager to tell him their private joke.

"The head-master was a proper churchgoer," began Hoag, as though he were the spokesman for the group. "He didn't have any use for devils or devil-worship. Went on record against them when he addressed us in chapel. That was what started us."

"Right," nodded Andoff, turning up his fat, larval face. "Anything he outlawed, we wanted to do. Isn't that logic?"

"Logic and reason," wound up Felcher. His hairy right hand twiddled on the sill near Setwick's thigh. In the moonlight it looked like a big, nervous spider.

Hoag resumed."I don't know of any prohibition of his it was easier or more fun to break."

Setwick found that his mouth had gone dry. His tongue could barely moisten his lips. "You mean," he said, "that you began to worship devils?"

Hoag nodded happily, like a teacher at an apt pupil. "One vacation I got a book on the cult. The three of us studied it, then began ceremonies. We learned the charms and spells, forward and backward——"

"They're twice as good backward," put in Felcher, and Andoff giggled.

"Have you any idea, Setwick," Hoag almost cooed, "what it was that appeared in our study the first time we burned wine and sulfur, with the proper words spoken over them?"

Setwick did not want to know. He clenched his teeth. "If you're trying to scare me," he managed to growl out, "it certainly isn't going to work."

All three laughed once more, and began to chatter out their protestations of good faith.

"I swear that we're telling the truth, Setwick," Hoag assured him, "Do you want to hear it, or don't you?"

Setwick had very little choice in the matter, and he realized it. "Oh, go ahead," he capitulated, wondering how it would do to crawl backward from the sill into the darkness of the room.

Hoag leaned toward him, with the air as of one confiding. "The head-master caught us. Caught us red-handed."

"Book open, fire burning," chanted Felcher.

"He had something very fine to say about the vengeance of heaven," Hoag went on. "We got to laughing at him. He worked up a frenzy. Finally he tried to take heaven's vengeance into his own hands—tried to visit it on us, in a very primitive way. But it didn't work."

Andoff was laughing immoderately, his fat arms across his bent belly.

"He thought it worked," he supplemented between high gurgles, "but it didn't."

"Nobody could kill us," Felcher added. "Not after the oaths we'd taken, and the promises that had been made us."

"What promises?" demanded Setwick, who was struggling hard not to believe. "Who made you any promises?"

"Those we worshiped," Felcher told him. If he was simulating earnestness, it was a supreme bit of acting. Setwick, realizing this, was more daunted than he cared to show.

"When did all these things happen?" was his next question.

"When?" echoed Hoag. "Oh, years and years ago."

"Years and years ago," repeated Andoff.

"Long before you were born," Felcher assured him.

They were standing close together, their backs to the moon that shone in Setwick's face. He could not see their expressions clearly. But their three voices—Hoag's soft, Felcher's deep and vibrant, Andoff's high and squeaky—were absolutely serious.

"I know what you're arguing within yourself," Hoag announced somewhat smugly. "How can we, who talk about those many past years, seem so young? That calls for an explanation, I'll admit." He paused, as if choosing words. "Time—for us—stands still. It came to a halt on that very night, Setwick; the night our head-master tried to put an end to our worship.''

"And to us,'' smirked the gross-bodied Andoff, with his usual air of self-congratulation at capping one of Hoag's statements.

"The worship goes on,'' pronounced Felcher, in the same chanting manner that he had affected once before. "The worship goes on, and we go on, too.''

"Which brings us to the point,'' Hoag came in briskly. "Do you want to throw in with us, Setwick?— make the fourth of this lively little party?''

"No, I don't'' snapped Setwick vehemently.

They fell silent, and gave back a little—a trio of bizarre silhouettes against the pale moon-glow. Setwick could see the flash of their staring eyes among the shadows of their faces. He knew that he was afraid, but hid his fear. Pluckily he dropped from the sill to the ground. Dew from the grass spattered his sock-clad ankles between oxfords and trouser-cuffs.

"I guess it's my turn to talk,'' he told them levelly. "I'll make it short. I don't like you, nor anything you've said. And I'm getting out of here.''

'We won't let you,'' said Hoag, hushed but emphatic.

"We won't let you,'' murmured Andoff and Felcher together, as though they had rehearsed it a thousand times.

Setwick clenched his fists. His father had taught him to box. He took a quick, smooth stride toward Hoag and hit him hard in the face. Next moment all three had flung themselves upon him. They did not seem to strike or grapple or tug, but he went down under their assault. The shoulders of his tweed coat wallowed in sand, and he smelled crushed weeds. Hoag, on top of him, pinioned his arms with a knee on each biceps. Felcher and Andoff were stooping close.

Glaring up in helpless rage, Setwick knew once and for all that this was no schoolboy prank. Never did practical jokers gather around their victim with such staring, green-gleaming eyes, such drawn jowls, such quivering lips.

Hoag bared white fangs. His pointed tongue quested once over them.

"Knife!" he muttered, and Felcher fumbled in a pocket, then passed him something that sparkled in the moonlight.

Hoag's lean hand reached for it, then whipped back. Hoag had lifted his eyes to something beyond the huddle. He choked and whimpered inarticulately, sprang up from Setwick's laboring chest, and fell back in awkward haste. The others followed his shocked stare, then as suddenly cowered and retreated in turn.

"It's the master!" wailed Andoff.

"Yes," roared a gruff new voice. "Your old head-master—and I've come back to master *you!*"

Rising upon one elbow, the prostrate Setwick saw what they had seen—a tall, thick-bodied figure in a long dark coat, topped with a square, distorted face and a tousle of white locks. Its eyes glittered with their own pale, hard light. As it advanced slowly and heavily it emitted a snigger of murderous joy. Even at first glance Setwick was aware that it cast no shadow.

"I am in time," mouthed the newcomer. "You were going to kill this poor boy."

Hoag had recovered and made a stand. "Kill him?" he quavered, seeming to fawn before the threatening presence. "No. We'd have given him life——"

"You call it life?" trumpeted the long-coated one. "You'd have sucked out his blood to teem your own dead veins, damned him to your filthy condition. But I'm here to prevent you!"

A finger pointed, huge and knuckly, and then came a torrent of language. To the nerve-stunned Setwick it sounded like a bit from the New Testament, or perhaps from the Book of Common Prayer. All at once he remembered Hoag's avowed dislike for such quotations.

His three erstwhile assailants reeled as if before a high wind that chilled or scorched. "No, no! Don't!" they begged wretchedly.

The square old face gaped open and spewed merciless laughter. The knuckly finger traced a cross in the air, and the trio wailed in chorus as though the sign had been drawn upon their flesh with a tongue of flame.

Hoag dropped to his knees. "Don't!" he sobbed.

"I have power," mocked their tormenter. "During years shut up I won it, and now I'll use it." Again a triumphant burst of mirth. "I know you're damned and can't be killed, but you can be tortured! I'll make you crawl like worms before I'm done with you!"

Setwick gained his shaky feet. The long coat and the blocky head leaned toward him.

"Run, you!" dinned a rough roar in his ears. "Get out of here—and thank God for the chance!"

Setwick ran, staggering. He blundered through the weeds of the driveway, gained the road beyond. In the distance gleamed the lights of Carrington. As he turned his face toward them and quickened his pace he began to weep, chokingly, hysterically, exhaustingly.

He did not stop running until he reached the platform in front of the station. A clock across the street struck ten, in a deep voice not unlike Felchers. Setwick breathed deeply, fished out his handkerchief and mopped his face. His hand was quivering like a grass stalk in a breeze.

"Beg pardon!" came a cheery hail. "You must be Setwick."

As once before on this same platform, he whirled around with startled speed. Within touch of him stood a broad-shouldered man of thirty or so, with horn-rimmed spectacles. He wore a neat Norfolk jacket and flannels. A short briar pipe was clamped in a good-humored mouth.

"I'm Collins, one of the masters at the school," he introduced himself. "If you're Setwick, you've had us worried. We expected you on that seven o'clock train, you know. I dropped down to see if I couldn't trace you."

Setwick found a little of his lost wind. "But I've—

been to the school,'' he mumbled protestingly. His hand, still trembling, gestured vaguely along the way he had come.

Collins threw back his head and laughed, then apologized.

''Sorry,'' he said. ''It's no joke if you really had all that walk for nothing. Why, that old place is deserted—used to be a catch-all for incorrigible rich boys. They closed it about fifty years ago, when the head-master went mad and killed three of his pupils. As a matter of coincidence, the master himself died just this afternoon, in the state hospital for the insane.''

SUCH NICE NEIGHBORS
by Chelsea Quinn Yarbro

Pauley liked them at once but Wanda took a while
before she decided that Mister and Missus Thistlewaite were welcome in the house behind theirs. Being
the only children under fifteen for two blocks around,
they were more demanding of the adults in the neighborhood.

"He calls her Pixie," Wanda said in her most con-
demning tone. She looked at her tattered daisy chain
as if the flowers would share her disgust. "And *she*
calls *him* Woozums. I heard her."

"Yech," Pauley declared, filled with six-year-old
scorn. He patted the ground beside the herb garden
and glanced at the fence between the Thistlewaite garden and theirs. "Jeremy said his name is Horace."

"Who'd believe Jeremy?" Wanda asked. She stubbornly disapproved of her new step-father and took
advantage of every opportunity to find him in error.

"Gran called him that, too," Pauley informed her.

Wanda wrinkled her nose. "Oh." Perhaps such a
name could excuse Woozums, she thought.

"Missus Thistlewaite works at the school library,"
Pauley added, parading this intelligence with pride.
He had wandered away from his older sister and now
busied himself among the last of the zucchini plants.

"I know that," Wanda said. She was a lean, coltish
girl, all knees and elbows, with a quick, frowning
glance that unnerved anyone she directed it at them.
Her hair was mouse-blonde and her eyes changed from
olive green to bronze with her moods. She wore faded

301

yellow jeans and a light cotton sweater of a nonde-
script shade of blue.

Pauley was sturdier than his sister, a square-built
little boy with wicker-colored hair and eyes like dutch
chocolates; he had already discovered how useful a
longing gaze could be, especially when Mama said no.
He was dressed in battered and thread-bare corduroy
trousers and a plaid flannel shirt. He pulled two forgotten, desiccated squashes from the vines and looked
at them critically. "Do you think they're going to
stay?"

"They bought the house," Wanda said understanding her brother's question. She had a look of resigna-
tion that was too adult for her features.

"I'd like them to stay. They're funny." He tossed
the withered squashes at Mama's compost heap, and
missed.

"They might move," Wanda suggested, and was
about to go on when the back door opened and a reed-
thin old lady stepped onto the porch.

"Wanda! Paul! It's time for lunch!" She flapped the
end of a dishtowel at them. "Hurry up now!"

"Yes, Gran," Wanda answered for both of them as
she got slowly to her feet and started across the back-
yard. "We were just talking."

Gran held the door for the children, shooing them
inside with an urgency that she did not feel. "There's
soup on the dining room table. Wash your hands before you sit down."

The children trudged off to the bathroom and made
as quick a job of their hands as they could. "I hope
Gran doesn't have that tomato gunk again." Pauley
whispered to his sister as they went into the dining
room.

"Sit down, the both of you," Gran said, taking her
place at the head of the table. As Pauley reached for
his spoon, she cleared her throat and lowered her head
over her bent hands. "Dear Lord, fill our hearts with
gratitude for Thy bounty, and remind us of Thy Mercy
when we are in the depth of sin. Amen."

''Amen,'' the two echoed impatiently

''Now, Paul, don't grab. There's plenty of crackers for both of you,'' Gran said as she poured herself some tea from the old crockery pot she had since she was a bride. ''I don't want to have to tell you more than once.''

''Gran, can you excuse me a minute?'' Wanda asked as she got to her feet, ''I've got to go to the bathroom.''

''Your mother should be willing to give you more time, to guide your steps properly,'' Gran said, waving to Wanda.

''Mama has to work,'' Pauley said brusquely. He kept doggedly at the tomato soup, hating the taste of it.

''It isn't a good arrangement. Women need to look after their families.''

Pauley said nothing. He held the spoon on his mouth, turned over so that it fit his tongue. He did his best not to look angry, but his deep brown eyes were hot as charring wood.

In the bathroom, Wanda took as long as possible on the toilet, and then washed her hands twice. She stared at herself in the mirror, trying to see what it was that so irritated Gran. She could not puzzle it out. She opened her mouth and looked at her teeth—no braces needed, luckily—champing them together a couple of times while making faces like fighting cats. When she could think of nothing else to do, she reluctantly returned to the dining room.

''Did you rinse out the sink?'' Gran asked

''Of *course*,'' Wanda answered with the appearance of meekness.

''Then finish your soup before it gets cold. You need the heat in weather like this.'' Gran reached over and patted Wanda's arm with a hand as light and brittle as twigs. ''When you're finished, I want both of you to lie down for an hour.''

''Aw, Gran,'' Pauley protested.

"Let's have none of that, young man. Children need to rest." With that horrible pronouncement, Gran got up from the table and returned to the kitchen to get two cups of hot chocolate that they were allowed every day. Gran's narrow mouth pursed in disapproval at this indulgence, but she was able to stretch her lips in a smile as she came back to the children.

PART II

I wonder what we could do to her?"

Wanda asked Pauley a few days later while they turned over rocks in the garden, looking for beetles and salamanders.

"To Missus Thistlewaite?" Pauley said in surprise.

"No, silly; to Gran." She grunted as she tried to work an ancient brick out of the ground.

"What's that?" Pauley wanted to know as the brick finally moved.

"What?" Wanda said, putting the brick aside.

"That." Pauley pointed to the strange thing that had been covered by the brick.

Wanda could not bring herself to touch it. "I don't know. It kinda looks like something dead."

Pauley poked at it with the popsicle stick he had been using for a prod on the black, stinky beetles. "It has something tied around it."

"Don't touch it," Wanda told him, "it's icky."

For once Pauley ignored his sister's order. With care he lifted it with the stick. "Look at that," he whispered, shoving the thing toward Wanda.

"Get it away!" She batted out with her hand, taking care not to let her fingers get too near their discovery.

"It's got a dead mouse in a little skirt." He giggled. "It looks like Gran, doesn't it?"

"Oh, Pauley," Wanda said, making a face. "It's just a dead mouse. Put it back."

"A dead mouse in a skirt. With hair on its head. Look; see that? Grey hair."

"Just drop it," Wanda insisted. "Go on. Right

now." She held the brick up, ready to clap it back into place.

"Okay, okay," Pauley agreed with obvious disappointment. "But who would want to make a thing like that?

"It isn't a thing. It's a dead mouse." Wanda had heard all she wanted to on the subject. "Come on. Let's see if there are any salamanders in the Thistlewaites' garden."

She started off at once toward the narrow gap in the fence that gave them access to the other yard.

Pauley followed along but with less enthusiasm. "I think somebody did it on purpose."

"Pauley!" Wanda threatened.

He scampered up behind her, jabbed her in the ribs with his fingers, then hooted with laughter as she shrieked and doubled over. "Wanda's got a tickle, Wanda's got a tickle."

"I'll tickle you," she vowed, and ran after him.

He got through the fence just ahead of her, breathless with mirth and panic. "You won't get me," he cried out, more in hope than certainty. "I'll get away." The sight of Wanda's arm coming through the gap made him sprint across the close-mowed lawn, watching over his shoulder for Wanda.

"Well, what have we here?" Moira Thistlewaite caroled in the voice she reserved for rambunctuous children.

Pauley stopped dead, flushing deeply. "I . . . uh . . ."

"Why, Paul how good to see you. And Wanda too," she went on as Pauley's sister careened into view. "I was wondering when you would come to see me."

"H'llo, Missus Thistlewaite," Wanda murmured, her ire leaving her completely."

"I'll bet you found that place in the fence, didn't you?" Moira Thistlewaite said with tremendous good humor. "Why, I told Mister Thistlewaite the other day that it would be such a nice surprise if you'd come for a visit.''

The two children exchanged glances. Neither one of them knew how to respond to this short, big-bosomed lady who smelled of a pungent fragrance and wore purple dresses. "Uh . . . Gran doesn't know we're here.''

"Well, then I won't keep you too long. I don't want her to worry about you.'' She reached down and put her hand on his shoulder. "Would you like to have . . . some nice hot cider?'' She looked expectantly from Pauley to Wanda. "It won't take a minute.''

"Oh . . .'' Pauley turned his big chocolate eyes up at her, paying no attention to Wanda's scowl.

"That's fine,'' Moira Thistlewaite said. 'Just follow me. The kitchen is through this door.'' She held it open for the two children, then hurried ahead of them. Her walk was light and springy, almost like a kid's walk. She stepped through the pantry door and pointed to the round oaken table near the tall windows. "You two have a seat there. It won't take me a minute to get the cider ready.'' She smiled again and bustled toward the stove, reaching for one of the copper pots that hung from the cast-iron rack over her head. "I can't tell you how pleased I am that you came to see me.''

Pauley looked at Wanda, hoping to get some idea from his sister of what they should do, but Wanda was frowning at the woven red placements and had nothing to say.

"Do you like a little extra cinnamon?'' Moira Thistlewaite asked as she poured cider from a large glass jug into the pot. "I always like a little extra cinnamon. There's something special about cinnamon, don't you think?''

"Sure; I like it,'' Pauley said, bewildered.

"The Egyptians used it in embalming and for magic, and the incense that . . .'' She turned and smiled. "That's a librarian for you—I bring the library home in my head.'' She gave her attention to the spice shelf. "Cinnamon, alspice, cloves, mace and nutmeg.

They're the same spice, of course, just that one is outside and the other is inside. The mace is the outside. The old herbalists used to make a liniment of ground mace for rheumatism that they claimed worked wonders.'' She took a large wooden spoon and began to stir the cider. "There I go again. Mister Thistlewaite says that I'm a walking encyclopedia. It's just a habit from the library and the kids.''

"You're at Thomas Paine, aren't you?'' Wanda asked suspiciously.

"Why, yes. It's a very pleasant school, with the teachers and students so curious.'' She bent over the pot and sniffed, though it was hardly necessary; the kitchen was redolent.

"My friend Emily goes there,'' Wanda volunteered.

"Emily?'' Moira Thistlewaite repeated.

"Emily Franklin,'' Wanda supplied.

"Oh, yes. She lives three blocks away, I believe, on Webster or Oak.'' She waved her spoon in the air, then looked about. "Let me see. I think this would be better in mugs. Soup mugs, so that you will have enough and I won't be tempted to drink the left-overs before Mister Thistlewaite gets home.'' For a moment she dithered, then went to one of the cupboards and opened it. Hanging on the inside of the door were a dozen large mugs. "The orange ones go so well with the kitchen, with the brick and all, and it *is* that time of year.'' She pulled three of the mugs off their hooks. "Wait a little longer now, and this will be ready.''

"Do you have any cookies?'' Pauley asked, pretending not to hear Wanda's disapproving hiss.

"Well, not cookies, but I do have some dried fruit— nice apricots and pears. You'll like them.'' She brought the filled mugs to the table, taking care not to spill the cider as she set them down. "I've left one stick of cinnamon in each mug.''

"It looks real nice,'' Pauley said.

"Why thank you, Paul,'' Moira Thistlewaite said. "Now, just give me a second, and I'll get some dried apricots for you." She went back to the pantry and returned with a pottery bowl. "There. Now you don't need to be shy; we're neighbors."

Pauley looked at the dried fruit, not sure what to make of it. "Gran doesn't give us anything but cookies."

"I'm surprised at her," Moira Thistlewaite said as she took her place at the table. "All those additives and that extra sugar. It really isn't good for you. She ought to read up on it, to find what goes into cookies."

"She makes them herself," Wanda announced, although it was not entirely true.

Moira Thistlewaite nodded. "That is the better way. But still, there is so much sugar. It is much better to have natural foods in our bodies. I noticed that your mother has a vegetable garden. I would have thought that she . . ." She paused, biting her lip. "Oh, dear. There I go again, butting in where I have no business intruding." She looked closely at her two guests. "You go to Florence Talley, don't you?"

"Yes," Wanda said, lifting her mug and tasting the cider.

"Yes," Moira Thistlewaite agreed. "That's the oldest school in the county, you know. Florence Talley willed the land and her enormous old house to be used for a school way back in eighteen-oh-nine. There were some hard feelings about giving it her name, back then. She was not well-liked in the community."

"Why?" Pauley asked innocently. From all he had been told at school, the lady it was named after had been a rich old woman without any kids of her own.

"Well, there were all those rumors about her, and some the local officials—ministers, for the most part— thought that it would be better if she was forgotten. But one of the conditions of the will was that the school be named after her, and since they really did need the school there was nothing to be done." She tasted her own cider, watching the children.

"What did she do?" Pauley asked, as he was expected to.

"That depends on whom you believe," their neighbor answered. "You know how unreasonable and superstitious people can . . . could be. Some said that she was a witch and that her brother, who had disappeared many years before she died, was a warlock, and they had practiced witchcraft and deviltry together." Moira Thistlewaite laughed. "You can imagine how upset that made some of the people."

"Was it true?" Wanda asked, her cider half-finished.

"What's a warlock?" Pauley wanted to know.

Moira Thistlewaite answered his question first. "A warlock is a leader of witches, a powerful man who is said to be able to summon devils and control spirits." She lifted her mug. "There are many books about them, most of them complete rot."

"Was it true?" Wanda repeated.

"Who knows? Gossip always exaggerates, you must know that by now. So it may be that Florence Talley and her brother went in for spiritualism or some other esoteric thing . . . astrology, crystal-gazing—that's called scrying—or other things, and people in town disapproved. According to the records we have, Miss Talley's brother was a very handsome man who . . . was not always well-behaved. Not that anyone would notice today, but back then, he was considered quite a rake."

"A rake?" Pauley echoed. "Why would they think that?" He tried to picture a man compared to the rake in the garden, and it made no sense.

"That means a man who isn't very moral and whose conduct is outrageous," Moira Thistlewaite explained. "He drank and wenched—chased girls—and was always up to something. Naturally it was easy for the townspeople to disapprove of him. He never married, and neither did his sister, which was unusual then. But since they had money, the town fathers could not afford to fight with them.'' She leaned back. ''Goodness. I didn't mean to go on like this. It's so close to All Hallows that we've been having many questions from students, for papers and all, about witches and the rest of it.''

''Yeah. Missus Anderson's been talking about it,'' Wanda said, turning to face Moira Thistlewaite. ''She said that there used to be a lot of witches around here.''

''Well, that was what people believe. Certainly it seems that there were a number of herbalists and other similar sorts of people.'' She got up from the table.

''And warlocks, too?'' Pauley asked. He had helped himself to half a dozen dried apricots and was stuffing a few of them into his pockets.

Moira Thistlewaite considered briefly. ''There are very few warlocks, according to the tradition. Each coven, or group of witches, has only one warlock.'' She hesitated, then went on. ''The library has some books on it, about the Sabbats and the rest of it.'' She coughed delicately. ''The Sabbats were the festivals of the witches, like the Christian Holy Days.''

''Oh,'' said Wanda. She drank the rest of her cider. ''What did they do?'' The image of the mouse under the brick came back to her. ''Awful things?''

''That depends upon which report you decide is correct,'' Moira Thistlewaite said, then looked at Pauley. ''I do rattle on, don't I? My husband tells me that he can't get a word in edgewise. I think it must be all those hours I spend in the library, where I have to be quiet. I have all this information around me, and I reach a point where I have to talk about it or burst.'' She laughed again, more heartily. ''It must seem silly to you, but when you reach my age, the world looks different.''

Wanda sighed, anticipating the sort of lecture Gran gave her all the time. Those lectures inevitably began with some reference to age. ''We . . . shouldn't stay too long, Missus Thistlewaite,''

''The apricots are real good,'' Pauley said, thinking

to delay their departure, though he recognized the tone in his sister's voice.

"Well, you can come back another day and have more of them. If we were going to be in on Hallowe'en, I'd give them out for tricks-or-treats." She got back to her feet, smiling at the children. "Don't wait to be invited back. You're welcome at any time." She pointed toward the pantry. "You know how to go out, don't you? I have a few calls I really must make. I'm simply delighted that you came to see me."

"It was good cider," Wanda admitted, leading her brother toward the back door. She was afraid that Gran would be mad at them for being gone so long.

That was the least of it. Gran told Pauley and Wanda that they had been rude to go into Missus Thistlewaite's garden that way, and even worse for accepting her hospitality. "What your mother will have to say about this," she ended shaking her head, "I can't imagine."

PART III

"It's bad enough your mother preaching her claptrap at them," Jeremy was saying to Pauley and Wanda's mother late that night as they lay in bed. "Now the neighbors are filling their heads with Sabbats and warlocks."

Pauley, sitting in the hall outside the bedroom, looked over his shoulder at Wanda. She lifted her finger to her lips, signaling him to be silent.

"Don't carry on this way, Jeremy," their mother countered, her voice light and teasing. "You're worrying about nothing. Kids are always hearing about goblins at this time of year."

"Goblins aren't the same thing as warlocks," Jeremy said, but he sounded less irritated.

"Naturally," she said, ending with a sound like a purr. "But they don't know that."

"I suppose you're right," Jeremy said softly.

"He's giving in," Pauley whispered. "Listen to him."

"Shush," Wanda warned.

"If you like, I'll talk to Mother again, and tell her we don't want her giving the kids religious instruction. She's likely to be upset, but I'll do whatever you want."

There was a long, moist silence, then Jeremy spoke again. "The trouble with Agnes is that she is so rigid in her beliefs. I wouldn't mind so much having her here if she just didn't preach all the time."

"It's her generation. Mother was raised like that." She whispered something more that neither child could hear, then said, more loudly, "So it didn't take with me, and it won't take with my kids."

"And what if they start asking questions about witches the way they asked questions about what Agnes has been telling them about burning in hell?" Some of the harshness was back in his voice, but not as severely as before.

"If they start asking questions, we'll discuss it, just the way we did about mother's religion. That's all." The silence this time was longer, and there was a slither of sheets to fill it.

"C'me on," Wanda whispered, pulling on the sleeve of Pauley's pj's.

"Not yet," he argued, holding his place in the shadow of the door.

"They're just making love," Wanda told him.

"I know. But they might talk." He folded his arms and kept listening.

"You're looking good, Camille," Jeremy said, his voice now soft and growly.

"Oh, boy," Pauley said, giving up in disappointment following his sister back down the hall and into her room.

"Grown-ups are a pain," Wanda announced as she closed her door so that she and Pauley could talk.

"Mama likes him, Wanda. You can't expect her to

be mean to him.'' He got on the foot of her bed and crossed his legs.

''He's icky,'' Wanda said, dismissing him as she sat on her pillow, her sheets pulled up to her knees.

Pauley shrugged. ''Do you think Gran will stop preaching?''

''No,'' Wanda said, not needing to think about it. ''She'll do more of it, the way she did the last time Mama had a talk with her. She'll tell us that it's her duty to bring us back from the path of sin. You know the way she goes on when she gets like that.''

''Do we have to listen?'' Pauley said, dejected.

''Of course not,'' Wanda told him. ''It's all silly, all of it.'' She leaned back against her headboard. ''Who cares about it, anyway.''

''Jeremy gets mad at Gran,'' Pauley pointed out.

''He likes getting mad at Gran,'' Wanda accused. ''He wants to have Mama all to himself. That's what he wants.''

''Not instead of us,'' Pauley argued, but with less certainty than before.

''Daddy didn't want us. He moved all the way to Alaska to get away.'' She lowered her head. ''Maybe we should just go away. Just you and me.''

''Hey, Wanda,'' Pauley said, nervously trying to reassure her.

''Or maybe the Thistlewaites would let us stay there for a while. That way Mama and Gran wouldn't argue about us.'' She clutched at her elbows.

''I thought you didn't like the Thistlewaites,'' Pauley said, unable to follow everything his sister said.

They're not too bad. *She's* not too bad, anyway. She liked having us at her house. Jeremy doesn't like having us here.'' Wanda sobbed once, then choked back her tears. ''It's no fun when he starts in on Mama.''

''Yeah, but that's cause he's trying to fit in. Gran said so, and Mama told me that he doesn't know that much about kids. We don't have to go yet, do we, Wanda? Can't we stay here for the time being?'' He was alarmed by the finality he heard in Wanda's tone. "Wanda, do we have to go?"

"Maybe not yet," she replied miserably.

"Maybe we could wait a while, until after Christmas. I don't want to miss my presents. Mama said she'd get me a bike," He leaned forward, trying to say the right thing. "You know how much of a fuss Mama makes about Christmas."

"She likes the tree," Wanda said, sniffing. "She likes hanging all those things on it."

"She likes the presents, too. She likes all the parties. You remember that she's going to a big party on Hallowe'en. Gran said that it was wrong and pagan to do that, but you know how Gran is about parties." He peered through the dark to see if Wanda was listening to him. "Gran would miss us, and Mama, too."

"Maybe," Wanda allowed. She wiped her hand over her face, spreading the tears.

"Don't worry about it," Pauley said, using the same phrase that their mother used when she was under pressure.

"I won't," Wanda said, "But it's awful sometimes."

"It'll be okay. You wait until Hallowe'en, and you'll see how much fun we can have. We can put soap in Jeremy's socks."

This made Wanda smile. "And toothpaste in his shaving things."

Pauley was filled with relief. "Yeah. And a dead mouse under his pillow." As soon as the words were out, he knew he had made a mistake. "Hey, I didn't mean that, Wanda. Forget the dead mouse, okay?" He tried to grab her arm, but she pulled away from him.

"It's still there. I looked. It's worse." She slid down into her bed, her face pressed against the pillow. "It stinks."

"But it's only a mouse," Pauley protested.

"With a skirt and hair and all of that. It's more than a mouse. It's supposed to be more than a mouse." She thumped her pillow with her hand. "Go to bed, Pauley."

"But . . ." He stood up, watching her in dismay.

"Go to bed." She would not look at him as he left her room.

PART IV

"It's no trouble at all," Moira Thistlewaite told Wanda's and Pauley's mother the day before Hallowe'en. "I'd love to have them with me for a little while."

"Thanks," Camille said with a hectic flash of a smile. "With Mother ill like this . . ."

"How is she doing?" She held the back door open wider and beamed down at the children. "You know where the kitchen is. Why don't you go and have a seat at the table. I'll be along in a minute." She gave her attention to their mother as the two youngsters did as she suggested, lingering just long enough to hear a few more words.

"They're doing tests today, but they say it doesn't look good. She's old, that's part of the problem, and they really don't know what's wrong." Camille shook herself. "I'm grateful you're willing to take them on such short notice."

"Don't be silly," Moira Thistlewaite said. "You go along and visit your mother. Strange, how she was taken suddenly like that."

"Yes," Camille said. "She claims she had no warning. One minute she was fine and the next she was in dreadful pain. I don't know what could have happened."

"Let the doctors figure it out," Moira Thistlewaite said, then motioned to Camille to keep her voice down. "They're listening, poor children. I suppose you can't blame them."

Camille flushed. "I'll call you later. When there aren't so many little ears around."

"They're whispering again." Wanda sighed. She

was picking at the edge of the woven placemat. "They want us to think Gran's okay."

"She might be," Pauley said, his eyes glowing with hope. "She said she'd be home in no time at all."

"But she doesn't know," Wanda said, her mouth turning down.

Moira Thistlewaite came back into her kitchen. "So you're here again. Let's go into the living room for a little while, until my husband gets home. You can help me put the candle in the jack-o'lanterns in the windows. How does that sound?"

"Sure," Pauley answered listlessly.

"Okay," Wanda said, getting out of her chair. "It should be fun."

The living room was large and dark-paneled with several old-fashioned lamps in sconces bracketted to the walls. The furniture was a reasonable compromise between comfort and formality, most of it upholstered in muted oranges and earth tones.

"There are candles in that cupboard over there," Moira Thistlewaite said, pointing across the room to some glass-fronted doors. "If you'll get them out for me, I'd appreciate it."

"The candles are black," Wanda said as she obeyed.

"Yes; for Hallowe'en," she said to the children. "Black and orange are the Hallowe'en colors, aren't they?"

"We did cut-outs of pumpkins at school," Pauley ventured, making it seem that this was remarkable. "We did cats and witches and kettles and everything."

"There are decorations at Thomas Paine, too," Moira Thistlewaite said, joining in the spirit of the occasion. "There was a contest to see who could do the scariest drawing. The judging will be tomorrow, after the students show off their costumes."

"We aren't allowed to wear costumes at Florence Talley," Wanda complained. "We asked."

"Well, there must be a good reason for that." Moira Thistlewaite went to her front porch and opened her

door. "Let me get the jack-o'lanterns. It will be only
a moment."

"What do you think of these black candles?" Wanda
asked her brother softly. "They're awfully thick and
greasy."

"Maybe they got them from a witch," Pauley suggested with a grin.

"That would be stupid," Wanda declared, but she
touched the dark wax reluctantly.

Your step-father will be here later," Moira Thistlewaite informed her as she came back into the living
room. She held five jack-o'lanterns awkwardly in her
arms, and almost dropped them before Pauley reached
her to grab a few. "Why, thank you, Paul," she said
a little breathlessly. "You see, there is one for each
window in the front of the house. Three downstairs
and two upstairs."

"Aren't you going to be gone?" Wanda asked.

"Yes, but that doesn't mean we can't add to the
occasion. The children appreciate it when they come
looking for treats." The last of the carved pumpkins
was set on the floor.

"Who did these?" Pauley wondered as he went from
one to another of them.

"Oh! My husband did them. They're quite original,
don't you think." Moira Thistlewaite leaned down and
patted the most hideous face. The carved features were
distorted and agonized as if the large pumpkin was
suffering unspeakable torments. The face beside that
was filled with malicious glee. "He's a very talented
man. He does other things—you know, little presents
and such—that are really marvelous."

Pauley and Wanda looked at each other, knowing
that once adults started to go on about people they
liked, it could get embarrassing.

"Are they all like this?" Wanda asked, trying to
shift the subject.

"See for yourself." She went from one jack-
o'lantern to the other, turning each of them toward the

children. One of the three remaining was frozen in
open-mouthed fury, one was consumed with grief and
despair, and the last was so contemptuous, so de-
monic, that Pauley hesitated to touch it, thinking that
it might do something to him.

"Well, you won't get many trick-or-treaters with
things like these in the windows," Wanda said; it was
the only thing that she felt was both true and polite.

"Mister Thistlewaite has a taste for the outer,"
Moira Thistlewaite said. Triumphantly she took the top
off one of them. "Now, if you'll bring me a candle,
we can set it in place."

Neither Pauley nor Wanda was in a hurry to touch
the candles or the pumpkins, but finally they set about
the chore, each of them trying not to look at the faces
or handle the greasy black candles for too long.

"There, now they're ready to put into place," Moira
Thistlewaite exclaimed. She had picked up the suffering one when the door opened and Horace Thistlewaite came in.

He was small and surprisingly dapper given rotund
build, like a beer-drinking gnome in a pin-stripe suit.
He grinned at his wife and then looked at Wanda and
Pauley. "Gracious, what have we here? Is Hallowe'en
early this year?"

"These are Paul and Wanda, from the house behind
ours. Their grandmother is in the hospital and I told
their mother that we'd look after them until their . . .
step-father comes for them." It was only when Moira
Thistlewaite stood next to her husband that it was possible to see that she was actually quite slight; the rest
of the time her large bust made her appear bulkier than
she was.

"That would be Jeremy?" Mister Thistlewaite
asked.

"Yes; Jeremy," Missus Thistlewaite said with a
quick look at Pauley and Wanda. "Camille is at the
hospital now and she doesn't know how long she'll
have to stay there."

Wanda made a sound like a cough, and touched Pauley's hand. She rarely did such things and it surprised her as much as it did him. "Gran got sick," she said.

"So your mother told me," Missus Thistlewaite said. "You must be concerned about her. She's taken care of you for some time, hasn't she?"

"Since Daddy went to Alaska," Wanda said, her mouth becoming a thin line. "Gran came then."

"Well, I'm sure you hope that she gets better soon," Mister Thistlewaite said, then looked at his wife. "Tell me, Pixie, are we having dinner in, or are we taking our little guests out?"

"Geez," Pauley groaned in an undervoice.

Moira Thistlewaite clasped her hands under her bosom. "I thought that since we don't know when their step-father will be here for them, it would be best to eat in. Nothing very fancy, just some good, simple food."

Mister Thistlewaite leaned over and kissed her cheek. "And tasty; very tasty."

"Oh, you," Moira Thistlewaite shrilled. She gave him a gentle push. "We have guests to think of," she said, nodding toward the children. "What would you like to eat?"

"Hamburgers?" Pauley suggested.

"What about a nice quiche?" Moira Thistlewaite offered. "And a big salad, and then some very special ice cream for desert?"

Pauley didn't know what a quiche was, but he didn't like the sound of it. "Well . . ."

"It's delicious," Horace Thistlewaite promised both of them. "You'll like it. It's like a custard pie, but not sweet."

Wanda shrugged. "We'll try it. Thank you." Gran would have been proud of her, she knew.

"Fine, fine, I tell you what, Pixie: you go into the kitchen and get dinner started, and these two guests and I will put the jack-o'lanterns into their windows. How would you like that?"

"Okay," Pauley muttered.

"That's okay," Wanda said, able to sound a bit more enthusiastic.

"Marvelous," Mister Thistlewaite said, rubbing his hands together. "Off you go, Pixie. We'll handle everything here."

Moira Thistlewaite did as he told her, waving to him as she reached the door between the dining room and the kitchen.

"I see you've got them all ready to go into place. Good for you." Horace Thistlewaite picked up the jack-o'lantern that his wife had set down. "This one goes downstairs—what do you think?"

"Yeah," Pauley said when Wanda did not answer.

"I think it turned out very well, don't you? Not like all those other comic book faces on the block." He patted the ghastly carving with affection.

"You're right," Wanda brought herself to say.

"Fine. This one, then, and what about this one for the living room window?" He touched the angry one with his toe.

"Great," said Pauley tonelessly.

Horace Thistlewaite made quite a ceremony of putting the jack-o'lanterns in place, and the better part of an hour had been used up by the time he permitted the children to go to the bathroom to wash up.

"They're icky," Wanda said, soaping her hands with unusual thoroughness.

"Sure are," Pauley said. "And all that stuff about festivals and witches and the rest of it." He wiped his hands on the towel as if he wanted to rub off the skin. "That great master he kept talking about. That wasn't real, was it?"

" 'Course not," Wanda said uncertainly.

"I hope Jeremy gets here soon." He opened the bathroom door.

"Me, too." She followed him to the dining room where everything was ready for them except the meal.

"I made you a nice, hot drink, so that you can have something while we have our drinks," Moira Thistlewaite said, offering each of them a fragrant, steaming mug.

"What is it?" Pauley asked.

"A secret. It has all sorts of good things in it. Taste it. You'll see." She smiled, apparently unaware of his suspicions, and waited for him to take the mug.

Wanda was slower to accept. "It's funny-colored," she remarked.

"Some infusions are," Moira Thistlewaite declared. "They're very difficult to make."

"It's pretty good," Pauley told Wanda when he took his first sip. "Kinda like those raspberry vine things you get at the movies."

"Really?" Wanda loved raspberry vines. She took the mug.

Another mug of the hot liquid was served with dinner, while the Thistlewaites drank wine. By that time, both Wanda and Pauley had grown used to the taste and did not mind it; in fact, they both preferred it to the quiche that Moira Thistlewaite gave them.

While Moira Thistlewaite was in the kitchen, the phone rang and Horace Thistlewaite hurried to answer it. He returned after a brief, inaudible conversation, to tell the two children, "That was Jeremy. He's going to be a bit later than he planned. He didn't want you to worry."

"Is he at the hospital?" Wanda asked.

"Yes. I'm sorry, but it isn't going well with your grandmother and your mother is making arrangements to spend the night there, in case she's needed." His face grew long and serious. "Your mother is very upset. You understand that."

"Yes," Wanda said for both of them.

"I told Jeremy that any time he or she needs to send you to us while . . . this is going on, then he should feel free to do so. We want you to know that you're welcome here at any time, but especially now."

"Is Gran gonna die?" Pauley asked, putting his hand to his mouth as soon as the words were spoken.

"We're all going to die," Mister Thistlewaite said slowly, "She's very ill, and she is elderly. Your mother is very concerned about her. You will have to be as patient as you can with her now, because of what has happened." He pulled out his chair and sat down again. "Pixie! Make those ice creams good sized for our company. They need something nice."

Moira Thistlewaite was full of sympathy as she bustled into the dining room with two large pottery bowls heaped with dark-colored ice cream. There was a butterscotch type of topping on the generous servings. "It's so sad about your grandmother. She's been very good to you, and you must be worried for her. Well, have some ice cream."

"Is this chocolate?" Pauley asked, pressing his spoon into the ice cream.

"Well, it tastes like chocolate. It's carob and a few other ingredients. The butterscotch is made a special way, too." She waited while Pauley and Wanda took first bites. "How is it?"

"Good."

"Fine."

"Wonderful. Now I'll go and get Woo . . . my husband's and my desserts." She started toward the kitchen again.

"Aren't you having any of this?" Wanda asked.

"Dear me, no," Moira Thistlewaite laughed. "If I ate that much ice cream, I'd be the size of a house. We're going out tomorrow night, and I'll be evil then, but not now." She was back in a few moments with a plate of cheese and sliced fruit.

Not long after dinner, Pauley began to feel drowsy. For a while he resisted the downward pull of his eyelids, but then he let himself drift into a half-sleep while Mister and Missus Thistlewaite told them about how they happened to buy the house.

"We wanted to be as near the great master as possible. This was the best we found." Moira Thistlewaite's good-natured face glowed with pleasure.

"Now, Pixie, they don't want to hear about that,"

Horace Thistlewaite said. "Are you getting sleepy, young fellow?"

"A little," Pauley admitted, his words slurring.

"I see you're looking a bit tired, too, missy," he said to Wanda. "What say we put you up in the guest room until Jeremy comes to get you."

"You don't have to," Wanda said.

"Thanks," Pauley said.

PART V

"Have they been asleep long?"

Wanda drifted out of her dream enough to recognize her stepfather's voice.

"Just under an hour," Moira Thistlewaite said.

"What did you give them?"

"Dinner," Horace Thistlewaite said heartily.

"Naturally," Jeremy said drily. "Any bella-donna?"

"Just a little," Moira Thistlewaite assured him.

"Good enough." He leaned over the bed where Wanda lay and she had the impression of a huge black cloud coming down over her.

"How is Agnes?" Moira was asking Jeremy.

"The poppet is finally working. Something must have disturbed it. She should have been dead two days ago."

"Well, no harm done," Horace declared. "It's working now."

Jeremy picked Wanda up in his arms. "Come on, my dear. We have places to go."

Horace lifted Pauley off the end of the bed; the boy was deeply asleep, hanging limply in Mister Thistlewaite's arms.

"Gran?" Wanda murmured as her step-father tightened his grip on her.

"Don't you worry about Gran now, Princess." He kissed her cheek. "My little, virgin Princess."

"I want to see Mama," Wanda said, but the words came out indistinctly and her head lolled to the side.

"That's right; back to sleep." He carried her down the stairs, Horace Thistlewaite coming behind him with Pauley. The night air was cold as they stepped out the front door and Wanda moved closer to Jeremy for warmth.

As she was put onto the front seat of the car, Horace Thistlewaite asked, "Will the Sabbat start at ten?"

"Yes; sacrifices at midnight, of course." Jeremy held the rear door open for Horace to put Pauley down.

"Of course." The rear door closed and Wanda could just hear the sound of Jeremy's footsteps as he came around to the driver's side. "Thanks for looking after them."

"Glad to be of help," Horace said.

Wanda's eyes tried to open; she knew, deep within her, that something was very wrong.

The car started.

"Until tomorrow," Jeremy called out.

"Until tomorrow, Great Master," the neighbors answered.

THE NEW PEOPLE
by Charles Beaumont

If only he had told her right at the beginning that he
didn't like the house, everything would have been fine.
He could have manufactured some plausible story
about bad plumbing or poor construction—something;
anything!—and she'd have gone along with him. Not
without a fight, maybe: he could remember the way
her face had looked when they stopped the car. But he
could have talked her out of it. Now, of course, it was
too late.

For what? he wondered, trying not to think of the
party and all the noise that it would mean. Too late
for what? It's a good house, well built, well kept up,
roomy. Except for that blood stain, cheerful. Anyone
in his right mind . . .

"Dear, aren't you going to shave?"

He lowered the newspaper gently and said, "Sure."
But Ann was looking at him in that hurt, accusing way,
and he knew that it was hopeless.

Hank-what's-wrong, he thought, starting toward the
bathroom.

"Hank," she said.

He stopped but did not turn. "Uh-huh?"

"What's wrong?"

"Nothing," he said.

"Honey. Please."

He faced her. The pink chiffon dress clung to her
body, which had the firmness of youth; her face was
unblemished, the lipstick and powder incredibly perfect; her hair, cut long, was soft on her white shoulders: in seven years Ann hadn't changed.

Resentfully, Prentice glanced away. And was
ashamed. You'd think that in this time I'd get accustomed to it, he thought. *She* is. Damn it!

"Tell me," Ann said.

"Tell you what? Everything is okay," he said.

She came to him and he could smell the perfume,
he could see the tiny freckles that dotted her chest. He
wondered what it would be like to sleep with her.
Probably it would be very nice.

"It's about Davey, isn't it?" she said, dropping her
voice to a whisper. They were standing only a few feet
from their son's room.

"No," Prentice said; but, it was true—Davey was
part of it. For a week now Prentice had ridden on the
hope that getting the locomotive repaired would change
things. A kid without a train, he'd told himself, is
bound to act peculiar. But he'd had the locomotive
repaired and brought it home and Davey hadn't even
bothered to set up the track.

"He appreciated it, dear," Ann said. "Didn't he
thank you?"

"Sure, he thanked me."

"Well?" she said. "Honey, I've *told* you: Davey is
going through a period, that's all. Children do.
Really."

"I know."

"And school's been out for almost a month."

"I know," Prentice said, and thought: *Moving to a
neighborhood where there isn't another kid in the
whole damn block for him to play with, that might have
something to do with it, too!*

"Then," Ann said, "it's me."

"No, no, no." He tried a smile. There wasn't any
sense in arguing: they'd been through it a dozen times,
and she had an answer for everything. He could recall
the finality in her voice . . . "I love the house, Hank.
And I love the neighborhood. It's what I've dreamed
of all my life, and I think I deserve it. Don't you?"
(It was the first time she'd ever consciously reminded
him.) "The trouble is, you've lived in dingy little

apartments so long you've come to *like* them. You can't adjust to a really *decent* place—and Davey's no different. You're two of a kind: little old men who can't stand a change, even for the better! Well, I can. I don't care if *fifty* people committed suicide here, I'm happy. You understand, Hank? Happy.''

Prentice had understood, and had resolved to make a real effort to like the new place. If he couldn't do that, at least he could keep his feelings from Ann—for they were, he knew, foolish. Damned foolish. Everything she said was true, and he ought to be grateful.

Yet, somehow, he could not stop dreaming of the old man who had picked up a razor one night and cut his throat wide open . . .

Ann was staring at him.

"Maybe," he said, "I'm going through a period, too." He kissed her forehead, lightly. "Come on, now; the people are going to arrive any second, and you look like Lady Macbeth."

She held his arm for a moment. "You are getting settled in the house, aren't you?" she said. "I mean, it's becoming more like home to you, isn't it?"

"Sure," Prentice said.

His wife paused another moment, then smiled. "Okay, get the whiskers off. Rhoda is under the impression you're a handsome man."

He walked into the bathroom and plugged in the electric shaver. Rhoda, he thought. First names already and we haven't been here three weeks.

"Dad?"

He looked down at Davey, who had slipped in with nine-year-old stealth. "Yo." According to ritual, he ran the shaver across his son's chin.

Davey did not respond. He stepped back and said, "Dad, is Mr. Ames coming over tonight?"

Prentice nodded. "I guess so."

"And Mr. Chambers?"

"Uh-huh. Why?"

Davey did not answer.

"What do you want to know for?"

"Gee." Davey's eyes were red and wide. "Is it okay if I stay in my room?"

"Why? You sick?"

"No. Kind of."

"Stomach? Head?"

"Just sick," Davey said. He pulled at a thread in his shirt and fell silent again.

Prentice frowned. "I thought maybe you'd like to show them your train," he said.

"Please," Davey said. His voice had risen slightly and Prentice could see tears gathering. "Dad, please don't make me come out. Leave me stay in my room. I won't make any noise, I promise, and I'll go to sleep on time."

"Okay, okay. Don't make such a big deal out of it!" Prentice ran the cool metal over his face. Anger came and went, swiftly. Stupid to get mad. "Davey, what'd you do, ride your bike on their lawn or something? Break a window?"

"No."

"Then why don't you want to see them?"

"I just don't."

"Mr. Ames likes you. He told me so yesterday. He thinks you're a fine boy, so does Mr. Chambers. They—"

"*Please*, Dad!" Davey's face was pale; he began to cry.

"Please, please, please. Don't let them get me!"

"What are you talking about? Davey, cut it out. Now!"

"I saw what they were doing there in the garage. And they know I saw them, too. They know. And—"

"Davey!" Ann's voice was sharp and loud and re-sounding in the tile-lined bathroom. The boy stopped crying immediately. He looked up, hesitated, then ran out. His door slammed.

Prentice took a step.

"No, Hank. Leave him alone."

"He's upset."

"Let him be upset." She shot an angry glance to-

ward the bedroom. "I suppose he told you that filthy
story about the garage?"

"No," Prentice said, "he didn't. What's it all
about?"

"Nothing. Absolutely nothing. Honestly, I'd like to
meet Davey's parents!"

"We're his parents," Prentice said, firmly.

"All right, all right. But he got that imagination of
his from *some*body, and it wasn't from us. You're going to have to speak to him, Hank. I mean it. Really."

"About what?"

"These wild stories. What if they got back to Mr.
Ames? I'd—well, I'd die. After he's gone out of his
way to be nice to Davey, too."

"I haven't heard the stories," Prentice said.

"Oh, you will." Ann undid her apron and folded
it, furiously. "Honestly! Sometimes I think the two of
you are trying to make things just as miserable as they
can be for me."

The doorbell rang, stridently.

"Now make an effort to be pleasant, will you? This
is a *house*warming, after all. And do hurry."

She closed the door. He heard her call, "Hi!" and
heard Ben Roth's baritone booming: "Hi!"

Ridiculous, he told himself, plugging the razor in
again. Utterly goddam ridiculous. No one complained
louder than I did when we were tripping over ourselves
in that little upstairs coffin on Friar. *I'm* the one who
kept moaning for a house, not Ann.

So now we've got one.

He glanced at the tiny brownish blood stain that
wouldn't wash out of the wallpaper, and sighed.

Now we've got one.

"Hank!"

"Coming!" He straightened his tie and went into
the living room.

The Roths, of course, were there. Ben and Rhoda.
Get it right, he thought, because we're all going to be
pals. "Hi, Ben."

"Thought you'd deserted us, boy," said the large, pink man, laughing.

"No. Wouldn't do that."

"Hank," Ann signaled. "You've met Beth Cummings, haven't you?"

The tall, smartly dressed woman giggled and extended her hand. "We've seen each other," she said. "Hello."

Her husband, a pale man with white hair, crushed Prentice's fingers. "Fun and games," he said, tightening his grip and wheezing with amusement. "Yes, sir."

Trying not to wince, Prentice retrieved his hand. It was instantly snatched up by a square, bald man in a double-breasted brown suit. "Reiker," the man said. "Call me Bud. Everyone does. Don't know why; my name is Oscar."

"*That's* why," a woman said, stepping up. "Ann introduced us but you probably don't remember, if I know men. I'm Edna."

"Sure," Prentice said. "How are you?"

"Fine. But then, I'm a woman: I *like* parties!"

"How's that?"

"Hank!"

Prentice excused himself and walked quickly into the kitchen. Ann was holding up a package.

"Honey, look what Rhoda gave us!"

He dutifully handled the salt and pepper shakers and set them down again. "That's real nice."

"You turn the rooster's head," Mrs. Roth said, "and it grinds your pepper."

"Wonderful," Prentice said.

"And Beth gave us this lovely salad bowl, see? And we've needed *this* for *cen*turies!" She held out a gray tablecloth with gold bordering. "Plastic!"

"Wonderful," Prentice said. Again, the doorbell rang. He glanced at Mrs. Roth, who had been staring thoughtfully at him, and returned to the living room.

"How you be, Hank?" Lucian Ames walked in,

rubbing his hands together briskly. "Well! The gang's all here, I see. But where's that boy of yours?"

"Davey? Oh," Prentice said, "he's sick."

"Nonsense! Boys that age are never sick. Never!"

Ann laughed nervously from the kitchen. "Just something he ate!"

"Not the candy we sent over, I hope."

"Oh, no."

"Well, tell him his Uncle Lucian said hello."

A tan elf of a man, with sparkling eyes and an ill fitting mustache, Ames reminded Prentice somewhat of those clerks who used to sit silently on high wooden stools, posting infinitesimal figures in immense yellow ledgers. He was, however, the head of a nationally famous advertising agency.

His wife Charlotte provided a remarkable contrast. She seemed to belong to the era of the twenties, with her porcelain face, her thin, delicately angular body, her air of fragility.

Nice, Prentice told himself.

He removed coats and hung them in closets. He shook hands and smiled until his face began to ache. He looked at presents and thanked the women and told them they shouldn't have. He carried out sandwiches. He mixed drinks.

By eight-thirty, everyone in the block had arrived. The Johnsons, the Ameses, the Roths, the Reikers, the Klementaskis, the Chamberses; four or five others whose names Prentice could not remember, although Ann had taken care to introduce them.

What it is, he decided, looking at the people, at the gifts they had brought; remembering their many kindnesses and how, already, Ann had made more friends than she'd ever had before, is, I'm just an antisocial bastard.

After the third round of whiskeys and martinis, someone turned on the FM and someone else suggested dancing. Prentice had always supposed that one danced only at New Year's Eve parties, but he said the hell with it, finally, and tried to relax.

"Shall we?" Mrs. Ames said.

He wanted to say no, but Ann was watching. So he said, "Sure, if you've got strong toes," instead.

Almost at once he began to perspire. The smoke, the drinks, the heat of the crowded room, caused his head to ache; and, as usual, he was acutely embarrassed at having to hold a strange woman so closely.

But, he continued to smile.

Mrs. Ames danced well, she followed him with unerring instinct; and within moments she was babbling freely into his ear. She told him about old Mr. Thomas, the man who had lived here before, and how surprised everyone had been at what had happened; she told hi how curious they'd all been about The New People and how relieved they were to find him and Ann so very nice; she told him he had strong arms. Ann was being twirled about by Herb Johnson. She was smiling.

An endless, slow three-step came on, then, and Mrs. Ames put her cheek next to Prentice's. In the midst of a rambling sentence, she said, suddenly, in a whisper: "You know, I think it was awfully brave of you to adopt little Davey. I mean, considering."

"Considering what?"

She pulled away and looked at him. "Nothing," she said. "I'm awfully sorry."

Blushing with fury, Prentice turned and strode into the kitchen. He fought his anger, thinking, God, God, is she telling strangers about it now? Is it a topic for backfence gossip? *"My husband is impotent, you know. Is yours?"*

He poured whiskey into a glass and drank it, fast. It made his eyes water, and when he opened them, he saw a figure standing next to him.

It was—who? Dystal. Matthew Dystal; bachelor; movie writer or something; lives down the block. Call him Matt.

"Miserable, isn't it?" the man said, taking the bottle from Prentice's hand.

"What do you mean?"

"Everything," the man said. He filled his glass and drained it smartly. "Them. Out there." He filled the glass again.

"Nice people," Prentice forced himself to say.

"You think so?"

The man was drunk. Clearly, very drunk. And it was only nine-thirty.

"You think so?" he repeated.

"Sure. Don't you?"

"Of course. I'm one of them, aren't I?"

Prentice peered at his guest closely, them moved toward the living room.

Dystal took his arm. "Wait," he said. "Listen. You're a good guy. I don't know you very well, but I like you, Hank Prentice. So I'm going to give you some advice." His voice dropped to a whisper. "Get out of here," he said.

"What?"

"Just what I said. Move away, move away to another city."

Prentice felt a quick ripple of annoyance, checked it. "Why?" he asked, smiling.

"Never mind that," Dystal said. "Just do it. To-night. Will you?" His face was livid, clammy with perspiration; his eyes were wide.

"Well, I mean, Matt, that's a heck of a thing to say. I thought you said you liked us. Now you want to get rid of us."

"Don't joke," Dystal said. He pointed at the win-dow. "Can't you see the moon? You bloody idiot, can't you—

"Hey, hey! Unfair!"

At the sound of the voice, Dystal froze. He closed his eyes for a moment and opened them, slowly. But he did not move.

Lucian Ames walked into the kitchen. "What's the story here," he said, putting his arm on Dystal's shoulder, "you trying to monopolize our host all night?"

Dystal did not answer.

"How about a refill, Hank?" Ames said, removing his hand.

Prentice said, "Sure," and prepared the drink. From the corner of his eye, he saw Dystal turn and walk stiffly out of the room. He heard the front door open and close.

Ames was chuckling. "Poor old Matt," he said. "He'll be hung over tomorrow. It seems kind of a shame, doesn't it? I mean, you know, of all people, you'd think a big Hollywood writer would be able to hold his liquor. But not Matt. He gets loaded just by staring at the labels."

Prentice said, "Huh."

"Was he giving you one of his screwball nightmares?"

"What? No—we were just sort of talking. About things."

Ames dropped an ice cube into his drink. "Things?" he said.

"Yeah."

Ames took a sip of the whiskey and walked to the window, looking lithe, somehow, as well as small. After what seemed a long time, he said, "Well, it's a fine night, isn't it. Nice and clear, nice fine moon." He turned and tapped a cigarette out of a red package, lighted the cigarette. "Hank," he said, letting the gray smoke gush from the corners of his mouth, "tell me something. What do you do for excitement?"

Prentice shrugged. It was an odd question, but then, everything seemed odd to him tonight. "I don't know," he said "Go to a movie once in a while. Watch TV. The usual."

Ames cocked his head. "But—don't you get bored?"

"Sure, I guess. Every so often. Being a C.P.A. you know, that isn't exactly the world's most fascinating job."

Ames laughed sympathetically. "It's awful, isn't it?"

"Being a C.P.A.?"

"No. Being bored. It's about the worst thing in the world, don't you agree? Someone once remarked they thought it was the only real sin a human could commit."

"I hope not," Prentice said.

"Why?"

"Well, I mean—everybody gets bored, don't they?"

"Not," Ames said, "if they're careful."

Prentice found himself becoming increasingly irritated at the conversation. "I suppose it helps," he said, "if you're the head of an advertising agency."

"No, not really. It's like any other job: interesting at first, but then you get used to it. It becomes routine. So you go fishing for other diversions."

"Like what?"

"Oh . . . anything. Everything." Ames slapped Prentice's arm good naturedly. "You're all right, Hank," he said.

"Thanks."

"I mean it. Can't tell you how happy we all are that you moved here."

"No more than we are!" Ann walked unsteadily to the sink with a number of empty glasses. "I want to apologize for Davey again, Lucian. I was telling Charlotte, he's been a perfect beast lately. He should have thanked you for fixing the seat on his bike."

"Forget it," Ames said, cheerfully. "The boy's just upset because he doesn't have any playmates." He looked at Prentice. "Some of us elders have kids, Hank, but they're all practically grown. You probably know that our daughter, Ginnie, is away at college. And Chris and Beth's boy lives in New York. But, you know, I wouldn't worry. As soon as school starts, Davey'll straighten out. You watch."

Ann smiled. "I'm sure you're right, Lucian. But I apologize, anyway."

"Nuts." Ames returned to the living room and began to dance with Beth Cummings.

Prentice thought then of asking Ann what the devil she meant by blabbing about their personal life to strangers, but decided not to. This was not the time. He was too angry, too confused.

The party lasted another hour. Then Ben Roth said, "Better let these good folks get some sleep!" and, slowly, the people left.

Ann closed the door. She seemed to glow with contentment, looking younger and prettier than she had for several years. "Home," she said softly, and began picking up ash trays and glasses and plates. "Let's get all this out of the way so we won't have to look at it in the morning," she said.

Prentice said, "All right," in a neutral tone. He was about to move the coffee table back into place when the telephone rang.

"Yes?"

The voice that answered was a harsh whisper, like a rush of wind through leaves. "Prentice, are they gone?"

"Who is this?"

"Matt Dystal. Are they gone?"

"Yes."

"All of them? Ames? Is he gone?"

"Yes. What do you want, Dystal? It's late."

"Later than you might think, Prentice. He told you I was drunk, but he lied. I'm not drunk. I'm—"

"Look, what is it you want?"

"I've got to talk with you," the voice said. "Now. Tonight. Can you come over?"

"At eleven o'clock?"

"Yes. Prentice, listen to me. I'm not drunk and I'm not kidding. This is a matter of life and death. Yours. Do you understand what I'm saying?"

Prentice hesitated, confused.

"You know where my place is—fourth house from the corner, right-hand side. Come over now. But listen, carefully: go out the back door. The back door. Prentice, are you listening?"

"Yes," Prentice said.

"My lights will be off. Go around to the rear. Don't

bother to knock, just walk in—but be quiet about it. They mustn't see you.''

Prentice heard a click, then silence. He stared at the receiver for a while before replacing it.

"Well?" Ann said. "Man talk?''

"Not exactly.'' Prentice wiped his palm on his trousers. "That fellow Matt Dystal, he's apparently sick. Wants me to come over.''

"Now?''

"Yeah. I think I better; he sounded pretty bad. You go on to sleep, I'll be back in a little while.''

"Okay, honey. I hope it isn't anything serious. But, it *is* nice to be doing something for *them* for a change, isn't it?''

Prentice kissed his wife, waited until the bathroom door had closed; then he went outside, into the cold night.

He walked along the grass verge of the alleyway, across the small lawns, up the steps to Dystal's rear door.

He deliberated with himself for a moment, then walked in.

"Prentice?" a voice hissed.

"Yes. Where are you?''

A hand touched his arm in the darkness and he jumped, nervously. "Come into the bedroom.''

A dim lamp went on. Prentice saw that the windows were covered by heavy tan drapes. It was chilly in the room, chilly and moist.

"Well?" Prentice said, irritably.

Matthew Dystal ran a hand through his rope-colored hair. "I know what you're thinking,'' he said. "And I don't blame you. But it was necessary, Prentice. It was necessary. Ames has told you about my 'wild nightmares' and that's going to stick with you, I realize; but get this straight.'' His hand became a fist. "Everything I'm about to say is true. No matter how outlandish it may sound, it's *true*—and I have proof. All you'll need. So keep still, Prentice, and listen to me. It may mean your life: your and your wife's and

your boy's. And, maybe, mine . . ." His voice trailed
off; then, suddenly, he said, "You want a drink?"
  "No."
  "You ought to have one. You're only on the outskirts
of confusion, my friend. But, there are worse things
than confusion. Believe me." Dystal walked to a
bookcase and stood there for almost a full minute.
When he turned, his features were slightly more com-
posed. "What do you know," he asked, "about the
house you're living in?"
  Prentice shifted uncomfortably. "I know that a man
killed himself in it, if that's what you mean."
  "But do you know why?"
  "No."
  "Because he lost," Dystal said, giggling. "He drew
the short one. How's that for motivation?"
  "I think I'd better go," Prentice said.
  "Wait." Dystal took a handkerchief from his pocket
and tapped his forehead. "I didn't mean to begin that
way. It's just that I've never told this to anyone, and
it's difficult. You'll see why. Please Prentice, promise
you won't leave until I've finished!"
  Prentice looked at the wiry, nervous little man and
cursed the weakness that had allowed him to get himself into this miserably uncomfortable situation. He
wanted to go home. But he knew he could not leave
now.
  "All right," he said "Go on."
  Dystal sighed. Then, staring at the window, he began to talk. "I built this house," he said, "because I
thought I was going to get married. By the time I found
out I was wrong, the work was all done. I should have
sold it, I know, I see that, but I was feeling too lousy
to go through the paper work. Besides, I'd already
given up my apartment. So I moved in." He coughed.
"Be patient with me, Prentice: this is the only way to
tell it, from the beginning. Where was I?"
  "You moved in."
  "Yes! Everybody was very nice. They invited me to
their homes for dinner, they dropped by, they did little

favors for me; and it helped, it really did. I thought, you know, what a hell of a great bunch of neighbors. Regular. *Real*. That was it: they were real. Ames, an advertising man; Thomas, a lawyer; Johnson, paint company; Chambers, insurance; Reiker and Cummings, engineers—I mean, how average can you get?'' Dystal paused; an ugly grin appeared on his face, disappeared. ''I liked them,'' he said. ''And I was really delighted with things. But, of course, you know how it is when a woman gives you the business. I was still licking my wounds. And I guess it showed, because Ames came over one evening. Just dropped by, in a neighborly way. We had some drinks. We talked about the ways of the female. Then, bang, out of nowhere, he asked me the question. Was I bored?''

Prentice stiffened.

''Well, when you lose your girl, you lose a lot of your ambition. I told him yes, I was plenty bored. And he said, 'I used to be.' I remember his exact words. 'I used to be,' he said. 'The long haul to success, the fight, the midnight oil: it was over. I'd made it,' he said. 'Dough in the bank. Partnership in a top agency. Daughter grown and away to school. I was ready to be put out to pasture, Matt. But the thing was, I was only fifty-two! I had maybe another twenty years left. And almost everybody else in the block was the same way—Ed and Ben and Oscar, all the same. You know: they fooled around with their jobs, but they weren't interested any more—not really. Because the jobs didn't *need* them any more. They were bored.' '' Dystal walked to the nightstand and poured himself a drink. ''That was five years ago,'' he murmured. ''Ames, he pussy-footed around the thing for a while— feeling me out, testing me; then he told me that he had decided to do something about it. About being bored. He'd organized everyone in the block. Once a week, he explained, they played games. It was real Group Activity. Community effort. It began with charades, but they got tired of that in a while. Then they tried cards. To make it interesting, they bet high. Everybody had his turn at losing. Then, Ames said, someone suggested making the game even *more* interesting, because it was getting to be a drag. So they experimented with strip poker one night. Just for fun, you understand, Rhoda lost. Next time it was Charlotte. And it went that way for a while, until finally, Beth lost. Everyone had been waiting for it. Things became anticlimactic after that, though, so the stakes changed again. Each paired off with another's wife; lowest scoring team had to—'' Dystal tipped the bottle. ''Sure you won't have a bracer?''

Prentice accepted the drink without argument. It tasted bitter and powerful, but it helped.

''Well,'' Dystal went on, ''I had one hell of a time believing all that. I mean, you know: *Ames,* after all—a little bookkeeper type with gray hair and glasses . . . Still, the way he talked, I knew—somehow, I *knew*—it was the truth. Maybe because I didn't feel that a guy like Ames could make it all up! Anyway: when they'd tried all the possible combinations, things got dull again. A few of the women wanted to stop, but, of course, they were in too deep already. During one particular Fun Night, Ames had taken photographs. So, they had to keep going. Every week, it was something new. Something different. Swapsies occupied them for a while, Ames told me: Chambers took a two week vacation with Jacqueline, Ben and Beth went to Acapulco, and that sort of thing. And that is where I came into the picture.'' Dystal raised his hand. ''I know, you don't need to tell me, I should have pulled out. But I was younger then. I was a big writer, man of the world. Training in Hollywood. I couldn't tell him I was shocked: it would have been betraying my craft. And he figured it that way, too: that's why he told me. Besides, he knew I'd be bound to find out eventually. They could hide it from just about everybody, but not someone right in the block. So, I played along. I accepted his invitation to join the next Group Activity—which is what he calls them.

''Next morning, I thought I'd dreamed the whole

visit, I really did. But on Saturday, sure enough, the phone rings and Ames says, 'We begin at eight, sharp.' When I got to his house, I found it packed. Everybody in the neighborhood. Looking absolutely the same as always too. Drinks; dancing; the whole bit. After a while; I started to wonder if the whole thing wasn't an elaborate gag. But at ten, Ames told us about the evening's surprise.'' Dystal gave way to a shudder. "It was a surprise, all right,'' he said. "I told them I wanted nothing to do with it, but Ames had done something to my drink. I didn't seem to have any control. They led me into the bedroom, and . . .''

Prentice waited, but Dystal did not complete his sentence. His eyes were dancing now.

"Never mind,'' he said. "Never mind what happened! The point is, I was drunk, and—well, I went through with it. I *had* to. You can see that, can't you?''

Prentice said that he could see that.

"Ames pointed out to me that the only sin, the *only* one, was being bored. That was his justification, that was his incentive. He simply didn't want to sin, that was all. So the Group Activities went on. And they got worse. Much worse. One thing, they actually plotted a crime and carried it off: the Union bank robbery, maybe you read about it: 1953. I drove the car for them. Another time, they decided it would ward off ennui by setting fire to a warehouse down by the docks. The fire spread. Prentice—do you happen to remember that DC-7 that went down between here and Detroit?''

Prentice said, "Yes, I remember.''

"Their work,'' Dystal said. "Ames planned it. In a way, I think he's a genius. I could spend all night telling you the things we did, but there isn't time. I've got to skip.'' He placed his fingers over his eyes. "Joan of Arc,'' he said, "was the turning point. Ames had decided that it would be diverting to re-enact famous scenes from literature. So he and Bud went down to Main Street, I think it was, and found a beat doll who thought the whole thing would be fun. They gave her twenty-five dollars, but she never got a chance to spend

it. I remember that she laughed right up to the point
where Ames lit the pile of oil-soaked rags . . . Afterward, they re-enacted other scenes. The execution of
Marie Antoinette. The murder of Hamlet's father. You
know *The Man in the Iron Mask?* They did that one.
And a lot more. It lasted quite a while, too, but Ames
began to get restless.'' Dystal held out his hands suddenly and stared at them. ''The next game was a form
of Russian roulette. We drew straws. Whoever got the
short one had to commit suicide—in his own way. It
was understood that if he failed, it would mean something much worse—and Ames had developed some
damned interesting techniques. Like the nerve clamps,
for instance. Thomas lost the game, anyway. They gave
him twelve hours to get it over with.''

Prentice felt a cold film of perspiration over his
flesh. He tried to speak, but found that it was impossible. The man, of course, was crazy. Completely insane. But—he had to hear the end of the story. ''Go
on,'' he said.

Dystal ran his tongue across his lower lip, poured
another drink and continued. ''Cummings and Chambers got scared then,'' he said. ''They argued that
some stranger would move into the house and then
there'd be all sorts of trouble. We had a meeting at
Reiker's, and Chris came out with the idea of us all
chipping in and buying the place. But Ames didn't go
for it. 'Let's not be so darned exclusive,' he said. 'After all, the new people might be bored, too. Lord
knows we could use some fresh blood in the Group.'
Cummings was pessimistic. He said, 'What if you're
wrong? What if they don't want to join us?' Ames
laughed it off. 'I hope,' he said, 'that you don't think
we're the only ones. Why, every city has its neighbor-
hoods just like ours. We're really not that unique.'
And then he went on to say that if the new people
didn't work out, he would take care of the situation.
He didn't say how.''

Dystal looked out the window again.

''I can see that he's almost ready to give you an

invitation, Prentice. Once that happens, you're finished. It's join them or accept the only alternative.''

Suddenly the room was very quiet.

"You don't believe me, do you?''

Prentice opened his mouth.

"No, of course you don't. It's a madman's ravings. Well, I'm going to prove it to you, Prentice. He started for the door. "Come on. Follow me; but don't make any noise.''

Dystal walked out the back door, closed it, moved soundlessly across the soft, black grass.

"They're on a mystic kick right now,'' he whispered to Prentice. "Ames is trying to summon the devil. Last week we slaughtered a dog and read the Commandments backward; the week before, we did some chants out of an old book that Ben found in the library; before that it was orgies—'' He shook his head. "It isn't working out, though. God knows why. You'd think the devil would be so delighted with Ames that he'd sign him up for the team.''

Prentice followed his neighbor across the yards, walking carefully, and wondering why. He thought of his neat little office on Harmon Steet, old Mrs. Gleason, the clean, well-lighted restaurant where he had his lunch and read newspaper headlines; and they seemed terribly far away.

"Why, he asked himself, am I creeping around backyards with a lunatic at midnight?

Why?

"The moon is full tonight, Prentice. That means they'll be trying again.''

Silently, without the slightest sound, Matthew Dystal moved across the lawns, keeping always to the shadows. A minute later he raised his hand and stopped.

They were at the rear of the Ameses' house.

It was dark inside.

"Come on,'' Dystal whispered.

"Wait a minute.'' Somehow, the sight of his own

living room, still blazing with light, reassured Prentice. "I think I've had enough for this evening."

"Enough?" Dystal's face twisted grotesquely. He bunched the sleeve of Prentice's jacket in his fist. "Listen," he hissed, "listen, you idiot. I'm risking my life to help you. Don't you understand yet? If they find out I've talked . . ." He released the sleeve. "Prentice, *please*. You have a chance now, a chance to clear out of this whole stinking mess; but you won't have it long— Believe me!"

Prentice sighed. "What do you want me to do?" he said.

"Nothing. Just come with me, quietly. They're in the basement."

Breathing hard now, Dystal tiptoed around to the side of the house. He stopped at a small, earth-level window.

It was closed.

"Prentice, *Softly*. Bend down and keep out of view."

In invisible, slow movements, Dystal reached out and pushed the window. It opened a half inch. He pushed it again. It opened another half inch.

Prentice saw yellow light stream out of the crack. Instantly his throat felt very dry, very painful.

There was a noise. A low, murmurous sound; a susurrus like distant humming.

"What's that?"

Dystal put a finger to his lips and motioned: "Here."

Prentice knelt down at the window and looked into the light.

At first he could not believe what his eyes saw.

It was a basement, like other basements in old houses, with a large iron furnace and a cement floor and heavy beams. This much he could recognize and understand. The rest, he could not.

In the center of the floor was a design, obviously drawn in colored chalks. It looked a bit, to Prentice, like a Star of David, although there were other designs around and within it. They were not particularly artistic, but they were intricate. In the middle was a large cup, similar to a salad bowl, vaguely familiar, empty.

"There," whispered Dystal, withdrawing.

Slightly to the left were drawn a circle and a pentagram, its five points touching the circumference equally.

Prentice blinked and turned his attention to the people.

Standing on a block of wood, surrounded by men and women, was a figure in a black robe and a serpent-shaped crown.

It was Ames.

His wife, Charlotte, dressed in a white gown, stood next to him. She held a brass lamp.

Also in robes and gowns were Ben and Rhoda Roth, Bud Reiker and his wife, the Cummingses, the Chamberses, and the Johnsons—

Prentice shook away his sudden dizziness and shaded his eyes.

To the right, near the furnace, was a table with a white sheet draped across it. And two feet away, an odd, six-sided structure with black candles burning from a dozen apertures.

"Listen," Dystal said.

Ames' eyes were closed. Softly, he was chanting:

All degradation, all sheer infamy,
    Thou shalt endure. Thy head beneath the mire.
    And dung of worthless women shall desire
As in some hateful dream, at last to lie;
    Woman must trample thee till thou respire
        That deadliest fume;
The vilest worms must crawl, the loathliest
    vampires gloom . . .

"The Great Beast," chuckled Dystal.

"I," said Ames, "am Ipsissimus," and the others chanted, "He is Ipsissimus."

"I have read the books, dark Lord. *The Book of*

Sacred Magic of Abra-Melin the Mage I have read, and I reject it!''

''We reject it!'' murmured the Roths.

''The power of Good shall be served by the power of Darkness, always.''

He raised his hands. ''In Thy altar is the stele of Ankf-f-n-Khonsu; there, also, *The Book of the Dead* and *The Book of the Law,* six candles to each side, my Lord, Bell, Burin, Lamen, Sword, Cup, and the Cakes of Life . . .''

Prentice looked at the people he had seen only a few hours ago in his living room, and shuddered. He felt very weak.

''We, your servants,'' said Ames, singing the words, ''beseech your presence, Lord of Night and of Life Eternal, Ruler of the Souls of men in all Thy vast dominion. . . .''

Prentice started to rise, but Dystal grasped his jacket. ''No,'' he said. ''Wait. Wait another minute. This is something you ought to see.''

''. . . we live to serve you; grant us . . .''

''He's begging the devil to appear,'' whispered Dystal.

''. . . tonight, and offer the greatest and most treasured gift. Accept our offering!''

''Accept it!'' cried the others.

''What the hell is this, anyway?'' Prentice demanded, feverishly.

Then Ames stopped talking, and the rest were silent. Ames raised his left hand and lowered it. Chris Cummings and Bud Reiker bowed and walked backwards into the shadows where Prentice could not see them.

Charlotte Ames walked to the six-sided structure with the candles and picked up a long, thin object.

She returned and handed this to her husband.

It was a knife.

''Killnotshaltthou!'' screamed Ed Chambers, and he stepped across the pentagram to the sheet-shrouded table.

Prentice rubbed his eyes.

"Shhh."

Bud Reiker and Chris Cummings returned to the center of light then. They were carrying a bundle. It was wrapped in blankets.

The bundle thrashed and made peculiar muffled noises. The men lifted it onto the table and held it.

Ames nodded and stepped down from the block of wood. He walked to the table and halted, the long-bladed butcher knife glittering in the glow of the candles.

"To Thee, O Lord of the Underground, we make this offering! To Thee, the rarest gift of all!"

"What is it?" Prentice asked. "What is this gift?"

Dystal's voice was ready and eager. "A virgin," he said.

Then they removed the blanket.

Prentice felt his eyes bursting from their sockets, felt his heart charging the walls of his chest.

"Ann," he said, in a choked whisper. "Ann!"

The knife went up.

Prentice scrambled to his feet and fought the dizziness. "Dystal," he cried. "Dystal, for God's sake, what are they doing? Stop them. You hear me? Stop them!"

"I can't," said Matthew sadly. "It's too late. I'm afraid your wife said a few things she shouldn't have, Prentice. You see—we've been looking for a real one for such a long time . . ."

Prentice tried to lunge, but the effort lost him his balance. He fell to the ground. His arms and legs were growing numb, and he remembered, suddenly, the bitter taste of the drink he'd had.

"It really couldn't have been avoided, though," Dystal said. "I mean, the boy knew, and he'd have told you eventually. And you'd have begun investigating, and—oh, you understand. I told Lucian we should have bought the place, but he's so obstinate; thinks he knows *every*thing! Now, of course, we'll have to burn it, and that does seem a terrible waste.'' He shook his head from side to side. ''But don't you worry,'' he said. ''You'll be asleep by then and, I promise, you won't feel a thing. Really.''

Prentice turned his eyes from the window and screamed silently for a long time.

DAW

Welcome to DAW's Gallery of Ghoulish Delights!

DAW

A feline lovers' fantasy come true ...

CATFANTASTIC

Edited by ANDRE NORTON and MARTIN H. GREENBERG

They prowl our homes, lords of all they survey. They gaze intently at seemingly empty space, spying on things no human is equipped to see. They choose their friends with care, and once they have chosen, their loyalty is unswerving.

This volume of original stories, selected and edited by two of the biggest names in the fantasy field, is for all the cat-friends upon whom these furry felines have worked their special magic, a unique collection of fantastical cat tales; some set in the distant future on as yet unknown worlds, some set in our own world but not quite our own dimension, some recounting what happens when beings from the ancient past and creatures out of myth collide with modern day felines.

So pad along this pawprint covered pathway to such fur-raising adventures as those of a noble Siamese out to defend its young mistress from evil, a bioengineered tabby who proves a diplomat beyond all human expectations, a wizard's hazardous encounter with his own familiar's kittens, and other imaginative escapades certain to capture the hearts of fantasy and cat lovers alike.

☐ **CATFANTASTIC** (UE2355—$3.95)

DAW

Don't Miss These Exciting DAW Anthologies

ANNUAL WORLD'S BEST SF
Donald A. Wollheim, editor
- [ ] 1986 Annual   UE2136—$3.50
- [ ] 1987 Annual   UE2203—$3.95
- [ ] 1989 Annual   UE2353—$3.95

ISAAC ASIMOV PRESENTS THE GREAT SF STORIES
Isaac Asimov & Martin H. Greenberg, editors
- [ ] Series 10 (1948)   UE1854—$3.50
- [ ] Series 13 (1951)   UE2058—$3.50
- [ ] Series 14 (1952)   UE2106—$3.50
- [ ] Series 15 (1953)   UE2171—$3.50
- [ ] Series 16 (1954)   UE2200—$3.50
- [ ] Series 17 (1955)   UE2256—$3.95
- [ ] Series 18 (1956)   UE2289—$4.50
- [ ] Series 19 (1957)   UE2326—$4.50
- [ ] Series 20 (1958)   UE2405—$4.95

SWORD AND SORCERESS
Marion Zimmer Bradley, editor
- [ ] Book I   UE1928—$2.95
- [ ] Book II   UE2041—$2.95
- [ ] Book III   UE2141—$3.50
- [ ] Book IV   UE2210—$3.50
- [ ] Book V   UE2288—$3.95

THE YEAR'S BEST FANTASY STORIES
Arthur W. Saha, editor
- [ ] Series 14   UE2307—$3.50

DAW

Creatures of Wonder

LAURIE J. MARKS

☐ **DELAN THE MISLAID** (UE2325—$3.95)

A misfit among a people not its own, Delan willingly goes away with the Walker Teksan to the Lowlands. But there, the Walker turns out to be a cruel master, a sorcerer who practices dark magic to keep Delan his slave—and who has diabolical plans to enslave Delan's people, the winged Aeyrie. And unless Delan can free itself from Teksan's spell, it may become the key to the ruin of its entire race.

☐ **MOONBANE MAGE** (UE2415—$3.95)

Here is the story of Delan's child, a spoiled royal progeny, who is kidnapped by an evil magician of its own species, and must tap reserves both personal and magical to save her race from a suicidal sorcerous war.

JACKIE HYMAN

☐ **SHADOWLIGHT** (UE2397—$3.50)

The Radiants have long ruled in the city of Ad-Omaq through their powers as adepts. Yet they are not the only magic wielders in the land. There is an older race, a horned people drawing strength from nature itself. To the Radiants, this race is a menace to be eliminated—but they have not counted on Shadow, born of both races and gifted with the special mind abilities of each. . . .

TAD WILLIAMS

☐ **TAILCHASER'S SONG** (UE2374—$4.95)

This best-selling feline fantasy epic tells the adventures of Fritti Tailchaser, a young ginger cat who sets out, with boundless enthusiasm, on a dangerous quest which leads him into the underground realm of an evil cat-god—a nightmare world from which only his own resources can deliver him.
